STICKS

Sleeping Bear Press
310 North Main Street
P.O. Box 20
Chelsea, MI 48118
www.sleepingbearpress.com

Printed and bound in Canada.

10 9 8 7 6 5 4 3 2 1

Library of Congress Cataloging-in-Publication Data

McMillen, William.
  Sticks / by William McMillen.
    p. cm.
  ISBN 1-58536-010-4
  1. City and town life—Fiction. 2. Real estate developers—Fiction.
  3. Golf courses—Fiction. I. Title.
  PS3563.C38714 S75 2000
  813'.6—dc21

                        00-010411

STICKS

by

WILLIAM MCMILLEN

Sleeping Bear Press

FOR CHRISTOPHER MCMILLEN

∽

But soft! What light through yonder window breaks?
It is the east, and Juliet is the sun.

ROMEO
Romeo and Juliet
ACT 2, SCENE 2

I hope it [the publication of *Uncle Tom's Cabin*] will
make enough so I may have a silk dress.

HARRIET BEECHER STOWE

Acknowledgements

My thanks go to Brian Lewis, Publisher, Danny Freels, Fiction Editor, and Adam Rifenberick, all of Sleeping Bear Press, for their support. May they always have low golf scores and play on courses as nice as The Candlesticks. Also thanks to my friend J. Michael Porter for his advice on the golf aspects of Sticks. Finally, thanks to my friends Bob and Karen Grauman and wife Barbara for their close reading of the manuscript during its creation.

TABLE OF CONTENTS

JULY 4, 1922

It was raining.

Not hard, but steady. Despite the early hour, it was already warm and humid. The branches and leaves of the large elms, oaks, and buckeyes overhead gave some shelter from the rain. But the woods and heat also produced a closed-in, claustrophobic atmosphere. In places, heavy underbrush choked the tree trunks.

Water pooled on the path through the woods as the two horses plodded along with their heads down. It was 7:00 a.m. and George August allowed his horse to carefully pick her way on the slippery trail. The horse, named Stanton, was one of Sheridan Howard's retired polo ponies. Most of Howard's polo ponies were named after Civil War persons or battles. This particular brown filly was misnamed after Lincoln's Secretary of War, Edwin McMasters Stanton. In Howard's stable, August could have chosen Abe or Mary Todd or even Gettysburg. But Stanton had a gleam in her eye that caught August's fancy.

Ahead of him, a man named Billy Barnes rode a jet-black horse with the more traditional name of Scout. Billy's white pug named Bandit wound his way in and out of Scout's legs. August was certain the little dog would be trampled at any second, but the mutt was nimble and seemed oblivious to the danger from Scout's hooves.

August had intended to explore the land set aside for the golf course by himself. However, when he arrived at the stable at 6:30, Billy had been there currying Scout. The man, whom August correctly judged to be about 30 despite prematurely gray streaks in his brown hair, immediately volunteered to help saddle a mount and accompany August as a guide.

August willingly accepted the companionship and within minutes they were underway into the forested area designated for the ambitious project. Now, peering past Billy and Scout, August could see that the green dripping trees thinned into a clearing. When they broke out of the woods, August pulled up next to Billy and they stopped. The rain also abruptly stopped although the clouds hung heavily. The weather gave all indications of hanging on for the day and ruining the holiday festivities planned, including the polo match set for the afternoon on the field behind the town square and later, of course, the traditional Independence Day fireworks.

"Are you a golfer, Billy?" George August asked his guide.

Billy grinned and wiped rain off his face with a red bandanna. He looked at the older man and said: "No, sir, baseball's still my game."

August nodded under his wide-brimmed leather hat. "Being a sportsman, I fully appreciate the game of *base*ball." He gave a funny accent to the word *base* as if it didn't belong with the word *ball*. "However," he continued, "as a Southerner, I find it hard to cheer for all those northern teams. The New York *Yankees*, in particular."

George August's Southern pose was somewhat disingenuous. Although George had been born in Virginia, his parents had immigrated to America from Germany before the Civil War. August had perfected the aloofness typical of an antebellum Southern gentleman despite his actually growing up in the era of Reconstruction. However, his lack of a true Southern drawl betrayed his heritage. Instead of using drawn out vowels and syllables, he spoke English like his German father with a flat precision, resulting in the unnatural splitting of words such as *base* and *ball*.

Billy chuckled. "Well, we're Cincinnati Red Stockings' fans here, sir. But isn't golf a game from Scotland? That's not the South either."

"Point well taken. Still, golf is a wonderful game. It has a universal appeal. Now, where exactly are we?" the older man asked, looking around.

"You see that stake over there?" Billy pointed a few yards off to their right at a small wooden stake. A yellow ribbon was tied to the top of the stake and trailed along the muddy ground.

Billy continued: "Last May, state surveyors came out. They marked that point as the southernmost extension of Pottawa State Forest. The Forest stretches about 20 miles to the north-northeast from here." Again, Billy gestured off in a direction with his hand.

August followed Billy's wave and then looked back at the stake. "Yesterday, Sheridan—ah, I mean, Mr. Howard—said that survey was irrelevant. The Ohio government does not care about this bit of land."

Billy shrugged. "Well, Mr. August, Mr. Howard does claim that the survey is not an issue. He may be right. Politics, you see. You do understand, don't you, sir, that Mr. Howard is from one of the families?"

"Now, that is interesting, Billy. In my two days here, I have heard a number of veiled references to these *families*. Are you in a position to explain what people are talking about? Who are these *families?*"

Billy swung down from Scout and pulled the reins over the horse's head. He leaned over and gave Bandit a rough rub on the head. "Let's walk the horses up to the Cascades, sir, if you don't mind. It's a little steep for them in the wet."

August dismounted. He was nearly 60, but still a fine horseman. He realized that Sheridan Howard knew that fact and had lured him out here not only for business, but also to see the polo match between the horsemen from central Ohio and the well-known Clubbers from Chicago. August led Stanton beside Billy, Scout, and Bandit. They plunged back into the woods for a few yards, but the path soon widened and the trees thinned dramatically as the men and animals made their way up a moderate slope.

Billy started talking: "It was the Civil War, you understand, sir. There were seven of them. Seven officers from Ohio. Only a couple of them knew one another before the war, although a number of them ran across each other during the war and even served together. Still, that's a common misunderstanding most folks have. That they were this band of brothers. Band of warriors. The statue is responsible for that."

August was surprised at Billy's tone. It almost seemed hostile and sarcastic. "The statue?" he asked.

"In town. On the square. Shows them all together at Gettysburg. Ain't true. Anyway, it was really the wives."

"The officers' wives, you mean."

"Yes, sir. And some of them weren't even wives, yet."

"I am not following your story here, Billy," August declared.

"Sorry, sir. Getting ahead of myself. You see the wives and betrothed all ended up in Columbus waiting out the war. They got to know each other real well. Knitting societies and things like that. Their specialty was knitting socks for the soldiers." Billy reached down and pulled up his blue pant leg. Sticking out above his brown boot was a bright green sock. "They specialized in green," he concluded.

August laughed. "I assume that is not 60-year-old hosiery."

"Might be. I understand that they were very durable."

They reached the crest of the slope. There was a large flat area with no trees in front of them. A natural place to put a golf green, August thought. Ahead of them to the left, the small Pottawa River swung out of heavy forest and fell on a set of flat, tiered gray rocks. The water washed over the rocks in a wide gentle waterfall onto another set of tiered rocks. Then another set of rocks and another set in a long slope until the water reformed into a small river off to their right where they could see that the land opened into farmland. A set of small boulders ran along their side of the gentle waterfall like a stone fence.

"Pretty view," August remarked. "We did not get this far yesterday when Mr. Howard showed me around."

Billy sat down on a rock and allowed Scout to graze. August did the same, releasing Stanton. The horses munched on the wet grass. Bandit, spotting a rabbit, tore off into higher grass. Billy rolled a cigarette and offered one to August who declined. The older man wished, though, that he had his pipe. This was a good spot for a pipe smoke. Instead, he took out a small silver flask from his coat's breast pocket and took a sip of whiskey. His morning bracer. He offered the flask to Billy.

"Thank you, sir, but I don't drink."

August nodded, took another nip, and put the flask away.

Billy continued with his story. "It turned out that one of the young ladies, who wasn't yet married, was an only child. Her father was very wealthy and owned all this land. Almost the entire county. Or, to be more accurate, what eventually became Pottawa County."

"I bet I can guess that his name was Stowe," August interrupted. "hence the town's name. Is that correct?"

Billy shook his head. "Ah, no, sir. His name was actually Percy, Josiah Percy."

"So, who was the Stowe of Stowe Towne? One of the soldiers?"

Billy laughed. "It was Harriet Beecher Stowe. The woman who wrote *Uncle Tom's Cabin*."

"How did Harriet Beecher Stowe get involved?" August asked, amazed.

"She didn't. But, you see, the wives all liked her book."

"So they named a town after her?"

Billy ignored the question. Instead, he said: "Sir, may I ask you a question?"

"Of course, Billy."

Bandit wandered back and rested at the feet of his master. But Billy ignored the dog and stared hard at George August. "This here golf course you're going to build, Mr. August. Do you know why you're going to build it?"

August looked at the stout, younger man sitting across from him. "What are you getting at, Billy? Mr. Howard and his associates, Mr. Hanover and Mr. Duke, are sportsmen. They already sponsor a well-known polo club. Now they're interested in having a golf course. It's true that most of the courses I've designed have been in or very near cities. But..."

"It's not the golf course, sir," Billy interrupted.

"Not the golf course?"

"The ladies want a clubhouse."

"Well, of course, there will be a clubhouse. Every country club golf course has a clubhouse. It will be a fine clubhouse too, I might add."

Billy was providing useful information, August thought, but he also was somehow becoming annoying. He seemed to know a little too much for his station in life.

Billy, perhaps aware that he was crossing some invisible social line, said, "No offense, sir. I'm sure it will be a very nice golf course. But no one really wants a golf course. I don't know one of the gentlemen who ever plays golf. It's just that the course has to come along with the clubhouse. The ladies want the clubhouse."

"You have said that twice now, Billy," August couldn't help but let annoyance creep into his voice. "Who *are* these ladies?"

"Well, mostly they're the granddaughters and assorted nieces, cousins, and the like of the original wives. The officers' wives who founded Stowe Towne. The ladies now all belong to the Daughters of the Union Army. The DUA. Nothing happens in Stowe Towne unless the DUA approves and gives its blessing."

"Nonsense!"

Billy flipped away his cigarette. "It's the truth, sir," Billy said without looking at the older man.

"Never even heard of the DUA," August declared with anger in his tone.

"Well, you wouldn't in the South," Billy said mildly.

August opened his mouth to reply and then thought better of saying anything. He couldn't be irked at the young man. Billy had provided him with much information. More information than he had received over two days from his host, Sheridan Howard. It was a bit ego deflating to be told by a stable man that your all-important project—your *raison d'être*—was just a front. Designing golf courses might be an odd profession. But it was a gentleman's profession. The August family was a prominent Tidewater family. George August did not need the money. He certainly did not need the insult either. Especially from these Ohio farmers with their polo ponies who for some reason wanted to be High Society and have their own country club.

Still, August thought, as he stood and looked over the Cascades, it is a beautiful place. He could do some things here that he had been wanting to try in design. Money apparently was no object. The land was boundless. So was the ignorance. He would be in charge and no one would tell him to lengthen or shorten a hole. No one here would question his golf wisdom.

Billy gathered the horses and handed Stanton's reins to August. "Thank you, Billy," August said kindly. "Will you be at the polo match this afternoon?"

"No, sir," Billy said, mounting Scout. "A few of us boys are driving down to Lancaster to play baseball. Rain or shine."

They mounted their horses and proceeded slowly down the gentle slope beside the Cascades.

Later, when torrential rain had indeed washed out the polo match, George August would casually mention Billy Barnes to Sheridan Howard. Howard said how much he liked the man. He mentioned that Billy had been in World War I serving under General "Black Jack" Pershing as a runner. Hell of a baseball player, too. Smart as a whip. Had recently been married and they were expecting a baby. Yet, Howard confided, the man was lacking ambition. Howard said he had tried often to promote him on the estate. Make him a manager, but the fellow always refused.

Nonetheless, when George August returned the next spring to oversee the construction of the golf course, Billy Barnes surprised everyone by agreeing to be the on-site foreman. He did an excellent job until his disappearance in the late fall of that first year when the basic course had been carved out of the trees and rocks and soil. One day he had been on the hill near the very rocks where he and August had sat and discussed the DUA—some of the workers had seen him there—and then he just disappeared. Some people speculated foul play. A hobo who had been hanging around Stowe Towne was blamed. But the hobo disappeared, too. No one ever knew what happened to Billy Barnes, although rumors of him being spotted playing baseball in Cincinnati persisted for many years. But those sightings were never confirmed. However, the little hill leading up to the seventh green, and indeed the seventh hole itself, was from then on known as Barnes's Knob.

chapter one

STOWE TOWNE, 1998

Louisa May Jones Miller, known to her Society friends as *May*, had been the president of the local chapter of the Daughters of the Union Army for 25 years. The Stowe Towne DUA was the most active chapter in the country and May had twice served separate two-year terms as president of the national Daughters of the Union Army organization in the mid-1980s in addition to her local presidency. But now, at 72, May was thinking that she should give up the presidency of the Stowe Towne chapter to one of the younger people like Emma Mitchell who was not yet 60 years old. It wasn't that the job was beyond her ability or energy. Oh my, no! But there was a time to pass the torch. Hadn't Jane Hanover designated May as president when May was a mere 47 years old? Jane was 78 at the time and had had a number of good years left. Nevertheless, in this day and age, May recognized that everything was geared to youth.

Oh my, it certainly was!

Just like that young girl who had just worked on her hair: Heather.

All the young girls in town seemed to be named Heather. May even had a granddaughter named Heather! May would never normally let Heather or anyone else except Elizabeth (of "Beth's Curl and Comb Beauty Salon") work on her hair. Her hair was very delicate. All the women who were born a Jones had very delicate hair. But Elizabeth was "out today" or so they said. Imagine, May thought, not being in your beauty salon on a Saturday morning. Saturday evening was when Society happened. Take tonight, for example. It was the DUA Spring Fling at the Maple Lodge. Granted, the Spring Fling was not the premier DUA event. The Fling came in third behind the formal Christmas Ball and, of course, the DUA's number one event, the July Fourth Arts Festival. Nevertheless, as president, May had to look her best for all events.

My, it was hot!

May stepped out of the salon and looked up and down the busy main street of Stowe Towne. Duke Boulevard (although not a boulevard now since it was redesigned in 1951 to accommodate angle parking) was filled with late Saturday morning shoppers. Those shoppers, mind you, who didn't drive over to the malls surrounding Columbus. May fanned herself with a handkerchief and touched her coiffured white hair. She prayed it looked all right. My, it must be a hundred in the shade! And so early in the year! Maybe it was the contrast to the air conditioning in the salon. Beauty salons always had the air conditioning turned up so high because of all those hair-dryers.

May blinked in the sun and turned right to walk down the block. She loved Stowe Towne. There was so much *history*. Just across the street there in the historic town square was the famous statue of the seven Civil War heroes who founded Stowe Towne with the help of their wonderful wives. May's great-great-grandfather Captain Job Jones was one of the soldiers depicted in the statue. Mr. Miller's great-great-grandfather Major Benjamin Miller was another. (May had claimed that Major Miller's nickname of "Simple" meant pure of spirit, although the nickname had always been an embarrassment to Simple's heirs.) On a hot day like this, May could just *swoon* thinking about those heroes and their exploits. And to think, they were part of her family!

May recovered and hurried along. Mr. Miller would be waiting for her at the Gettysburg Café just a few steps away. He was having coffee and his favorite—cherry pie. May knew he was meeting some of the old fellows for golf this afternoon at The Candlesticks. *But only nine holes,* she had warned him. He had to be ready for the Spring Fling. They had to be there first to greet the guests. Of course, they should be having the Spring Fling at the country club. That was the right setting for such an event. But the club wasn't even a club. It was so *commercial.*

She sighed as she walked to the Café. She kept monitoring her hair carefully with her left hand. Joyce Thompson *Yoo-Hoo'd* passing by in her car. "See you tonight, May." May waved back with the handkerchief in her right hand. Momentarily, both of May's hands were waving above her head. *Rather indiscreet of Joyce shouting from the car,* May thought. She knew Joyce was interested in being DUA President, but something or other would have to freeze over before that ever happened.

Maybe Mr. Miller could be persuaded to wait a few more minutes so she could have a piece of pecan pie at the restaurant. It was so delicious. Although she really shouldn't. But it would lift her spirits. She felt depressed thinking about giving up the presidency of the DUA. She knew it was the right thing to do—turn over the reins. Yet, there was something not quite right about it. She couldn't put her finger on it. Something was in the wind. She had an intuition about these things. *No doubt about that!* May was seldom wrong. That's why she'd been president for 25 years. Still, she wasn't sure what was wrong. It irritated her. She cautioned herself, however, as a gentleman in bib overalls held the door of the Café open for her, that she couldn't take it out on Mr. Miller. She needed him to be in a good mood for tonight.

⌣

Sticks Bergman and Howie Howard had been in the same high school class in the late sixties. The high school, the only high school in Stowe Towne and all of Pottawa County, was the Harriet Beecher Stowe High School. Home of the Union Generals and the Lady Union Generals. The nicknames were awkward, especially for the girls' teams. In addition, every once in a while some literary-oriented sports opponent would taunt the Union Generals by calling them the Uncle Toms. This was racially confusing to the traditionally white Stowe High School athletes, but it nevertheless made them mad.

Sticks and Howie, although they had known each other since kindergarten and occasionally had fallen in and out of friendship as children do, were not friends as adults. It was not active dislike, just disinterest. Their lives had taken different paths despite the small orbit of the small town of Stowe Towne, Ohio.

Howie Howard was a true Howard, meaning he was from one of the seven original families who founded Stowe Towne in the late 1860s immediately after the Civil War. The principal streets of the town immortalized the seven families: Howard Street; Thompson Street; Miller Lane; Jones Street; Mitchell Street; Hanover Avenue; and Duke Boulevard. All good English names. For 130 years, the families belonging to those names ran most of what was important in Stowe Towne.

Sticks Bergman's family did not have a street named after it. Not that his family did not consist of good people. The Bergman boys' father and grandfather owned a large farm that Sticks now owned. He had replaced the old farmhouse with a modern home. The barn had burned down long ago and now he mostly rented out the land for farmers in the area to farm. His two brothers owned a prosperous lumberyard, Bergman Bros. Lumber, in Stowe Towne. Sticks owned an interest in the business and often helped out at the lumberyard.

But the lives of Howie Howard and Sticks Bergman were inexorably linked because their homes and property bordered the two sides of The Candlesticks Golf Course. The Candlesticks. That was what the golf course designed and built by George August in 1922 and 1923 had been named. August had wanted it to be called The Cascades after the rippling waterfall at the back of the property that he had first viewed with Billy Barnes. But unbeknown to him, the ladies of the DUA had, as Billy Barnes predicted, already picked out the name Candlesticks because that was the name *they* wanted for the clubhouse.

The Candlesticks was built on land south of the Pottawa River, directly to the east of the Howard family property, directly west of the farmland now owned by Sticks Bergman and his wife, Sammi, and a few short miles to the northeast of Stowe Towne proper. The Candlesticks Golf Course property was on the very southernmost tip of a large tract of land owned by the State of Ohio. The land, stretching north-northeast, was part of a long geological ridge and was heavily wooded. It contained some picturesque rock formations and waterfalls. When Ohio was settled, this tract of land was never farmed because of its terrain. The state government always owned it and eventually created Pottawa State Park on the northern end 20 miles northeast of Stowe Towne. The state turned the rest of the land into Pottawa State Forest except the southern tip where the ridge ran out to a reasonably flat area intersected by the Pottawa River. The state eventually gave this relatively small parcel of land to a group of Stowe Towne investors (from the seven families, of course) with the proviso that the land be turned into a recreational area. An exclusive country club was probably not what the state had in mind. Except, many state legislators, after passage of the legislation giving over the land, became members of The Candlesticks. Down to the present, legislators wanting to play golf were always accommodated at the golf course.

So, when the families joined together in the early 1920s to build the club and golf course on this newly acquired property, they did it up right. When completed, George August's course was magnificent, although it later became old-fashioned in golf terms. The Candlesticks' course was short and tree-lined despite covering a generous amount of land. The bunkers were deep and isolated like Scottish bunkers and not like contemporary bunkers that are beach-like and shamrock-shaped. The greens were small, lush, and slow. The vistas were beautiful from the tees for the golfers' benefit, not from the greens for the galleries' benefit. It was a pleasure and honor back then to play The Candlesticks. To hit your niblick or your brassie or your spoon. To discuss distance with your caddie. To tip your cap in honor of a fine shot.

The layout of the course was dictated by both the Pottawa River and by the stone ridge that finally petered out on the downside of the course near the clubhouse. But the river met what was left of the ridge at the back of the course. The ridge, eons ago, had caused the river to dip down back southeastward for about 300 yards in a wide, slightly cascading, near-waterfall before the water hit a rock buildup that turned it back to its natural eastern flow. The whole course, but especially around the Cascades, was heavily wooded.

George August ultimately decided to build a "low" nine and "high" nine. The low nine was the front nine of the course and mostly occupied the flatter, western side of the property that adjoined land owned by the Howard family. However, the seventh hole, a 420-yard par 4, the most difficult hole on the course, went uphill to an undulating green at the top of the Cascades. This was the hole that became known as Barnes's Knob after Billy Barnes's disappearance. The eighth hole, a dogleg par 5, immediately played away from the water. The shortest par 4, the 340-yard ninth hole, then came back to the clubhouse.

The high nine or the back nine started back toward the river with the 10th hole. The rest of the holes played back and forth and along the Pottawa and among occasional rock outcroppings. Only the long, 568-

yard par-5 18th hole returned to the clubhouse near the flat eastern edge of the property, which was owned by the Bergman family.

Trees lined all the fairways, although, over the years, many of the trees on the low nine had been pruned away and those holes were much more friendly to the golfers who hit wayward drives. Trees still flourished along some of the fairways of the high nine and, with the rock formations, made that nine one of the most difficult nine holes most golfers ever played. Despite its difficulties, it was still a gorgeous course. It was the type of course to play by yourself on a misty morning. However, it was *not* the type of course that could well accommodate Saturday afternoon hackers lined up two foursomes deep on every tee.

In the '50s, despite President Eisenhower's love of golf, the game overall fell into the doldrums. The Candlesticks Country Club and Golf Course fell into the doldrums too. Arnie Palmer had not yet come along to reinvent golf, and country clubs were out of fashion for World War II vets raising families and staying home nights to watch Ed Sullivan and big money TV quiz shows. Some of the Stowe Towne families wanted out of the ownership deal, which was easier said than done. In fact, the ownership of The Candlesticks was a legal quagmire caused by an increasing number of family heirs and heirs apparent, and a less than specific original handshake agreement. The Howard family, led then by Howie's father Grant, was aggressive and vociferous during the legal wrangling. The Howards, after all, had the most at stake because the family's property adjoined the course. The Howards, including Howie's grandfather Sheridan who was one of the original handshakers, always felt that the course was "sort of" their private domain.

Finally, an Ohio Supreme Court justice who was a frequent club guest was called upon to mediate the dispute before it ended up in the courts. His name was Richard Summers and he was a hell of a golfer. He was only 34 in 1956, the youngest justice on the Court. In the late fall of that year, he crafted what would become known as The Candlesticks Accord.

The Candlesticks Accord formalized The Candlesticks Golf Course into a business with the seven families as shareholders. The number of shares per family was determined through a complicated formula devised by Justice Summers based on the original handshake, various contributions made by the families over the years (both monetary and in-kind), and current concerns and considerations. Shares could be sold, but only among the original families unless all the families agreed that shares could be sold to outsiders. However, no shares ever were sold to outsiders and only one family ever divested to the other families.

The course itself was turned into a semiprivate club essentially opening it to public golf. The phrase "Country Club" was dropped from the title. The club's restaurant was closed and remodeled into a large, fully stocked golf store. The old Men's Grill became a bar and lounge. Much of the building's classic country club facade was torn down and the building was streamlined in a pseudo 1950's Frank Lloyd Wright style.

This customer-oriented, public remodeling was very unusual at the time and opposed bitterly by a few members of the families who remembered the club's glorious Society days in the late 20s and 30s. However, the move was shrewd. The Candlesticks prospered from public play and the pro shop, the first of its kind in the area, became extremely profitable.

Justice Summers refused payment for his consultation and mediation but accepted a lifetime membership, including lifetime free golf at The Candlesticks.

⌣

All others paid cash.

Including the Saturday foursomes that trudged past Howie Howard and Bip Jordan on the eighth tee. Three benches formed a semicircle well behind the gold championship markers at the very back of the tee. Behind the benches, the ground sloped gently for about 15 yards to the edge of the Cascades. Sitting on the benches gave golfers three spectacular views of the course. They could look to their right back to the tiered seventh green. Or, they could look to their left down the normally trickling Cascades and Pottawa River and see the large 11th green and beyond most of the fairway and green of the 12th hole beside the stream. Or, they could look straight ahead away from the river down the long par-5 eighth fairway.

Howie and Bip sat on the middle bench, their golf bags on the ground in front of them, and watched two carts squeal up to the white tees 30 yards in front of them. The white tees were way up to facilitate crowded Saturday play. It was the first weekend in May and it was also the first truly beautiful weekend of the spring. The sun was warm and there was a light breeze in their faces.

Howie waved the foursome to play through. Bip sighed audibly as a goofball golfer in red shorts and a Cleveland Indians T-shirt sliced a drive to the right over the trees and far into the seventh fairway. "He doesn't even care," Bip muttered as the man guffawed with his friends. "We have no standards. Golf has gone to the dogs." The other three golfers sprayed equally bad shots down the fairway and got back into their carts and sped off.

Bip, The Candlesticks' resident pro, was offended by everything: the golfers' play, their dress, their attitudes, the fact they used carts... one of them even had a yellow neon bag with the word *PROSTAFF* on the side.

"Shitheads," Bip said. Bip's father had been a coal miner in West Virginia and that had been his favorite term. Bip had grown up hearing his father call everybody and everything *shitheads*. But that was a long time ago. Bip was going to be 65 in mid-July. His father had died at age 47 of Black Lung Disease.

Howie laughed. "Bip, I've told you before to take Saturdays off. It's just too hard on your soul. Besides, each of those guys paid $45 for the privilege of hitting a slice. Then there's $24 for each cart. Not counting the money they'll spend for beer and dogs." He did some quick math in his head. "That's about $270, more or less."

Bip leaned forward shaking his head. "I'm sure they've done at least that much damage to the course, Mr. Howard."

Bip had known Howie for 30 years and had called him Howie for most of that time. But he had started calling him Mr. Howard a year before when Howie had taken over chairmanship of the owner's committee from Tom Duke, Senior. Howie had never served the three-year term as ownership chair. It was a royal pain in the ass even though the only two things the members of the committee wanted were a decent profit check and free golf on demand. But the person who held the ownership chair still had to function like an owner, which was occasionally time-consuming at best and a severe migraine at worst. It was certainly Howie's turn. He made appropriate and expected noises about his reluctance. Nevertheless, his demeanor was all a facade. Howie had big plans which all hinged on his being committee chair. However, one of the less portentous outcomes was that from the day Howie became Bip's official boss, Bip started calling him Mr. Howard.

Howie hated it because he truly loved old Bip. But he understood. Bip had rules because golf had rules. You didn't mess with the rules. Howie, for example, from his very first round of golf under Bip's instruction, had never taken a mulligan. You just didn't do that.

Yet, things do change. And Howie had two immediate goals that involved Bip. The first was that Howie needed Bip to help him get his daughter, Julie, a full golf scholarship at Ohio State University in the fall. The second was that he needed Bip to retire before Bip's next birthday. Bip would do all he could for Julie. That wasn't a problem. But Bip's retirement was going to be tricky.

Thinking about Julie, Howie asked, "What did you think of her today?" The three of them had played the first seven holes together, but

Julie had some sort of school obligation and had left. Senior graduation planning and partying was eating heavily into her golf practice time. Besides, for all Howie knew, it wasn't even practice. She hadn't committed about what college she was even going to, much less whether or not she was going to play golf. High school golf had happened the past fall. Statistics were in for her. She had been a close number two on the squad to the Miller girl. Not that it mattered, but Heather Miller wasn't even interested in golf any longer. She was going to some school out East and Howie bet she hadn't picked up a club since the state high school tournament. Meanwhile, he had taken Julie on two winter golf trips to warmer climates to keep her edge and interest. But now her future and her golf were hanging in the balance.

"Julie's golf?" Bip said. "Her swing was ragged. No concentration, especially on the greens. But she's a little bigger and a little stronger. The drive on seven was great. Her first drive, for that matter, on one, was strong. A little left. Anyway, she seems to have picked up 15 or 20 yards off the tee."

Howie agreed. "I noticed it, too. On *all* her shots. On number four, she decided to hit a three-iron instead of a wood for her second shot. She put it on the green. I've seen her hit from there before and she's always used a wood. But she cranked that three-iron."

"But then she three-putted from 18 feet. No concentration, I tell you."

Howie's shoulders sagged. "I know. I know. We have to get through this graduation and get her a scholarship and get her set. She has to go to Ohio State."

Bip looked out of the corner of his eye at his boss. Bip's own two sons had never done a thing he asked of them once they reached 16. He—well, mostly his wife Dorene—had managed to get them through high school, but that was it. The boys hit the highway running. The older of the two, Jerry, now sold real estate in California, had a big family, and was reconciled enough with Bip and Dorene to spend an occasional Christmas or Thanksgiving back in Stowe Towne. The other,

Jack, was long gone. Supposedly, Jerry knew how to get in touch with Jack. But Bip had given up caring. He, unfortunately, saw a little bit of Jerry and Jack in Julie Howard.

"Well," Bip said, "Doug Kreuger is bringing a couple of athletic boosters over tomorrow for a round. I'll work on him for Julie. We'll see."

That made Howie feel better. Kreuger was the assistant men's coach at OSU. It was something, at least. There was a break in the parade of golfers in front of them. "Come on, Bip," he said getting up, "let's play the last two holes and get some lunch."

Just as Howie stepped up and ripped his drive 240 yards down the middle of the eighth fairway, Sticks Bergman was duplicating Julie Howard's three-iron shot on the fourth hole. His Titleist carried the green and came to rest 15 feet shy of the pin. His three playing companions were not even near the green with their second shots. He gave up a stroke to each of them on the fourth, but, if he sank his birdie putt, he would probably sweep them on this hole too, just like the first hole. Overall, he would be three up on all three bozos after only four holes.

It scarcely mattered to Sticks that he was also shooting par.

In fact, Sticks would have happily given up the possibility of making upward of $100 on bets in exchange for playing a single round with his son Randy. Randy had driven home yesterday from Kent State University in order to celebrate his mother's birthday. He had about a month to go in his freshman year. Last night Sticks and Sammi, the birthday girl, Randy, and their daughter Sissy (who was four years older than Randy) and her husband Chuck had all gone to dinner at the Maple Lodge. The Maple Lodge was Stowe Towne's best restaurant. It was the only expensive restaurant in town. The children had always loved the Maple Lodge and it seemed the right place to go for Sammi's birthday.

Sticks wanted to play golf with Randy on Saturday. He was even willing to cancel the business foursome, but Randy explained over shrimp cocktail that he already had other plans. He didn't elaborate. And Sticks didn't press. Randy was a good kid and had had a hard time in school. Sticks had wanted him to go to Kent State because that's where Sticks had gone. Sticks had played football there and now Randy was playing football for the Blue and Gold. Randy was a good high school linebacker and center, but Stowe High was a Division II high school and Randy was a marginal college football player. That meant no scholarship consideration. But he had walked on, and the woeful Golden Flashes had kept him on the squad. He took a lot of punishment in practice and didn't get to play much. But then, as Sticks explained after going to every single Kent game (including road trips to East Carolina and Navy), Randy was just a freshman and was putting in his time for later glory.

The putt broke about a club head left to right and Sticks rolled it in with no problem. Birdie. *Well, whatever Randy was doing, Sticks thought, he wasn't making money like his pop was.*

‚úĆ

What Randy Bergman was doing at that moment, panting heavily, was attempting to remove Julie Howard's panties. He was not having much success. In fact, it got so awkward that he fell off the sectional in the Howard family room. "Is there something wrong here?" he asked from the deep plush tan carpet.

Julie rolled on her back on the sectional and fingered the top buttons of her "Lady Union Generals" blue and white high school golf shirt. "I was watching TV the other day," she said, "and there was this show that said that Amazons used to cut off their breasts so that they could shoot bows and arrows better. Maybe I'd be a better golfer if I cut off my breasts. Like that guy on TV said who they fired."

Randy moaned. "That's just great. You can already beat me at golf. Now you want to cut off your boobs so you can beat me worse and I lose the boobs, too."

"You're a boob, too."

"Great. I'm a big boob sitting on the floor."

"I played rotten this morning. I don't like golf anymore." She brushed back her long honey blond hair from around her face. "Maybe I should cut my hair short so I don't have to wear it in a ponytail when I golf."

"What about sex? I thought this was about sex, not golf."

"For God's sake, Randy, I'm in high school."

Randy gazed at his girlfriend's prominent breasts. "Is this the twilight zone or what? We've been going together for two years. We've had sex in cars, in your bedroom, in *my* bedroom, in Heather Miller's bedroom, and even right here on this couch. And that was with both your parents in the house. Which they aren't now."

But Julie wasn't paying any attention to him. She reached her arms up toward the ceiling as if she were shooting an invisible bow and arrow. "Archery and golf have a lot in common. Ever think about it? Strong arms. Holding the body still. The release. Did you ever think about it, Randy?"

"Can't say that I have, Julie." Actually, it sounded to him like she was describing sex, not archery or golf. He stood up and felt stupid rezipping and rebuttoning his pants. He had just unzipped and unbuttoned himself moments earlier. But he had seen her in these moods before. He used to think she was just immature. But now he was starting to become afraid that this was the way she really was.

"When are you going back?" she asked.

"You want me to go back?"

"No." She suddenly sat up. "Come on, you can watch me change clothes and then you can take me to McDonald's."

She marched out of the room and Randy hesitated for a second. Then he shrugged. "What the hell," he muttered and hurried after her before she changed her mind. Again.

chapter two

THE SPRING FLING

Sticks Bergman said good-bye to his pigeons after collecting their money and buying them beer and brats, and walked home from The Candlesticks. The club let him keep his King Cobras in Bip's office. His house was a quarter of a mile down County Road 12, better known as The Pike, toward Bryce Bridge. Actually, he didn't even walk down the road. He cut past the club's maintenance building and cart shed, eased himself through a break in the out-of-bounds fence on number 18, and strolled along the south end of one of the fields he rented out for farming. The soybeans, he noted, were just coming up. He picked up a brand new Top-Flite XL from some poor golfer's wayward second shot. He'd give it to Randy. Sticks didn't play Top-Flites.

It was past four when he entered their ranch house through the deck and into the family room. Their old golden retriever, Bertha, raised her head but didn't get up from where she was lying just inside the sliding glass doors. He scratched her behind the ears. Weren't the Reds playing in LA? Sticks remembered seeing it listed on cable. He picked up the remote and flicked on the big-screen TV. But Sammi heard him from the laundry room and yelled something. He punched the mute. "What, honey? I just came in the back."

"You didn't forget about tonight, did you, Sticks? You know the old ladies. Dinner will be at 6:30 and not a second later."

Damn, Sticks muttered to himself. *The dreaded Spring Fling.* He composed himself as he surfed through the channels silently and finally found the Reds' game. He said loudly and as pleasantly as he could manage: "No, honey, I'll be ready. I just need a quick shower." He suppressed a belch from the beer and brats.

An hour or so later, Sticks stood in his good white boxer shorts and best undershirt and stared morosely out the window of their master bedroom that overlooked the soybeans and the 18th fairway beyond. He had had three eagles on that hole in his life although not today. In fact, he was damn lucky to make par. He had mishit his third shot into the green—way right. Then his chip rolled by the hole a good 20 feet. But he had drilled the putt. Not that it mattered. The match was long over by then and he had won all the money that there was to be won. Still, that par had given him 11 pars, two birdies, and five bogeys for a 75. A couple strokes over his usual score for The Candlesticks. On other courses, even though they were often much easier than The Candlesticks, he usually shot in the high 70s to low 80s. But he had played The Candlesticks so often that he was almost a scratch golfer on the course. He knew how to avoid all the trouble on the course, knew the greens by heart, and had supreme confidence in shooting well there. He loved The Candlesticks.

"Hurry up, Sticks, don't you want a Rob Roy before dinner?" Sammi said as she came out of the bathroom. "The old ladies haven't outlawed liquor, you know."

Sticks sighed. "If the husbands couldn't drink at these affairs, they'd make their wives disband the stupid DUA."

"That's not likely to happen. Anyway, be nice...and get dressed. And take a look at how your birthday present looks on your grateful wife."

Sticks turned away from the window. He looked at his wife whose right hand fingered the delicate pearl necklace at her throat. Their daughter, Sissy, had picked it out and had spared no expense. But that was all right. At the restaurant last night, the pearls had been a big hit, so Sticks felt good about his gift.

Sticks gave his wife a smile. "They look very nice," he said. Actually, Sammi looked very nice. She had on a pale yellow dress and her light brown hair was pushed back from her oval face. Not bad looking at all for someone who now—with her birthday yesterday—was as old as he was.

"Thank you," she answered. "Now please get dressed."

Sticks sat down on the bed and pulled on gray socks. Sammi had laid out his clothes. Looked like he was wearing gray slacks, blue shirt, double-breasted blue blazer, and a sporty red and blue striped club tie that he had never seen before. Sammi had very good taste.

"Why do we have to go to these things?" Sticks moaned.

Sammi chose to ignore her husband's question because she knew that he knew the answer. Of course, Samantha Bergman was not now or ever would be a member of the Daughters of the Union Army. However, Sammi was partners with Bruce Dean. Dean and Bergman Associates was the leading real estate office in the county. So, naturally, DUA members who owned much of the land in and around Stowe Towne were very interested in socializing with the leading real estate agents. In addition, Bruce Dean had once been a member of Town Council. The Spring Fling, in other words, was *business* for Sammi.

Sticks finished dressing and tied the tie. It did look smart as he gazed at himself in the mirror. He was just over six feet tall. Sort of husky, but he had kept his weight under control for a guy in his mid-forties. Brown hair receding a bit; he self-consciously brushed it a little forward now. Sammi stood beside him. They were a handsome couple. You *could* take the boy out of the country. Speaking of boys...

"Has Randy been around?" he asked.

Sammi nodded. "He was. Then Julie stopped by after she finished golfing, I guess. She was wearing her high school golf shirt. I think she only wears it to please her father. That's what she told me once. Anyway, Randy went off with her and I haven't heard from him since."

Sticks smoothed his tie and Sammi murmured her approval. He said, "I thought those two would kind of drift apart. Not that I have anything against Julie, of course. But I just thought Randy would get more interested in college girls. You know what I mean?"

Sammi murmured something again and turned away from the mirror. Sticks wasn't sure what she had said and concluded that he did not really want to know anyway. Sissy had been easier to raise than Randy. She just went off to college at the University of Cincinnati, became a teacher, came back to Columbus to teach, found another young teacher (Chuck), and they married last fall. Neither of them played golf. It had all been effortless. But Randy was a different story.

Sticks shrugged and grabbed his sports coat. *Well,* he thought, *it's Spring Fling time. Who should be so lucky?*

⌒

Margaret Emerson Howard was only a junior member of the Daughters of the Union Army because she would not turn 45 until the first of July. But a mere three days after that, at the DUA July Fourth Arts Festival, she would be inducted as a full member. The Arts Festival was the only time of the year when new members were inducted into the DUA or when junior members were promoted to full membership. Being married to Howie, of course, made her eligible for DUA membership. It was a common misconception that only members of the seven families were members of the DUA. Membership did go beyond simply being a blood descendant of one of the original seven families or marrying into one of the families. About a third of the current DUA membership came from "outside." Nevertheless, figuring out exactly how the outside members were chosen was not a matter of public record.

Twenty years earlier, when Margaret Emerson came to Stowe Towne with her new husband, DUA members quickly discovered that Margaret out-blue-blooded most, if not all, of them. She was from the Boston Emersons and had forefathers who were officers not only in the Civil War but also the Revolutionary War. Margaret came from serious money and was the younger of only two children of a thin, bookish man named John Paul Emerson who was, of all things, a Professor of Geology at Ohio State University. He had come to Ohio directly from Harvard and had taught at OSU for 32 years. Margaret had been born at University Hospital in Columbus. Professor Emerson now had been retired for almost 20 years, and despite being 83, he lived by himself in a very comfortable older home just blocks from campus. Mrs. Emerson, Margaret's mother, had died in a car accident when Margaret was just five. The professor never remarried.

Margaret was thin and severe and thought of herself in Audrey Hepburn-like terms, although her perpetual frown suppressed any Audrey Hepburn-like charm. She looked more like her father than her mother, although her daughter Julie was full-figured and looked very much like her late mother, whom Margaret could barely remember. But the professor remembered and it endeared him greatly to his grand-daughter. Margaret, for the Spring Fling, chose to wear a dark green dress that during some previous fashion year might have been called a sheath. She also wore pearls almost identical to Sammi Bergman's birth-day present.

Margaret sat in the living room smoking cigarettes and listening to

Vivaldi and made Howie go back into the bedroom and change clothes three times before she approved a light gray, glen plaid Brooks Brothers suit with a deep paisley maroon tie. Howie was slightly smaller than Sticks, his neighbor on the other side of the golf course. Howie had the traditional Howard black hair that he slicked down—a style encouraged by his daughter. And Howie always indulged Julie. His most distinct feature was his sharp gray eyes.

Howie breathed a sigh of relief when Margaret finally okayed his suit selection for the evening. He glanced at the clock. It was only 5:30. Just a mite early to leave, although Howie wouldn't mind more than a couple of drinks tonight. It was the only way to really survive the Spring Fling.

"You look very nice," Howie said. He always told his wife she looked very nice just before they went out. "Did you get that in Columbus this morning?"

"No," she answered, "I just visited with father. I've had this old thing."

Howie knew his wife would never be caught dead in just any *old thing*. She may not have bought the dress this morning, but he would have bet that she had never worn it out before. He would have won that bet.

"Have you heard from our daughter this afternoon?" he asked to pass the time. He sat on the piano bench across from the couch.

That music she has on seems to be playing very fast, he thought.

Margaret paused before she answered and then said: "She called before you got home. I think she's spending the night at Heather Miller's."

"I didn't think she liked Heather Miller."

"Oh, you know girls," Margaret said. "One minute they're friends and the next minute they're sworn enemies."

"Well, I know she didn't like her during golf season. Heather never played up to her potential. She dragged the team down and she dragged

Julie down, too."

Margaret blew a horrific amount of smoke into the air above her head. "I heard Randy's home this weekend. Was he at the course?"

Howie bit his lip. "I saw Sticks, but I didn't see Randy. He could've been there. It was crowded."

The Vivaldi played on. After a pause, Margaret said: "I hope they aren't together."

The "they" of her statement lay on the deep tan carpet between Margaret and Howie; the couple stared at it as they listened to the *Concerto for 2 Flutes in C Major*.

Indeed, together, and separately, they wondered about "they."

When the concerto ended, it was time to go.

⌇

The Spring Fling was not actually being held in the Maple Lodge whose restaurant was buzzing with its usual heavy Saturday night trade. Instead, the Fling was next door in what the Lodge staff called derisively "The Barn," but what was known to the public as "The Grove." It was really an annex to the Lodge and was serviced by the same staff and kitchen. "The Barn" was the more accurate description. Despite its cavernous, exposed-beamed, dark, and dank interior, it had been the home for three generations of homecomings, proms, reunions, anniversaries, wakes, ballroom/line dancing marathons, and, of course, wedding receptions. May and Mr. Miller, Sticks and Sammi Bergman, and Howie and Margaret Emerson Howard all had had their wedding receptions in The Grove. Everyone felt at home in The Grove.

Howie slipped away from Margaret in quest of her Chardonnay and his Chivas on the rocks as soon as they cleared the receiving line headed by May Miller. Green and yellow crepe paper seemed to be hanging everywhere and there were huge, riotous collections of pots of flowers on all the round dinner tables. It was like a florist had died and all of his fellow florists tried to outdo each other to honor the dearly departed rival. Even Howie, who cared or noticed little about such things, thought it was way too much.

The bar, as usual, was tucked in the rear corner. It was too small and would be overcrowded all night by men seeking refuge. Tommy Smith, Joe's kid—not so much a kid anymore—was bartending and Howie just flicked his finger and Tommy nodded. He finished making a gin and tonic by plopping a lime in the glass, handed the drink over to a heavy-set man Howie didn't recognize, and then uncorked a liter of Taylor Chardonnay and poured a glass. Then he poured a heavy double of Scotch for Howie. Howie slipped Tommy a ten, waved, and retreated. He would be back.

Truthfully, Howie had other things on his mind and, as he handed Margaret her wine, his eyes glanced around the room. Specifically, he was looking for Bruce Dean, the realtor, and Chuck January, the President of the Pottawa County Commissioners. He saw neither of them yet, although he knew they would be here. The Spring Fling was too important an occasion for Stowe Towne society. This was where real estate deals were made and politicians lined up money for the next election. And, if Howie got the good news, this year's Spring Fling would also be the confirmation of the biggest announcement in Stowe Towne since Allied Pipes put up a new plant just south of town. But only if everything was handled very carefully.

Howie kept his eye out for Dean and January as he drifted into a conversation with a couple of the old fellows. The fellows, who were DUA spouses, were arguing, as always, about golf. Usually, it was some irrelevant topic like who was better, Palmer or Nicklaus, or some obscure rule concerning drops or scorecards or such. But this discussion was something different.

Lincoln Jones, sporting a lime green sports coat, was saying, "Sixty thousand for the lot. And, it's just on a fairway. Not at a green or tee."

"He's got to be out of his mind," Paul Mitchell said, shaking his bald head.

"That's right," Lincoln agreed. "And when he builds, the house has to have a value of at least four hundred thousand. That's actually written in the land deed. How does he have half a million dollars?"

"Who?" Howie asked, intrigued.

Mitchell turned on Howie. "George Simmons, that's who. That man never made an honest nickel in his life."

Howie righted himself from Mitchell's vodka martini breath. "Well, Paul, that's what happens when you marry well."

Mitchell sniffed and took another drink. "Hannah Hanover is as dumb as a fence post. But that's still no excuse for her marrying that jerk."

Of the seven original families, the Hanovers had always had the most money and had consequently been the most foolish and the most extravagant.

Jones chuckled. "Give it up, Paul, that's 40 years ago that she dumped you for George. But you're right, she is as dumb as a fence post, although she's still a looker."

Howie interjected before Mitchell could respond: "Anyway, gentlemen, where are they building a house?"

"Somewhere north of Naples," Jones answered. "Up near Ft. Myers Beach. It's in a development called The Glades."

"That stands for everglades," Mitchell added, "and that means swamp. You know, hit your golf ball and then burp a 'gator to get it back."

Howie humored the men by laughing with them.

Sticks, who had just arrived with Sammi, was passing near the three men as they erupted in laughter. He glanced over and saw that the group included Howie Howard and kept on going. He had to have at least one drink before he talked to Howie.

Sticks got both Sammi and himself Rob Roys from Tommy and they drifted into a conversation with Matt and Laura Robinson. Laura worked as a secretary for Sammi in the real estate office and Matt built homes for a living. It was also business for Matt to pony up the $150 per couple cost for the Spring Fling. He was a loyal Bergman Lumber customer and the brothers gave him extremely favorable rates on building supplies.

After joking about the number of trees that had to be sacrificed to paper the room, Matt said, "Laura told me that Bruce got a call from Cliner on Friday. He wasn't in at the time, but Laura gave him the message. She doesn't know if he called back."

Cliner was a large Cleveland real estate development firm that specialized in upscale housing developments. Sticks shrugged. He would like some Cliner Columbus business for the lumberyard, but Cliner mostly, if not exclusively, bought wholesale because of the number of houses the firm developed.

"Sammi didn't mention it, Matt," Sticks said. "Sammi, did you know Bruce got a call from Cliner?"

Sammi shook her head. "No, Laura just mentioned it to me. Bruce didn't say anything to me on Friday. But I was in and out a lot."

"Well, I'm worried," Matt said. "Just mentioning Cliner can cut my income in half. Or worse."

Sticks glanced at the hulking builder who looked extremely uncomfortable in an ill-fitting light blue sports coat. He knew the man was a pessimist at heart—it always showed in his golf. He could hit the ball a ton, but then one bad hole and he would be done for the day. Matt could be working on half a dozen houses at once and have money to burn, but still cry on your shoulder about what he was going to do two or three months down the road. He and Laura were seriously in need of a financial planner.

Well, this was a social event, so Sticks felt an obligation to try to make Matt feel better. "Doesn't a company like Cliner ever subcontract to somebody like you? I mean, you've got an excellent reputation. You did houses in that subdivision over in Gahanna, didn't you?"

"Sure," Matt acknowledged, "but Cliner doesn't work like that. They do it all themselves and keep all the profits."

"So, why would they call Bruce?" Sticks wondered aloud to his wife.

Now it was her turn to shrug. "I don't know. Bruce was talking to a fellow who owns a piece of property south of the airport in Columbus. But that's just a little piece of land. Six or seven houses at the most. You couldn't even put a strip mall there, plus it's not on a main road. Cliner wouldn't be interested in that, I don't think."

Matt took a long gulp of his Molson's. "I don't know, but I bet you that I get screwed."

Being the screwer, not the screwee, was actually on Bruce Dean's mind as he slipped in the kitchen entrance door of The Grove so that he could avoid the receiving line. Bruce, later that evening, was picking up a young woman friend who was more or less separated from her husband. She lived on the north side of Columbus and he had a motel room reserved up in Westerville. The woman was distinctly younger, maybe 14 years, than Bruce, who was a youthful 39. Bruce was also more or less separated from his second wife, Melinda, who was on an extended vacation with her parents in Indianapolis. Bruce didn't really expect her to return to Stowe Towne anytime soon.

He slunk along the wall, hiding behind dangling green and yellow crepe paper, and worked his way to the bar. It was somewhat paradoxical that he was only here to see people although he preferred not to be seen. A further paradox: real estate people only survived by meeting people, but tonight he'd prefer not to meet anyone. Bruce knew, though, what his real problem was. He couldn't keep a secret. It was his failing. And now he had a pretty good secret to keep.

He made it to the bar with only a couple of cursory, *Hi, how you doing tonight?* to friends and former clients. Tommy poured him Skyy vodka on the rocks with a lemon twist. Bruce gratefully took a sip and surveyed the room. God, he thought, it looks the same as the first time I was invited 15 years ago. He knew he had only been invited then because his first wife was a Jones girl. Now he knew he was only invited because so many of the old families owed him for real estate deals. Some of them, in fact, owed him a great deal.

Bruce spotted Howie Howard making a beeline for him. Well, that's why he was here. He stepped away from the jostling at the bar and the two men hovered behind a potted bush decorated with green and yellow crepe paper tulips.

"Well, did they call?" Howie demanded immediately.

"Yeah, but I missed it. Then I couldn't get back through to Morgan. That's why I didn't call you." Actually, the real reason he didn't call Howie was the possibility of getting Margaret on the phone. Bruce thought Margaret a cold fish and hated talking to her. Plus, he didn't know how much Howie had told her about the project.

"So, you don't know."

"Howie, when I know, you'll know. You're too anxious about this. Situations sometimes have to percolate, if you know what I mean."

Howie had no idea what Bruce meant. "I just talked with Chuck and he and Barney are ready to go. We got the two Republican Commissioners on our side and you know that Barnes will do whatever they say."

Barnes was Kenny Barnes, the first-term state senator who, as everyone knew, had his head so far up his ass that he wouldn't see the light of day until his second term. If there *was* a second term. He was also the grandson of Billy Barnes of Barnes's Knob fame.

Suddenly, Sammi was at their elbows. "Did you talk to Cliner on Friday, Bruce?" she asked her partner directly, without acknowledging Howie.

She didn't notice Howie turn as white as May Miller's hair. Holy shit, he thought, if Sammi Bergman knows about this...

But Bruce was up to the challenge. He always subscribed to the theory that the best defense was a strong offense "Why are they calling us?" he shot back at Sammi. "Those guys eat agencies like us for lunch."

"I don't know," Sammi said, a bit wide-eyed at Bruce's tone.

"Why didn't you take the call? We're partners."

"I guess they didn't ask for me."

Bruce shrugged. "Well, we can call them back on Monday. Or wait until they call again, which they'll do if they want something."

Sammi returned the shrug and, still without acknowledging Howie, slipped away.

"Goddamn," Howie muttered and gave Bruce a baleful look. He turned away to find Margaret. The Golden DUA Liberty Bell was ringing for dinner seating.

It was precisely 6:30 p.m.

~

It had originally been Heather Miller's idea. Four years ago when they were freshmen in high school it had been little more than a somewhat out-of-control pajama party. Now FSF had grown, changed locations, and was clearly going to be out-of-control by the end of the night. Supposedly, you could come only if your parents were invited to the real Spring Fling. But even that rule was routinely broken. Julie Howard nudged Randy Bergman. He looked where she was looking and saw Scooter Scotland wandering up the woodsy road with Wayne Schultz. Wayne's parents would be at the Spring Fling. His father was a banker in town and his mother, like Margaret Howard, was about to be admitted to full membership in the DUA. But Scooter's parents ran the local computer store and were not members of Stowe Towne society. Scooter couldn't blend in very well either. The Scotlands had adopted him and he was black. The only African-American, in fact, who attended Stowe

High School.

Heather's shrill laughter distracted Julie and Randy. Heather was overseeing the set-up of a second beer keg. Some senior guys were lifting the keg out of the back of the pickup truck she had commandeered from her father. No one knew how she always came up with more beer than even a bunch of thirsty and horny high schoolers needed. And Heather wouldn't tell. Julie suspected that some of Heather's father's race car friends were the suppliers. Julie also suspected that that was where Heather got her steady supply of grass.

"She's going to be a handful tonight," Randy muttered shaking his head. Randy and Julie often had to rescue Heather from whatever nightly mess she fell into and then escort her home. Sometimes it was not a very pleasant responsibility.

"At least the Allied Pipes' thugs aren't here," Julie said. Heather, lately, had been dating a guy in his 20s who worked at the Allied Pipes' plant south of Stowe Towne. Julie intensely disliked the guy and his crowd. But Heather had assured her that tonight only privileged Stowe High School students would be present, with a few acceptable exceptions like Randy and a few marginal exceptions like Scooter Scotland (who at least was a varsity basketball player).

"I hope they don't show up," Randy said taking a sip from his beer. He was drinking from a 20-ounce plastic cup that was labeled Hank Distribution, Columbus, Ohio. Must be where the beer comes from as well, he thought.

Julie and Randy took some comfort in the fact that not too many outsiders knew about the FSF or about where they were. Although they were parked just down the logging road and driving would take them 10 miles on a circuitous route to get home, they were actually less than a mile from their homes and The Candlesticks Golf Course. The logging road wound through the south end of Pottawa State Forest and ended in a large clearing that had once been a logging camp during the

Depression in the 1930s. There had been a barracks for about 20 men who worked for the WPA. The camp had been used for five years and then abandoned well before World War II. At some point, someone had come in and dismantled about half the building, probably just stealing the lumber. The cooking/sitting area of the building had been left with, of course, one full wall missing. The structure had weathered into a rustic, open-air shelter.

Julie and Randy, ever since they were little kids, had walked up Barnes's Knob on the golf course, carefully stepped across the placid waterfall of the Cascades, and walked straight through the woods (there was a faint path if you knew where to look) until they came to the abandoned camp. Sometimes, even now when they were almost grown-up, they pretended they were being chased by the ghost of Billy Barnes. The camp, however, held some nostalgia for the young couple since it was there that they had first made love. Condom wrappers, in fact, along with beer cans, were the chief litter around the clearing.

More kids were arriving and someone cranked up the music. There were four or five battery-powered camper lights scattered around the clearing and in the shelter. Heather had friends borrow the lights from family camping equipment. Randy had brought one but, since the Bergmans didn't go camping any more, he had had to buy a new battery. Fires were strictly forbidden. Everyone knew that the park rangers were aware that kids hung out at the camp. Over the years, a mutual understanding had evolved. The kids were left alone, but there could be no fires.

Randy drained his beer. "Are you ready for another?" he asked Julie. She shook her head. "No, not yet."

Julie shifted uncomfortably and swatted at a bug. They were sitting on two of the half-dozen cheap lawn chairs that had been abandoned over the years at the camp. Knots of students clustered around the beer kegs, but kept their distance from Randy and Julie. The couple was an intimidating presence. Randy had been a major sports star at Stowe High before graduating a year ago and going on to Kent. Julie, if not the outright best-looking senior girl, was certainly the sexiest and had an almost menacing personality. She did not suffer fools lightly. Except for a few close friends like Heather, nobody would dare casually walk up to the couple to pass the time of day.

"Is something wrong?" Randy asked.

"Did I tell you that I have to play golf with a guy from Ohio State tomorrow? Or, at least hit a few balls with him."

"No, who's that?"

"He's the assistant coach on the men's golf team. Mr. Jordan set it up."

"On the men's team? Why wouldn't it be the women's team?" Randy asked.

"I guess the guy's coming with some alumni or somebody. I don't know. But Mr. Jordan thinks it's a way to make my case for getting a scholarship at Ohio State."

Randy nodded. "Well, I think Bip knows about things like that. I can't believe your father's still insisting that you go to Ohio State..."

"...and my mother and my grandfather." Julie sighed and then took a sip of beer.

Randy glanced over at his girlfriend in the fading light. "Well, I ended up at Kent State because that's where my Dad went. And where he obviously wanted me to go." He paused. "It's all right, I suppose."

Heather Miller slid by, arm and arm between two senior guys. "You two aren't much fun," she challenged Randy and Julie. "You forget this is the Fucking Spring Fling?" Heather shook her head and her very pale blond hair whirled around her face. Despite being more than 50 years younger than her grandmother, May Miller, one could clearly see the family resemblance.

"Hey, Tony, Marty," Randy said acknowledging Heather's companions who had both played football with him at the high school. "Heather," he said, "I hope you saved some beer for us."

"I can get another keg just like that," she said and released Tony's arm and snapped her fingers. "Come on," she said, "let's go dance. You, too," she said to Randy and Julie.

"We're right behind you," Randy assured her.

The trio of Heather, Tony, and Marty spun around in place kicking up dirt and marched over toward the shelter that was serving as the dance floor.

"You up for dancing?" Randy asked Julie.

"I don't think so."

"You up for another beer?"

"Sure, it's going to be a long night."

Randy agreed, took Julie's cup, and went for refills. She, meanwhile, stared straight ahead. Graduation in a month. Golf. College next fall. Randy. Her father and mother. She had a lot to think about. A real lot to think about at the Fucking Spring Fling.

chapter three

GENERATIONS

The private boardroom in The Candlesticks Clubhouse was the one room in the club that had never been remodeled. It was located on the upper level of the building in the southwest corner and the only windows in the room were three tall ones that overlooked the first tee. It originally was an anteroom just off from the large combination dining room and ballroom that had been remodeled and divided into the pro shop and grill. The paneling in the boardroom was rich, dark walnut. Heavy forest-green drapes framed each of the three windows. Around the large mahogany conference table were 14 deep brown leather executive chairs. There was a functioning black marble fireplace whose mantle always held a cut glass vase of fresh flowers. Today, there were purple, mid-May lilacs in the vase. Next to the fireplace stood a pink marble floor stand on which rested the slightly battered brass Candlesticks Cup, the original club tournament cup. The Candlesticks Cup was last awarded in 1953. On the wall opposite the fireplace were six ornately framed oil paintings of men who had served as chairmen of The Candlesticks' Board. Not all the chairmen were represented since each portrait had to be paid for by the subject himself. The most recent was a dark, brooding portrait of Howie's father, Grant Howard. The only touch of whimsy in the portrait were the three golf balls he clutched in his massive left hand symbolizing the three holes-in-one he had shot in his life.

Howie loved this room. He loved its look and smell. But mostly he loved it because it was the only place where he ever really connected with his father, the only place where his father treated him with some respect and collegiality. Grant Howard was a tough, uncompromising SOB. In effect, he had driven away both his daughters, Howie's older sisters. Linda, the oldest of the three siblings, had fled to Stanford for college and had married a physician. They now lived in Santa Barbara and were very well-off. Gwen had fled to Swarthmore College and had married a Philadelphia attorney. Neither Linda nor Gwen ever returned to Stowe Towne and wanted nothing to do with their hometown. This split had, in the end, benefited Howie. When his father died (his mother had died before Linda had even graduated from high school; his father, suffering from prolonged grief, had never remarried), Howie had inherited everything in Stowe Towne. All three children had each received a large payment from the old man's substantial insurance policy. His sisters hardly needed the money, although they didn't turn it down. Howie needed the money, but also wanted the Howard property next to the golf course. In an uncharacteristic act of generosity by a Howard, both sisters signed away their property inheritance to Howie for only token payments. The sisters felt guilty because Howie had shouldered the burden of taking care of their father during the old man's cranky last years. As a result, Howie's inheritance of money and property along, with carrying on the Howard name, made him an important citizen of Stowe Towne.

Not that Howie hadn't suffered at the hands of his father. But since he was a male and, by chance, had a more submissive personality than either of his sisters, he was able to survive. His father liked to do manly things and liked to sit down with Howie in the boardroom and talk business with his son. It was the only time the two ever really talked. This room was where Howie had had his first drink of Scotch, straight up, on his 18th birthday when he and Grant had a business talk. It was where Howie learned about the *Howard Tradition*—although he still was uncertain years later what that actually meant. It was where he learned about the Howard finances—which he understood better. It was also where he learned that the philosophical and mental side of golf was just as important as the physical side of playing the game.

Only seven of the chairs were now filled on this Wednesday May morning. Howie requested that The Candlesticks' Board enter into executive session, which meant that Bip, the club pro, and Warren Alexander, the club manager, were both excused from the meeting. Bip and Warren always sat in on the Board meetings because the Board usually only talked about items concerning the club's operation. Bip and Warren were surprised, but did not argue and exited the room quickly. Now, Howie gazed around at the men who were left. He had talked to each of them as well as the absent Board members privately about transforming The Candlesticks into a housing development. However, he had not discussed the matter with David Canello, the club's attorney.

Canello was the managing partner of the Columbus office of Mr. Miller's old law firm, Miller, Duke and Hanover. The firm had been formed in the 1890s by three sons of three of the original seven Civil War heroes. But when Mr. Miller retired he was the last person connected by either name or heritage to Stowe Towne or the law firm's founding. In fact, Miller, Duke and Hanover had offices now in Dayton, Indianapolis, and Tampa Bay, besides Columbus. The firm did maintain a one-room office with a part-time secretary in Stowe Towne in the Merchant and Farmer Cooperative bank building for two reasons: tradition (the town was still listed on the firm's letterhead) and because of the firm's longtime interest in The Candlesticks. Miller, Duke and Hanover had always handled the golf course's legal matters which had never been that much bother (or profit) until Justice Summers had written The Candlesticks Accord. Then, as the course and the pro shop became more profitable, the firm's interest picked up. Plus, it was a useful golfing perk for the firm's lawyers and clients.

David Canello dealt personally with The Candlesticks. The golf course was one of his few active clients beyond his expansive managing partner administrative duties. It just so happened he liked golf although he played poorly. He was a slender, balding man who at 54 had already outlived his father and two brothers, who had all died at a younger age from heart disease. His heart, he knew, was not in the greatest of shape. But he was still alive...and playing golf. Instead of being grateful for that fact, he had become increasingly cynical. The golf wasn't to blame.

As Howie outlined the development plan, Canello sat stunned. He was not a man who enjoyed being stunned. He couldn't believe Howie was proposing what he was proposing. He didn't think Howie had the brains to conceive such an idea or the guts to even carry it this far. Plus, it sounded like he had covered all his bases to this point in time and covered them very well. Of course, it all went back to the goddamn Candlesticks Accord. He hated the Accord mostly because it tied the hands of the club's attorney and effectively gave all the decision-making power for the club to the chair of the family Board. This was never much of a problem since the chair usually ran the club as a hobby and not a business.

Now, however, a Board chair was clearly proposing something way beyond the scope of anything ever proposed before. Not since The Candlesticks had been fundamentally changed by the adoption of the Accord had this sort of transformation been considered. The golf course was going to be modified into an upscale housing development. And, as Canello stared in turn at the nodding heads of the five Board members listening to Howie, he realized that this deal was greased. Silent Keith Miller, the son of Mr. Miller. Tom Duke, Jr.—his old man must have approved the idea because Tom would never cross Tom Senior. Albert Thompson who was 80 years old and semisenile. Paul Mitchell who was often three sheets to the wind. And George Simmons who had his wife's, Hannah Hanover's, proxy and had pointed out repeatedly since the meeting began how he had made the trip up from Florida just to be present here today.

Howie was wrapping up his presentation: "And, next week, Don Morgan from Cliner Development will be visiting for his first look-see at the course. Bruce Dean will be accompanying us. I ask your indulgence to let me handle this alone for now. Since we have a very unusual management structure, I don't want to scare off Cliner. Of course, nothing of a financial nature will be committed without the full knowledge of the Board. Please keep this confidential. Especially wives, except that George better tell Hannah."

Everyone except for Canello laughed. George included.

"Unless there are questions," Howie continued, "I think we stand adjourned."

Everyone stood up except Canello. "Howie, I have some questions," he said.

"Sure, David," Howie said glancing around at the Board members, "but let's let everybody else go. No need stretching out these meetings."

Canello protested: "This is the most important item this Board has discussed in four decades. We're not exactly stretching out the meeting."

"David," Tom Junior said, "I gotta run. You ask Howie whatever you want."

The rest of the men murmured agreement and within a minute or two, with Paul Mitchell helping old man Thompson, the room had cleared except for Howie and Canello.

The echo of the door closing sounded around the paneled room.

Howie spoke first: "David, the lawyers will be involved when the time comes. You'll be involved. Cliner has their own lawyers. I'll have to have a lawyer because my property is involved. The State Attorney General may be involved because of the State Forest land. Everyone will have their shot at this."

"That's fine, Howie, but I don't sit on this Board just to drink coffee. Why didn't you ask my advice?"

Howie shrugged. "We talked about it at previous meetings. Talked around it, at least, when you were here. Next year is the seventy-fifth anniversary of when the course opened for play in 1924. We talked about doing something special to mark the occasion."

"Having a birthday cake and giving out free logo golf balls is a lot different than redesigning the course into a housing development," Canello objected.

"Still, it's an excuse to do something like this," Howie answered.

"A flimsy excuse at best."

Howie reached down and picked up the brief meeting agenda that he had left lying on the table. He didn't like David Canello very much. But he didn't want to say that. He didn't want to argue. He folded the paper over once before he spoke. Then, he said, finally: "David, this is family business. You're an outsider. Don't press me on this. I'm the Board Chair and I have the power and authority to do what I'm doing. That's just the way it is. You know that. You know the Accord by heart."

Canello was taken aback. He shook his head. "Okay. You're right. It's not even that I think it's a bad idea. I don't. I'm just a little puzzled by your attitude."

Howie looked at the lawyer and shrugged again and then left the boardroom and the ghost of his father without another word.

~

Mr. Miller was not close to his only son Keith. It was a bit odd because his son had been a good son by most objective measurements. Most parents would have been glad to have him as a son. But May and Mr. Miller were a little eccentric. Had always been a little eccentric. Keith had recognized that fact early on.

Keith Miller had gone off to college at the University of Indiana where he had completed a degree in English and writing. Keith was very smart. But then he had surprised both May and Mr. Miller by coming home to Stowe Towne to marry his high school girlfriend, Rachel McDermott. Rachel had gone to college at Ohio State University, a McDermott tradition. The McDermotts were not one of the original seven families, but the original McDermotts had been one of the first families to settle in the area after Stowe Towne was established. The first McDermotts were heavy into horse trading.

Keith and Rachel had two children including Heather—Julie's best friend—and a younger daughter named Stacey. Mr. Miller was convinced that Keith married Rachel because he had always been best friends with her brothers, Toby and Phil. At the turn of the century, the McDermotts had made the transition easily from horses to automobiles. Now, nearly a hundred years later, they had their hands in practically everything involved with cars in the town. Gas stations. Car washes. Buying and selling. Racing. Keith loved cars as much as the McDermott boys and he had made a career of doing car deals with the McDermotts. They had actually been involved off and on with the NASCAR circuit. In addition, Keith took to writing about cars. He wrote for car and truck magazines. Did freelance manuals for various automobile components. Rachel, meanwhile, was a high school math teacher from the get-go. Overall, they had a pretty good life.

However, it just was not the type of life that Mr. Miller could appreciate very well. Mr. Miller dearly would have loved his son to have become an attorney. But Mr. Miller was smart enough to recognize that the *problem* between him and Keith was a lot more *his* problem than his son's problem. They worked it out. They had give and take. For instance, Keith was now serving on The Candlesticks' Board in the Miller seat because Mr. Miller had asked him to serve in the interest of the family. Keith golfed about once a year. But he knew the course was important to his father and, besides, he didn't mind the steady extra income that came the way of the *greater* Miller family. (The greater Miller family now consisted of just the two men.) Keith had also allowed his father to introduce golf to both Heather and Stacey. Heather had taken to it, although Stacey had rejected it out of hand.

Mr. Miller had received a call from Keith the next afternoon after The Candlesticks' Board meeting to stop over and see him at the McDermott Marathon Station going east out of town near Bryce Bridge. Keith and the McDermott boys spent a lot of time at the station, although it was actually owned by the boys' Uncle Joe. Mr. Miller parked his Lincoln off to the side of the pumps and gave Joe a wave. Mr. Miller and Joe McDermott had played high school baseball on the same team, way back.

"Keith's out back if you're looking for him," Joe yelled.

Mr. Miller walked through the busy station and out the back door. A paved lot was littered with haphazardly parked cars. To the right, a small building sported a red and white sign that read "McDermott Foreign Car Repair." The sign stretched above two garage doors that opened into two repair bays. Both the garage doors were up and Mr. Miller could see the figure of his son in the shadows inside the garage. Keith had turned 40 in January but still was slim and had the features of his mother. With his jet-black hair and wearing jeans and a black T-shirt, he looked much younger.

"Keith," Mr. Miller called.

"Hey, Dad," Keith said turning around from the small dark green car he was looking at. "What do you think of her?"

"The car, you mean?" Mr. Miller stepped out of the May sunshine and into the garage.

"It's a '72 Triumph TR-6 convertible," Keith explained. "Toby is thinking of buying it and we're going to check it out tonight. Owner just dropped it off."

"Awfully small, I think." Mr. Miller didn't know a thing about cars. "Rare, I suppose, something like that."

"Not really. What do you think the guy's asking?"

"I have no idea, Keith."

"Guess."

Mr. Miller hated guessing. "Oh, maybe ten thousand. Twelve thousand."

"Whoa! I said *not* rare." Keith squatted down and rubbed a cloth on the dark green car door. He concentrated on one spot and rubbed hard. "It's not what they call mint condition. He's asking $4,800."

"Somebody from around here?"

"No, a guy from Columbus. We know him a little from racing. Nice guy. Toby might buy it if he can get him down to forty-five or a little lower. We'll get under the hood tonight after we do the test drive."

Mr. Miller walked to the back of the garage and sat on a stool in front of a cluttered workbench. "When I first saw the car, Keith, I thought you might try and sell it to me."

Keith laughed. "Well, Toby might. You can stand to be a little more sporty in your old age."

"I'm sure it will impress your mother and the ladies of the DUA," Mr. Miller said dryly.

"You never know. Anyway, I hope you didn't mind coming over. I wanted to tell you something without the chance of Mom overhearing us."

"What's that?"

Keith walked over and retrieved a can of Coke from the workbench.

"I don't think you're going to like this. I don't know. Maybe you don't care." He paused, shrugged, and then continued. "Yesterday, there was a Board meeting at The Candlesticks. Regularly scheduled meeting. I went since I was in town. You know, I miss a lot of meetings when I'm out with the racing crew or I'm doing some writing. So, I went."

Keith hesitated and after a very long moment, Mr. Miller said, "Is anything wrong?"

Keith got a little grin on his lean and tan face. "Well, what I just told you isn't exactly true, Dad. Never could lie to you very well. The truth is that Howie Howard called me and asked me to come to the meeting. He told me in advance what it was about. He's proposing to turn the golf course into a housing development."

"What?"

"Now don't get your blood pressure up, Dad. He's going to keep the golf course. He's going to build on his land. Then around the course. You know, between holes. Stretch it out into the State Forest on the other side of the river. Says he has permission already to do that."

"And you agreed to this?"

Keith shrugged. "Sure, why not? It's going to make more money. Lots more. Both from the upscale golfing and from the housing, of course. Besides, it's a done deal. Howie's the Board chair and he can do it. What do you think?"

"I think Howie Howard's a bastard."

"That might be," his son agreed.

Mr. Miller restrained himself with effort. He couldn't jump all over Keith. Why would he oppose it? All The Candlesticks meant to him was a quarterly dividend check. Besides, it was ultimately his own fault. He knew he shouldn't have given up his seat on the Board to Keith. But Keith was the only Miller left. There really had been no choice once Mr. Miller himself wanted off the Board. Tom Duke, Senior, had done the same thing for his son. But now...

"What do you think, Dad? I mean besides Howie being a bastard."

Mr. Miller shook his head. "I don't know, Keith. But why don't you give me the rest of the details. I need to give this some thought."

"Are you going to tell Mom?"

"Do *you* want to?"

Keith laughed. "I don't think so. Besides, you're the lawyer. You know how to do things diplomatically."

Mr. Miller grunted. "The toughest judge in Ohio was easier to deal with than your mother." Then he warned his son: "When she calls you, don't call *me*. Now, give me all the details you can remember."

⤻

It's odd how sometimes a person knows something is wrong even though it appears that nothing is wrong. That's the way Sticks Bergman felt all Thursday morning and into the afternoon. He had gone to the lumberyard because his brothers had wanted him to sit in on a meeting with their paint wholesaler. The wholesaler had consistently been raising prices while providing less service over the past six months. The wholesaler was a good old boy who played a bad game of golf and lost generously with good humor. But even in a small town there are limits and—business being business—something had to be done. The meeting did not go well, lasted too long, and got bogged down in contradictory financial reports. It ended inconclusively and for a little while Sticks just thought that the *paint problem* was what was upsetting him.

Sticks got out to the golf course about 4:00 p.m. and teed off just in front of the Rotary Club Golf League. This was the first day of league play for the Rotarians. From now on until the end of August, Sticks would have to adjust his playing time to accommodate league play. It was a pain although he knew full well that league play was a huge money-maker for the course. The leagues teed off Monday through Thursday in the late afternoon. Sticks didn't play league golf any more even though he had, off and on, over the years. Guys were always asking him to be their partner since he was such a good player, especially playing The Candlesticks. But he had had enough of tedious, two-dollar, nine-hole league play and always politely declined.

Sticks's playing partner today was Dan Ofman, the high school football coach. Dan also taught history. He was a burly fellow in his early forties who played golf like many one-time good team athletes: great power and drive, but little finesse and understanding of the game. Dan might eagle any par 5 at any time, but he could never complete a round without putting a half a dozen balls either out-of-bounds or in the water.

Sticks couldn't shake his feeling of doom and dread despite the beautiful late afternoon spring weather. It had to be more than paint. The gnawing sensation affected his play and he did poorly. Bogeyed the first two holes. Had to make a 20-foot putt just to bogey number three. By the sixth hole, he wasn't even keeping score. Plus, they caught up to a foursome of slow-playing ladies. Waiting next to the tee, Dan practiced chipping at one of the white tee markers. "Jesus Christ!" he exclaimed as he bladed a shot and it flew way over the marker. "Why don't I look up a little sooner? Why do I look at the ball at all?"

He turned and spoke to Sticks, who was pensively staring at the white markers on the tee. "Anyway, you know, Sticks, that I'm teaching a modern history class after lunch. College prep class."

Sticks nodded. Dan's problem wasn't looking up; he was swinging too damn hard. That had always been Dan's problem. "I think Randy took your class," he said.

"Sure he did. That's right. Last year. Anyway, I'm leaving class after the bell rings and Julie Howard's walking out with Heather Miller and I ask if they've been golfing any with the warmer weather. Julie says she has, but she doesn't know how much more she will if her Dad sells the course."

"What?" Sticks stared at his partner.

"That's what *I* said, '*What?*' But she had another class and I only got a quick comment about her father building condos or something. Do you know anything about it?"

"No, I don't know anything about it."

"Julie said she overheard her father talking on the phone or something like that."

Sticks shook his head. "I can't believe it."

Dan changed clubs and stepped up onto the tee with his driver. "Well, we better find out. We wouldn't want to lose The Candlesticks!"

After they finished nine (they couldn't continue—even if they had wanted to—because the Rotarians teed off from both the front and the back for league play), Sticks charged into Bip's office to find the club pro with his feet propped up on his desk reading a copy of *Golf World*.

"What the hell do you know about turning Candlesticks into condos?" Sticks demanded. He flung his bag into the corner of the office where he usually set it down carefully next to a water cooler. The clubs rattled against the wall and slid unceremoniously down to the carpeted floor.

Bip looked at Sticks with such a wide-eyed, innocent expression of amazement that Sticks knew at once that Bip knew nothing about the scheme. At least he was pretty sure he knew nothing about it.

"Howie's idea? You know anything about it, Bip?"

Bip straightened up, his feet falling to the floor. He flipped the magazine onto his desk. "What are you talking about, Sticks? Condos? I haven't heard anything like that."

"But you've heard something?"

"No, I mean I haven't heard anything. What are you talking about?"

Sticks quickly repeated Dan Ofman's story.

Bip whistled when Sticks finished. He then motioned for Sticks to close the office door and sit down in the single padded side chair next to the desk. He opened the bottom drawer of his file cabinet and pulled out a bottle of Jim Beam and two small liquor glasses. "I think we need a drink," he said. "I was going to have a drink anyway because it's the first day of Rotarian golf. But now I have an even better reason."

Sticks sat down and accepted the generous shot of whiskey. "You don't know anything about this?" he asked Bip yet again.

"No, nothing. But somehow I'm not surprised. Something's been brewing ever since Howie took over as Board chairman. Yesterday, at the Board meeting Howie asked Warren and me to leave because they had to go into Executive Session. Whatever that means. No one would talk to me afterward. About the Executive Session, I mean. So we were left in the dark."

"So, you think they talked about selling the course?"

Bip shrugged. "Maybe it's just Howie's attitude. Sometimes he's an arrogant SOB. But I never thought he would propose something like selling The Candlesticks."

"Maybe it's not even selling. Selling is one thing. Selling might even be all right. But turning it into a condo course? I don't even want to think about it." Sticks shook his head unhappily.

Bip stared into his drink for a minute before he spoke again. "I've been thinking about retirement. Natural thing to do at my age. Howie keeps bringing up the subject of my retirement. You know, with a positive spin. About how the club has an obligation toward all its employees. That sort of crap."

Sticks scratched his head. "I don't know if I'm following you, Bip."

"I assume Howie would want me out of the way if he was planning some sort of change here. I taught him to love this course. I taught him that myself when he was just a kid. He would know that I would oppose any change. Especially any major change like that."

Sticks nodded. "You'd probably be less inclined to oppose any change if your generous retirement depended on being in Howie's good graces."

"Exactly."

"You think there's really any truth to this?"

"I suppose we could always ask," Bip said.

But Bip spoke without much conviction and Sticks looked at the old fellow carefully. He was a good man and it was obvious he wasn't involved in any nefarious plot. Bip was the golfer and teacher. Sticks knew the man was as honest as the June day was long. Bip had a stake, certainly, in what Howie might be planning. But it also, obviously, wasn't his responsibility...or fault.

"Why don't we keep this quiet, Bip? Until something else surfaces. Maybe it's just teenage girl talk. Believe me, girls tend not to listen very well, although it never stops them from jumping to conclusions."

"I wouldn't know, Sticks, I raised boys."

Sticks managed a weak laugh. "Sure, Bip, I know."

Sticks finished his drink and then continued: "Here's what I'll do. I'll call Dan and tell him not to spread the rumor. Tell him to keep it quiet. I'll see if he's told anyone else. Then I'll call Randy at Kent. You know, he still dates Julie. Maybe she mentioned something to him. Sound like a good plan?"

"Sure," Bip nodded. "And I'll keep my ears open around here. At least sound out Warren if he's heard anything."

"Good, you do that."

Sticks sat back and stared at the 1985 calendar behind Bip that the old pro hadn't changed for more than 10 years because he liked the photo of Pebble Beach.

Sticks also remembered one other small piece of information, which he wasn't going to share with Bip, at least not now: the Cliner call to Sammi's office. Big real estate developers. Were they part of this? Well, he better get home. He had some serious phone calls to make.

⌇

Randy Bergman was working out in the basement weight room of the Sig Pi Fraternity house a block from the Kent State campus. Randy had resisted pledging Sig Pi partly because he basically hated frats and partly because his best friend on campus, Tom Yahney, a sophomore starting linebacker for the Golden Flashes, already was a Sig Pi and invited Randy to anything interesting or fun that the Sig Pi's ever did. Which was actually damn little in Randy's opinion.

The weight room was dark and dimly lit and smelled to high heaven of sweaty men's bodies. Randy loved it because no one ever bothered him and because there were always one or two guys grunting at the weights. The problem Randy had was that weights didn't do his body much good. He just didn't tone up very much. He didn't have one of those bodies that took to it. That's why—he was finally beginning to realize—he wasn't, nor ever would be, a very good football player. Not Division I, not even Mid-American Conference quality. High school competition and an overwhelming burning desire to impress his father and uncles made him a better than average high school football player. But now the competition was much better and his desire was dimming. Not that he didn't like running out on the field on a crisp fall afternoon in his blue and gold uniform and jumping up and down and getting in a few licks. He would probably play next fall, although he was not offered a scholarship and he knew that his place on the team was far from assured. But he would like to keep up with Tom and give it another try. And his father, he knew, still expected it of him.

He went and sat on the ratty blue couch in the corner of the basement. On party nights, the weight room was closed (but not off-limits) and a rather expensive couch cover came out of the closet. The cover was thick enough to muffle most of the sweaty guy smell. At the top of the stairs, just above the basement door in the hallway, there was a bent nail driven into the wall. If the nail was turned up, the couch was in use; if the nail was turned down, the couch was free. Twenty-minute limit if you didn't want someone pounding hard on the door.

Randy had only used the couch once with some girl he didn't think he could recognize now. They were both pretty drunk. Otherwise, he had been pretty faithful to Julie. Surprisingly so, in fact. He hadn't planned on being so faithful while away at college. But now with only one day of classes left in spring semester before exams next week, it seemed to have turned out that way. He thought of her most of the time.

She was the reason, of course, that he didn't mind going home for the summer to live in his parents' house and work at his father and uncle's lumberyard. He had worked in the lumberyard every summer since he was 14. He earned great money through family generosity. His two uncles, Hal and Paul, fawned on him since they both had daughters and no sons. It wasn't so bad. But he also knew that he wouldn't go back home if it weren't for Julie. He didn't know what he would do otherwise. He had no desire to stay in Kent over the summer. But he knew he wouldn't go back to Stowe Towne. He would only go back to be near Julie.

Less than a hundred miles away, Julie, at that moment, sat in the passenger seat of Heather Miller's white Neon and stared at the Memorial to the Seven Heroes. Heather was half a block away, probably in the backseat of Matt Pawlicki's car. Matt was five years older than Heather, was from Columbus, and worked at Allied Pipes. Heather was specifically forbidden to see him by her parents. So, Julie was Heather's cover story for the night.

The early spring evening was warm and the sun was just fading over the Civil War statue. The Neon was parked on Mitchell just off Duke Boulevard. Mitchell, Duke, Jones, and Howard were the four streets that formed the town square in the center of Stowe Towne. Julie lit a Salem Ultra Light—her mother knew she smoked; her father didn't. She stared at the Memorial of the seven interlocking statues of the seven founders of Stowe Towne. The word "FOUNDERS" on the base of the Memorial was not quite accurate. Technically, the seven Civil War officers depicted were the spouses of the real founders of Stowe Towne. But the distinction was lost on most people except for members of the DUA, who made certain the truth was kept alive.

Even in the fading light, Julie could easily pick out her direct ancestor, Major John Howard. He was the one on the far right with his left hand raised pointing. His right hand at his side held a pistol. The scene of the seven men staring and gesturing at something before them, of course, never happened. Some of the men were together for about a year, but only four of them were at Gettysburg. The base read: "GETTYSBURG JULY 3, 1863." However, the officers never were all together during any battle. But the scene still was heroic and because of the oddity of the seven figures together, it was one of the better-known statues among Civil War aficionados.

Julie had trudged out to the Memorial all her life. Endless grade school treks. (Now let's see, the teachers would say, who in this class is related to any of these great heroes? Julie Howard, yes. Heather Miller, yes) Even this year, her art class had had to come out to sketch the Memorial coated with snow. Yuck! Fucking John Howard. What the hell is he pointing at and doesn't his arm ever get tired?

Julie sighed.

It was times like this she missed Randy. He had been well-known in high school and they had been a hot couple. That was last year. This year, which should have been fun for her since it was her senior year, had a pall cast upon it by his general absence except for certain events like the recent FSF. It wasn't his fault. But she was still his girl in everyone's eyes. She didn't disagree; after all, who wanted to date the guys left in high school? Still, she was so far into the "in" group that she actually had gone out the other side. No hassle, but no fun either.

Matt, Heather's friend, had set her up a couple of times with one of his thug friends. But she wasn't much into the older pipefitting crowd. So, she moped a lot. And then, when Randy came home, she moped around him because he was only home temporarily and she was confused about where their relationship was going. Which now put her into a contemplative mood because she knew he had finals and would be home in a week or so. What was she to do? *What was she to do!*

Darkness settled in and now the soldiers were lit in shadows by the streetlights and the lights from the storefronts. She always thought the cast iron figures were creepy at night. They seemed to meld into one figure with multiple arms and legs and heads that seemed to move suddenly as headlights turned and swung across the statue. This was when she thought the old guys were staring back at her.

She shuddered, slumped down in her seat, lit another cigarette, turned on the radio loudly, and tried to think good thoughts about Randy.

And, as far as thinking about condos on The Candlesticks: She wasn't and didn't.

chapter four

AWESOME!

As Howie Howard promised the Board members of The Candlesticks Golf Course, a potential developer—a really big developer, as it turned out—agreed to visit Stowe Towne and The Candlesticks. Bruce Dean, who Howie thought could meet the man on professional grounds of realtor to developer, was designated as the initial contact person.

Bruce Dean sat across from Cliner Development Vice President Don Morgan at the Bob Evans Restaurant where State Highway 37 intersected I-71. After breakfast, Morgan would leave his Cadillac in the parking lot and Bruce would drive them over to look at Stowe Towne and The Candlesticks. They eventually would have lunch at Howie Howard's house. Not that Morgan needed more food, Bruce thought. The man was enormous. He literally was sitting on two chairs. He had ordered something called the "Lumberjack Special" which consisted of waffles, scrambled eggs, breakfast meats (both bacon and sausage), and biscuits with gravy. It was a very scary meal.

Bruce put the food out of his mind and said, "In the top 35 markets in the United States, there are only two cities that do not have a major league professional sports franchise. You know, baseball, football, hockey, or basketball."

"Is that so?" Morgan responded as he emptied the contents of the small white syrup pitcher onto his waffles. "I suppose that you want me to guess." He rolled his eyes as if bored by the challenge.

"Well, no," Bruce stammered, "it's just an interesting..."

"Columbus, of course," Morgan interrupted. "I assume that's the point you're making. Although aren't they getting a hockey team in the future? Of course, I don't consider hockey a major league sport. But just give me a second for the other one."

Morgan delicately picked up a strip of bacon with a pudgy finger and thumb and ate the whole strip in one gulp.

"I got it!" he exclaimed after a moment of deep thought. "Providence, Rhode Island." Morgan smiled expansively.

Bruce sucked in his breath and picked up his cup of coffee. "That's amazing. You're absolutely right."

Actually, Morgan was absolutely wrong. The correct answer was the metropolitan area of Norfolk/Virginia Beach. But Bruce Dean was an expert at sucking up and this seemed harmless enough. But how in the hell did Morgan ever come up with Providence, Rhode Island? That wasn't even on the radar screen.

"Still," Morgan said after swallowing another bacon strip, "some people would argue that Ohio State athletics is a bigger deal than any pro team."

"True," Bruce agreed, "but that just confirms my point. Central Ohio is huge and it's growing."

"And you don't think Stowe Towne is too far away for the commute to Columbus?"

"Hell, no. Columbus is growing out to meet us anyway. Look at the developments already in Gahanna and Sunbury."

Morgan waved a fork in the air. "Stowe Towne's farther."

"A little. But part of the development will actually be in a state park. Great selling point. Golf. State park recreation..."

"Two hour commute," Morgan interrupted.

Bruce sat back with a pained look on his face. "It's not two hours, Don. Come on. Two hours is Cleveland, for Christ's sake. You just drove from there."

Morgan shrugged and dug away at his food. After a minute he said. "We think there are some obstacles here. Cliner Development does not go lightly into just any project. We're very thorough. For example, a state park is an excellent marketing device. Just as long as you don't have any goddamn environmentalists in Stowe Towne."

"Don, I assure you that we've done our homework. The people in Stowe Towne are pro-growth."

"It only takes one, you know. One fucking environmentalist."

Bruce glanced around at the clientele in the red-checked tablecloth family restaurant. The old folks having their morning coffee probably wouldn't appreciate Morgan's language. Not that the big man would be intimidated by anyone's stare. However, the two of them were off in a corner and it appeared that no one was within hearing distance.

Bruce turned his attention back to Morgan and gestured with his hands up. "Don, you can't expect me to guarantee that no one will object. But we can handle it. First of all, the deal will be done before most people even know about it. Secondly, the people who do know about it are all for it."

"So, who might object?"

Bruce was frustrated. "I don't know. But I know who won't object. The state senator's in our pocket. The editor of the weekly paper isn't a factor. The paper's just an advertising rag and the editor's an alcoholic. The banks are in on it, of course. The county engineer is on board. So, we're ready to take the next step."

"Why aren't you using a Columbus developer? Like Mertz, for instance. No one in Columbus would touch it?"

"You already asked me that on the phone."

"I know," Morgan said as he patted his sweaty brow with a napkin, "but now we're face-to-face so I'm asking again. After all, you're telling me that Columbus is such a hot shit town."

"Well, my answer's the same as before. We didn't ask anyone in Columbus or anywhere else. We know what the people in Columbus are doing. We are aware of their projects and plans. The fact is that no one else except Cliner is big enough in Ohio to handle this. You're the biggest and the best."

Bruce paused and looked at Morgan's bulk sitting across the table. *At least you're the biggest*, Bruce thought to himself.

"That's very flattering," Morgan said dryly. He surveyed the empty plates in front of him. "Well, then, let's go have a look."

⌐

Later, while Don Morgan gorged himself on a luncheon of lobster bisque, salmon, pecan pie, and the trimmings catered by Chef Jeff, Margaret Howard's personal friend, who was the current fashionable caterer in Columbus, Sticks Bergman, Randy Bergman, and Bip Jordan teed off on the first hole at The Candlesticks. Sticks, in the week and a day since he had heard about the potential "condo-mizing" of the golf course from Dan Ofman, had not been able to track down any firm or even unfirm confirmation. He had dropped some subtle and not-so-subtle comments around town at places like the lumberyard, Abe's Tap (where he often ate lunch with his brothers), and The Gettysburg Café. But people had stared at him blankly. The "solid" lead from Sammi about the call to the real estate office from Cliner Development in

Cleveland seemed a dead end. Bruce had called Cliner back, she reported. He told her that Cliner was just planning a summer real estate seminar on one of the Lake Erie islands. They were soliciting attendees. At $495 a person plus lodging! Bruce explained. Sammi didn't know if Bruce was reporting the truth or even part of the truth to her. Although she did know Cliner put on seminars and she had, in fact, gone to one herself some years back in Cleveland.

Sticks watched his son pop up his first tee shot about 90 yards down the fairway. "Sorry, Dad," Randy said sheepishly, "you know this is my first time out this year."

Sticks nodded and stroked his own tee shot 250 yards down the middle of the fairway. Randy also had been no help on the development rumor. Sticks had quizzed Randy by phone at Kent last week and again when Randy got home last night for his summer break from the university. But Randy swore Julie had never mentioned any changes for The Candlesticks. He was, of course, going to see her after she got out of school today and he promised he would give her the *third degree.* Randy had noted to himself that his sarcasm seemed to have little effect on his father.

On down the first fairway, Sticks watched his son swing at a fastball and foul it in the dirt. Unfortunately, Randy was playing golf, not baseball. His second shot, a three-wood, trickled 50 yards up the fairway. He trudged ahead and hit another weak three-wood, but at least he finally got his ball by his father's and Bip's drives.

"Watch my swing," Bip advised Randy sternly. The old pro took his three-wood back slowly and hit a high fading shot which cut the corner of the dogleg and bounced out of sight down the middle of the fairway of the par-5 hole.

Bip slung his club back into his bag. "Now remember: slow take back, shift your weight, follow through, keep your head down. That's just for starters. How long have I been telling you that? Fifteen years?"

"Thanks, Mr. Jordan," Randy whispered as they watched Sticks power his second shot out of sight around the dogleg. It would end up 20 yards in front of the green.

"You young people," Bip said. "Sometimes you just don't keep your concentration. Did Julie tell you about playing with Doug Kreuger from Ohio State about three weeks ago?"

"She told me on the phone that it didn't go well."

"Well, Kreuger was with a couple of guys who were bastards, which didn't help. Made her nervous, I think. She just played three holes. But she rushed every shot. Kreuger was nice enough about it and I pumped up her ability. I mean, told him she was good."

"She's got a great swing," Randy volunteered.

"That's right, she does," Bip agreed. "Kreuger could see that. But, like she told you, it didn't go well and Kreuger was pretty noncommittal afterward."

"I don't know what's on her mind about golf and college," Randy said as they trudged along toward their balls.

By the time they finished five holes, Bip was shooting par, Randy was nine over, and Sticks was two under. Sticks was invigorated. He loved playing with his son. He was glad Randy would be home again for the summer. He was glad—at least as far as he knew—that The Candlesticks would not be undergoing any changes. He was glad he was well into another season of golf.

On the sixth tee, Bip excused himself to use the port-o-john. Sticks could remember years ago when Bip bitched endlessly about port-o-johns on the course. Now, with his aging prostate, Bip never complained.

Sticks and Randy waited on the tee, both of them swinging their pitching wedges. The sixth was the shortest hole on the course. A mere 134-yard par 3. But the green sloped severely left to right and any shot not on the left edge of the green (no matter where the pin placement) tended to roll off the green.

"What's the story with you and Julie?" Sticks asked suddenly.

Randy stared out at the green. The hole was about the length of a football field if you included the end zones. They would all hit their shots in a minute and probably clear that distance effortlessly. But that same distance on the football field would have 22 men beating each other's brains out for every foot. Seemed strange.

"Randy? You and Julie?" Sticks repeated.

"Oh, sure, Dad. I don't know. I guess we'll just wait and see."

"Well," Sticks said, "just remember that the acorn never falls far from the oak."

Randy hesitated in the middle of a practice swing. "Did you learn that in biology class 25 years ago?" he asked sarcastically.

Sticks was a little chagrined. "You know what I mean."

"No, Dad, I don't know what you mean."

"Look, all I meant was that Julie's all right, of course, but Howie and Margaret are, well, you know what I'm trying to say."

Randy knew full well that the Bergmans and the Howards didn't get along. He decided, as they waited for Bip, that this was a good time to confront the issue. "What's that all about, Dad? Why aren't we friends with the Howards? They're our neighbors, aren't they?"

Sticks shrugged. "They're just different. You understand, I'm sure."

Randy pulled at the sleeves of his dark blue Kent State sweatshirt that he was wearing over a white golf shirt. He looked at his father and said: "Different? Let's see. We live in pretty much identical houses. Drive similarly expensive cars. Play at the same golf course which happens to be located right between those two houses. We eat at the same restaurants. I think both families bank at the Huntington. Or, maybe they're at the Huntington and we're at the Merchant and Farmer. Big difference! Can you see where I'm going with this, Dad?"

Sticks fidgeted nervously and looked at his club head to see if he really was holding his wedge. Of course he was. He could tell what club he was holding with his eyes closed at midnight in a thunderstorm. Truthfully, he didn't really understand all the dynamics that went on between the Howards and Bergmans. He had known Howie all of his life. But there was something...

After a moment, he realized he had to respond to his son and he said, "The Howards have a hell of a lot more money than we do."

"Maybe that's true, Dad. Julie's told me her mother's family is from the East. Boston, I think. But that doesn't make any difference. I mean, you and Mom go over and play euchre at the Green's. Right? I know we have a lot more money than the Greens."

Sticks grunted and stooped down to get more tees out of his bag even though he already had a pocketful. David and Marsha Green had a big Jewish family of five kids. They had moved to town because David was a foreman with Allied Pipes. Sammi had sold them their house and she and Marsha had just hit it off. Then it turns out David's a good golfer—about a 12 handicapper. So, they all just got along, all four of them. Nothing special, cards or dinner in Columbus once a month or so.

The port-o-john door slammed shut as Bip came out. It was a distinctive loud bang that echoed across the golf course.

"All right, let's play some golf," Bip said.

Sticks and Randy, father and son, eyed one another. Obviously, their conversation about friendship and social standing in Stowe Towne would continue at some later point.

"Let's go," Bip repeated.

As Sticks teed up his shot, Randy asked, "Any holes-in-one here yet this year, Mr. Jordan?"

"No, we got a little spring fungus problem on the right side of the green at the bottom of the slope. So, we've been keeping the pin high left. It's almost impossible to even get it near the hole much less *in* the hole." He paused as Sticks swung. It was a beautiful-looking shot, but all three of them saw at once it would be long. The ball hit on the green but past the hole and its momentum and the slope of the green carried it to the back right fringe. Sticks had a long, curving uphill putt. It would be a difficult putt just to get close.

Bip picked up his thought as he teed up his ball. He chose an eight-iron instead of a wedge. "Most holes-in-one come when the pin is plunk in the middle of the green. You'd be surprised how many holes-in-one are bladed ground balls that simply roll straight to the green and in the hole. One of the holes-in-one I've had was like that."

Bip swung and hit what looked like a good shot. But when it hit the left fringe of the green, it took a wicked bounce right and rolled all the way across the green. He also had a very long putt coming back.

"Shit," Bip muttered shaking his head.

Randy teed up his Top-Flite. He had no confidence whatsoever. He hung over the ball and went through the mental checklist. Head down, etc., etc. Finally, he took the club back and swung easy. He knew at once, as golfers do, that he had hit a good shot. The ball was a little off-line to the hole. A little left, which was good. But not too high. A little less power than either his Dad's or Bip's shots. The ball hit just behind where Bip's ball hit, but instead of kicking right it took two short bounces along the left fringe and then rolled onto the green and dipped down toward the pin.

"Oh, my God," Sticks said as the three of them held their collective breath.

The ball rolled just past the pin and stopped no more than two feet below the hole.

"Great shot," Bip exclaimed, "great shot!"

"That's my boy!" Sticks crowed.

"Awesome," Randy whispered to himself.

At the same time, May Miller called to order the emergency meeting of the Daughters of the Union Army's executive board. They convened for convenience sake in May's elegant Victorian dining room. DUA Vice President Emma Mitchell and Treasurer Sylvia Duke Smith sat in obedient attendance. They were slightly awed—as most people were slightly awed—when surrounded by a 130 years of Jones/Miller antiques. Even though they had both been in the Miller house countless times, the women were overwhelmed anew. DUA secretary, Hannah Hanover, was apparently, again, in Florida. That meant that May, again, would have to do minutes. May believed that Hannah's tenure as an officer of the organization was certainly in jeopardy if her attendance and, quite frankly, her attitude did not improve.

May took a moment to record the date and time and names of those attending on the top of one of Mr. Miller's yellow legal pads. He still kept them all around the house, a legacy of his years as one of the area's leading attorneys. Finally, she looked up and spoke:

"Ladies, I've called you together on a matter of vital importance. There is a rumor that the Board at The Candlesticks is proposing to turn the golf course into a housing development. I believe they call it a *project*."

Sylvia gasped. "A project? Like in a city?"

"Isn't that one of those things Jimmy Carter does?" asked Emma. "I believe he calls it a 'Habit for Humility.' He's very religious, you know."

"I don't have the details," May said, "but I intend to get them."

"Aren't projects usually for, you know, our minority friends?" Sylvia asked hesitatingly.

"That's my understanding," May agreed.

"My, I'm not sure we want that," Emma said pulling Kleenex out of her black purse and dabbing at her face.

May observed the vice president with disdain. Emma's face-dabbing was a very annoying habit and one she would have to stop if she ever expected to be DUA President. She must make a note to speak to

Emma about it in private.

"I understand that it's Howie Howard's idea," May said.

"How can Howie do such a thing?" Sylvia gasped.

All three of the lady officers had known Howie Howard all his life. He was, after all, one of the few remaining male direct descendants of the original seven officers who carried one of the seven original names. And now, in fact, since the Howards had only had Julie and were unlikely to have another child, the Howard line would end. May's own Jones line had no male sons and would soon end. It was very sad if one dwelt on it.

"May?" Sylvia asked.

May looked up startled. She had drifted off, thinking about dynasties ending. It strengthened her resolve about The Candlesticks. She answered Sylvia, "He can do no such thing. He may be president of the Board at the club, but we'll see who's boss."

"Isn't Keith on the Board, May?" Emma asked.

May sat up primly. "Yes, I'm sorry to say that he is. I spoke with him on the phone and Mr. Miller actually went to see him at that place where he *hang*s out. That *garage!*"

May spoke with disdain. In her eyes, her son was permanently a 19-year-old juvenile delinquent (even though when he had actually been 19 he was a sophomore at Indiana getting mostly all As). He had definitely married below his station, she thought. While she did adore Heather and Stacey, her two granddaughters, Keith and Rachel had had no sons and probably wouldn't have one and so the Miller name would soon end, too.

"So, what did he say?" Sylvia asked pressing the matter.

Before May could answer and describe how her son had infuriatingly insisted in a cool and calm tone that it was "only business," the ladies heard the rattle of golf clubs as Mr. Miller passed by the open dining room double-doors on the way out the front door to play golf.

"Mr. Miller!" May shrieked at her husband.

Uh, oh. Mr. Miller thought. *I'm in for it now. She hates it when I clean my clubs in the kitchen sink.*

He turned and stepped into the dining room. "May. Emma. Sylvia. Having a little meeting, are we?"

May, who was sitting at the head of the table with her back to the door, turned in her seat. "How are *you* going to stop Howie from turning The Candlesticks into a *project?*" she asked imperiously.

Mr. Miller could clearly see storm clouds on the horizon. He did not want May and the DUA actively involved in this yet. He had told her that when he had told her about his conversation with their son. But he knew she would call Keith as well. And he knew the rumor mill in Stowe Towne was vicious and highly tuned. Still, he needed some planning time.

So, Mr. Miller acted dumb. "Well, ladies, The Candlesticks' Board is thinking about putting a couple of fairway bunkers at the dogleg on the first hole. And they may have to rebuild the green on the sixth hole. But that's considered normal maintenance. I wouldn't call it a project."

"No, no," May said, "I mean the housing project." *Mr. Miller could be so dense sometimes*, she thought.

Mr. Miller put on a stern face. "I'll ask the boys today what they know. We'll get to the bottom of this, you just wait and see."

Mr. Miller, however, did not feel as confident as the brave face he was showing to the ladies. He had, of course, fretted about what Keith had told him. Fretted and worried. But he knew it was coming. The club had been in the process of changing for a couple of years now. For example, old fellows like himself were more tolerated than welcomed at the club. Computer registration, 18-hole play only on the weekends, price increases (and no senior discount), and other more subtle changes had made them all uncomfortable. Mr. Miller had even spoken to Howie about it when he took over the club presidency from Tom

Duke, Senior. Howie had been polite but distant. The golf course had to modernize to survive, Howie had said earnestly.

And now this.

May excused her husband with a wave of her hand. "You do what you can do," she said as she turned back to the ladies, "and we'll do what we can do."

He shook his head. *This is not good*, he thought as he retreated. His bag of clubs on his back rattled like bones as he left through the front door.

                                               ~

Don Morgan seemed to bond with Howie and Margaret Howard. Or, so it appeared to Bruce Dean.

Either that or Morgan was a genius politician or genius marketer. He certainly was a genius eater. When they had arrived at the Howard's after a tour of Stowe Towne and some of the surrounding countryside, Margaret's catered brunch by Chef Jeff progressed into lunch and more lunch until the early afternoon had slipped by and Morgan started to verbally speculate on the cocktail hour.

Bruce called the office to hand off a couple of showings to Sammi. He did not offer an explanation for his absence and ruefully noted to himself that the office staff would chalk it up to a sexual liaison. How ironic, considering he was actually working on the biggest real estate deal of his life.

The only downside to the Morgan-Howard bonding was that they waited so long to tour the "properties" that a spring thunderstorm blew in from the southwest. The rain, which also made Sticks, Randy, and Bip scamper through the last hole of their round, thoroughly drenched Morgan, Bruce, and the Howards. Howie had borrowed one of the club's two four-passenger golf carts for the tour. The cart had a roof, but the rain slanted in on them from the sides and there was no escaping it.

Thunder suddenly cracked above them and Howie headed full-speed from the back edge of his property across the second and fourth fairways to the large wooden shelter just beyond the third green. About a dozen golfers had already found safety in the shelter, but there was plenty of room for more.

Bruce and Margaret both hated to be wet and looked like drowned rats. But Howie and Morgan seemed to revel in the thunder, lightning, and rain. A bolt streaked across the sky followed by a cannon shot of thunder. Everyone huddled together for safety near the back of the shelter except Howie and Morgan who stepped forward to the edge of the cement floor. Rain whipped about their faces.

"I haven't asked you, Don," Howie shouted into the fat man's left ear, "if you're a golfer."

"I play a couple of times a summer, but I hate the fucking sport," Morgan shouted back. "But it's been great for business. We can inflate the price of a house thirty to fifty percent just by putting it on a fairway. The closer the better. Put the house so close that the kids can't play in the backyard for fear of getting brained by a golf ball and you can up the price seventy percent."

"How does this course look?" Howie shouted as another clap of thunder rocked the shelter.

"Like a million bucks. Maybe ten! I can cram houses on this course up your ass."

Howie gestured toward the par-3 third hole and toward the stand of trees that blocked the view from the shelter of the Pottawa River. "Like I said in the house, Don, that's where we'll expand into the Pottawa State Forest. Beyond those trees up there. Make a couple of new holes up into the park across the river. Give us even more room for houses down where we are now."

Morgan nodded his rain-soaked head. "So, we have the course, the park land, and your land behind your house."

"That's right," Howie said, "and it'll all be known as 'Candlesticks Acres.'"

"Awesome!" Morgan yelled above the thunder. "I tell you that it's fucking awesome!"

chapter five

LE ROI DE SADE

Randy went straight from the golf course and picked up Julie outside of the high school library an hour after school was dismissed. The
rain had swept through Stowe Towne and the surrounding Ohio countryside leaving clear, deep yellow, late afternoon sunlight and a strong,
earthy smell of late spring. It was beautiful.

Julie had attended her final meeting of the French Club. The members were planning their upcoming annual spring trip. The club was
traveling to Cleveland to see the new French film based on King Lear,
Le Roi de Sade. The film was being shown without subtitles at The
Spocket, a small art house in the Flats that specialized in foreign films.
It also was the only place in the Flats where you could not purchase an
alcoholic beverage.

Julie, while being an average student overall, had a flair for languages. She had taken all the school's courses in French and Spanish and
also had informally acquired a working knowledge of Italian and Greek
from her mother. Margaret knew seven languages well, including

Japanese. Julie acquired her language talent entirely from her mother.

Julie was happy about planning the trip to Cleveland and she was also happy to see Randy. All of which put her in a good mood. Randy was also upbeat because of Julie and because after his near hole-in-one, his golf game improved markedly. He had ended up shooting a 41 on the back nine. He described the near hole-in-one and the 41 several times to Julie on the drive back to her house; she described what went on at her French Club meeting three or four times. Neither heard much of what the other said and, like an old married couple, it didn't matter at all.

They weren't quite sure what they were going to do that night. Randy was planning to suggest that they go to a club in Columbus where the John Tempest Band was playing. But he kept thinking and talking about golf as they drove over the Bryce Bridge and then a couple of miles later pulled into the Howard's drive.

"Whose Beemer is that?" Julie asked as they parked next to Bruce Dean's car.

"Oh, that's Bruce's car. You know, the guy who's my Mom's real estate partner."

"Why is he here?" she wondered.

Randy never liked Bruce, although he had had little to do with him over the years. He thought the guy was a phony. He shrugged as he got out of the car. "Who knows?"

Inside the house, the young couple was greeted with an extraordinary sight, especially for the usually pristine and austere Howard residence. In the spacious family room that overlooked the expansive wooden deck that itself overlooked the crook of the dogleg of The Candlesticks' first hole, sat an enormous man draped in the floral pink and mauve bedspread that usually covered Howie and Margaret's bed. (But never would again after today!) The man had a ruddy face that seemed to beam at the young people. Neither Julie nor Randy would have known the reference to Bacchus, but the man was the very image of the Roman god of wine and debauchery.

Julie also noticed, after she got over the shock of seeing Morgan, that Bruce Dean was inexplicably wearing the white and gold LaJolla golf shirt she had purchased through a catalog for her father last Christmas. Meanwhile, her father was wearing one of his old green Candlesticks' golf shirts—not a shirt he normally wore for company. Only her mother was dressed appropriately in a light blue spring dress. But even her hair was disheveled as if she hadn't fixed it after her shower. Julie knew that Margaret *always* fixed her hair. What was going on?

Howie and Margaret were taken aback to see their daughter arrive with Randy at that precise moment. But Howie made an instant decision that keeping the project a secret any longer was now a moot point. Don Morgan was obviously not the secretive type. In fact, he had been telling them just before the kids arrived that the community needed to know about the project just so hidden opposition could surface now at the early stage and be dealt with quickly and efficiently.

Of course, Howie didn't share with Morgan the fact that part of any opposition could come from the father of the young man who was standing in front of them staring in disbelief at the Buddha-like figure draped in their bedspread. Howie was sure Sticks Bergman would oppose changing the golf course. But he also knew that Sticks and Sammi could see opportunities. After all, Sammi was Bruce's partner. She would profit handsomely if she played along. Plus, Sticks was sitting on a fair piece of land that eventually could become "Phase II" of Candlesticks Acres. Howie knew Sticks loved golf and loved The Candlesticks. At first blush, he wouldn't want the course altered in any way. But Howie also knew Sticks and Sammi liked their money and their lifestyle.

Howie took the bull by the horns.

"Julie, Randy, I'd like to have you meet Don Morgan from Cliner Development in Cleveland."

For an awful second, everyone in the room thought Morgan was going to get up from the couch. The thought of the bedspread slipping off and exposing his body was frightening. But the huge man was only maneuvering his Beefeater martini on the rocks from his right to his left hand so that he could offer to shake hands. Both Randy and Julie came forward hesitatingly as Howie continued the introductions.

"Don, this is our daughter Julie and her friend Randy Bergman."

"Julie, Randy," Morgan boomed out as he vigorously shook hands. "Excuse the rather unusual dress. We all got caught in that downpour and your Dad didn't have anything to fit me. He could have ordered a tent if he had known."

Morgan laughed uproariously while everyone else sort of tittered. Randy and Julie backed away after shaking hands.

"Are you here on business?" Randy asked. His father's persistent questions about a housing development on The Candlesticks echoed loudly in his brain.

"Absolutely, Randy. Howie, Bruce, and I are discussing a project involving the golf course here."

Holy shit, Bruce thought to himself. Of course, unaware that Howie had just decided to go public using Randy as the catalyst, Bruce was beside himself. Sammi was already suspicious and would blow up as soon as she found out. People usually didn't like business being conducted behind their backs by their partners. Plus, this was personal because of her own home's location. But, at this moment, he was paralyzed as Morgan expounded on the project.

Morgan acted like he was a young real estate agent again, selling a house to newlyweds. He waved his arms at the wall of windows that looked out at the pastoral rural landscape as he spoke directly to Julie and Randy. Soon, he said, there would be quarter to half-million dollar homes and roads and the newly expanded golf course running through the development. He wasn't sure about Candlesticks *Acres* as a name —too bovine—but the homes would be something that would attract professionals from all over central Ohio.

"Can you see it?" Morgan concluded. "Can you feel the excitement?"

Both Julie and Randy were a little shell-shocked. Suddenly, they could feel they were center stage. Somehow, what they said next mattered to the adults in the room. That hadn't always been the case.

Finally, Randy said, "Well, do you have to change the golf course? Can't you just put the houses over there or someplace?" He gestured vaguely with his hand away from the direction of the golf course.

"Oh no, son," Morgan said in a fatherly tone. "People want sites that are integrated with recreational opportunities. Golf, water, the park."

"The park?" Julie asked.

"Of course, we'll extend right into the park."

"Can you do that?" she asked looking at her father.

"Just a little bit of the state forest, not the state park," Howie said nervously. "No one will have a problem with that. You know, economic development."

"What exactly would you do with the golf course? How would you change it?" Randy persisted.

"Very little," Bruce said quickly. "You can assure your parents that it would change very little."

Howie glared at Bruce. They didn't need Sticks Bergman's approval to go ahead with this development. Or Sammi Bergman's permission, either. "Well, kids," Howie stepped forward and made to usher Julie and Randy out of the room, "we've still got some talking to do. But we were just discussing having a news conference at the end of next week. So, we'd appreciate it if you didn't spread this all around. You understand. Just keep it to yourself for now."

Julie and Randy retreated to the double doors leading from the family room to the house's large country kitchen.

"Nice to meet you," Julie said with a little wave of her hand toward the giant man wearing her parents' bedspread. She was always very conscious of her manners when in the presence of her mother.

"You too, Julie. Randy," the voice boomed back. "I'm sure we'll see a lot more of the two of you."

Backing them a step into the kitchen, Howie, smiling, slid shut the door to the family room in their faces.

Julie glanced at Randy. "Let's get a couple of beers," she said softly, "and go for a ride." They quickly got out of the house, flustered and confused.

⌐

The game was gin.

Mr. Miller was not doing well because his mind was on his conversation with the ladies about the golf course. He kept staring past his brother-in-law Lincoln Jones's shoulder and out the window of the clubhouse at the 10th tee. No one had been there since dinnertime on Friday. But the course, cleansed by the soaking rain in the afternoon, looked beautiful. The setting sun cast a golden glow over the shades of green. You could look all the way down the long par-5 10th hole and see the trees along the edge of the Pottawa River. It was a glorious place.

"Gin!" Bip said, snapping his cards on the table.

"You bastard," Lincoln cursed, flipping his cards away. "I'm getting another drink. Anyone else?"

Mr. Miller, Bip, and their fourth, David Canello, declined.

"David," Mr. Miller began (he had been waiting for just the right minute), "what do you know about any changes at the course?"

"What do you mean?" Canello asked. He liked Mr. Miller even

though he considered him an old fart. Mr. Miller had been his mentor when he had joined the firm although their relationship had been strained at the end just before Mr. Miller retired.

Mr. Miller shrugged. "I don't know. Anything at the Board meeting? Changing the course? Selling it?" Mr. Miller, out of the corner of his eye, caught Bip arching an eyebrow.

"No, don't know what you're talking about," Canello lied. He glanced at Mr. Miller and Bip as he slowly gathered up the cards. He knew that they knew. Bip would have found out from Howie by now or just from being around the club. Keith Miller would surely have told his father.

Bip shifted uncomfortably; he knew he had to say something. He instinctively decided to leave Sticks and Howie out of it. "Some fellows mentioned to me that Dan Ofman heard a rumor at the high school. Some kids told him that they were going to build houses on the course, condos or something."

"Kids said that?" Canello scoffed. "What do kids know? Ofman never gets anything right. Poor excuse for a teacher and a poor excuse for a football coach."

"What's the real story, David?" Mr. Miller asked.

"Who knows? I'm just The Candlesticks' lawyer. Seems no one needs my opinion."

The three men lapsed into silence waiting for Lincoln to return.

Bip didn't like David Canello. He didn't like him because he cheated at golf. All the time, on almost every hole. Took fairway mulligans. Always improved his lie. Assumed gimmes on putts three or four feet from the hole. Took every break he could and still shot piss-poor golf.

Mr. Miller, meanwhile, wondered what Canello might be hiding. He knew the man was a bulldog on finances. That's why Canello was his old firm's managing partner. This was all well and good, but Mr. Miller knew Canello didn't have an ounce of sentimentality. *Witness his lack of rever-*

ence and respect at my retirement party, Mr. Miller thought. So, if there was a penny or dollar more to be squeezed out of The Candlesticks, the man would agree to it and grease the wheels. Still, Mr. Miller noticed that Canello had a scowl on his face. He wondered why. Maybe there was something Canello really didn't know.

David Canello, on the other hand, felt paralyzed. He hated being out of the loop. He hated lying, or at least playing dumb, to these men he had known for decades. *The goddamn familes*, he thought. *The goddamn families!* His whole life he had had to deal with the Stowe Towne families. He would rather have dealt with a Mafia family or a labor family or the First Family. One of the great accomplishments of his life was leading the effort to wrestle control of Miller, Duke and Hanover from the last tenacious remnant of the Stowe Towne Seven Families. Mr. Miller had not gone graciously, but at least he went. And the old codger had come around pretty fast afterward so that they now could at least play a civil game of gin.

Lincoln finally returned with two fingers of Canadian Club on ice and the game continued in a grim and methodical manner. Lincoln was oblivious, but the other three men mulled over their thoughts as they mulled over their cards. Finally, the game ended, bets were paid off, and the men went their separate ways. Still deep in thought.

∽

Later that same evening, Sticks Bergman sat alone on the new metal bleachers lost in his own thoughts. The bleachers were part of a three-field softball complex that Allied Pipes had built next to their new plant. It had been part of the tax abatement deal the Stowe Towne Town Council had cut with the company in order to entice the new industry to relocate. The deal had worked out well, although so far Allied Pipes and the softball complex were the only two tenants in the

Stowe Towne Victory Industrial Park south of town.

The softball game was over and Sticks should have gone over to the shelter area where his brother Paul and the lumberyard team were celebrating their 15 to 7 victory over a hapless team of county employees. The game was only that close because the muddy infield and rain-soaked outfield softened the usually rock-hard softballs and turned normal lumberyard home runs into fly ball outs. Sticks had been an original member of the lumberyard's team, but had given up playing softball 10 years before when he concluded that his batting swing was screwing up his golf swing. However, right now he wasn't thinking about softball. Instead, he couldn't stop thinking about The Candlesticks' dilemma. He couldn't even decide if it was really something to worry about. He knew just from being married to a real estate agent that many real estate proposals never came to fruition. And he knew that Howie Howard was not necessarily the most savvy or dynamic business leader in the community. Nevertheless...

"Sticks?" a voice interrupted his thoughts.

Sticks focused on the scruffy figure of Will Boyd. Boyd was the current town eccentric. He had appeared in Stowe Towne about five years before, just when the deal Sammi and Bruce had been putting together to turn the Hanover Mansion into condos had come apart. He had bought the old home on the rebound and had spent a ton of money remodeling it extensively. He supposedly was living off an inheritance— old Kentucky horse money was the rumor. Although Sticks always suspected the fellow was really a lottery winner living off his winnings.

"How are you, Will?" Sticks greeted the man. "You don't look like you're playing tonight."

Will was the shortstop and the best player on a team made up of *Stowe Towne Bugle* employees, the best team in the league behind the lumberyard. Tonight, however, Will was dressed in work boots, jeans, and a blue plaid shirt that looked too hot for the pleasantly warm evening. He had a scraggly brown beard and longish brown hair streaked with gray. He looked more like a lumberjack than either a softball player or Stowe Towne resident.

At his feet, Will's white bulldog plopped down in the mud. The dog accompanied his master everywhere and was the gentlest dog anyone ever knew. At ball games, kids would come up and pet and sometimes tease the dog, yet Bandit (as Will called him) only responded with panting and wet face licks.

"No, we had a bye this week. You don't look like you're umpiring tonight, either," Will answered back.

"No, but that's actually why I'm here. My brother called and said they needed a substitute ump. Old Harry was supposedly on his deathbed. Again. But when I got here old Harry was right there behind the plate as usual."

Will laughed. "Harry's going to die behind the plate, not in bed. I'll give him credit, though. He still makes the right calls. Usually."

The men laughed. Most people acknowledged that Harry couldn't see farther than the pitcher's mound. But that was far enough to call balls and strikes.

"Read that article you wrote last week in the paper about Bryce Bridge," Sticks said changing the subject. "Didn't know it was named after a guy from the Civil War. Your story was interesting." Will occasionally wrote feature stories for the newspaper, often on historical topics.

"Thanks. I guess most people had forgotten about Bryce."

Sticks stood up and stepped over a couple of bleachers to the muddy ground. He said, "You know, if you grow up here, all you hear about are the goddamn seven heroes. You'd think they beat the South single-handedly."

Will nodded. "I can assure you that wasn't the case."

"Like this Bryce fellow. You said that he was in the fighting at

Gettysburg."

"Indeed he was. Right in the middle of it. Three of the seven heroes weren't even at Gettysburg, despite what the statue says."

Sticks shook his head. "Then you said he disappeared."

"No one knows," Will replied. "People said at the time that he took off for out West. It was about the time of the silver strikes in Nevada. Late 1870s. Left a wife who never heard from him. Sad story."

"I guess. Well, at least he got the bridge named after him."

Will nodded. "At least he got the bridge."

"Come on, let's go have a beer with the lumberyard team," Sticks said clapping Will on the back. "Those guys got to be generous as long as they're in first place."

"Thanks, I don't drink beer, though I might have a Coke if they have one. But, Sticks, when I saw you, I thought I'd ask you about The Candlesticks. Since you live next door and all, I figured you'd know what's going on. I hear there's some rumors."

"Is this for the newspaper?" Sticks asked.

"No, just for me."

"You don't play golf."

"Sometimes I do. I've played The Candlesticks. Not recently, but I have."

Sticks shrugged; he had never seen Will on the course and this was the first time he could remember the man mentioning golf. "I don't know, Will. There are some rumors, I guess. I tried to track the sources down, but I didn't find out anything for certain. First I heard that the course was up for sale. Or already sold. Then, they were going to start building houses on it. Or condos. Who knows?"

"It would be too bad to lose that course, or even have it significantly altered in some way."

"That's what I think," Sticks agreed. "Hopefully, it's just hot air. Howie's been known to blow hot air before. My son, you know, dates

Julie Howard. I keep pumping Randy for information, but he's given me nothing concrete yet."

"Well," Will concluded as they crossed the edge of the large gravel parking lot toward the picnic shelter, "let's hope nothing happens or else we'll have to do something about it."

He said the words in such a tone that made Sticks glance sideways at the strange man. Sticks wondered what stake this relative newcomer to Stowe Town could possibly have in The Candlesticks.

But instead of pursuing the subject, Will reached down and scratched Bandit behind the ears. "Good boy, Bandit," he muttered. "That's a good dog."

~

"Juliet, please come in here!" Margaret's voice rang out in the dark, silent house.

Howie tapped out the seconds with his right index finger on the arm of the chair. He had sat in the chair in the living room across from where Margaret sat on the couch for about an hour. The Scotch on the rocks, which he clutched in his left hand, had long since turned to Scotch and water. He knew that Morgan, more or less unwittingly, had pushed Margaret to the brink today. He also knew that before Candlesticks Acres or whatever it might be called became a reality, Margaret would be pushed to the brink over and over again. That was why he quickly and meekly agreed to her demand to sit up and wait for their daughter.

But he had been here before. That's why he tapped his finger. He knew that before the tenth tap, Julie would say from the hallway:

"Please, Mother, I'm tired. I don't want to do this tonight."

Now the unseen clash of wills.

Tap, tap, tap. The wait for her to appear at the door was growing longer as she grew older. *Tap, tap, tap.* The first time this scene had happened Julie had flown to the door to plead her case. To offer her defense. To accuse them of spying—although, how they could be spying by sitting silently in a darkened living room was beyond Howie. *Tap, tap, tap.* One day soon she just would not come. Would go to her room. And then—Howie shuddered—he and Margaret would be left alone with each other. *Tap, tap, tap.*

"All right. What is it?" Julie was standing in the door, her arms folded defiantly across her chest.

Margaret ground out her cigarette in the large glass ashtray that dominated the rectangular glass and walnut coffee table. "Your father and I have decided, Juliet, that you no longer will date Randy Bergman."

Howie's jaw dropped. It was inconsequential to him that Margaret had not discussed this decision with him despite her implicating him, but even Howie knew enough elementary psychology that such a statement was like waving the proverbial red flag in front of the proverbial bull. And here he was trying to be so careful with Julie because of her pending college decision. And now, in one sentence, Margaret had probably blown months of delicate negotiations.

Julie, too, was stunned. "What? What did you say?"

Howie couldn't let this one go. He had to salvage something. "I think what your mother is saying is that you can't devote all your time to Randy. End of the school year. Graduation. We've still got to get that college choice nailed down." He tried desperately to sound upbeat.

"Excuse me, Howard," Margaret said. "Juliet is not to see Randy Bergman. That's perfectly clear."

"You can't order me not to see him," Julie responded her voice still shaken by her mother's dictum.

"I most certainly can. We're your mother and father, and you live in our house. Until that changes, you follow our rules."

Holy shit! Howie thought, *she's burning the goddamn bridges.*

"I'm eighteen, I'm dating who I want. And you can go fuck your-self." Saying that, Julie turned and disappeared.

"You'll regret that attitude, young lady," Margaret responded in a sharp voice.

"What the hell..." Howie started.

"You don't say a word, if you know what's good for you," Margaret said in the same sharp voice. Then she lowered her voice to a whisper and leaned across the gulf of the carpeting toward him. "You make me go through that charade today with that...that man from Cleveland and made plans to totally disrupt our lives and meanwhile your daughter is dating the enemy."

"The enemy? You mean the Bergmans?"

"Of course the Bergmans," she spat.

"I think Sticks might see this as an excellent business venture. I don't think he'll necessarily oppose..."

Howie's voice trailed off. Margaret was right. He was only fooling himself. He sat for a minute thinking it through. Sticks would organize and lead the opposition. And Julie would become a willing or unwilling spy against her own parents and their interests. They were risking alien-ating her. But they were also drawing the lines clearly for her. And, who knows, maybe this would just push her to making that college choice.

It wasn't quite clear but, as usual, he was beginning to see Margaret's point.

Sticks was in the kitchen making a liverwurst and Velveeta sandwich on whole wheat toast when Randy got home after dropping off Julie, and delivered the news about The Candlesticks. Sticks took it very calmly. After all, it wasn't a big surprise. He had been certain that the rumor must have had some basis in fact. But he was surprised at the scope and, yes, even the audacity of the project. Proposing to take state park land? Sticks was fully aware that—technically—part of the property in question was the tail end of the state forest and not a state park. It was undeveloped land that had no trails or camping or anything else recreational. He was sure that most people in Stowe Towne didn't even know that the golf course abutted the state forest or even that the course itself had long ago been part of the state forest. It was simply that land on the other side of the Pottawa River that in and of itself— except for its little cascade through the golf course—was a pretty unscenic and unremarkable stream. Sticks wondered momentarily if he had any obligation to call Will Boyd and tell him the rumors were true since they were just talking. No, probably not. Will would know on his own pretty soon.

Sticks munched on his sandwich and sipped a glass of orange juice. He motioned for Randy to get himself a beer and sit down opposite him in the breakfast nook off the kitchen. The little alcove was too cutesy for men, Sticks thought, and he usually avoided eating there. But this was late at night. He also seldom offered his son a beer or liquor of any kind. Sammi was absolutely opposed to the practice, but she was sound asleep. Again, it was late at night and Sticks wanted to hear everything Randy knew.

Sticks noted that Randy popped the Bud Light with a familiar ease that indicated that he had drunk his share of beer. Not surprising. The kid had been away at the university for a year. Randy proceeded to tell his father in detail about the bizarre encounter with the bedspread-clad Don Morgan. Sticks listened intently and then questioned Randy on a couple of his statements. Still, in the end, Sticks was unsure of exactly how far along the project was.

"Bruce didn't do a lot of talking, you said?" Sticks asked.

Randy shook his head. "No, I suppose he was surprised to see me. Mom doesn't know anything about this?" he asked.

"No, not really. I guess there were some phone calls from Cliner Development down at the office a few days ago. But she didn't know it was about this. She thought they were advertising some seminar or something."

"So, he's going behind Mom's back?"

Sticks knew that Randy knew that he didn't like Bruce very much. They both knew that Sammi didn't like Bruce very much either. There had been plenty of discussions at home on the topic. But they also knew that Sammi had done quite well in partnership with Bruce. Bruce's peccadilloes and general sleaziness aside, the man still managed a pretty good real estate agency and through aggressiveness and a little luck had made it very profitable. Sammi worked hard, but liked her work and made a hell of an income.

"Well, Randy," Sticks finally answered after a long pause, "I'm not sure he's exactly going behind her back. You know that real estate people are working deals all the time."

"What? You aren't in favor of this?"

"Oh no, I didn't say that."

"You're going to fight this, aren't you?"

His son's indignant attitude took Sticks a little by surprise. Randy now suddenly seemed mad at him and not Howie and Bruce. He quickly recanted: "Sure, we have to fight it. It's The Candlesticks. Our golf course. But we have to think about your mother's situation. Work situation, I mean. We can't put her in an awkward spot."

"Bruce is a real asshole."

"Right, I know. But your mother has a job, has a career. She may want to stay neutral here."

"If I know Mom, I don't think she'll want to stay neutral."

Sticks nodded slowly and ran his finger around the rim of his orange juice glass. He thought about his wife, but he also thought about his two brothers and the lumberyard. The yard was doing okay, but it could use a shot in the arm. If a deal could be worked out concerning the new project...

He glanced up and saw his son staring at him.

"Oh, well, Randy, you're right. But I just think we have to see what develops. You know that real estate people sometimes hallucinate. Remember a couple of years ago when Mom and Bruce were going to get the Hanover mansion and turn it into six apartments or condos or something like that. They had the blueprints right here on the table for a month because they didn't want anyone else, even at the office, to know about it. And then it all fell through just like that."

"Why are you bringing that up?" Randy asked.

"Oh, I saw Will Boyd tonight at the ball fields. Remember how he came in and saved everybody's ass by buying the place?"

Randy shrugged and polished off his beer. "I don't know, Dad, this is something different. Anyway, I guess I'll go to bed."

Sticks watched his son leave the kitchen. He cleaned up his dishes, buried the beer can deep in the trash, and then went to bed himself. He lay quietly and rigidly next to Sammi. His stomach was churning. *The goddamn liverwurst! How could he be so stupid?* But he knew it was more than that. It was the whole idea of changing The Candlesticks. He hated condo golf with a passion. Hitting past backyards. Neat little greens beyond bedroom windows. Trophy greens! Having sex and watching a guy blow a four-foot putt. It was like going to a football game in November and sitting in a warm comfy sky-box drinking cocktails. That wasn't watching football! And condo golf wasn't playing golf. At least not to Sticks.

Plus, they would change the course itself. They would have to. It wouldn't be his own private course any longer. It would be different. And then he wouldn't be as good a player. He'd be going backward. He was already afraid enough of growing old. This would only make it worse.

Eventually, he fell into a fitful sleep. About 4:00 a.m., another thunderstorm rolled over Stowe Towne and Pottawa County and the thunder and lightning woke both him and Sammi. When Sammi woke up during a thunderstorm, she always got up and checked things out. Of course, as usual, everything was fine. Everything was secure. When she finally came back to bed, Sticks told her what Randy had reported and they talked about it lazily for a half hour. They came to no resolution. Eventually, they both fell back to sleep.

chapter six

WHAT DO YOU EAR?

Peter Onear, the chief legislative reporter for the *Columbus Dispatch*, reached for his ringing desk phone with his left hand while at the same time grabbed his morning coffee mug with his right hand. The newspaper supplied the white mugs that had red lettering reading PRINT PEOPLE GET IT RIGHT. The newspaper had recently launched a self-promotion campaign trumpeting newspaper accuracy and thoroughness. Fortunately, for Peter's own mental health, he was always more concerned about other people's hypocrisy than his own. He was of that school of journalism that allowed that only in journalism did the means justify the end.

It was not yet 8:00 in the morning, but the newsroom was already active. This was Onear's first phone call of the day, but it wouldn't be his last by far. The man lived and died by the phone.

"Is this O'Near?" a male voice asked.

Onear ignored the mispronunciation of his name—he was all too used to it.

"Yes, who's this?"

"Never mind, just listen."

Onear sighed; people watched too much TV. He'd normally get two or three calls like this a week, many more if there was an election coming up. Most were bogus. Some guy would want him to investigate the Columbus Water Department because his water bill went up five bucks. Or some lady was convinced the post office was shredding her mail. Still, Onear always tried to be polite. One never knew.

"All right, how can I help you?" he asked the voice.

"You know State Senator Barnes?"

Onear put down his coffee and pulled a piece of paper toward him. These types of calls usually didn't start like this. "Sure," he said, "I know Kenny Barnes."

"He's on the take."

"Hey, they're all on the take, fella. What have you got for proof?"

"He's going to sell off state land. You know, like a state park."

"What state park?"

"Do you know, where he's from?" the voice asked.

Onear hesitated for a second. *Barnes*, he thought. One of the younger members of the Senate. Essentially a nonplayer. Voted straight party line. "Well, he's from around here. Up by Stowe Towne. That district stretches north, northeast..." He paused and thought for a second. Then Onear said, "Pottawa."

"Bingo!" the voice said and then hung up.

Onear put down the receiver and picked up a blue Bic pen and wrote POTTAWA in large letters on the clean white paper. Then he reached for the guide to the state legislators published yearly by the Truckers' Association and looked up Barnes. The bio was sketchy mainly because the guy had done nothing. From Granite City, a town just northeast of Pottawa State Park. Law degree from Michigan. A three-year stint in the Prosecutor's Office in Akron. Won the Senate seat because he was handpicked by the retiring incumbent.

Onear grabbed his notepad and put on his tattered herringbone sports coat. He wasn't planning to wander the Senate hallways this morning. But then, why not? Stop in and talk to Barnes about something. Something innocuous, like the education bill or the lottery reorganization bill. If he dropped a reference to Pottawa and if Barnes reacted, then...

Onear was a clever man. There had been clever Onears for almost 200 years. In 1805, Napoleon won his greatest victory at Austerlitz over the Austrians and Russians. One of the heroes of the battle was a young French soldier who nearly single-handedly turned an enemy cavalry charge by pulling the Austrian captain leading the charge off his horse. The heroics, however, cost the young soldier his right ear that was sliced clean off by the captain's saber.

The soldier, who was only 15 years old and an orphan, acquired the name Monsieur Unorielle, *The Sir With One Ear*. The youth was an engaging fellow and became the equivalent of a celebrity in Napoleonic and even post-Napoleonic France. Monsieur Unorielle produced a large family, but by the end of the nineteenth century one branch of the family, in disrepute, decided to immigrate to America.

Pierre Unorielle was determined to become a true American and transform his family of a wife and three boys into true Americans. He learned enough English to know that his name translated into "One Ear" and believed that the fame of his brave ancestor would be recognized and probably revered in the United States. Of course, at chaotic Ellis Island, the named became *Onear* in the paperwork. Pierre was indignant and forever insisted the name was "One Ear." The sons, ultimately there were seven of them, were embarrassed by their old man and eventually Onear—pronounced Oneau—won out. Unfortunately, most people thought the name was an odd Irish variation and pronounced it O'Near.

Peter Onear found few people this early on a Thursday morning in the Senate hallways of the newly renovated State Capitol building. The door was locked to Barnes's office. Onear shrugged his shoulders and wandered away. No matter. He had a major story on the lottery reorganization coming out in the Sunday paper. It was a good story, although not significant. The lottery was unimportant to state government, but a popular people topic. Gambling was always a popular topic. Onear would have liked to have found corruption and theft of funds. But all he really found was management ineptness and political featherbedding. The technicians/accountants who actually ran the show were honest and boring.

Onear was coming out of the building when he ran into his prey. Barnes was stout, if not overweight, and laboring up the steep steps. He was wearing a brown wool suit that was too heavy for the spring morning. His hair was disheveled. Looks, Onear thought, will not get this man reelected.

"Senator?"

Kenny Barnes looked up, startled to see the reporter a couple of steps above and directly in front of him.

Onear held out his hand. "Peter Onear. *Dispatch*. We've met before, I think."

Kenny shook hands weakly. "Nice to see you, Mr. Onear." He pronounced Onear's name correctly in a surprisingly strong voice.

"Time for a couple of questions?" Onear asked.

Kenny glanced at his watch. "I've actually got an agriculture committee meeting."

"Sure," Onear nodded. Did Barnes think he didn't know the committees didn't start until 10:00? It was barely 8:30. "Well, I'll make it quick. What do you think about requiring that twelfth grade students pass the proficiency test before they're allowed to graduate?"

Kenny's ample brow wrinkled. "Well, I've never understood why you'd give a test if passing it wasn't required. But I don't know why you're asking me about that. That issue's been referred to the State Superintendent of Public Education. It's not a legislative issue for now. I'm sorry, but I've got to run."

Onear moved aside as Kenny stepped past him. He was a bit surprised at the deftness that the man had displayed in parrying his question.

"Oh, well, Senator, just background. Say, just one quick nonpolitical question."

Kenny stopped and turned back. Now he was a couple of steps above the reporter. "All right," he said quickly.

Onear gave a little smile. "My girlfriend and I, this weekend, thought we'd have a little getaway. Maybe drive up to Pottawa State Park. She's new to the area. Any suggestions on where we might stay? Some rustic inn?"

Kenny paused and Onear searched his face for any sign of nervousness. He really couldn't tell, yet it seemed to take the man just a bit too long to come up with an answer. Finally, the senator said, "Well, there's the lodge in the park, of course. It's off Highway 37. Can't miss it on the map. It's very nice. I've stayed there."

With that, he turned and continued up the steps. Onear stood watching him until the politician disappeared into the capitol.

⌁

Kenny Barnes did, in fact, have an agriculture committee meeting, but he left the committee room after 15 minutes in the middle of a very boring report on soybean blight. He changed clothes in his office and, by noon, he was hauling out his late father's golf clubs from the trunk of his dark blue Taurus in the parking lot of The Candlesticks. Kenny hated golf; he hated everything athletic. But one political lesson he had

learned early was that to survive he had to be (1) completely knowl-
edgeable about Ohio State University athletics, (2) fairly aware of local
high school athletics in his district, and (3) at least dimly coherent about
Ohio's professional sports teams. To that end, he was wearing a white
golf shirt with a red and gray OSU Buckeye logo and a dark blue
Cleveland Indians' windbreaker with a Chief Wahoo patch on the
shoulder.

Kenny was under the mistaken belief that his golfing partner today,
Supreme Court Justice Richard Summers, was a law graduate of Ohio
State. In fact, Summers had gone to Marietta College and then to Ohio
Northern University for his law degree. But Summers was a master
politician, since Supreme Court justices in Ohio were elected and
Summers had survived on the bench for more than 40 years. He never
made a point about being an ONU grad. Instead, he acted like a rabid
Buckeye fan.

Kenny found Judge Summers having a sandwich on The
Candlestick's large deck overlooking the pond adjacent to the 18th
green. Kenny panicked, thinking that he was supposed to have met the
justice for lunch.

"Am I late, Judge?" he asked anxiously.

The gray-haired justice looked up with a thin smile.

"No, Kenny, in fact, you're early. Our tee time isn't for another 45
minutes. Sit down and have a hot dog."

"Thanks, but I had a late breakfast," the senator lied. He was much
too nervous about golfing with Summers to even consider eating. Kenny
sat down in a green metal chair across from the justice and plunked his
clubs next to him. He realized that he should have left the clubs down
on the bag rack. He looked around as he caught his breath and the judge
finished his sandwich. It was a beautiful spring day—the fresh earth
smell of spring in the air. Yet, there were only a handful of people on the
deck.

After a moment, the justice's silent munching got to him. "I just thought I'd get here early and practice putting or something. I'm afraid I'm not a very good golfer."

"I know," Summers said nodding his head. "There are some of us who know the skill level of everyone in state government who plays golf. It's the only way you can hope to win in scrambles. If you know what I mean."

Before he ran for the Senate—his first elective office—Kenny barely knew the rules of golf much less the definition of "scrambles." But then Howie Howard had offered to sponsor a fund-raiser at The Candlesticks for him. That had been the beginning of his golf education. *Now*, he thought, *for some reason Judge Summers is about to take me to Golf Graduate School.*

"When I was a little kid, my Dad used to bring me out here all the time. You know, for obvious reasons," Kenny said.

"Oh yes," the judge said, finishing his iced tea. "The infamous Billy Barnes and Barnes's Knob. Your father was fascinated with what happened to your grandfather."

"You knew my father?"

"Well, everyone knew Ace Barnes," the judge replied.

William Ace Barnes had not even been born yet when his father had disappeared on Barnes's Knob. Of course, all of Stowe Towne had felt sorry for the tragic widow burdened with a new baby. The Howard family had supported Alice Barnes for years and the Hanover family had employed her at their grocery store through the twenties, the Depression, and the war years.

Young William Barnes had been wild for airplanes and had learned how to fly by harassing area crop dusters into teaching him during summer vacations. He had actually acquired the nickname Ace before the war and his name became a self-fulfilling prophecy. The day he turned 18, he entered the Air Force and became a fighter pilot in the European

Theater. He was handsome, flamboyant, and, in 1944, saved a planeload of VIPs who had strayed off course over the North Sea and were about to be picked off by a Luftwaffe patrol. Barnes shot down two planes and shielded the VIP plane until help arrived. It earned him the Medal of Honor.

He stayed in the Air Force, had a brief and disastrous marriage to a general's daughter, and flew in the Korean Conflict. Finally he retired and came home to Stowe Towne because his mother insisted. He married Kenny's mother and tried unsuccessfully to be a gentleman farmer up near Granite City. He died of a massive heart attack in 1968 when Kenny was 10 years old.

"Your father was a hell of a pilot and a hell of a nice guy. I always wanted him to go into politics, but he insisted that he didn't know enough. That doesn't usually stop the normal politician, so I guess your father must have had integrity, too. Unfortunately, what he didn't have was any talent for golf."

"I probably inherited that gene," Kenny said.

"Well, golf is a game for patient men. I don't suppose fighter pilots are very patient men, in general." The judge smiled and pushed away from the table. "Let's play a little golf, Kenny."

An hour later, the senator finally put together a decent drive and four-iron on the short par 4 fifth hole. He was on the left fringe of the green close to the pin placement. Judge Summers, on the other hand, had hit his first poor shot of the day off the tee and then bounced a six-iron into the near right side bunker.

Summers stopped their cart behind the bunker and got out. "Oh, these creaky bones act up. I need some July heat to get loosened-up." He plucked his sand wedge out of his bag and stood looking down into the sand. "Come over here, son," Summers said.

Kenny came around the cart and joined the older man staring down at the half-buried white ball. He shuddered. If he were down there, he might never get out.

"Let me teach you a little about golf, politics, and life," Summers said. "We can just barely see my ball down there. Then there's your ball over there. Just off the green and about 20 or 22 feet from the hole. It would appear that you're in better shape than I am on this particular hole. Wouldn't you agree?"

Kenny stared down at his beat-up Converse tennis shoes. He didn't even own golf shoes. He made a mental note to buy a pair.

Suddenly, Summers dropped the head of the sand wedge on his playing partner's left foot. "Are you listening to me, Kenny?"

"Of course, sir. I'm sorry. I was just staring at your shot. It's impossible."

"Well, we will see. Now, I'm 74 and how old are you...?

"40."

"So, you've got 34 years on me. But, do you think you can get your shot down before me?"

"What? Oh, well, I don't know. You're an excellent golfer. Much better than I am."

"I am. I am a much better golfer. But consider this particular case. You see, we both lie two. But I'm buried in the sand and you're very close to the hole. You might even make that putt for a birdie."

"Well, I don't know about that."

"But it's possible. Step up and stroke the ball. I'm an old man. I have to climb down into the pit."

Kenny shrugged. "Maybe, sir."

"No maybe about it, you're home free."

Summers stepped down into the sand and took an exaggerated open stance over his ball. Kenny thought he was going to hit his shot, but then the old man stepped away.

"You wouldn't want to put a little wager on this, would you, Senator?"

"Wager? Like what?"

"I don't know. Why don't we just make it an unspecified political favor? I owe you or you owe me. No strings attached. No payback."

Kenny Barnes was no fool. He could feel himself starting to sweat. Justice Richard Summers was a figure to be reckoned with both within the Party and across the state. When the justice's secretary called to invite him for golf, Kenny would have shown up no matter what. Even if he had had a meeting scheduled with the governor. Now, this was the payoff. Done with a little flair. A little style.

Kenny managed a weak smile. "Sounds like a good bet to me, sir."

To Kenny's surprise, Summers offered his hand. The senator shook it, a little unnerved by the formality. He backed away as the judge reset himself. After a moment, the judge swung easily and the ball just cleared the lip of the bunker and landed halfway to the flag and rolled in an arc left to right and ended up six feet to the right of the pin.

"Great shot," Kenny breathed out. He realized that he had been holding his breath.

"Thanks," Summers said climbing out of the bunker. "You're away."

Kenny was halfway across to his ball when he realized he was still holding his four-iron. He retreated to get his putter. Meanwhile, Summers marked his ball. "Leave the flag in?" he asked.

"Sure, why not?" Kenny was in the first cut of rough. Now that he was standing over his ball, he realized that the green sloped away quite sharply. From a distance, it hadn't appeared that the green had any slope at all. He would have to hit his ball hard enough to get it off the fringe, but then the ball might definitely roll by the hole. In fact, the more he looked at the putt, the more certain he was that there was no way he could stop the putt.

He stood over his ball. His (or rather his father's) putter was just a mallet head putter. He needed a new fancy putter. One with a big head. But he couldn't do anything about that now. He stared at the ball. And then decided to hit it. But then he let up. The ball trickled off the fringe and stopped after only a yard. He was still at least 15 feet from the hole.

"I believe you're away," Summers said softly.

Now Kenny struck the ball too quickly and it rolled past the hole and stopped a foot beyond Summers' marker. The judge didn't have to say anything again. Kenny's next putt stopped six inches shy of the hole. "That's good," the judge said and the young man stooped down in humiliation and picked up his ball.

The judge calmly sank his putt for par. Kenny had a six.

Back in the cart, Summers said, "Don't take it too hard, Kenny, I'm sure nothing of importance will ever come up. By the way, how about those Indians?"

~

Delia Long owned the "other" golf course in Stowe Towne, a nine-hole country course six miles southeast of the town on the edge of the Hocking Hills. It was named "George Long's Golf Club" for Delia's husband who had died at the age of 55 on one summer morning in 1990 just after changing the hole position on the first green. Besides renaming the course from "The Hocking Hills Golf Course" to "George Long's Golf Club" to honor George, Delia also refused to move the hole on the first green. She'd declared loudly to anyone who complained that it was her beloved George's last hole and she couldn't bear to see it changed. While the sentiment was noble, the constant traffic around the hole wore down the green until the hole was like a big brown drain. Any reasonable putt within a six-foot circle rolled into the hole. Players, who complained for a year or so, learned to live with it and love it.

Few people who played George Long's Golf Club (the GLGC) played The Candlesticks. Or vice versa. The GLGC clientele mainly consisted of kids who were charged the "junior" rate of $3 per nine or $5 all day or older folks who were charged the "senior" rate of $3 per nine or $5 all day. About the only full-paying customers were nearby farmers who occasionally took an afternoon off to play nine holes and then drink a little beer with Delia in the squat, cement-block clubhouse George and Delia had built with their own hands in 1972. The place was like an oven in the summer despite the window air conditioner. But the heat encouraged beer sales and that's where Delia made most of her golf course income now.

Brash and bossy 60-year-old Delia Long, with her dyed red hair and abnormally long arms (she could belt a golf ball longer than about any woman in the county, but she couldn't make a putt, even on George Long's first hole), normally wouldn't have had anything to do with the plan to change the venerable Candlesticks Golf Course. Neither Howie Howard nor Sticks Bergman had played George Long's Golf Club since they were teenagers, when it had been owned by George's father Earl. In fact, few of the prosperous people in Stowe Towne ever went on the southeast side of Stowe Towne, which was thought to be where farmers and poorer people lived. So, Delia Long wasn't a player in the controversy over the condo conversion of The Candlesticks, except....

Delia Long was President of the Central Ohio Chapter of the National Golf Club Owners Association.

⌒

The next week was surprisingly uneventful. When Sammi confronted Bruce, he put her off, saying that Morgan had been in town to talk about a number of things and they had just been free-associating when the kids had walked in. Randy and Julie had jumped to some conclusion no doubt assisted by Morgan's flamboyance. Howie, meanwhile, was away on a "business" trip, although no one ever quite knew Howie's business. The other members of The Candlesticks' board demurred over the issue. Yes, there had been some talk of changes, they said, but it was just speculation. Bip slipped into a funk and told Dorene at home that she had better be ready for a change of some sort. No one else seemed to know anything, although both Mr. Miller and May Miller kept the rumor mill hopping. David Canello went into the complete deep freeze and hid away in his Columbus law office.

As the late spring days hurried by, nothing happened except there was one change: Julie Howard was not seen in public with Randy Bergman. Margaret Howard, free of any restraint with Howie's absence, put the clamps on her daughter in no uncertain terms.

Julie had an interesting reaction. While the outrageousness of her parents' action in banning her from seeing Randy overwhelmed everything, she still had been her mother's daughter for 18 years. She shared her mother's view that Howie was a lovable dolt although she was unaware that Margaret had two important additional insights into her husband, Julie's father. First, Howie was much better in bed than one might ever suspect and second, Howie was much smarter than he looked.

Julie also had been her mother's pal. She was an only child, an only daughter. She had adopted her mother's ways, her mother's demeanor. They would smoke together in secret out on the deck. They shared intimacies (but not that intimacy) and gossiped about school and the townspeople. They went shopping together and ate chicken salad in the Galleria in Columbus. Occasionally, on a Sunday afternoon, they took grandfather to the foreign films he so much favored that were showing on the Ohio State University campus. They were coconspirators in life. Until now.

Of course, Julie had seen Randy. She had left school at noon on Tuesday; senior monitoring at the overcrowded high school this late in the spring was lax. She and Randy had spent the afternoon in Heather's deserted house (her parents were at some auto race in Florida).

Lying naked in Heather's parents' bed, Julie railed against her parents while Randy, lying on his stomach, eyed her wrath and bouncing breasts out of one eye. Finally, he lifted his head slightly to speak: "My parents, uh, suggested that I don't see you any more either. Think there's a connection?"

Julie was incredulous. "What? They said what?"

"They said we weren't the same kind of people," he said slyly just to get a rise out of his girlfriend.

"What the hell is that supposed to mean?"

"Exactly my response. But it didn't seem to make much of an impression on them."

"Assholes."

Randy let his head flop back on the soft bed. Quite frankly, Julie had tired him out. Not that it wasn't enjoyable. Anger seemed to be...he searched for the right word...an aphrodisiac. He had never really thought about aphrodisiacs before. He contemplated their potency.

He brought himself back to the conversation. "I guess being an asshole is catching," he muttered into the sheets.

"What?" Julie demanded shrilly.

He sighed and turned on his side. "Julie, calm down. It's just us here."

She hunkered down in the bed and pulled the pale blue sheet up to her neck. She stared straight up at the ceiling. "What are we going to do?" she asked. Her voice was still tense.

"Well, what can we do for the time being? You're graduating from high school and I'm working in a lumberyard. Where I'm supposed to be right now, incidentally."

"Rather be there than with me. Is that what you're saying?"

"No, that's not what I'm saying, Julie. But we have limited alternatives at the moment."

Julie snorted. A very annoying snort, Randy thought.

"Look, these things tend to blow over," he continued. "Remember when you ran into old man Blake's car when you first got your driver's license. Your father knew you were drinking, too. He grounded you for eternity. A month later he completely forgot about it."

Julie continued to stare at the faint circles swirled into the beige ceiling paint. Randy was right. The car incident had blown away faster than even she could have hoped for. However, this situation somehow seemed different. Maybe because her mother—and not her father—was the enforcer. But there was something else as well and she couldn't put her finger on it. She knew it was somehow connected with golf and the golf course. There was the continuing ever-present pressure from her father about her playing golf in college. But he had to get real about that. Not that she had totally dismissed it, but there were plenty of other things to think about right now.

Randy had now reached over and was caressing her flat stomach. Maybe she should forget the condom, she thought. But that was so juvenile. Besides, Randy was Mr. Straight. He wouldn't go for it. No, she had to think of something else. There *had* to be something else, she thought, as she turned and gave "that Bergman boy" a really big kiss and grabbed his balls in the process.

⌇

The NGCOA, the National Golf Club Owners Association, Central Ohio Chapter, held its spring meeting on Monday afternoon in a downtown Columbus hotel. The members would have dinner in the hotel and then they were scheduled to go to a road company performance of *Phantom of the Opera*. In the spring, they always met away from any golf course; at their fall meeting, they always met at a course and had their annual tournament. But the spring meeting included spouses and a lot of socializing. Delia Long, without a spouse, just did a lot of socializing. She amused the other owners who called her "their own Marge Schott."

But not to her face. Still, typical of such an organization, she was willing to do the work and so she got the glory—whatever that might be.

The general meeting in the afternoon had taken care of what little business the association had as well as featuring a talk on "Golf Course Fungi Diseases" by an Ohio State botanist. Then there were a half-dozen 90-minute seminars on such topics as "Food Management: Untapped Profits in Ethnic Dishes," "Mowers for the Twenty-First Century," and "New Horizons in Public Course Golf: Soft Spikes and Required Carts." Most of the spouses went across the street and shopped at Lazarus.

For the fifteenth time, Delia checked with the banquet manager who would have killed her on the spot if he had been holding a knife or gun or any blunt object. Finally satisfied, she headed for the hotel bar. She had about an hour before the official golf cocktail hour started in the atrium outside the banquet room. When she entered the bar, she noticed David Canello right away. He was sitting at the mahogany bar staring at an overhead TV tuned to the Golf Channel. Delia sat down beside the lawyer for The Candlesticks; she had known him for a long time.

"Didn't see you at the business meeting, David," Delia chided in greeting.

"Tell me you weren't elected to a third term unanimously. It was greased."

"I earn my keep. I got a 15% discount off the *Phantom* tickets and 10% off the banquet."

"It's Monday, they were giving those tickets away."

"Now that's just not true. Give me a double Cutty on the rocks, honey," Delia instructed the bartender.

"See that?" Canello held his drink up toward the TV. "Those are highlights from yesterday. Hale Irwin won on that putt. Goddamn."

"You thinking of having a Seniors' event at The Candlesticks?" Delia waved her hand at the bartender. "Not too much ice there, honey."

"Now that's an idea, Delia."

"All of you at The Candlesticks are so progressive. What are your plans? Maybe one of those private walled communities I read about in the papers. Million-dollar homes. Resort in the park. Senior tournament, at least." Delia paused as her drink was served. "Thank you, honey, and you come back in a minute."

"Well, the rumors are flying in Stowe Towne no doubt."

Delia held up her glass of Scotch. "Cheers, David."

"Cheers, Delia." They clinked glasses. After a sip, he continued: "So, what do you care, anyway? Hell, it'll just mean more people golfing at your course if they can't get on The Candlesticks. You should take this opportunity and expand to 18. How many times have we talked about that?"

"I don't need nine more fairways to mow."

"Delia, you don't have nine fairways to mow now. The distinction between fairway and rough on your course is marginal at best."

"You guys always lorded it over us."

"Not me guys. I've been your pal."

"I know, David. I could be in the roofing business for all it matters to Howie Howard. So, is that really what's up with The Candlesticks?"

Canello turned halfway around to look at the older woman. "Howie doesn't want me involved. Says I'll be involved when *all* the lawyers are involved."

Delia laughed. "The Families strike again. The little Kingdom of Stowe Towne. Us peasants will be informed at a later date."

Canello nodded and muttered, "On a need to know basis."

"Exactly. What about Bip?" Delia asked. She had been friends with Bip and Dorene Jordan for years.

"Bip knows nothing. You know, he's going to retire."

"Sure, and I'm going to offer him a job and I bet he takes it." She finished off her drink and waved the glass at the bartender down the bar. "Honey, one more please before I turn ugly."

Canello laughed and stared up at yet another replay of Hale Irwin making that same damn putt again.

⌒

At that moment, along the South Carolina coast, Howie watched Sean Donaldson tee off on the 18th hole of the Sand Cliff Golf Course. Sand Cliff was a semiprivate club that was closed to public play on Mondays. Donaldson was a minority owner of Sand Cliff and also used it as his home course for his golf course design business. Ironically, Donaldson did not seem to be much of a player. Howie was up by five strokes. But even Howie could tell that Donaldson could care less about his round. Donaldson, a transplanted Scot, had designed Sand Cliff and throughout the round had been more concerned with erosion, seagull droppings, and the height of mower cuts than he had been with any of his shots. He was a feisty little 40-year-old man and Howie didn't like him much. But, as daughter Julie (a pang of guilt raced through Howie) would say, the man was Hot! Hot! Hot! At least he was hot in the trendy and mercurial world of golf course design.

Normally, Donaldson would not have even talked to Howie. He employed a young associate who was an expert at giving the brush-off. However, Howie had offered ample money for an easy project (a simple redesign) in a market area (Great Lakes Region/Upper Midwest) that Donaldson had not yet penetrated. He had not designed a course in Ohio, Michigan, or Indiana. Plus, at The Candlesticks he would have the opportunity to redesign a George August course. Always good to develop one's own reputation by doing the greats one better. So, he had been as cordial as he could manage—which wasn't very cordial—to this dope from Ohio.

Howie was perfectly happy to act the country half-wit and get to play for free at one great golf course. Plus, he was so conveniently out of town. Away from Margaret and Julie. Bruce and Morgan. Sticks and Sammi. Bip and Mr. Miller. And every other person in Stowe Towne.

"This is a tight finishing hole, Mr. Howard," Donaldson said as they strolled down the 18th fairway. The offhanded remark surprised Howie. The tee shot had been open to a wide fairway. The hole had appeared to Howie to be a typical long par-5 finishing hole trek to the clubhouse. Not unlike The Candlesticks' last hole.

"Well, we both look to be in good shape down the middle, Sean," Howie responded in up-tempo.

A late afternoon sea breeze had been blowing up and swirling the air.

"Perhaps, Mr. Howard. Unfortunately, your shot is a little left and a little farther than mine. That means you're in trouble, I'm afraid. You'll see when we get there."

Howie began to grasp what Donaldson meant. The fairway narrowed dramatically and an out-of-bounds suddenly loomed along a line of sand dunes that hid an access road on the left side. Donaldson from the right side still saw a lot of fairway and he hit an easy long-iron shot along the right edge of the fairway. Howie's lie, however, had a dramatically different perspective. From his angle on the left side, Howie's only option seemed to be to hit his ball out-of-bounds left. If he tried to aim right toward Donaldson's shot, it appeared that he was hitting directly into a row of two-story, sea-grey condos that edged the right-hand side of the fairway. After a long minute, he asked for a four-iron from the silent, sullen teenager who was caddying for them both. He knew he could generally control his four-iron. He realized that he was looking into an optical illusion of sorts. He knew the fairway was right out in front of him. But there seemed to be no room. He kept adjusting his feet and when he finally swung, he pulled up from his swing anxious to see where the ball was going. Consequently, he hit a vicious line drive slice that skidded into some poor sucker's patio. There was a loud bang as the ball hit a trash can or grill or something.

Howie sighed and dropped another ball, switched clubs, and hit a soft, safe six-iron 140 yards. He finished with an eight (his first eight of the spring) to Donaldson's birdie four. Donaldson had made up four of five strokes on one hole. Howie realized as they walked to the clubhouse that Donaldson probably could have made up four strokes on any given hole if he had cared. Howie was glad the Scot had refused to bet "on a business deal." He would have nailed Howie.

In the small, but sporty clubhouse, Howie came straight to the point. "Sean, I've visited and talked to three architects this past week." That was more or less true. The other two architects had simply turned down Howie and the project. "I like you, and Sand Cliff is a magnificent course. Just like *Golf Magazine* said. I'd like to have you come up and see The Candlesticks. I think you'll be impressed. It's a great old course."

Donaldson nodded. The man seldom smiled. "Thank you, Mr. Howard. I think I'll take you up on your offer. Let's look at our calendars."

chapter seven

EYE TO EYE, TOE TO TOE

The morning of the third Thursday in May was beautiful, the fairest May morning that anyone had ever experienced. The trees were filled with new leaves. The grass was an emerald green. May flowers were bursting with new colors—yellow and pinks, violets and reds. There was the faintest of breezes that just managed to stir the scent of the flowers so that the very air turned soft and gentle. And, to complete the picture, no one showed up to play golf.

Practically no one.

Sticks dragged his King Cobras out of Bip's office. Bip wasn't around. Some Thursday mornings he gave lessons to ladies at a driving range midway between Stowe Towne and Columbus. He gave lessons at The Candlesticks too, of course, but since the club did not have a driving range, he was somewhat limited—especially with beginners who weren't ready to go out on the course. In any case, Bip wasn't around to partner with Sticks.

Chet, behind the check-in counter, just waved Sticks out to the first tee without a thought. Sticks didn't have to bother to check-in on a day like this, but he usually did so as a courtesy. He was one of a dozen people left who still held what was called a "Master Pass." About 20 years earlier, in one of its first reorganizational moves, the club had restructured its "membership" system. Membership for the course had meant that open play was available for people who wanted to pay a flat fee for the season. Members could play all the time, any time.

However, public play had increased so dramatically and become so profitable, that members were in the way and reserving too many prime weekend tee times. The club instituted a tiered membership scheme that severely restricted weekend play and created such categories as junior and senior memberships. Many of the members, led by Sticks who was the youngest of the group, were furious. They organized and mounted a passionate and aggressive response. The Board quickly caved in and grandfathered in all members of record as long as they continued their membership. The Board took some measure of revenge by upping the membership fee by 25%. Still, for someone like Sticks who played all the time, it was a deal. Gradually, holders of the new "Master Pass" had died off, dropped out, or moved away and only a handful of players now had free run of the course.

Normally, Sticks didn't play on Thursday mornings. But he was committed to spend the afternoon and evening at the lumberyard overseeing the business. Brother Hal was taking the afternoon off for a road trip to Logan with his daughter who was the starting catcher for the high school softball team. His other brother, Paul, and his wife were flying out of Columbus on one of those weekend gambling junkets to Las Vegas. Neither Sticks nor Sammi enjoyed casino gambling and did not like Vegas much. But Paul and Cathy were crazy about the place.

The tee for the 490-yard, par-5 first hole was long and narrow and edged on both sides with a row of severely cut, two-foot high shrubs. Sticks stood his dark blue Titleist bag upright with his left hand and stooped down to rummage through the pockets with his right hand to find his golf glove and a couple of Titleist balls. He pulled out a handful of natural wood tees. As he straightened up, he yanked out his Cobra driver and lowered his bag by the strap to the ground. He loved this ritual. The preparation for battle. Being armed and dangerous.

He took some practice swings. He never warmed up enough. He knew that was a fault. He rarely sought out any driving range to hit a bucket of balls. He didn't spend enough time on the putting green and seldom used the practice bunker beside the green. That was a serious flaw. Sand had always been a real problem for Sticks. He did well at The Candlesticks because the course did not have a lot of sand in the first place and Sticks had learned to deftly avoid what sand there was. But sand often cost him strokes when he played other courses.

He stepped up to the gold "Championship" tees. This was the first year the club had put in gold tees. Now there were red (traditionally ladies'), white, blue, and gold tees. The gold tees, though, were where the blue ones used to be for the most part and the blues were now just plopped between the gold and white. Sticks had razzed Bip about the new gold tees, but Bip had just shrugged, saying that it was the decision of the "Course Play Committee" of the Board.

"Sticks," a voice spoke behind him.

Sticks continued to stare down the fairway and did not at once respond to the voice. He took a breath to compose himself and then turned around and said, "How you doing, Howie?"

Howie Howard stood a couple of yards in back of the tee. He was holding his soft-side red golf bag, the one he used just for hacking around. But he was still carrying his good Taylor Burners. He had just transferred them from his travel bag to his practice bag after he returned from South Carolina.

"Mind if I join you, Sticks? Looks like we're the only ones here."

"Sure, why not? You and I haven't played together for a while."

Out of courtesy, Sticks took a step away from the tee. But Howie waved him back. "You're all set. Go ahead and hit."

Sticks went back to his setup. He focused on the ball and hit a good drive down the left side of the fairway, far enough to get around the dog-leg. Howie stepped up and hit the same shot. They ended up within five yards of each other. They both parred the first hole and the next, play-ing almost in silence through the clear, quiet morning air. They acknowledged good shots. They showed each other courtesy on the green. They remarked on the beauty of the day. And, they said nothing else.

On the par-3, 185-yard third hole, the pin was in the back corner and Sticks chose to hit his three-iron instead of four-iron. Playing into a slight breeze. He blasted the ball and it bounced over and off to the left of the green. Howie, undecided about what club to hit, ended up mishitting his four-iron and coming up 20 yards short of the green. Both men's chips weren't near the hole and they two-putted for bogeys. The hole unnerved them and they both missed the green again on the par-4 fourth hole scoring bogeys. But they regrouped and scored pars on five and six.

On the seventh tee, playing Barnes's Knob, with adrenaline pump-ing, Sticks airmailed his drive left into the woods running along the side of the uphill fairway. The woods at this point was a stand of trees which separated the seventh fairway from the Pottawa River. Sticks couldn't believe his shot. He literally could not remember the last time he had hit a ball into those trees. Howie, meanwhile, hit safely down the mid-dle of the fairway. Sticks cursed his shot as they walked together.

"Goddamn ball took off like a shot straight to the woods. I never hit a ball like that. Maybe I was standing too close."

Howie laughed. "Christ, Sticks, sometimes even *you* hit a bad drive. Chalk it up to the curse of Billy Barnes, if you want. Anyway, you might be all right. The ball landed before it got to the trees. Those trees are pretty sparse for a few yards in."

Sticks grunted and was silent for a minute. Then he glanced over at his playing partner. Howie was wearing a yellow golf shirt with the Sand Cliff, South Carolina logo. Sticks couldn't help but resent the fact that Howie had played so many more exotic courses than he had.

As they reached the trees, Sticks could not contain himself any longer: "Well, I suppose if there were condos here I'd just be on somebody's patio. Are there going to be condos here, Howie?"

Howie didn't miss a beat: "I don't know yet. I think you're up a few yards. There." Howie bent over and looked at a ball and then reached down and picked it up. "I assume you're not playing Pro Staff. I'll keep this for Julie's shag bag."

"How is Julie these days?" Sticks asked as he peered into the shadowy trees. He knew Howie wouldn't respond to him honestly about the condos. "Randy says she's not supposed to see him."

Howie was prepared for this question as well. He knew the odds were that he would run into Sticks or Sammi at some point. And he knew that after Sticks asked him about the condos he would immediately ask him about Julie. He was "right on" as they used to say back in the '70s.

"Well, Sticks, I must confess something. That was pretty much Margaret's idea. I agreed with it, but you have to understand that it doesn't have anything to do with Randy really."

"What do you mean? Damn, where the hell is my ball?"

"You've gone through this with kids," Howie said giving up the ball hunt for a second and concentrating on his remarks to Sticks. "You have two kids who graduated from high school here. Hell, you and I graduated from high school here for that matter. It's still called senioritis. Julie is, well, nuts. For example, I can't pin her down on a college. Nothing. It's getting to be a desperate situation, if you know what I mean."

"I thought she was going to Ohio State."

"We're waiting for the scholarship to come through."

Sticks paused in his search to look at Howie. "You surely can afford to send her to Ohio State without a scholarship."

"Of course. It's not the money, obviously. It's the golf scholarship. I want her guaranteed a place on the team."

"Can they guarantee that? *Do* they guarantee that?"

"That's what we're waiting to find out."

Sticks suddenly spotted his ball. "Oh, shit, look at that."

Howie came up behind him. A Titleist was nestled against a tree trunk away from the hole. "You sure that's your ball, Sticks?" he asked

"Sure I'm sure. That's my red dot below the name." Sticks surveyed the situation. The ball was almost underneath a root of the tree. An angle of trees and brush cut him off entirely from seeing the green. "I'll have to take a drop and punch out." He looked out at a right angle at the fairway and could see Howie's ball. "I'll be about where you are in three. If I'm lucky. Damn!"

Sticks got out of the woods, but ended up with a double-bogey while Howie scored a routine par. On the eighth hole, the long and wide-open par 5, they both had to sink longish, 15-foot putts to salvage par. Howie remained two up going to the ninth, a straight par 4 that was rated as the fourth easiest hole on the course.

Looking down the fairway toward the clubhouse, Sticks shook his head. "What are you going to do with the clubhouse? Tear it down? Why do you want to screw this up?"

Howie stuck his white tee in the ground and carefully placed his Wilson ball on the tee. Howie was the only person Sticks had ever played with who almost always stuck his tee in the ground separately from the ball and then placed the ball on the tee. Most people teed up the ball and tee together as a unit. Sticks always wondered where Howie picked up the habit. But he had done it ever since they had first played together as kids.

Howie straightened up and turned to look at Sticks. "You know, Sticks, this isn't *your* private course. Never was and never will be."

Sticks was surprised by the anger in Howie's voice. Sticks paused a second, considering, and then said: "Well then, with ownership comes responsibility. Don't you have a responsibility to the playing public? The people who have played this course for decades? And have paid for the privilege?"

"Oh, please, spare me the civic pride lesson. And the economics lesson for that matter as well. Besides, turning the course into an exclusive club and housing development will do a lot more for Stowe Towne than keeping it as a second-rate out-of-date course."

"Out-of-date?"

"Pros won't play this course. It's out of fashion." Howie turned back to address his ball.

"Who wants pros to play here?" Sticks crinkled up his face with the question as Howie swung. For the first time in the round, Howie missed his drive. And he missed it badly. The shot sliced far to the right almost to the fifth tee. He would have to hit his second shot over the edge of the putting green and over a line of evergreens that separated the putting green from the ninth green. It was a blind shot to the green.

Sticks stepped up to the tee, took a deep breath, and blistered a drive nearly 275 yards down the middle of the fairway. Somehow, it seemed a fair measure of revenge.

Howie, for his second shot, hit a seven-iron and got his ball up over the trees with no difficulty. But he pulled the shot and it buried itself in the hole's only bunker on the left front of the green. Sticks hit a short wedge to within five feet of the hole. He made the putt for a birdie three. Howie struggled out of the sand and two-putted for a bogey five. It could have been worse, but he still lost two strokes to Sticks.

At the end of nine holes, the men were even—both at three over par.

As they walked toward the clubhouse, Howie said: "Sorry, Sticks, but I have to go. You know, stuff to do."

"That's okay, me too," Sticks answered.

Howie stopped suddenly. "We had a good match going. Not our best golf necessarily, but a good match."

Sticks also stopped and slung his bag off his shoulder and looked Howie in the eye. "You're right, a good match, even up. Would've been an interesting back nine. Especially if we had bet something."

"That's what I was thinking."

"Like you dropping your plans for the development."

"You mean, at least on the golf course?" Howie paused and then added, "Against your full and unconditional support?"

Sticks shrugged. "Maybe, like you said."

Howie smiled. "It would be ironic, you know. I mean if you lost the bet and I won the match, your property would end up being worth 10 times more than it's worth now. Maybe more. You'd tie right into the development. All that land you got out there."

Sticks bit his lip. "I'll tell you, Howie. I like my land. Just the way it is. And I like this golf course, too. Just the way it is."

Howie took a step away. "It's going to happen someday, Sticks. You might as well be in on it. You know what I mean? Well, I really got to get going. At least you could think about it. Think about it rationally."

Sticks didn't reply and stood holding his bag, staring not at his retreating rival but back at the number nine green and on down the lush green fairway.

⌐

Kenny Barnes sat at his State Senate office desk in the capitol and looked at the draft of the supplemental bill for "improvements at the south end of Pottawa State Forest." Nearly a page was devoted to surveyor language exactly pinpointing the acreage that would be "improved." Not very much land at all. Scrub brush and a portion of a meandering creek. That terminology wasn't in the bill, of course. His legislative aide, Terry Bourne, who had had the bill drafted, had suggested the language in case the Press called. "It's just scrub brush and a creek if anyone asks, Senator."

Bourne had an annoying habit of sneering when he called Barnes "Senator." But Barnes had learned to put up with it. He had inherited Bourne from his predecessor and had had no choice but to keep him. But the man was a young, snot-nosed, 30-something who had a talent for paperwork and didn't mind making squat for a salary. He performed his work thoroughly and efficiently despite his sarcastic attitude. He even did a good job when he thought it boring and unnecessary, such as this little project. Barnes could recall his exact words: *Why are you running this risk, Kenny? Screwing around with public property—and a park at that. You're giving the loonies in your district a cause.*

Barnes had thanked his aide for the advice, but still requested that he get the language written as soon as possible.

Bourne didn't know everything, of course. That's what always finally got to legislative aides. No matter how many years they worked in state government and no matter how well connected they might be, the rawest rookie representative or senator or even governor always knew something more. Something on the inside that the aides just couldn't find out. It frustrated them to no end. Some it drove mad. Some it drove into lobbying. And some even ended up running for office themselves.

Meanwhile, Senator Barnes let thoughts of politics and his irritating assistant seep away and he slipped into his lawyer mode. After all, he did have a law degree from one of the most prestigious law schools in the country. He read slowly. Thinking. He made some notes in the margin. This would do, he thought. However, it needed just a few changes.

⤳

Peter Onear and his current temporary girlfriend Polly stopped at the Gettysburg Café for lunch. What a glorious day to take off. Two days off, actually, and then the weekend. They were going to stay tonight and tomorrow night at the Pottawa State Park Lodge. Onear had reservations.

He was having reservations about Polly, too. They'd been together about three months, a longish time in terms of any Peter Onear relationship. She was a secretary at ODOT, the Ohio Department of Transportation. He had started dating her *after* she had helped him get information for a story he was doing at the time about highway signage contracts. He had achieved getting a couple of administrators fired—an indication in Peter's mind that the story was a great success. Somehow, Polly's involvement had fortunately slipped through unnoticed even though the documents she had provided had been crucial. She had her own ax to grind as it turned out.

Peter started dating Polly not because he felt any guilt about putting her in jeopardy, but because she looked vaguely French. Or, at least he thought that she looked like what French girls should look like. In truth, she wasn't French at all. Her last name was Harris and if anyone would have bothered to trace her history back, they would have found ordinary Pennsylvania and New York farmers. Still, she was curiously attractive with straight black hair and a smallish oval face. Very white skin. Few other people would have thought of her as French, however.

Getting out of the car, Peter stared around at the town square of Stowe Towne. He really couldn't remember ever being here, although it looked like many other small Ohio town squares. Old buildings. A couple of them were vacant although the place was fairly bustling for a Thursday noon. A couple of antique stores. A "Basket Boutique" on one corner with dozens of wicker baskets sitting around outside. Must be a real Chinese fire drill if a thunderstorm ever blew through. In the center of the square was a three-story red brick courthouse. From this angle, it looked like a modern annex had been slapped on the back. Not too large. Probably didn't have a jail inside like some of the county courthouses. To the right of the building's front steps was the usual mounted cannon with a pyramid stack of cannonballs cemented together.

The statue then caught Peter's attention. Odd hunk of metal. Collection of soldiers huddled together with arms and rifles jutting out. Maybe stroll over and take a look at it after lunch.

"Come on, Pete, let's eat," Polly called from the other side of the car. Polly was the only person who called him Pete.

"All right, all right." He locked the car and they walked into the Gettysburg. Normally, he would have stopped at a McDonald's or Taco Bell, but he hadn't felt like eating fast food. That's okay, he thought. Got to get a little feel for the town anyway. Nothing better for local color than the local café.

Inside, the restaurant was bright and cheery. No Civil War motif. Wooden tables with blue paper place mats. The only problem—the place was packed. Dishes rattled and waitresses rushed around. One older waitress with red hair stopped in front of them. "A couple places at the counter," she advised. "Busy time, sorry."

"No problem," Peter said as the waitress whisked herself away. "We'll take the counter."

He and Polly wended their way through the tables and sat down at the counter on dark blue swivel seats with backs. They picked up menus as a young woman with very large breasts beneath her white uniform appeared in front of them with a coffee pot and two mugs. "Coffee?"

"Ah, sure," Peter said. Polly ordered an iced tea. They looked at the menus.

A voice on Peter's left: "Try the hot roast beef sandwich. It's today's special. Not on the menu."

Peter looked at the voice. It had come from an older man who was finishing up a piece of cherry pie.

"That sounds pretty good." he responded. "I might take your advice. Must be a good place to eat. Filled up."

"Good place for lunch. Place across the square, Maple Lodge, is where everybody has supper. That's pretty good, too."

"Well, maybe we'll try that sometime."

"Name's Mr. Miller." The old man put down his fork and turned partway to hold out his hand to Peter.

Peter awkwardly shook it. "Hello, ah, Mr. Miller. I'm Peter Onear. And this is my friend, Polly Harris." Peter had the distinct feeling he should have introduced himself and Polly as *Mr. Onear* and *Miss Harris*. That felt odd.

When Mr. Miller had turned to shake hands, Peter noticed that his green v-neck sweater carried a breast logo of two candles circled by the words, *The Candlesticks Golf Club*, in white stitching.

"The Candlesticks, that's near here? Up by the state park?" Peter asked.

Mr. Miller frowned for a second. "The park? Well, it's not a park down here, it's a state forest, I think. No one calls it a park. But The Candlesticks is about four miles north of town."

"I guess I was thinking of Pottawa State Park, Mr. Miller. There's a lodge there. We're going to stay there tonight."

"Oh, sure, the park. But that's up there a ways. Off 37. Not by the golf course."

Peter nodded. "I see. Well, that's where we're headed. Up to the lodge, I mean. But I hear that's a good golf course. The Candlesticks? I'd like to see it."

"You a golfer?" Mr. Miller asked pointedly. "A real golfer would say he'd like to play it, not just look at it."

"You got me there. That's very astute. You're right, I'm not a real golfer. Not a golfer at all."

"I'm a lawyer, son. Retired. I made my living knowing people's motives." Mr. Miller took a big bite of cherry pie.

The voluptuous waitress returned and Peter and Polly ordered. Polly only ordered a small salad. Peter could tell from the tone of Polly's voice that she wasn't a happy camper in the Gettysburg Café. Well, screw her; he was on a story. Besides, he could fall in love with their waitress and dump Polly in a second.

"Anything going on at the golf course?" Peter asked turning back to Mr. Miller.

"What do you mean?" the old man asked suspiciously.

"I don't know. Changes?"

"There's talk of it being developed. The course, that is. Houses and so on. Like one of those goddamn Florida courses. You ever golf in Florida? No, you said you're not a golfer."

"Sorry, never golfed in Florida," Peter confirmed. Then he asked: "Is it serious? Those plans, I mean."

"Over my dead body. And lots of others of us, too." Mr. Miller looked at his wristwatch. "Well, I have a tee time. Nice talking to you. You too, miss."

Peter shook hands with the old man again. "Nice talking to you, too. You have a nice town here." Then he baited Mr. Miller. "It would be a shame to lose it to outsiders, if you know what I mean."

But Peter saw that the old fellow didn't take the bait. Instead, his eyes narrowed and face hardened. Peter realized that he would not have wanted to be a hostile witness under Mr. Miller's cross-examination. "There's no outsiders," Mr. Miller said. "We take care of our own business here in Stowe Towne."

" Ah, good luck," Peter managed to stutter in response. He watched as the old fellow left the restaurant.

Peter turned back to the counter and contemplatively sipped his coffee while Polly groused about the service and remarked on the hair-styles of the waitresses. He shook off the chilling effect of saying good-bye to Mr. Miller and formed the news feature in his head that *he* wanted to write. Always from the same angle: Somebody always out to screw the public for personal gain. He worked it in his mind. Old golf course on public property. Sell or maybe just take for private development and profit. The citizenry loses a public playground so a few rich SOBs can play golf without co-mingling with the riffraff. Sounds like a hell of a front page Sunday feature. *Liberty, Equality, Fraternity*.

Peter Onear took his notepad and Bic pen out of the breast pocket of his short-sleeved plaid shirt. He always carried his notepad and a Bic pen. And, as his ample plate of white bread, sliced roast beef, real mashed potatoes, and gravy was served, he took notes.

∽

State Senator Barnes met Howie Howard, Bruce Dean, and County Commissioner Chuck January for dinner at the Kahiki, an ostentatious Polynesian restaurant on the east side of Columbus. The restaurant, shaped like a huge Polynesian native longboat, was a favorite of high-school students out for their proms and married couples out for their twentieth wedding anniversaries. Local legend had it that in the days of Woody Hayes at Ohio State, the football team always ate at the Kahiki the night before a big game. But for this meeting, it was useful. Politicians and reporters seldom, if ever, stopped at the restaurant. And, it was divided up into little alcoves with very dim lighting so that it was hard to identify your fellow diners.

The four men ordered drinks straight up, eschewing the exotic fruit juice, umbrella drinks that were carried past their table by sarong-clad waitresses who were often OSU coeds from Chillicothe and Zanesville. Barnes passed out copies of the draft of the "Improvements" bill to

Howie, Bruce, and Chuck. Everyone sipped their drinks in silence as they reviewed the language. It was difficult to see the print in the dim light so they tilted the pages this way and that. Plus, they were sitting on the aviary side instead of the aquarium side of the restaurant. The aviary stretched along the full east wall and every few minutes a mock thunderstorm coursed through the aviary complete with lightning, loud thunder, and a dousing of rain. The birds scrambled for cover.

How would you like to live in that environment? Barnes thought. *Not that it's so much different than the Ohio Senate.*

"I can't make out half of what's here and I don't understand a god-damn word of it anyway," January grumbled as he tossed the bill down on the table. January was short, stocky and 46 years old. He was a two-term Commissioner and most of the people in the know around Stowe Towne considered him an ass. But he was very compliant. He agreed to everything. He was uncorrupted because he never had an ulterior motive. Until now. He was a contract electrician and worked mostly in Columbus. In his mind, at least, it was implicitly understood that he would do all the electrical work for Candlesticks Acres or whatever the hell the development was going to be named. He didn't give a rat's ass as long as he got his fair share.

"Well, let me summarize the important points then," Howie began. "Let's make sure we all have the same understanding. There are really two provisions in the bill. One modifies the original agreement that allowed the golf course to be built on state property. It now allows for improvements to be made to the course including, specifically, housing. The second appropriates new land from Pottawa State Forest for the same improvements."

"That's right, Howie, although understand that it's actually a lease," Barnes explained. "The state is leasing the land to your Pottawa Enterprises, Inc. for a dollar a year for 40 years with a succeeding 40-year option."

Bruce leaned forward. "It's guaranteed that anyone who buys a house will own it for 80 years before the state can even think about reclaiming the land."

Barnes nodded. "Absolutely."

"Is that legal?" Bruce asked.

"Legal? It's state law." Barnes enjoyed, for a change, not being intimidated by these guys.

"Done before?" Bruce persisted.

"Bruce," Barnes explained patiently, "the State of Ohio owns a lot of land. Not just parks and forests. Universities, mental hospitals, prisons. Lots of just plain land. It buys and sells and leases land all the time. There's no problem, I assure you."

Bruce sat back and smiled. "I know that, Senator, I'm in real estate. I was just testing you."

Have you always been an asshole? Barnes wondered to himself. He took a sip of his drink and ignored the real estate agent.

Howie put his copy of the bill aside. "It looks great to me, Kenny. It doesn't seem to raise any more red flags than necessary. Looks pretty innocuous. Good job."

Barnes reached over and gathered up the bills from the men. He added his own and put all the copies in his briefcase underneath the table. "My new idea is to change the format slightly into an amendment and attach it to a coal reclamation bill. That bill's coming up in the Senate in a week or so. It has a lot of state property language in it already because of some strip mine leases. Building houses on a corner of state land instead of ripping it up to jerk out coal will make us look like saints in comparison."

"That's a great idea," Howie said.

"But what if that bill doesn't pass?" January asked. He at least knew something about passing legislation, for Christ's sake!

"Oh, it'll pass because the environmentalists have signed off on it.

Remember, I said reclamation. It allows strip-mining, but with more reclamation of the land afterward."

There was a pause as the men all finished their drinks. January caught the sarong of a passing waitress and told her to bring another round.

"So, gentlemen, what's the strategy?" Howie asked. "We know that people in Stowe Towne know that we're thinking about a development. But, of course, there hasn't been any announcement. Just lots of rumors. Do we hold a press conference? Or, do we wait until the legislation passes? Seems to me to be a no-brainer."

January looked puzzled. "Meaning?"

"We wait," Barnes said. "If the legislation passes, we're home free because we have the law on our side. In effect, it's a done deal. However," he paused for dramatic effect, "what if the media discovers the amendment and breaks the story before the vote? Then we'll have to scurry around and make it public. Or, you three will. I'm staying out of it."

"Except your name will be on the amendment," Bruce said.

"Don't worry, I'll handle that," Barnes responded curtly.

Their drinks arrived and all four men relaxed and tried to look down the front of the waitress's sarong. It was a little too tightly wound. But then, all of them were a little too tightly wound as well.

Thunder rattled in the aviary and the birds headed for cover.

chapter eight

THE PEOPLE'S RIGHT TO KNOW

The article appeared in the *Columbus Dispatch*'s Real Estate Section the Thursday before the Memorial Day holiday weekend. Peter Onear had gotten into a hassle with his editors about the article and, on this occasion, had been overruled. The loss was a rare occurrence in Peter's recent professional life. The problem was that Peter had stumbled across a story that in and of itself was news independent of any corruption, political dealing, or other catch phrases used by so-called investigative reporters. The basic information itself was important: the possibility of a substantial new upscale housing development in a potentially fashionable, soon-to-be-overrun by Yuppies and DINKS, near suburb of Columbus was news. No doubt about it. It was news to home buyers, builders, persons who supplied builders, landscapers, interior decorators...in other words, most of the people who carefully read the weekly Real Estate Section featured in every Thursday edition of the *Dispatch*.

Corruption be damned! Houses are being built! Communities are growing!

Peter stewed and stormed and screamed that the story could rot in hell for all he cared. The editors finally assigned a young woman named Mara Fish, a recent graduate of the journalism program at Ohio University, to finish the goddamn story. They also sent a photographer out and ended up printing a picturesque photo of The Candlesticks' 18th green taken from the clubhouse deck. The photo appeared with the article that was now *co-reported* by Peter Onear and Mara Fish, although Peter never saw the final copy until it was in print.

Housing Development Proposed
for Historic Area Golf Course

A new upscale housing development has been proposed near Stowe Towne, 30 miles northeast of Columbus.

The planned development, called Candlestick Acres, will incorporate The Candlesticks Golf Course. The course, designed by legendary golf course architect George August and first opened in 1924, is four miles north of Stowe Towne. It was listed as one of the 50 classic golf courses in America in 1989 by *Golf Magazine*. The course frequently makes lists of the best public golf courses in Ohio and the country.

Speculation is that between 125 and 150 houses and condominiums will be built around the golf course.

Howard G. Howard, a lifelong resident of Stowe Towne, is a part-owner of the golf course. He declined to go into many details on the project, but said that plans for refurbishing the golf course and adding homes have been under consideration for some time. He stated that members of the golf course's Board of Directors are enthusiastic about the project.

"The course needs an upgrade. We concluded that we need to prepare it for the next century," Howard said in a brief phone interview.

An unusual feature about the course is that a small portion

of it is located on land that is part of Pottawa State Forest. The land was ceded by the State of Ohio long ago, according to Howard, for development. He believes adding houses to the course is within the spirit of development.

Jeremy Trumann, a spokesperson at the Ohio Department of Natural Resources, said he was unaware that the golf course was on state forest property. He did not know if the department had been contacted concerning the proposed development.

Pottawa County Commission President Chuck January said that county officials are aware of the proposal. He stated that sewer, water, and other utilities already existed in the area and no county monies would have to be spent to accommodate the development.

"It will be a wonderful economic boon to Stowe Towne and Pottawa County," January stated.

Both January and Howard said that no commitment to a developer has been made. However, a source indicated that a representative from Cliner Development in Cleveland has visited the site. Cliner is one of the largest residential real estate developers in Ohio. Cliner's Erie Bay development west of Elyria was cited by the source as a project similar to the Candlestick Acres development.

Howard declined to speculate on a time frame for the project.

Residents interviewed around the town square in Stowe Towne were surprised at news of the proposed development. A number of people expressed concern about maintaining the golf course for public play. Don Paulson, a retired physician, said that he plays the course at least twice a week. "I wouldn't want anything to change that." He also stated that he didn't think there was anything wrong with the course and didn't know how it could be upgraded.

The development would be the largest construction project in the Stowe Towne area since Allied Pipes built a plant two miles south of the town in 1990.

The source, of course, was Bruce Dean. After Howie and Chuck got the calls from the woman reporter, Bruce decided he needed to get into the act. It wasn't that he didn't trust Howie and Chuck. They told him what they had said to the reporter. But he wanted some feedback from her as well. So, he called and was perfectly up-front with her. But he insisted that for the time being, he remain anonymous. She reluctantly agreed and was rewarded for her confidentiality with the Cliner information. Bruce wanted to get Cliner's name in print for two reasons. He could tell Cliner that he was promoting their company. However, if some other developer was interested, they would know who they were up against and wouldn't waste anybody's time.

The day the article came out, Bruce ducked around town avoiding any questions. Of course, almost no one knew that he was directly involved. Finally, he settled in his office behind closed doors with specific instructions that he was not to be disturbed. An odd request, he realized, since he usually lived to be disturbed. When he arrived, he had checked to see if Sammi was in her office. He knew he was destined to have a confrontation with her. But she was out showing the Portman farm, one of those white elephant properties that Dean Realty had been trying to unload for nine months. The secretaries didn't know when Sammi would be back.

Bruce sat at his Packard Bell surfing the net, alternately looking at real estate sites and supermodel home pages. It was amazing how many different pictures there were of Kathy Ireland. He idly looked at the Cliner Development Home Page. Cliner was really pushing their Erie Bay development. It looked good. They had all sorts of links to Northeast Ohio. Anyone surfing the web in anticipation of moving to the Cleveland area would be bound to eventually link into Cliner.

Dean Realty had its own home page. But Bruce wasn't very happy with it. He had had a high school kid do it a year ago and it looked pretty cheesy. Plus, the kid usually blew him off when Bruce would try to get the kid to update the thing. He had just heard that the Scotlands, the husband and wife couple that owned the only computer store in Stowe Towne, were getting into web page design. He would have to give them a call one of these days. He would certainly want to promote Candlestick Acres in a big way on the web. People who surfed the web for real estate always had a lot of money, Bruce assumed rightly or wrongly.

Suddenly, his office door banged open and he automatically clicked off from a new page he was hunting down purporting to offer real nude photos of celebrities. Before he could turn away from the screen, he knew that Sammi had arrived. He took a deep breath and looked at her. She was dressed in a dark blue business suit and white blouse. He noticed that her blue pumps were streaked with mud. Probably from the Portman farm barnyard. He hoped against hope that she had made the sale. A sale would blunt her temper.

"You're an asshole, Bruce."

No sale, he guessed, wincing.

"You're a lying SOB," she continued. "How can you talk to me about being your partner with a straight face? You hypocrite."

"Sammi, close the door, would you? Come in and we'll talk about it."

Sammi flicked the door and it slammed shut with a bang. She marched into the spacious office and sat in one of the wingback chairs in front of Bruce's desk. "There's no explanation that can make this right," she said.

"Sure there's an explanation," he countered. "You obviously read the article. You know the people I'm dealing with. Who's mentioned in the article? Howie Howard and Chuck January. If you added a couple more posts to those two, and a little barbed wire, you could make a pretty nice fence. Am I right about that?"

Bruce thought it was a pretty clever line, but Sammi just glowered at him.

Bruce sucked it up and continued: "Look, Sammi, you're the least of my worries. How are you going to help me now? You're not. The initial real estate part of this deal is no big thing. I can handle that. Our work—your work!—comes later. That's when we make money selling lots and houses. Lots of lots and houses. I can't do that alone. We're partners. There's enough to go around."

"Your generosity overwhelms me, Bruce," Sammi said dryly. "But pardon me if I don't understand why you didn't tell me."

"It's very simple, Sammi, it's your husband. We had to keep Sticks in the dark as long as possible." Sammi started to speak, but Bruce held up his hand. "Wait, let me explain. We aren't picking on Sticks. It's other people around town, too. It's the Millers and some of those other old farts. Like Doc Parsons. Old Doc Parsons of all people was quoted in the article. In other words, anyone who might have opposed the development."

"Opposed it?"

"Sure, opposed it." Bruce stood up abruptly. Time to go on the offensive with Sammi. "Opposed it in principle before we had our ducks in order. Fortunately, they're in order. Just barely. The article doesn't hurt us. In fact, it's great. It ended up on the real estate page and not the front page. Front page is later, maybe, when we break ground."

Sammi was fully aware of Bruce's tricks of intimidation. She was a successful real estate agent. She used them herself. Standing up just at the precise moment that a client started wavering was a great trick. Clients got distracted and backtracked, hoping that you'd sit down. It was a useful maneuver. But she didn't give a damn now. Bruce could walk around on the ceiling for all she cared.

"I really hate being lied to, Bruce. I asked you about Cliner at the Spring Fling."

Bruce shrugged. "So, I'm sorry. I apologize about lying to you at the Spring Fling. That aside, are you with me on the Candlestick

Acres development?"

Sammi bit her lip and eyed her colleague. He was wearing blue and gray suspenders and had his hands dug so deep into his pants' pockets that he was stretching the suspenders. He rocked back and forth on his heels.

Finally, she said: "We both know the difficulty here, don't we?"

Bruce nodded. "I think so. You mean the fact that you and Sticks own a large piece of land right beside the golf course. The development will impact on your property. The problem you have is that your property could appreciate in value five, ten, maybe fifteen times its current worth."

Bruce sighed with dramatic exaggeration. "You're in a very tight spot, Sammi. Making thousands and thousands of dollars in new commissions as well as owning what will soon be the absolute prime piece of real estate in Pottawa County. I see what you mean by—what word did you use—*difficulty?*"

"Cut the sarcasm crap, Bruce."

"Am I wrong?" he asked.

Sammi brushed an imaginary piece of lint off her skirt. Of course, Bruce wasn't wrong and, of course, this was what was motivating Howie Howard. The Howard property was on the other side of the golf course. She had seen it happen more than a few times around Columbus. Some guy sitting on some piece of property. Maybe an old family farm. Maybe an inheritance from a favorite uncle. Then boom! It's suddenly the hottest piece of land in the universe. Housing development. Strip mall. Plant expansion. It had even happened right here in Stowe Towne when Allied Pipes came to town. Kay and Vern Smolinski had owned a dairy farm right where the Allied Pipes' people decided they had to build. Kay and Vern live someplace in Florida now. They don't write much.

Sammi hesitated. "We're talking my home here, Bruce," she said. "It's my husband's home, too. And the children."

"Your children are grown, Sammi," Bruce unnecessarily reminded her. "Look, why don't you just think about it? Talk it over tonight with Sticks. Nothing new is going to be decided today or tomorrow."

Sammi stood up slowly and turned and walked back to the door. She opened it and then looked over her shoulder at Bruce. "By the way," she said, "they made an offer on the Portman place. I think the owners will take it. I'm sure they will." With that she left, closing the door behind her.

⌐

The moral, ethical, famial, and financial dilemmas confronting Sammi Bergman did not exist for May and Mr. Miller in regard to The Candlestick Matter. That was how May began to refer to it: The Candlestick Matter.

It was interesting. The Candlestick Matter riveted them together as a couple like nothing else in literally decades of marriage. They felt invigorated and energized and inspired and motivated. They felt alive! Yet, ironically, they conspired together in the deepest and darkest and nastiest terms.

They hated Howie Howard. A man in his prime, who should be championing the seven original Stowe Towne families and their interests. And such a wonderful wife. Surely Margaret wasn't a part of this.

They hated Chuck January. The turncoat. The traitor. Good, dependable Republican Chuck. A pillar of their church. Not a member of one of the original families, of course, but the January clan had lived in Stowe Towne for generations. They'd always been made welcome. But now he had turned on them.

And, they hated the golf course's Board members, except, of course, son Keith. All good original family members. But now they wouldn't even take calls. *Well*, May had said to Mr. Miller, *their wives would certainly take calls from her. Then we would all get to the bottom of this.*

But it turned out to be not as easy as May thought. Some of the wives were not family members, but had married into the families. Some of them were quite young. A couple of them, May realized, were not Daughters of the Union Army members and, in fact, were a little uncertain just who May was and why she was calling. Her last call finally tipped her off to what was going on. It was to Cynthia Duke who was Tom Duke Senior's daughter-in-law. When Tom had given over the chairmanship of the club to Howie, he had also resigned in order to give his seat to his son Tom, Jr. Cynthia, who May erroneously believed had the I.Q. of a can of hair spray, let slip that the committee members were going to make a lot of money on the deal.

Horrors! May whispered to Mr. Miller. *They're doing it for the money!*

Mr. Miller, meanwhile, had better luck with his golf cronies, both the ones who were family members and the ones who were not. The potential loss of the only 18-hole golf course nearby struck deep into the golfers' hearts. Plus, it was a prestigious course. The kind that people traveled to just to say they've played it. But these guys could brag that it was their "home" course. They knew a housing development would wreck it. Even if the course didn't go private (which would probably happen), public play would certainly be restricted. In addition, the course itself would be negatively affected. Houses would line the fairways. There would be new out-of-bounds. In fact, as they talked, they concluded that there would no doubt be new holes. Many of the holes on the current configuration paralleled each other. It would be impossible to line those fairways with new homes. New holes would have to go off in some direction. Probably across Howie's land.

"It'll be one of those goddamn gated communities," Doc Parson groused to his fellow golfers. Seven men were crowded around the back corner table in the Gettysburg Café.

"I never should've got off that goddamn Board," Lincoln Jones sputtered.

"You were on the Board?" Coach Ofman asked in surprise. "I didn't know that."

"I was on the Board, too," Mr. Miller volunteered.

"You were? Really?" Ofman asked. "What happened? I mean I don't know anything about the Board. I just know there is one. I thought Bip was on it. I know he attends the meetings."

Mr. Miller nodded. "Bip as the club pro, along with Warren as the club's general manager, serve as staff to the Board. They really work for whomever is chair of the Board. The chair of the Board is where the real power lies. That's how it was set up in the Accord."

"The what?" asked Dick Ofman. Dick was Dan's younger brother and an insurance agent in town. He played The Candlesticks, although he was not an avid golfer; he just came along to the meeting because Dan had asked him.

Mr. Miller explained: "The Accord was signed in the mid-'50s to establish a structure to manage the golf course. The Candlesticks was originally created by the seven families way back, sort of as their own golf course. Kind of a society club. Actually, what was really important in the 1920s was the clubhouse. Very fancy back then. Well, you know, there's those paintings that are still hanging at the front entrance."

"I never knew those paintings were of The Candlesticks," Coach said. "I just thought they were nice paintings of some other place. Like Scotland or someplace."

Jones snorted. "That was when all the families supposedly had money. But you see, some families had more money than others. That was the problem. You know, I'm the last Jones male. I inherited my share of the course when my father died in 1962. That was fine, except taxes and assessments cost me more than any money I got back from profits. At the time, I was just a guy in my 30s with a family trying to make a living. But the Accord said I could only sell to one of the other families."

"Who did you sell to, then?" Dick asked.

"Grant Howard, Howie's father. You see, the rich get richer. Fortunately, my sister May is smarter than me and married well."

"And she's made a damn fine wife all these years, thank you very much, Lincoln." There was the faintest hint of sarcasm in Mr. Miller's voice. He knew his brother-in-law could be kidded, but only to a certain extent. Money was a delicate issue. One did not discuss it in a crowd or bring up the fact that Mr. Miller and May had put their two nieces, Beth and Grace Jones, through college.

Dick persisted in trying to understand the situation. "So, the Howards gained controlling interest in the course."

Mr. Miller shook his head. "No, the Accord isn't structured like that. Although Grant was very aggressive in running the show before he got Alzheimer's. And then, of course, he died. In fact, Grant is eventually why I left the Board. You couldn't suggest anything. I got tired of his bullying. Nevertheless, even though I quit the Board, as the lead Miller family representative, I never sold the family shares. Keith took over my seat."

"So, you make money from the course?" Dan asked.

Mr. Miller nodded. "The Millers do and I represent the Millers. I divide up our share, which means Keith and I split it."

Dan pressed the issue: "Then as a shareholder you must have some say. You can just stop this housing development. If you have enough votes, I guess."

"Well, that's one problem, having enough votes," Mr. Miller explained.

"But it all goes back to the Accord," Jones jumped in to explain further. "You see, no one knew or could figure out what arrangements the old guys who built the course back in the 20s had with each other. But they somehow managed it and invested in it and took money out right up until World War II. The war sort of screwed up everything. Some guys didn't come back, other guys got old, and the course limped along."

"That's when things got desperate," Mr. Miller picked up the story, "and Ohio Supreme Court Justice Richard Summers was prevailed upon to straighten it all out. In fact, my father and Grant Howard and Tom Duke's father were the key people in engaging Summers. Summers produced The Candlesticks Accord. It wasn't the U.S. Constitution, but Summers managed to tiptoe around most of the problems and reach compromises when he had to."

"Funny how I've never heard the whole story like that," Doc Parsons commented.

"The families weren't obliged to make it public," Mr. Miller explained. "One of Summers's strategies was to give management power to whomever headed the Board. Someone had to be the authority for running the place. Some of the chairs have been good managers. But there was always the possibility for abuse like Grant Howard and now Howie Howard."

"But I still don't understand, exactly, why the Board agreed to this," Dick said. "At least I assume they agreed. Maybe they haven't voted on it yet."

"But that's what I'm trying to tell you, Dick," Mr. Miller said leaning forward. "First of all, the Board doesn't have the power to stop Howie. The course is still going to be there. This is a management decision. A business decision made by the Chair. Secondly, Howie is promising the Board members a ton of money. Maybe not a ton, but enough to blunt any internal criticism."

At this point, the seventh man around the table spoke up. Hal Bergman had not yet said a word. Sticks had called him up and asked him to attend. Hal assumed that his brother would be here, but Sticks hadn't shown up. Hal felt out of place. He knew these fellows, of course, but he wasn't their golfing buddy. And, he really didn't give a rat's ass about The Candlesticks. He knew the lumberyard probably wouldn't make any money from building the new houses there. If Cliner was involved, they'd wholesale out all the lumber.

So, tentatively, Hal asked: "What happens now? By the way, I don't know what happened to Sticks. Sticks, Paul, and I have a meeting with the wine merchant at the lumberyard in half an hour. He said he was going to meet me here before that."

"Wine merchant?" Jones asked.

Hal turned his attention to the old fellow. "We're thinking of starting a fine wine section at the lumberyard."

"A what?" Doc Parsons exclaimed.

"Well, there's no place in town where you can buy a good bottle of wine."

"That's the damn truth," Parsons agreed.

Mr. Miller rubbed the right side of his cheek and chin with his hand. It was an old lawyer habit that he did whenever something struck him as odd or offbeat. "You're going to sell wine at the lumberyard?"

"We've got the space," Hal explained. "And you know our younger brother Paul is a wine expert."

"That may be, but I don't see the two-by-four crowd also interested in a full-bodied Merlot."

"Why not?" Hal asked.

There was a moment of silence around the table as the men contemplated a full-bodied Merlot. Finally, Mr. Miller said, "Anyway, back to The Candlesticks. I don't know what happens now, Hal. Anybody have any ideas?"

After a pause, a few ideas floated around the table. How about a boycott? We'll all start playing down at George Long's Golf Course. Won't Delia like that? Maybe a letter-writing campaign? Send a letter to the *Dispatch* or in town to the *Stowe Towne Bugle*. But who reads letters to the editor? Call some of the other politicians. But no one thought any politician would jump at being their champion. The conversation drifted off and the guys finished their coffees and started to fidget like they would rather be somewhere else.

That's when Mr. Miller made his suggestion. "Let's have a rally, boys. May and I have talked this over. Right at the statue immediately following the Memorial Day ceremony on Monday. Keep the crowd here on the town square. Have a *Save The Candlesticks* rally. Bound to get good media coverage."

Mr. Miller glanced around at the faces of the other six men. He knew instantly that he had come up with a winner.

"And don't worry, boys," he said enthusiastically, "May and I will do all the planning."

⤳

Ohio Supreme Court Justice Richard Summers swung around in his high-backed, creaky leather chair and looked out the window. The newspaper, carefully folded and creased to the Real Estate Section, rested on his lap. Out the window, two stories below him, he watched the cars on the street. He did not have the best office. The Chief Justice had the best office, which was the way it should be. However, since he was by far the longest serving of any of the justices, he had the second best office. It was very dark and very paneled. It oozed authority and wisdom. It intimidated the weak and cowed the mindless. Most of the attorneys and judges in Ohio who had any prominence whatsoever had at one time or another been humbled in this office by Justice Summers. It was his great legacy.

Justice Summers would not tolerate a member of the bar who did not possess humility.

There was a discreet knock at the door. "Did you want to see me, sir?"

Justice Summers swung back around to see a very attractive young woman standing just inside his office door. Black hair. High cheekbones like a model. Tailored dark green suit with a pale yellow blouse open at the neck. He was partial to green and yellow. "Miss Avery, get me The Candlestick Accord," he ordered politely.

Miss Avery was one of his law interns. She was fairly new; a midyear graduate of the Law School at Ohio Northern. Justice Summers always had one law intern from Ohio Northern, his alma mater. That intern was automatically his favorite. None of the other interns disputed that fact. It was just the way the world functioned.

Miss Avery hesitated for a second. "The Candlesticks Accord, sir?"

"It's in the gold file, Miss Avery."

"Yes, sir," she said and disappeared. The gold file was the judge's personal file. Miss Avery would have to get the special gold file key from Mr. Vance who controlled all the files. This would be quite a feather in Miss Avery's cap. Fetching something from the gold file.

Justice Summers swung back to the window. It was starting to rain. Big raindrops splattered noisily on the tall window. *Not a good day for golf*, he thought to himself, *not a good day at all*.

⤻

In the dilapidated and musty Hanover mansion, William Boyd sat at a table in the sunroom. A copy of the *Dispatch* opened to The Candlesticks' article lay off to one side on the old oak table. Will patiently sorted through the coins, carefully placing them in order in cylindrical watertight containers. Mostly Buffalo Head Nickels. Mostly in very good condition. Dates still clearly visible, although the coins had not been minted for decades. The date had been the problem with the Buffalo Heads. It had been raised and had rubbed off early in circulation. So, the coins with visible dates had become valuable. Will Boyd knew all about rare coins. That was how he made his living. He was packing the rolls of coins in flat, metal boxes about the size of necktie gift boxes. Maybe a dozen rolls per box. And then he would bury them at selected spots in Pottawa State Forest. For safekeeping. Will was very eccentric and he had reasons not to trust banks.

He finished packing another box, sat back in his chair and reached down and scratched Bandit's ear. The sunroom with its old curving windows was one of the few rooms that he had remodeled. He had converted the library to a study and that was where he did his writing. He had put on a new roof because he had to. He had repaired water damage throughout the second floor and made one bedroom at least tolerable for his own use. But there was still much to be done. The kitchen, for example, was barely functional.

But Will doubted that he would ever get around to the rest of his house. In his will that was lawfully filed with a law firm in Columbus, he deeded over the mansion to Stowe Towne and set up a trust fund that it be converted into a museum. Stowe Towne, despite its professed love of history, had never had a museum. *Not big enough for a museum*, the town fathers had always maintained, thus avoiding ever having a museum line item in the town's budget. But Will knew that that was not the real reason. No, the fact was that the descendants of the seven original families didn't want a museum. They jealously guarded their own histories and kept hold of their own historical artifacts and antiques. It would be an interesting dilemma for Stowe Towne when his will was made public someday in the future. The Hanover Mansion. The trust fund.

But that will be then, this is now.

Will picked up the paper and read the article for the third time. Stowe Towne had faced "progress" before. Everything from paved roads to parking meters. City water to bottled water. Bathtub gin to the FSF. (He was one of the few adults who knew all about the FSF.) The last livery stable closing to the opening of Allied Pipes. And now it was The Candlesticks' turn.

Maybe.

He took the paper with him and wandered back through the dusty rooms to his study. It was time for him to do a little writing.

chapter nine

RAY'S STICKS

The rain on the judge's window turned into a full-fledged spring thunderstorm in Stowe Towne when Sammi got home at 5:30. She opened the garage door and pulled in next to Sticks's dark green Jeep Cherokee. Randy's old clunker was not in the drive and she assumed he was still working at the lumberyard. But she was more interested in her husband's whereabouts. She hadn't talked to him all day, which was somewhat of a rarity. And they certainly had some things to talk over.

The house was quiet and seemed deserted. No TV sounds; Sticks always had the TV on. He was probably over at the club playing cards, she thought as she dumped her purse on the kitchen counter and thought idly about what to fix for dinner. There were some leftovers. Maybe that would have to do for tonight. Normally, if she made a sale as big as the Portman farm, they'd go out to dinner at the Maple Lodge or even drive into Columbus to eat. But her argument with Bruce and the festering dilemma over The Candlesticks' housing development dulled her desire to celebrate.

She passed by the entrance to the family room on her way to change her clothes and was startled to see her husband looking out the patio doors at the rain. He was sitting in the rocking chair that they had bought a few years ago as a joke on their twentieth wedding anniversary. Getting old, you know. He had pulled the chair halfway across the room so that he could sit in it and stare out the window at the rain. Bertha was curled up at his feet. Sticks had a beer in one hand and there was an empty beer can tipped over on the carpet beside the rocker.

"Sticks, I didn't know you were here. Is there anything wrong?"

"Oh, hi, honey," Sticks answered flatly. "No, nothing's wrong."

Sticks often was in a funk when it was raining and he couldn't play golf. But somehow this seemed different to Sammi. "I didn't know where you were," she said. "Hal called me at the office about 4:00 and said that you missed a couple of meetings. He said he had tried to call you here."

"Yeah, I guess I missed those meetings." He didn't offer any further explanation and silence hung heavy in the room as the rain pelted the windows and the sliding deck door. Thunder rumbled briefly overhead. Bertha raised her head listening to it.

Sammi sat down on the end of the couch a few feet from the chair. "Sticks, this isn't like you. Are you feeling all right? Are you sick?"

"I'm fine, Sammi," he said and looked over at her. "And don't worry, this is only my second Bud and it's still almost full."

"I didn't think you were drunk, Sticks. I can't remember the last time you were drunk."

"I know, but I was actually thinking about getting drunk. I guess you saw the article."

"Oh, sure, I saw it. Bruce and I had a fight about it."

"You did?"

"And, I sold the Portman farm."

"Really?"

"Really. It's been quite a day."

Sticks paused and stared back out at the rain. Finally, he said: "The Portman farm, congratulations. That one's been a pain in the ass, hasn't it?"

"It sure has. Thanks. So, what meetings did you miss?"

"Oh, Mr. Miller got a few of the guys together to oppose developing the golf course. I asked Hal to meet me there and then I stiffed him. I guess I stiffed all of them."

"Why?"

Sticks paused for a minute and then said: "Well, I wanted to know what was going on and who was there, but I didn't want to go myself. So, I talked Hal into going so he could tell me. But that doesn't matter. It's not important. What did you argue about with Bruce?"

"His lying to me. Not that he hasn't lied to me before, but generally not about business. You know what I mean? He's been pretty honest about the business. He lies about his social life and what he's thinking and he's generally a sleazeball. But he's always been pretty fair about the business. Until now. If something was in the works, he has always shared it. If it was significant, like this."

"How did he react to you?" Sticks knew that his wife could come on as a strong personality at times. But then, Bruce had seen her in action before.

"Oh, he took the easy way out. He said it was still in the talking stage. Too early to discuss. That's a load of crap and he knows it. But...well..."

This time it was Sammi's turn to pause. After a moment, Sticks looked over at her again. She flushed. "Anyway, you know that's not the issue, Sticks."

Sticks nodded. "I know."

"So, what are we going to do?"

"I don't know, Sammi. I've been thinking about it. You know, it's like buying a lottery ticket. I buy one and then I ask myself: Do I really want to win? You hear stories about how lottery winners always end up miserable. Family gets greedy and all that sort of stuff. I get to thinking: Why do I need more money? I have a great life. Good kids. Play golf practically seven days a week, if I want. Yet, finally, I still go and buy the ticket. You know?"

"I know. I know," Sammi agreed.

"We'd make money, wouldn't we? Not on the lottery. I mean on a housing development."

Sammi nodded. "If we wanted to, we'd probably make a ton of money, Sticks."

"That's what I'm thinking. But we don't need to make a ton of money, especially this way. Besides, you just sold the Portman farm. But, if the development is going to happen anyway..."

"Is it going to happen anyway?" Sammi interrupted.

Sticks put his beer down on the carpet next to the empty can and turned the rocking chair so that he fully faced his wife. "That's it. That's exactly the point. I don't know. Is it going to happen anyway? Do you know for sure that The Candlesticks will be turned into a condo development?"

Sammi shook her head. "I don't know, Sticks. I've been thinking about it all day. All the angles. And I don't know. I just don't know."

"Of course," Sticks argued, "we wouldn't have to participate. We could just keep the farm. The housing development would be over there. On the other side of the club. On Howie and Margaret's land. Let their land be ruined."

"We don't do a lot with *our* land, Sticks. You rent it out to the Curtis boys to farm if they're interested. Which they sometimes are and sometimes aren't. We pay pretty hefty taxes on it just to let the Curtises harvest soybeans every other year. It's not great farmland, plus farmland is hardly at a premium around here."

Sticks nodded. "I know. It's not exactly a retirement nest egg. But it's something."

"That's right, it is something," Sammi agreed. "And in five or ten or twenty years when we want to move, it might be worth more."

"And it could be worth more, too, for a housing development right now," Sticks suggested.

Sammi grimaced and sat back on the couch. "Well, maybe, but you've heard the cliché about being *in on the ground floor*. I think that came from real estate. Maybe the development won't be wildly successful. Maybe there won't be a phase two or phase three. Maybe the expansion will take place on the other side of the Howard's property. There's the Schmidt land and Hanover farm over there. Or maybe they'll just keep going up into the state forest. Lots of unknowns."

"Yeah, but the river cuts through over on the other side of Howie's," Sticks argued.

"The river is at the back of our property, too, Sticks. Besides, people like the water. They like homes overlooking a river."

"It's a trickle. It's little more than a stream."

"So? It's labeled a river."

Sticks sat back and rocked in silence staring at a spot on the wall above his wife's head. After a couple of minutes he sighed and said, "I suppose I better call Hal. I'll tell him I got the flu or something. Make up some excuse for not being there today."

"Is Randy working?" Sammi asked abruptly.

"Do you think he'll believe me about the flu?"

"Hal's your brother. He'll know you're not telling the truth before you finish the sentence. You might as well tell him the truth. Tell him you're suffering from indecision. Anyway, Sticks, what about Randy?"

"Oh, Randy. I thought he said he wasn't working today. But I haven't seen him. I don't really know."

Now it was Sammi's turn to sigh. "Well, I'm going to change and then I'm going to treat you to leftovers. I sure don't feel like going out and seeing anybody."

She wandered out of the family room and went to change clothes. It was a half hour later when she went to get the mail that she found Randy's note on the little table by the front door. The note said he was going up to Kent to spend the night with a buddy. He didn't leave a phone number.

~

However...

The Bergman's only son, at that very moment, was discreetly purchasing a ticket for the showing of *Le Roi de Sade* at the Cinema Paradiso in the Flats on the west side of downtown Cleveland. The film had been running for about 10 minutes, which was according to plan. Julie and her fellow French Club members were supposed to be by then fully engrossed in the film. Randy was to sit in the back row, right side, and about half an hour into the film, Julie was going to excuse herself for the bathroom and, depending which way the wind was blowing, she was either going to leave with him or tell him it was no dice. The wind in question consisted of her language teacher Wendy Price. Wendy was young and very cool. It was quite an accomplishment, being a cool high school teacher. But, in the eyes of her students, Wendy was cool. Although, Julie knew, you must never forget that Wendy was still a teacher.

The plan, such as it was, consisted of this: after the film, Heather Miller would tell Ms. Price that Julie went home with her mother and wouldn't be taking the high school van home. Heather would insist that Julie had brought Ms. Price a permission letter. Ms. Price would insist not. Surprise! Julie forgot her purse and look, there inside, was the undelivered letter from Mrs. Howard to Ms. Price. A very nice forgery, thank you, on Mrs. Howard's own personal stationery. What a dope—Julie forgetting to give Ms. Price the letter and now forgetting to take her purse. But why did she leave early? Well, Heather would explain, you know Mrs. Howard (Wink!). Being cool, Ms. Price would understand and wouldn't want to meddle.

Julie had reserved the option with Randy of calling off the plan if (a) Ms. Price somehow figured it out in advance and couldn't be tricked or (b) Julie just was having too good a time. Fortunately for Randy, neither "a" nor "b" happened. He was not surprised, after watching 30 minutes of the film. Not even any subtitles. It was one of those foreign films that seemed to have been shot underwater. It was in color, but the only color was pale, washed-out blue. This old guy wandered around yelling and he cut an ear off a horse and an ear off some young girl who might have been his daughter. What's this *ear* business all about?

Randy quickly followed Julie out of the theater after she breezed by his seat and gave him the thumbs up. Outside, he grabbed her hand and they dashed down the street deeper into the Flats. The mostly one-story buildings were a mixture of new and old divided by cramped parking areas and inlets of water from Lake Erie. Pleasure boats were tied up along many of the docks.

The day was warm, but cloudy with rain starting to drizzle on them. It was also the Thursday night before the long Memorial Day weekend and the place was filling up. Music blared out of sleek bars and restaurants along the docks. Cars honked looking for the few good parking spots. There was a mixture of young suits—both men and women—from the office towers downtown and the post-college age 20-somethings.

"Where are we going?" Julie yelled at Randy as they hurried along. Even though it was only a very remote possibility, they both felt they were being followed.

"Just up there," Randy said and pointed. "That white sign, The Salt

Mine. That's where my buddy's a bouncer. Here, take this."

Julie took the card Randy handed her. "What is it?"

"It's a fake I.D. my buddy confiscated. I got one too. They don't look much like us, but they're not bad. I'm Tom March. You're like, Sarah somebody."

"Sarah Smith. How original."

Randy stopped abruptly. "There, he's the guy on the right. Green T-shirt."

"How do you know him?"

"He's the starting offensive left guard on the Kent football team. Big guy."

"I'll say," Julie agreed.

"All right, stay cool and don't get jostled into the other line. The guy with the white Salt Mine T-shirt. Our guy is the *green* shirt."

After all the intrigue, getting in ended up being a snap. Randy's teammate even told him which bartender to go to. It was all fixed. They found a couple of seats in the corner by a window overlooking the water so they could drink their beers inconspicuously.

"I don't get the name," Julie said looking around at the bar's decorations that consisted of shovels and pick axes, Morton Salt signs, and big drill bits.

"It's the salt mine under the lake," Randy explained. "Just offshore here. Most of the salt they use on the roads is mined here. You know, in winter."

"You're kidding."

"No, a couple of guys I know at school work there off and on. There are only two mines like it in the country. The salt from here is shipped all over the United States."

"It's underwater?"

"Well, it's under the lake, not on the bottom of the lake. The mine's very deep, I guess."

Julie shrugged as if the concept of a salt mine below Lake Erie was just too bizarre for contemplation. She glanced around for a minute as the bar filled up with the early evening drinking crowd. Finally, she remarked: "Well, this is a nice place anyway." She said it as if she hung out at bars every weekend. She turned her attention to her boyfriend: "So, what did you think of the article today?"

Randy set down his plastic cup of Miller Lite on the tiny round table between them. "The what?" he asked.

"In the newspaper? Duh."

"I didn't see a paper today."

"It was all over school, Randy. What planet are you living on?" In mock exaggeration, Julie recounted as best she could The Candlestick development story from the *Dispatch*.

"Holy shit," Randy whistled. "So, that guy in your house was for real."

"He was real enough all right. What do you think your parents are going to do?"

"My Dad was really pumping for me to get information from you. But not lately. I don't know. It's really hard to say."

"I saw Mr. Ofman in the hallway this morning just before we left..."

"By the way, why did you leave so early if the movie wasn't until now?" Randy interrupted.

"Oh, we went shopping," Julie explained. "We always go shopping when we go on our French Club trip."

The logic of that statement slipped past Randy, but he let it go.

Julie continued: "Anyway, Mr. Ofman was plenty upset. He didn't yell at me or anything, but he said that he didn't think that The Candlesticks should be changed."

"Well, I'm with him on that. Aren't you?"

Julie squinted at Randy's broad, square face. Sometimes he looked and acted too much like a dumb football jock. "No, I'm not. I think. I mean, this past winter Dad took me to Florida and Arizona to play golf. You know? And we played on some courses with houses and condos and stuff. They were fine. They were nice, in fact."

"As nice as The Candlesticks?"

"Right. Right, they were." Julie grimaced. The courses were crowded and not very friendly to a teenage girl. Old guys would yell at her. Old women, too. And the courses tended to be tight. Intimidating. Lots of water in Florida and lots of snakes (or at least threats of snakes) in Arizona. It was nice to go on the trips. Even get some days off from school. But, to tell the truth, she also liked The Candlesticks and did not really want it changed. Yet, she also felt a family loyalty that disturbed her. And she knew she couldn't talk about *that* to Randy.

Randy drained his beer. "Drink up. I'll get us another one. But I don't know, Julie. I like things the way they are. My house. Your house. The golf course in between. I don't want things to change."

Julie looked at her beer and then took a deep breath and drained half a glass. She had no idea where they were going to sleep tonight. She had no idea what arrangements Randy had made. And she was absolutely certain that her mother would find out. But, what the hell? She didn't know if she wanted things to change either. However, somehow, she knew they were going to change no matter what she thought.

⌒

The phone rang at 6:15 Friday morning and Sticks groaned. One of the luxuries of having kids out of the house was not having to get up for school anymore. Since Randy had graduated from high school, Sticks and Sammi's rise and shine time had gradually gotten later and later. The ringing persisted and since the phone was on his side of the bed, Sticks finally answered it.

"Sticks, this is Bip, are you awake?"

"What time is it?" Sticks had never had a phone call like this from Bip.

"I got a problem; you got to help me."

"What is it?" Sticks said suddenly alert. "Is somebody sick? Is something wrong?"

"Not yet," Bip answered. "Listen, I've got a buddy who's the pro over at River Hills Country Club in Cincinnati. You ever play there?"

Sticks swung his feet onto the floor. Oh, it was early. He'd sure like a cup of coffee. He had had a couple more beers before he'd gone to bed last night. More than he usually drank.

"What was the question?" Sticks asked.

"River Hills in Cincinnati. Ever play there?"

Sticks had heard of the course; it was one of the more prestigious courses in Cincinnati. An old course like The Candlesticks. "Never had the opportunity, Bip. Why? Why is that important this time of the morning?"

"Well, this might be your lucky day. My friend will give you unlimited play there if you can do him a favor."

"What favor?"

"There's this guy who wants to play The Candlesticks this morning. Apparently, has to play for some reason. He's a member of River Hills and he's all over my buddy to get him on The Candlesticks."

"So what do you need me for?"

"He has to have a playing partner who'll play him straight up."

"For money? A hustler? Why should I get out of bed in the middle of the night to lose money to some strange golfer? Have you lost your mind, Bip?"

"It's not the middle of the night, Sticks. I'm looking at the sunrise right now. My friend said this guy's not a big better. Likes to bet things like dinner. My friend and I will cover you if you lose. Look, Sticks, I really have to do my friend a favor. I really owe him. Please, I'm not being a shithead here."

Sticks sighed. "All right. All right. I'll be there. What time? And what's this guy's name?"

"Just Ray. That's all my friend would tell me. Ray. He called my friend at 5:00 a.m. Said he was leaving for over here right away. So, I suppose he could be here any time between 7:00 and 8:00. I didn't call you right away, Sticks. I didn't call you at 5:10."

"I'm eternally grateful, Bip." He paused and got his bearings. "All right, I'll be there." Sticks resisted the overwhelming temptation to go back to bed and forced himself into the shower.

An hour and fifteen minutes later at 7:30, Sticks was standing near the first tee with Ray. Bip and Ray had been waiting for him. Bip had Sticks's clubs for him. Bip had even gone to the trouble of cleaning them. Sticks sized up his opponent as they small-talked for a minute about the warm morning. The man defined the word nondescript, Sticks decided. He was just under six feet tall, medium weight, brown hair, early 40s. He was wearing a plain white golf shirt (no logo), tan slacks, and brown Foot-Joy soft-spike golf shoes. What was most remarkable (or unremarkable, as the case may be) was his clubs. First of all, the clubs were in an absolutely plain, generic, dark blue bag. Regular shoulder bag. No stand. No sheepskin strap. No brand name anywhere. No commemorative tags from golf courses, tournaments, or country clubs. The only thing hanging from the bag was a blue towel exactly the color of the bag. His clubs also appeared to be generic. He did not have head covers or iron covers. There were no identifying marks on the clubs. Even the putter appeared to be a mallet head putter from a starter's set.

Bip had slipped them in behind a foursome. But the foursome had carts and looked to be pretty good players. There was no one scheduled behind Sticks and Ray for 30 minutes. As they walked toward the tee, Bip slipped away.

They stopped a discreet distance away and Sticks took his King Cobra Titanium driver from his bag and swung it a few times. He felt okay; not quite loose enough yet.

"Cobras," Ray noted. "Do you like them?"

Sticks took a full practice swing. "I've had them for about a year. I've played all right with them. Sometimes they're a little quick, if you know what I mean." Sticks was trying to make conversation.

"Sure, you tend to whip them. When you start doing that, it's back to Golf 101."

Sticks was amazed at how plain and vanilla the guy was. He didn't even have an accent or a speech impediment. "I couldn't help noticing your clubs," Sticks remarked. "No identifying marks on them anywhere."

"Oh, I have them custom-made. Graphite shaft and titanium head, of course. No insert. The grips are nice. Calf skin. Here, take a swing."

Sticks put his own driver back in the bag and accepted the no-name one from Ray. Since he was about the same height as Ray, the club fit comfortably. He swung easily. It was a beautiful club. Very nice. Very, very nice. "That's a great stick," Sticks said handing the club back. "Whoever did these for you did a great job."

Ray just smiled. The foursome finished teeing off and headed for their carts. Sticks and Ray walked up to the tee.

"What made you so anxious to play The Candlesticks?" Sticks asked.

"Oh, I've heard about the course for years," Ray answered. "Late yesterday afternoon I found out I had to come to Columbus and so I thought about playing here this morning."

"Well, I'm glad we could accommodate."

"Your pro was most helpful. His name's Bip? Just like the Reds ballplayer Bip Roberts?"

Sticks nodded. "I think so. I guess it's some family name. He's from West Virginia." Sticks looked around, but Bip was nowhere to be seen.

He had vanished almost immediately after the introductions. Curious.

"And your name's *Sticks*. Is that family, too?"

Sticks laughed. "No, it's from right here. This course. Played it all my life. The nickname stuck."

The players in the foursome down the fairway were hitting their second shots. "Well, Sticks, it looks like we need to establish the bet. Eight handicap for you, I understand." Sticks nodded. "Well, I'm a six," Ray said. "Two strokes, but it's your home course. I'd call us even."

"That's fair," Sticks agreed.

"I don't like to bet money," Ray said. "Who needs more money? Right?"

"Sure," Sticks agreed, "it just gets in the way."

"So, what about the clubs? My custom-made clubs for your Cobras. Minus the putters and sand wedges, of course. Doesn't look like either of us has any odd clubs. Straight stroke play. Lowest score at the end of 18. Just like on TV."

Sticks pondered the deal. His Cobras were expensive clubs. Even used, he didn't think Bip and the River Hills pro would want to cover the replacement price. Plus, he didn't know the real value of Ray's clubs. But the driver seemed terrific. And the man was going to use them to play now. Just a second, he was going to play with them, wasn't he?

"Point of clarification, Ray. Are you going to use these clubs for this round? We're talking about at the end of the round, one person walking off with both sets, meaning these two sets of clubs here."

"That's right. Absolutely." Ray nodded.

"Just the sticks, not the bags or anything in the bags."

"Right again."

Sticks pondered the situation for a moment. "I'll tell you what, Ray, I'd just as soon just bet the irons. I really don't want to risk my woods."

Ray nodded. "I can understand that. All right, just the irons."

"No gimmies. Putt all putts."

"Of course," Ray agreed.

"No play-off if we tie. Just keep our own clubs."

"Fine with me. I won't have time anyway."

"And no money."

"No money."

"All right," Sticks said, "let's play ball."

The first three holes didn't reveal much as both men played excellent golf, shooting par. Ray just missed a birdie on the first hole as his putt hung on the lip. On the second hole, Sticks rimmed out a 12-foot birdie putt. Both men had beautiful long-iron tee shots to the green on the 185-yard par-3 third hole. They both made pars. Sticks couldn't see any weakness in Ray's game, except he was an extremely slow player. They were in no danger of overtaking the foursome in front of them. It was odd, though. Few players as good as Ray were as slow and deliberate.

Sticks blinked first on the easy par-4, 380-yard fourth hole. His drive rolled into high damp rough on the right side of the fairway. The rough turned his seven-iron and his ball landed in the sand to the right of the green. He managed a bogey, but Ray scored a routine par.

After two pars on number five, both men scored bogeys on the short par-3 sixth hole. It was the hole Randy had had his near hole-in-one. Sticks cursed silently. The sixth was one of the holes he should have had a tactical advantage from knowing the course. But he couldn't cash in on it. The men also scored bogeys on Barnes's Knob, the long, difficult uphill seventh hole that ended at the Cascades.

They paused, as most serious golfers did, on the eighth tee and took in the view. The fairway of the long par-5 eighth stretched in front of them.

"This is a beautiful course. Everything I ever heard or read about it is true," Ray remarked.

Sticks nodded. "It's a classic course."

"Kept up well, too. Looks great for a public course."

"We've had lots of rain this spring. I think the rain has kept play down and given the grass a chance."

Ray teed up his ball. "Well, Sticks, you're a good player. I'd say I'm lucky to be one up at this point." Ray took his time as usual and belted his ball straight down the fairway.

Maybe it was the pause in the action or maybe it was Ray's words that got him to thinking about the course, but Sticks had a disastrous hole. He put his drive in the right rough again. He managed to hit his three-wood a long ways, but the ball landed even further into the right rough. He came up way short with his eight-iron. Overhit his wedge to the back of the green and then three-putted for a seven. Ray had another par.

Both men scored pars on the ninth hole although Sticks's was shaky. He had to sink an 18-foot putt to make it. For the front nine, Sticks had a five-over-par 41 and Ray had a two-over-par 38. Sticks was down three strokes and was not playing very good golf. Ray was burning up a course he claimed he had never even seen before.

At the turn, Ray excused himself to pee while Sticks stewed in that odd no-man's land on a golf course between the front nine and the back nine. He looked around again quickly for Bip, but the pro was still absent. *Wait until I get my hands on the old fart! Getting me in the middle of this match. With a goddamn golf pro! Besides I have more important things to think about. Damn!*

Ray returned and they started on the "high" nine as the back nine was sometimes referred to at The Candlesticks. Both men scored pars on the 10th and the 11th and Sticks, to his dismay, still didn't notice any chinks in Ray's golf armor. Sticks had to make up some strokes before he ran out of holes. Maybe the 12th, another hole where Sticks thought he might have a tactical advantage because of experience.

The short 12th was a severe dogleg left par 4 that started next to the bottom of the Cascades and then ran along the Pottawa. It was possible for a good player to hit over the rocks and trees and cut the dogleg. Except the fairway was narrow and one could easily fly the fairway and end up in the trees along the right side. The tee was also slightly elevated which made it all the more tempting to cut the dogleg.

Ray stood studying the scorecard trying to figure out the hole. Having honors was definitely a problem for Ray in this instance. Sticks knew that Ray would dearly love to have him hit first and show him what to do. But Sticks just stood at the back of the tee holding his golf bag. He didn't even remove a club. Ray could see that the dogleg was so short down the fairway that he couldn't dare hit more than a seven-iron or he would run into the trees at the turn. But even a perfect shot to the fairway would leave a long 200-yard second shot into a heavily bunkered green. Not a great situation.

Finally, Ray selected a club, his driver. A small smile passed over Sticks's face. The smile turned into a grin when he saw Ray set up for the shot. Ray was making the usual mistake good golfers made the first time they played this hole. Ray was, of course, confident that he could clear the trees and rocks and cut the dogleg. But, since he did not know the angle of the fairway coming into the green, he was aiming too far right. After a long pause, he swung and hit a towering drive, but Sticks instantly knew it would be in the trees across the fairway.

Ray turned and looked at Sticks. Sticks shrugged and said, "Good-looking shot, but you might be across the fairway into the trees." Ray nodded and picked up his tee and made way for Sticks. Sticks selected his three-wood instead of a driver and lined up dramatically to the left of Ray's line. It looked like Sticks was hitting directly into the trees and rocks. In fact, he was aiming over the highest rock, a marker the experienced golfers on the course used. He swung and his three-wood gave him great height. He knew at once that it would come down gently in the middle of the fairway about 120 yards from the green.

Sticks put his wedge six feet from the hole and made birdie. Ray finally found his ball all the way through the trees and on the edge of the 13th fairway. Because he was too close to the trees, he had to play up the 13th to the 13th tee. Then his wedge shot across to the 12th green found a bunker. He got out of the sand and two-putted for a double-bogey. The score was suddenly tied. Sticks had picked up three strokes on a single hole.

After that, chaos reigned for the two golfers. There was a flurry of birdies, bogeys, and pars, although neither golfer was ever ahead or behind by more than one stroke. On the 17th hole, Ray's six-iron to the green actually hit the pin and stopped four feet from the hole. His birdie putt tied him with Sticks going to the last hole.

On the 18th tee, the long par-5 finishing hole, Sticks felt a rush of emotion as he looked across the out-of-bounds fence and saw his house. Was this a doomed sight? Would new houses soon wipe out this view? He tried to shake the thought from his mind. He had to concentrate.

Ray stepped up and stroked a drive down the middle. Sticks followed suit and they both then hit solid second shots. Sticks was 10 yards behind Ray about 100 yards out. Sticks stared ahead at the flag. It was positioned a little left of center and slightly to the back of the green. But not too far. Suddenly, it dawned on him that Bip had probably supervised the pin placements at dawn. Yes, of course he had. It all made sense now.

Sticks selected his nine-iron and hit a high shot into the narrower left side of the pin. The ball stopped up well short of the pin, but safely on the green. "Too bad," Ray commented. It was the first time he had said anything about any of Sticks's shots. Ray also selected a nine-iron, but hit directly into the middle of the green. His ball stopped no more than four or five feet to the right of the pin.

"Nice shot," Sticks said encouragingly. He hoped to boost Ray's sense that he had just won the match with that shot.

The match was dead even on the 18th green. A classic situation. The golfers took out their putters and flopped their bags on the edge of the green. It appeared that Ray had the definite advantage for the win. Sticks had a 22-foot putt. Ray had a 5-foot putt. But Sticks knew one small, but important fact that Ray didn't know. The pin was placed just to the left of an invisible break in the green. Sticks was above the break and Ray was below the break. Sticks had an absolute flat, straight putt. Ray's putt looked flat and straight from every angle. But it wasn't.

However, it was hardly a sure thing. Sticks would have preferred to be 10 or 15 feet closer and have Ray 10 or 15 feet farther away. Still, he had an advantage. He had been here before.

Sticks marked and cleaned his ball. He took his stance and looked down the line to the hole. The green was perfectly cut. The hole beckoned. He knew he would make the putt. He stroked the ball, kept his head down, and then looked just as his ball curled into the hole.

"Jesus Christ," Ray muttered. It was unnerving enough that Sticks had made the putt. But, in addition, Ray never saw the break. His ball broke two feet away from the hole and slid on by to the right. The putt never had a chance.

Ray picked up his ball and walked over to Sticks. "It was a pleasure playing with you, Sticks. You're a fine golfer."

"Thank you, Ray."

The men shook hands. They picked up their bags and walked over to the clubhouse deck where Ray took his irons out of the bag and leaned them against the steps going up to the deck. "I think you'll enjoy these. Use them in good golf."

"Can I get you some lunch? A beer?" Sticks offered.

"No, no, I really have to run. Ah, thank Bip for me. Maybe we'll have a rematch later in the summer."

"I'm always here, Ray."

The man smiled briefly and hurried away to the parking lot with his nearly empty bag over his shoulder. Sticks sat down on the deck steps with his own bag at his feet and the strange, unmarked clubs he had just won next to him. He picked up his new three-iron and hefted it in his hands as he looked back at the 18th green. *Some match, all right*, he thought.

And at that moment, Sticks made up his mind.

chapter ten

RALLY 'ROUND THE STATUE, BOYS

By early Saturday evening of Memorial Day weekend, May and Mr. Miller's life had turned into a circus. This was a very unusual situation for the sedate, older couple who prided themselves on their sophistication. But now their exclusive Miller Lane residence most resembled—*Horrors*—a Democratic Party campaign headquarters the Saturday before a Tuesday election. May established her Daughters of the Union Army rallying room in the front dining room while Mr. Miller established his golf buddies' rallying room in the back kitchen. Mr. Miller suggested the arrangements. He argued that the Maple Lodge could cater food and beverages to the front dining room for the ladies while the boys only needed pretzels and beer from the fridge. May was quite agreeable to separate her ladies (who came in through the front door) from Mr. Miller's boys (who came in through the back door). Just because their cause was the same, it didn't mean the sexes had to mingle.

Defining the cause, actually, was a crucial point. In that regard, the boys had it a little easier. They had a simple purpose: they did not want to lose their golf privileges. It was a tougher sell to the ladies of the DUA. Not that May's force of personality couldn't carry the day. Still, many DUA ladies had never actually been out to The Candlesticks. Maybe their grandmothers had partied once upon a time at the old country club, but most of them had not even stepped through the front door of the clubhouse. All of them, of course, had driven by it on some pretty Sunday afternoon excursion. But the ladies seldom, if ever, had had any occasion to actually stop in. Not only that, but the thought of a new housing development was not entirely displeasing to them for a number of reasons. Carefree condo living appealed to some of the ladies who were sick and tired of maintaining drafty and dusty nineteenth century homes. *(Not everyone could afford a daily housekeeper like May Miller had!)* Some ladies had children and grandchildren who might be inclined to stay or move back to Stowe Towne if new contemporary housing was available. And, finally, some of the ladies were interested in house design and interior decorating. Just think about *that* Parade of Homes!

Nevertheless, one could not exactly say *no* to May Miller, although one could demur. A few ladies dropped off 20-dollar bills or casseroles for whatever reason and pleaded that they had to be out of town for the holiday. Memorial Day was a holiday, after all. Many of the DUA ladies traveled on Memorial Day because they all were expected to be in town to work in some capacity at the July Fourth Arts Festival that included the once-a-year induction of new DUA members. May realized this and had to be somewhat gracious. Anyway, there were still enough ladies around and there even were some who worked up a decent indignation. The Candlesticks Country Club was part of the tradition of Stowe Towne and where would we all be without tradition? Theirs was a town founded because of history. You just didn't throw history away to put up condos and make money.

The ladies decided to make some signs. Or, to be more precise, they decided to arrange to have someone else make some signs.

Mr. Miller in the kitchen with his legal pad was being a little more practical, although he had an equally hard time focusing the boys on the project. The boys tended to talk in no particular priority about the Cleveland Indians, bowling, the Cincinnati Reds, fishing, boating, the weather, Donna Dougall's large breasts (she was the waitress in the Gettysburg Café and always had one too many buttons unbuttoned on her uniform), how much the new houses might cost at The Candlesticks, and golf. But at least they were enthusiastic about stopping any alteration of the golf course. Not necessarily, however, about stopping the construction of a housing development next to the golf course.

Let Howie put it in his own backyard if he wants it so badly, they said. Just make him leave the damn course alone.

Mr. Miller had to keep bringing the boys back to the point. Since Howie in effect *controlled* the golf course, why wouldn't he want to integrate it with the housing? That was the whole selling point behind the development. Otherwise, it could go in anybody's cow pasture. After all, County Road 12, "The Pike," was not the most accessible or well-traveled road in the area. In fact, the convoy of construction trucks necessary to build a housing development would probably destroy the road over a couple of years. That would be a hidden cost to the taxpayer. Mr. Miller made a note.

Charley Johnson, who was a retired county engineer, also raised the point that he doubted—no matter what that asshole Chuck January said in the paper—that utilities out on The Pike would support a large housing development. It really depended on size, he admitted, because new water and sewer lines were run out along The Pike about five years ago well past the golf course. Still, it was a point of argument and Mr. Miller made a note.

Dan Ofman raised the question about schools. He had read an article in some paper recently about a proposed school tax levy for a school district on the west side of Columbus. Dan liked to keep up on such issues as a matter of self-interest. That district was working with a formula of 1.1 additional school-age children for every new home in the district. One hundred and fifty new homes at The Candlesticks would mean 165 more students in the district just from there. Stowe Towne's two grade schools, junior high school, and high school were full now. In fact, he could tell the boys confidentially that he thought the School Board was soon going to propose a levy for a new high school. It was all hush-hush.

Dan seriously overstepped his bounds. He invariably made stupid, rash decisions. Without fail, in every football game he coached, he would decide to go for a first down on fourth down. He could be ahead by two points on his own 10-yard line and needing three yards and still go for it, and later justify the failure to make first down and subsequent loss by a point as believing the Union Generals had the element of surprise on their side. If Dan Ofman had been a Union officer during the real Civil War, the South would no doubt have won. In this instance, the boys he took into confidence about the proposed school levy would all, of course, oppose it vigorously being mostly retired and reactionary fellows. In fact, for many of them, this new information leapfrogged in importance over the golf controversy. A new school levy meant money out of their pockets. Golf was just recreation. And fishing was a lot cheaper anyway.

Mr. Miller made another note. Actually, he made two notes: *School Crowding* and *Oppose Levy*.

The boys made a couple more beer runs on the refrigerator and Mr. Miller tried to keep them on track. Eventually, he had to give up, although he did elicit a pledge from each to show up at noon on Monday at the statue. They had permission to use the Memorial Day Ceremony stand that was always erected next to the statue of the Seven Heroes in downtown Stowe Towne. It was a portable metal stand the Town Council finally had to invest in 10 years ago after years of building, tearing down, and rebuilding the speaker stand next to the statue. The Memorial Day Ceremony would start, as always, at 10:00 a.m. and conclude by 10:30. The ceremony would open with the Union Generals Marching Corps playing the *Star-Spangled Banner* and close with *America the Beautiful*. Then the band would lead a marching procession west on Jones Street to Hanover Avenue and then south on Hanover to Union Cemetery. In fact, the cemetery was only a couple of blocks from the Millers' house that was in the "well-off" southwest corner of the city. Finally, after the flag raising, prayers, and the playing of the *Battle Hymn of the Republic* at the War Memorial obelisk, the American Legion commandant would invite everyone to go back to the square for the "Save The Candlesticks" rally.

No one had the faintest idea how many people would come to the rally. News had to be spread by word of mouth. *The Stowe Towne Bugle* only came out once a week on Wednesday and one couldn't (or shouldn't) advertise the rally by radio or television. May and Mr. Miller had called the religious leaders in town and had strong-armed promises from them all to announce the rally from their pulpits. Exactly why the clergy would agree to this might be a little mystifying to an outsider. However, the Millers simply, and with great dignity, threatened the financial well-being of all the churches if there was no cooperation. The Families ran the churches; the churches did not run the Families.

Program-wise, the rally was a little weak. Mr. Miller and May would both speak and they were well-experienced and effective public speakers. But after that, the program was thin. Dan Ofman politely declined to speak—he wasn't a complete idiot. No politician would agree to be on the platform: the mayor, town council members, county commissioners, even school board members. They said no before Mr. Miller could get around to suggesting that political donations would not be forthcoming in the future. Everyone had other plans. They all were sure he understood. Memorial Day was a busy time, you know, for politicians. Lots of speaking engagements. Finally, the boys had to agree on Lincoln Jones making brief remarks on the importance of recreational golf and Charley Johnson making brief remarks on the possibility of the utilities costing the taxpayers more money. Not exactly a rally lineup to die for.

May and Mr. Miller went to bed exhausted. Sunday would be church and another day of nervous planning.

⤳

Howie and Margaret Howard pulled up to the Professor's house a few blocks from the Ohio State University campus. When Margaret was growing up, the pretty, tree-lined street had been mostly populated by the families of Ohio State faculty members. But gradually the old homes had been converted into apartments filled mostly with graduate students. Stereos now blared out of windows. Cars were pulled off driveways onto the edge of the smallish front yards. Beer bottles and cans littered the sidewalk from Thursday through Sunday night. Howie and Margaret pleaded with the Professor to move. But he was adamant. He would *not* move. Besides, just because they didn't like the kids didn't mean that *he* didn't like the kids. Plus, he was so deaf he hardly noticed the music. And occasionally when he did, he liked it.

But today, Howie and Margaret would not plead with the old man to move into one or another of the beautiful assisted-living residences that they had found. Instead, they were at the house to pick up their wayward child. Julie had never come home. Instead, she had had Randy drive her all the way to Columbus to her grandfather's house in order to hide out. That was yesterday, Friday. She called her parents and she and her mother had carried on lengthy negotiations with the help of the Professor. Howie was away on business, making a quick trip back to South Carolina to see the golf course architect, Sean Donaldson. It was imperative Donaldson make an appearance at The Candlesticks as soon as possible. The issue of the course being somehow "wrecked" had to be blunted. What better way to blunt it than to show off a golf architect with a worldwide reputation?

Margaret had picked up her husband at the airport in Columbus and had headed straight for the Professor's house. The Professor had greeted them cordially at the door and had escorted them into the front parlor. The parlor was an unusual octagonal-shaped room, the signature room for the house. The room had no television or radio. It was furnished in a comfortable '50s style with overstuffed chairs and a big sofa. There were plenty of lamps. This was the room where the Professor read books. On a table by the front window (where the Christmas tree always stood) was a pitcher of iced tea and glasses. The Professor loved making flavored iced teas.

"It's raspberry today," he said as he went to pour glasses for the three of them.

"Well, has our daughter run away again? Where is she now?" Margaret asked from the doorway as Howie slunk over to his favorite chair, an overstuffed lounger with a blue and white flower pattern and a rectangular hassock. He was tired. He and Donaldson had stayed up late drinking Glenfiddich.

"She'll be along presently, Peg. Why don't you sit down?" The Professor handed her a glass of tea. He was the only person in the world who could get away with calling her Peg. But then, he was her father, which neither he nor she ever forgot.

The Professor fixed iced tea for Howie and then for himself. He took a painfully long time. Margaret was fully aware of how much longer the simplest tasks in the world now took her father. Eating was particularly excruciating. But you couldn't just reach over and grab the knife out of his hand and cut up his meat into the tiny morsels he preferred. Finally, he sat down on a side chair next to the table with the iced tea. But then he began fidgeting with his hearing aid. Howie was half-asleep and didn't care, but it was driving Margaret nuts.

"Well, our Julie was a naughty girl, so it seems," the Professor finally said.

"She's not eight years old, Dad. I wouldn't call her naughty," Margaret responded.

"Oh," the Professor said looking at his daughter, "then she's an adult."

"I'm not going to play your word games with you either. She's not an adult."

Howie roused himself. "She lied to us. I mean, well, I was out of town. But she lied to Margaret, Pop." Howie had settled on calling the Professor "Pop" a long, long time ago.

The Professor ignored his son-in-law and spoke directly to his daughter. "She said you demanded that she break up with her boyfriend. I've met him a couple of times. Yesterday, you know, he drove her here. Randy, isn't it? I don't know what you think is wrong with him."

"Julie can do better," Margaret responded icily. She hated that her father was meddling in this. She was furious that Julie had dragged him into it.

"I'm sure your mother could have done better, too," the Professor said dryly.

Mrs. Emerson was a *verboten* subject between Margaret and her father.

"Bring me up to speed here, Pop," Howie said. "What was Julie's excuse?"

"Excuse, Howie?" the Professor said as he leaned slightly in the direction of his son-in-law. "She didn't have an excuse. She said she went to Cleveland with the film club or some group and came home with her boyfriend."

Margaret jumped in. "Yes, except she was supposed to come home with the *French* Club. Instead, she forged a note from me to her teacher excusing her from the group. That's the lie," Margaret declared. "I have no idea where she stayed or with whom she stayed Thursday night."

"Well, that's the rub, all right," agreed the Professor.

"Did you happen to ask her about college?" Howie ventured from his comfortable chair. "We just can't pin her down."

The Professor raised his hand and Howie realized he hadn't heard the question. He repeated it loudly. Maybe if Julie was listening somewhere in the house, she would hear it too.

The Professor nodded. "She talked about it. But she's not ready to decide. I wouldn't rush her."

"Rush her?" Howie exclaimed taking his feet off the hassock for emphasis. "I'm sorry, Pop, but everyone else in her class who's going to college is all set."

"So, you're sure she's going to college?" the old man asked.

Howie sunk back in his chair in exasperation. Margaret chipped in: "Aren't you, of all people, encouraging her to go to college, Dad?"

"Oh, I'm sure she'll go to college, Peg. But it won't be because you or Howie or I tell her to go. Or Randy either for that matter."

"We want her to play golf," Howie pleaded.

"I don't know if she wants to play golf," the Professor said. "It's not you, it's what *she* wants."

Margaret's own exasperation finally broke through: "Where is she, Dad? I think it's time for her to join the conversation."

"She'll be along," the Professor said absently as he again fiddled with his hearing aid.

Margaret found a seat and the three of them waited in a silent triangle in the octagonal room. They waited and waited. Barely talking. They waited half an hour and then Margaret went looking around the house. The rest of the house was empty. They went into the kitchen and fixed sandwiches because Howie hadn't eaten all day. They waited again. Finally, they were tired of waiting and they got back in the car and drove the 30 miles home to Stowe Towne.

They were mad and worried; concerned and frustrated. *This is a god-damn no-win situation*, Howie kept muttering over and over to himself until Margaret told him to be quiet.

⌒

It had sprinkled at dawn, scaring the Millers to death. But now, as rally time approached, it was a beautiful Memorial Day morning. The Millers attended the Memorial Day service. There were upward of 200 Stowe Towne citizens clustered around the speakers' platform, although the Millers were fully aware that half the people were band parents following the Union Generals. The Union Generals Marching Corps was a large, award-winning high school band that had a very aggressive booster organization and a very dedicated following. If any of the Union Generals' athletic teams had half as much support, they'd be state champs. They did not and never were.

The Millers did not go to the cemetery and had to endure more than an hour of nervous waiting as the clock on the front of the red brick courthouse crept toward noon. Part of the time they were preoc-cupied stringing the red and white **SAVE THE CANDLESTICKS** sign across the front of the platform. But they still worried to each other: Would anyone show up? Was this a complete bust? They had called all the television and radio stations in Columbus. How embarrassing would it be if *they* came and no people showed up? May thought to herself that perhaps she would just have to resign from being president of the DUA out of pure humiliation. Of course, they had called Peter Onear and Mara Fish at the *Dispatch*. Perfect follow-up story, Mr. Miller thought. He felt somewhat more confident than his wife. He considered himself media-savvy. And he truly thought there would be an adequate crowd. He had made too many personal phone calls. His friends better not let him down.

A few cars began to park around the square, although a number of the folks were obviously on their way to the traditional Sunday brunch at the Maple Lodge. But gradually people drifted through the beautiful pink and white flowering trees that dotted the square and stood in front of the platform and its sign. Then the truck from Channel 10 in Columbus showed up and stopped in a no-parking zone right in front of the statue. Mr. Miller rushed over to meet the reporter, a young black woman named Jolene Walters whom he recognized from the station's nightly news. He thrust a news release in her hand and then after a few pleasantries made to rush away. Had to give her the impression that this was very important business.

Charley and Lincoln arrived all combed and in suits. May was at the side of the platform surrounded by a gaggle of DUA stalwarts. Mr. Miller worked the gathering crowd, shaking hands and thanking people for coming. He felt good in one sense because he was obviously going to be in front of friends. However, that mostly meant he was also going to be preaching to the converted. But wasn't that what news coverage was all about?

Speaking of news, Mr. Miller spotted Robert Redford, the mid-'50s former owner and current editor of the *Stowe Towne Bugle*. Redford was distantly related to the Hanovers, one of the original families. But obviously on the distaff side. He was a sourpuss and it had more to do than unfortunately ending up with a movie star's name. The *Bugle* was the town rag that no longer even covered town council meetings or school board meetings in depth. Redford had been a good enough fellow for many years, in Mr. Miller's opinion, but had gotten screwed up by his son.

It was ironic. Redford had groomed his son to take over the paper and the kid had dutifully gone off to college and gotten a journalism degree. He came back and took over the paper all right; however, what he really did was use it to create an expanded printing business. In almost no time, the new Redford Printing became a very, very successful printing business that allowed the son to buy out his own father. The business became the fourth largest employer in the county behind Allied Pipes, the school system, and local government. The kid, Tim, did not give a damn about journalism, but kept the paper going because of his father. So Bob ended up working for his kid (who lived a pretty high life-style for Stowe Towne) and the paper was downsized about fifty percent. It printed school lunch menus, garbage pickup schedules, Cub Scout meeting announcements, and not much more.

When Mr. Miller went over to shake hands with Redford, he noticed that Will Boyd was with the editor. What a pair, he thought. Those two prove that you don't have to be an old coot to be eccentric.

"Bob, good of you to come. Will, I think we've met at the café. I'm Mr. Miller."

"Of course, Mr. Miller," Will said shaking hands.

"Quite a turnout," Bob said.

Mr. Miller could not tell if the newspaperman was being sarcastic or not. "I'm happy with it on such short notice. Just glad you're here."

"Well, we always got to do a feature on Memorial Day. Thought I'd stick around and see what you had to say."

Mr. Miller smiled, but felt sorry for the guy. He looked a wreck wearing an old green cardigan. Was a heavy drinker, of course, and had reason to be. His wife long ago sided with their son and worked on the printing side. Very sad story.

"Here's a press release," Mr. Miller offered. "Summarizes our major points."

Redford accepted the paper and shrugged. "Frankly, it doesn't seem like a big deal. Something about this business bothers me. But I can't put my finger on it. Anyway, do you know what you're doing?"

Mr. Miller bristled at both Redford's tone and insinuation, but his years of being an attorney hid his reaction. Thank God, he thought, at least May wasn't nearby. She would be offended by the way Redford looked, acted, and talked. Plus, he had a peculiar smell. Maybe it was Boyd who smelled.

"Well, Bob, I hope we say some convincing things for you. Show you how important this is to Stowe Towne. If you'll excuse me, I guess it's time to get started."

The platform party was gathered at the bottom of the five step metal stairs. Mr. Miller led May, Charley, and Lincoln up the steps and realized at once that he had made a mistake. He had not cleared away all the chairs from the Memorial Day presentation. There were eight chairs. It would look like speakers didn't show up. Well, nothing could be done about it now.

In addition, some kids were making a racket playing over on the old cannon by the front door of the courthouse. He knew he would have to ignore them; couldn't yell at little kids in front of people.

Mr. Miller stepped up to the microphone and podium. He had had to pay $125 for the town to leave up the stand and sound system for a couple of extra hours. It was robbery. They wouldn't have even taken it down by now. Everybody at the planning meetings at the house Saturday night had chipped in some cash and some of the DUA ladies not present had contributed. The total had come to $162.50. But for now Mr. Miller was going to save that for the start-up cash for a Save The Candlesticks Fund. He had paid current expenses out of his own pocket.

He surveyed the mostly familiar faces spread out in front of him. Decent enough crowd. The Channel 10 crew was set up slightly off to his left. He noted that Bob Redford and Will Boyd had actually boosted themselves up and were sitting on the edge of the memorial to the heroes, to the platform's right. They were lounging right under the outstretched arm of Major Howard. It was a no-no to climb on the statue. You could chase kids off, teenagers off, and strangers off. But no one, not even Police Chief Hank Anderson, who was probably sitting in one of Stowe Towne's blue cop cars parked across the street by the Gettysburg Café, would chase Bob Redford. He didn't do it often any-more, but Redford occasionally still wrote nasty front-page editorials. Will Boyd might get chased by the police if he was alone, but he would be safe as long as he was with the editor.

"Thank you for coming on this beautiful Memorial Day," Mr. Miller began. "Most of you know me. I'm May Miller's husband." He paused to embrace the mild laughter. The comment did not have quite the same charm as JFK saying that he had only accompanied Jackie to Paris.

Mr. Miller continued: "We're here to save The Candlesticks, our historic golf course. But we're not here just because some of us like to play golf on a wonderful old course. We're here because everything about this proposed housing development is bad news for the citizens of Stowe Towne.

"Now, we have three speakers who will address important, different points and then I'll be back to sum up. First, to speak about The Candlesticks' historic importance is my wife and the President of the local chapter of the Daughters of the Union Army, May Miller."

As May stepped up smartly to the podium and started in on the Stowe Towne history related to the golf course, Peter Onear lurked at the back of the crowd. He was estimating the number of people much lower than Mr. Miller's guess. If he hadn't been so bored and pissed about being here at all, he would have just counted the people. The old lady was going on and on about Stowe Towne. Who gave a good god-damn? But the crowd seemed hypnotized. God, he didn't want to be here. He had been happy to throw a fit and hand off the story to Mara Fish. This story was going nowhere. But Mara was on another story and his editor insisted that he come out and see if he could do a follow-up to their coauthored real estate page article. Memorial Day, after the traffic fatality count, was always a slow news day.

Peter's eyes drifted over to an attractive young woman who was trying to keep a toddler in tow. The woman wore blue shorts and what looked like one of those designer-type T-shirts. Long brown hair pulled back. She bent down to admonish the toddler and presented an outstanding view from behind. No husband or boyfriend seemed to be around. But Peter wasn't about to get stuck with a kid like that. No, sir. But then, maybe the kid wasn't hers. Maybe she was only babysitting for her sister or friend. He started, almost unconsciously, to drift over toward her when the crowd began applauding, marking the end of May's remarks. Hmm, he thought, I hope she didn't say anything important.

Like watching a tennis match, Peter kept moving his head back and forth from the rear of the young woman to the speaker's stand. The old man had returned to the microphone to introduce the next speaker. Peter remembered him from the Café when he had had lunch with Polly on their way up to the Pottawa Lodge. Mr. Miller had called him on Sunday and Peter had remembered the way he had identified himself as *Mr. Miller*. But he did not let on that they had had the conversation in the restaurant. Miller was announcing the next speaker as some sort of retired county engineer when a voice out of the crowd suddenly interrupted. That got Peter's full attention. This had not appeared to be a crowd that would do any protesting. He strained to see who had spoken up.

"Mr. Miller! Mr. Miller! I'd like to have a word. Can I speak?"

Mr. Miller, like Peter Onear, was surprised to hear a voice from the crowd. He had not expected any protest or opposition. The choir in church never interrupts the minister. But the voice was familiar. He peered off to the right past the front of the statue.

"It's me, Mr. Miller, Sticks Bergman." Sticks made his way through the crowd toward the platform.

"Sticks?" Mr. Miller asked too loudly into the microphone so the name boomed out to everyone.

Sticks stopped below the podium and spoke to Mr. Miller. "Believe me, Mr. Miller, I fully support what you're doing here and I think you'll want to hear what I have to say. I meant to be here when you started, but I got hung-up on an errand."

Mr. Miller realized that anything would be better than listening to Charley Johnson drone on about sewage volume. "Come on up, Sticks, and say your peace."

Sticks didn't bother walking around to the steps, but instead hoisted himself up onto the stand and ducked under the single metal railing. He straightened himself up and stood at the podium. He was wearing blue Docker slacks and a white Candlesticks golf shirt. Of course, he spoke too loudly into the microphone and it squeaked back at him. He laughed nervously and adjusted his voice.

"Thank you, Mr. Miller. Mrs. Miller. Friends, most of you know me. I'm sure that most of you also know that my wife Sammi and I live next to The Candlesticks Golf Course out on The Pike. We've lived there for about 20 years now. And you know that I occasionally play a few rounds of golf at The Candlesticks."

Mild laughter, but the crowd edged closer, sensing something more interesting than a Stowe Towne history lesson.

"I came here today because I wanted to let everyone know, especially Mr. Howard and the Board that runs The Candlesticks, that my wife and I are opposed to changing the course in any way and building a housing development there. Now it's conceivable that my wife and I could profit from such a housing development. After all, we own the land in back of our house that is right next to the course. Right next to the 18th fairway, if you've played there. You can make a lot of money subdividing land for new houses.

"However, we like our property the way it is and we like the golf course the way it is. We don't see any reason to change it."

There was a smattering of applause as Sticks stopped to catch his breath. He looked over and saw Randy and his brother Hal. When he had made his decision, he had called up and apologized to Hal and explained the situation. That's when Hal had told him about the rally.

Sticks continued: "My wife knows real estate here in the county and there are much better places to put a housing development than to put it here and destroy a famous golf course. Sammi is a real estate agent and is partners with Bruce Dean in Dean Realty. Most of you know that. However, it is not generally known because his name wasn't in the article in the *Dispatch*, that Mr. Dean is one of the main movers behind this housing development. He has contacted Cliner Development in Cleveland, one of the largest housing developers in Ohio. A man from Cliner has already come down here to tour the course. My son Randy was introduced to him. If Cliner gets control of this, there will be no local control or business. Believe me, any of you who think that you'll make money from this development won't make a cent."

The crowd stirred and edged closer. This was news. Big news tinged with gossip.

Onear, reluctantly, got his pad out of his hip pocket and started taking notes.

The Channel 10 cameraman moved closer for a better shot of Sticks.

"Sammi isn't here with us at this rally. That's because she's meeting right now with Mr. Dean and she is dissolving their partnership. And I'm here to announce that Stowe Towne and Pottawa County will soon have a new real estate firm, Bergman Realty."

Now this was real news. The crowd almost surged forward. Robert Redford even hopped off the base of the statue, abandoning Will Boyd. The police could close in.

"And you have our word on it, Bergman Realty *will not* be selling lots on The Candlesticks Golf Course!"

Now there were even a few cheers. This was unbelievable. Sammi Bergman and Bruce Dean together had sold or bought houses for more than half the people in the crowd. They had sold and bought houses for *all* the people on the speakers' platform. If May Miller hadn't been sitting down, she'd have fallen down. She glanced at her knot of DUA supporters just a few feet from the platform steps. They were all in the act of swooning. Good Lord!

Sticks was warming to his task. In fact, he was damn hot. This was fun!

"I don't know exactly how we can stop Mr. Howard and others from developing The Candlesticks. I guess that's for lawyers like Mr. Miller here to figure out. We owe a debt to the Millers for getting this opposition organized.

"I do know, though, that Stowe Towne is a small, friendly town where we do things the right way. We don't go sneaking around. We don't get outside people to come in and hand over our public *treasures* like The Candlesticks. We support each other and we work together."

Sticks paused. He didn't have any other surprises to drop on the crowd. In fact, he didn't really have anything else to say. But he had to finish up somehow.

"Well, thank you all for letting me say these few words. And, ah, now I'll turn it back over to Mr. Miller."

Sticks stepped away from the microphone and the crowd now loudly applauded. Mr. Miller, who always had a keen sense when to push a jury and when to leave a jury alone, seized the moment. No one wanted to hear Charley or Lincoln. That was obvious. What they wanted was some plan. All right, he had a plan. He stepped up and gripped the side of the podium. The applause subsided.

"No one could speak more eloquently than Sticks Bergman has. Tomorrow at the Gettysburg Café there across the street, there will be a petition to save The Candlesticks. You stop in and sign it. We've already started a fund to save the golf course. There's more than $150 in it already. You can donate at the café if you want. And then in next week's *Bugle*, there will be an announcement about our next plan of action. We will investigate our legal options. But I will tell you now, that this battle to save the golf course can best be won in the court of public opinion. Talk to your friends and family members. Tell them we don't want strangers in town. Tell them that we want to save the golf course. Thank you, and have a great rest of the Memorial Day."

Onear smiled at the old man waving his arms on the podium. Quite a performance. He had underestimated the fellow when they shared a hot roast beef sandwich at the Gettysburg. Well, this headline would attract some attention: "Proposed Housing Development Splits Town." Peter hurried forward to talk to this Bergman fellow who already was cornered by some guy in a ratty green sweater. He noticed that the Channel 10 people were also moving forward.

Mr. Miller, meanwhile, was trying to calm down both Charley and Lincoln who had both been inspired by Sticks and then suddenly canceled and deflated by Mr. Miller. May flew down the steps to the ladies and the gossip about Sammi Bergman and Bruce Dean twittered among them. They talked as they hurried off to their cars. There were other ladies to call right away who would be very interested.

Randy and his Uncle Hal stood back observing the scene in front of them. The energized crowd. The TV camera and trucks. The knots of animated citizens. It was quite a remarkable scene in Stowe Towne terms.

"Is your mother really forming a new real estate agency?" Hal asked after a minute.

Randy shrugged his broad shoulders. "It's news to me, Uncle Hal. It's all news to me."

chapter eleven

CELEBRATE! CELEBRATE! DANCE TO THE MUSIC

Sticks and Sammi had planned to have a Memorial Day cookout at their house with a few friends in celebration of their respective morning announcements. Sticks had gone to the new Kroger's on the road out toward Allied Pipes and had stocked up on hot dogs, hamburger, potato salad, chips, and picnic supplies. The store was crowded. Many of the citizens of Stowe Towne had, at least temporarily, abandoned the ancient Hanover's Grocery in town for the glitzy new Kroger Super Store that was next to the town's first fast food restaurant, a McDonald's. The crowd in Kroger's resulted in Sticks having to wait in line. Not to mention the fact that he couldn't find the mustard. It ended up being in the Gourmet Section. *Yellow French's Mustard is not gourmet food*, Sticks thought. Anyway, that's why he was late to the rally. He had intended to talk to Mr. Miller beforehand about speaking. Nevertheless, his late arrival at the square and his subsequent dramatic entrance at the rally had worked out rather well, he concluded.

Almost too well, in fact, in terms of the food. Afterward, Sticks kept telling people to "Stop on out!" as they congratulated him. Of course, his brothers and their families were already coming. And Sammi had invited Matt and Laura Robinson since Laura was jumping ship with Sammi and would be her assistant at the new Bergman Realty. So people told other people and pretty soon the Bergmans had a full house and a full deck. Cars filled their large driveway and were parked in front of the house up and down The Pike. Sticks had to send Randy with his young cousin Cheryl to pick up extra beer at Hal's house and a few more franks at the store. Randy had the good sense to go to Hanover's Grocery in town since it was much more convenient.

Sticks fired up the Weber with hickory-smoked charcoal. Meanwhile, off to his right, the older fellows, Budweisers in hand, stood in a row along the deck railing looking at The Candlesticks' 18th green and fairway. They were like passengers on a cruise ship waiting to dock at a golf resort and salivating at the scene. The course was crowded since it was a holiday. The men weren't really close enough to follow play—especially with their fading eyesight—but they could see a good shot into the green and they could watch players do little war dances or high fives when they made good shots or toss clubs and kick their bags when they made bad shots.

"It's a beautiful sight, don't you think, Lincoln?" Mr. Miller said to his brother-in-law.

"Yes, it is," Lincoln agreed, wishing he had a gin and tonic instead of a Bud in his hand.

"The course is in great shape despite all the rain this spring," Doc Parsons added. Doc had played in the morning with his son Pat who was an otolaryngologist in Columbus. Pat had had to get home to the family so Doc, seeing the crowd on Sticks' deck, had just wandered over from the 18th green. Everyone was glad to see Doc.

Doc went on to ask about the rally. The old fellows gave him a detailed account. The news that Sammi was forming her own real estate agency especially intrigued him. He had not yet confided in anyone, but he and his wife Brenda had pretty much decided to sell their Jones Street house and move permanently to a condo down in Fort Myers Beach. Maybe Sammi would be willing to work out a deal. After all, their house on Jones Street was a well-known "historical" home. It was bound to be a high-profile sale. He wondered if Sammi might even waive her commission just for the privilege of listing the house.

At that moment, Sammi was not thinking about real estate or commissions. Nor was she able to enjoy the moment or savor the remembrance of the look of surprise and shock on Bruce Dean's face when she told him she was dissolving their partnership and opening her own agency. Instead, she was stuck in the kitchen frantically preparing food for this horde of people who had suddenly descended upon their house. Her sister-in-law Cathy, Paul's wife, was offering minimal assistance. Cathy was more interested in Sammi as a captive audience who had to listen to her colorful recountings of her recent trip with Paul to Las Vegas. *The Luxor is fabulous!* Cathy could have been at least minimally excited about Sammi's news. But Sammi knew from long family experience that if something didn't impact Cathy or her two "precious" daughters directly, she had little interest.

"I have some cans of baked beans," Sammi said pulling down cans from the cupboard, "and I think we'll need them. Sticks didn't buy nearly enough potato salad to go with things. Would you mind opening these, Cathy?"

Cathy audibly sighed and reluctantly got off the kitchen stool where she had been sitting at the far end of the kitchen counter. She had a pretty, round face and natural blond hair, but she was overweight and moved slowly. Sammi had originally given her the job of separating the hot dog buns from one another. But by the end of 15 minutes, she had only finished two eight-packs of buns.

"So," Cathy asked, "how did Bruce take the news?"

Sammi looked up from where she was searching for her big stoneware casserole. "Oh, well, he was surprised. Didn't see it coming. That's what he said. 'Sammi, I didn't see this coming.'" She smiled as she remembered the apoplexy reflected on Bruce's face.

"Well," Cathy said in a tone that carried a distinct edge, "*no one* saw it coming. You could've called, you know. It does affect your family." Cathy pressed the lever and the can of Campbell's baked beans whirled around the can opener.

"First of all, Cathy, Sticks and I just decided this last night. Secondly, I'm not sure how it affects you. Unless you might want me to sell your house." Sammi spied the casserole in the very back of the cupboard. "Ah-ha! There it is."

Another can whirled around under Cathy's less than watchful eye. "I was just thinking about your income and all. Doesn't it cost money to start something like that?"

"Of course, but . . ."

"Maybe you could use that room in the lumberyard's office. Paul's not sure they can afford to turn that into his wine store. They still haven't finalized the loan from the bank, you know."

So, that's it, Sammi thought as she ran water to rinse out the seldom-used casserole. Cathy was probably worried about Sticks asking for a larger share of the lumberyard's profit if Sammi suddenly lost her real estate income. Well, if Cathy was really worried about money, all she had to do was stop buying those little girls new wardrobes every month.

The third and last can of beans whirled around the opener.

"I don't think that would work out," Sammi said. "Really, Cathy, I plan to hit the road running. Bruce agreed...actually, he didn't have a choice. I plan to take most of my clients with me. I might lose a few who will decide to stay with an established firm. True, I won't get new listings until I get my name out there. Do some advertising."

"Which costs money," Cathy noted.

"You could help by talking to your friends," Sammi suggested. "You know, if they want to trade up."

Cathy didn't respond and retreated back to the buns while Sammi retrieved the cans and started dumping the beans into the casserole. She opened her mouth and was going to explain about a new office requiring less overhead and other economies that she had already thought about. But then she closed her mouth. Cathy wouldn't have a clue. Sammi decided she might as well let it go.

On the deck, Sticks retrieved a beer from under the melting ice in the dark green Coleman cooler. He passed a hand over the coals and decided that they were hot enough to start the dogs and burgers. He was feeling pretty pleased with himself. He really thought he and Sammi had made the right decision. The right financial decision and, as Sammi had pointed out, the right moral decision. Sticks was a little surprised by the ethics aspect of the question. He thought he was a moral person. He just seldom, if ever, thought about morality. But he felt he understood that this was the right thing to do: oppose the development of The Candlesticks.

Why ruin something old and beautiful just to make money?

Sticks recalled Sammi's explanation of real estate morality, although a question had occurred to him that he wisely suppressed. What about Sammi's efforts a while back to convert the Hanover Mansion into apartments? She had explained that apartments were desperately needed in Stowe Towne. At the time, Sticks had little interest in the project or her explanation. However, like Sammi had argued then, Howie and others were arguing now that a new upscale housing development was desperately needed in Stowe Towne. So, was Sammi being a hypocrite? Which was more historically important: the Hanover Mansion or The Candlesticks Golf Course?

Sticks thoughtfully turned the meat as the party buzzed behind him. Occasionally, someone clapped him on the back and peered over his shoulder at lunch. He thought about selfishness—another topic he seldom contemplated. From one point of view, they were not being selfish. They could have gone with the flow. Turn this farmland stretching out beyond the deck into prime real estate. Sold lots and houses and made money. Well, they've decided against that now. Yet, he realized, he and Sammi were still being selfish. She was going off on her own forming her own company and he was preserving his comfortable life style. Work when he pleased and play golf all of the time.

He never thought of it as selfish before. It was just the way they lived. Or, rather how he lived. Is it moral to do something for purely selfish reasons? Whoa! This type of thinking could give him a headache.

Fortunately, before he needed an aspirin, Delia Long came up beside him and punched him on his right arm causing him to drop the barbecue tongs on the grill. "Hell of a speech, Sticks," she said.

"Delia, I didn't see you at the rally." Sticks retrieved the tongs with his Homer Simpson barbecue mitt. The mitt was last Christmas's traditional humorous "Dad" present.

"Oh, I was there. Off behind the statue. I wouldn't have missed it."

Sticks noted that Delia was drinking what looked like Scotch on the rocks. So, the liquor cabinet had been breached. Delia also had to be the most festive party-goer present. She was wearing an orange tent-like top and yellow slacks. A beacon of poor taste.

"So," Sticks said recovering his composure, "did it do any good? My talk, I mean."

"I had the impression that you were singing to the choir. But you'll get some media coverage and that's what you were really after. Correct?"

"I suppose so. I wasn't in on the planning stage."

"Well, I'm all for tradition, you know," Delia said staring off at the golf course.

Sticks piled up some of the burgers and dogs on the edge of the round grill as they finished cooking. He started fresh meat in the middle of the grill where it was hottest. They would need it. If Delia Long had found her way to their deck, the whole world must be here. "How's your course this spring?" he asked, since Delia somehow seemed mesmerized by the view.

"Wet," she finally replied. "Slow and wet. But two months from now the guys will be complaining that I never water."

"They ought to know by now that you never water anyway."

"Hey, I might this year. I'm also thinking about cutting the fairways shorter than the rough."

"Are the guys who play your course really ready for fairways?" he asked smiling.

"Careful, Sticks," Delia warned. "After all, my course might be your only alternative in town. What's to stop Howie now from banning you from The Candlesticks?"

Delia's comment affected Sticks like an errant second shot on number two slicing into the lake. How could that happen? But, of course, it *could* happen. He just hadn't thought of it. Now that he publicly announced his view, Howie could ban him from the course. Play my game or don't play at all. Was that legal? Could you ban someone from a golf course open to public play? Sticks didn't know. But even if he couldn't ban me, he could make life miserable. Bad tee times. No services. Certainly, no privilege.

Sticks remained motionless, thinking for so long, that Delia poked him again to warn him that the dogs were charring.

About then, Randy and Cheryl finally arrived with supplies. Sammi was just starting to serve the food. Food was spread out haphazardly on the dining room table. Piles of buns. Beans. Two big bowls of chips. Pickles. Potato salad. Macaroni salad that Randy had gotten. Ketchup. Mustard. And Sticks's first platter of dogs and burgers.

Sammi was thankful that Sticks had bought heavy-duty Chinet

plates. Maybe no one would spill food on the carpets. Particularly the light beige living room carpet. The old folks, of course, were heading into the living room complaining about the heat on the deck. Sammi decided to retreat back to the kitchen. Cathy was no longer there, having arranged it neatly to be the first one in the food line.

The kitchen, in fact, was empty except for Randy on one knee in front of the refrigerator restocking the shelves with his Uncle Hal's beer. He saved a few to take out to the deck to replenish the cooler.

"I think, after the last few hours, I deserve a beer," Sammi said to her son.

Randy looked up and handed his mother a cold Miller Genuine Draft.

She took pity on him. "Look, Randy, if you're not going to drive this afternoon, you can have one, too."

Randy finished his job, stood up, and closed the refrigerator door. He stacked three extra six packs on the counter. "That's okay, Mom, I already opened one." He walked over and retrieved his MGD from the counter. He didn't tell her, but actually this was his second beer. He and his 15-year-old cousin Cheryl—who was very mature for her age—had each had a can on the drive home from her house.

Sammi watched Randy gulp the beer and smiled a wan smile. She sat down in the breakfast nook. "So, did I do the right thing?" she asked.

Randy sat down across from her. "I guess. What do *you* think?"

"Randy, first of all, I want to assure you that there's money set aside for you to continue at Kent."

Randy grinned. "Mom, I really hadn't given that a thought."

She smiled back. "What do I know? Listen, how's it going with Julie? I'm thinking that there might be problems."

"Why do you think that?"

"Well, I mean now that we've drawn the line in the sand. Isn't that what they say these days?"

"By 'we' you mean you and Dad and Mr. and Mrs. Howard. You

haven't exactly been friends with them anyway."

"True, but..."

"And I'm still going out with Julie. Despite what you guys say."

Sammi sighed, "Randy, we..." She paused. His matter-of-fact defiance was so open and cheerful that it disarmed her. Her son had grown up and they had no control. That realization somehow took hold for the first time. She took a sip of beer and then said: "I guess you can't take everything your parents say seriously."

He laughed. "Don't worry, Mom, I don't."

Meanwhile, in the living room, May Miller sat at the very end of what she considered a very unattractive floral-patterned sofa. May was not comfortable in the Bergman home. She knew and liked Sammi, but considered her a "tradesperson." One didn't generally socialize with tradespeople, although there were exceptions. The Hanovers, or at least a branch of the Hanovers, had owned their grocery store in Stowe Towne for more than a hundred years. One of the dark secrets of the families, that May knew full well, was that during Prohibition, the Hanovers had imported the best liquor in all of central Ohio. The availability of good booze at The Candlesticks had been one reason for the golf course's early popularity.

But real estate agents were a little different than other tradespeople who were acceptable. Real estate agents often bordered on being unseemly, which was certainly the case with Bruce Dean no matter how charming he could be in person. Sammi projected a more honest front than Bruce, and May would absolutely use her if—horrors of horrors—she and Mr. Miller would ever need to sell their house. Yet, that was not a reason for her, May Miller, President of the DUA, to be out here on the Sunday of Memorial Day weekend eating *picnic* food.

In the center of her large white Chinet plate, May had deposited one single scoop of white potato salad. She poked at it with a flimsy white plastic fork. Suddenly, a young red-haired woman she vaguely recognized plopped down next to May. Did she know this woman from the Spring Fling? The woman sat down so exuberantly that even May's gelatinous ball of potato salad bounced up and down. She almost dropped her whole plate.

"Hi, I'm Laura Robinson," the young woman said. "I'm going to work with Sammi at the new agency." Laura balanced an enormous plate of food and a full can of Bud.

"Hello, I'm May Miller," May said, worried to death now that something from the young woman's plate would spill on her Ann Taylor skirt.

"Oh, I know who you are, Mrs. Miller. My husband and I met you at the Spring Fling. Everyone knows who you are."

May smiled at the compliment, although way in the back of her mind she wondered if it really was a compliment. Well, she had to respond nicely. "Isn't this a beautiful day?" she said.

Laura bit off a mouthful of hamburger. "Issh surf isf. Arff youff gonna ell youf hooose?"

"What?" May asked startled.

Laura tried to laugh and held up her beer to her mouth. After a second, she swallowed and said, "I'm sorry. I asked if you were going to sell your house?"

May stared wide-eyed. "Why, of course not, dear."

"That's all right," Laura said. "Sammi wants me to be more aggressive."

"Oh, but we don't have to be rude, young lady."

Laura, her ears clogged by the sound of her own chewing, said, "Please don't apologize, Mrs. Miller."

"I didn't apologize," May said.

"No, I mean it, don't. Just call us when you're ready to sell. Now, enough business," Laura said primly. "Tell me about those adorable grandkids. You do have grandchildren, don't you? May I call you May?"

That set Laura off giggling again and May resolved to get up out of the soft couch no matter how much effort it took.

A little after 3:00, Sticks, Randy, Matt Robinson, and Dan Ofman snuck out of the house to go play golf at The Candlesticks. Sticks was a little nervous that maybe Howie had already banned him from the course. However, everything seemed normal. They were getting off at 3:24 in place of a cancellation. The course was still packed with holiday and weekend golfers. Sticks normally would not have played at such a prime time. In fact, he should have been home saying goodbye to the last of the guests and then helping Sammi clean up. He left telling her to leave things until he got home although they both knew she would have it all done.

Sticks went in the clubhouse and down the hallway to Bip's office. He opened the door hoping Bip was there. He wanted to know the old pro's opinion about the possibility of his being banned from the course. But Bip wasn't there. Sticks looked over at his two sets of clubs, his regular Cobras and his new irons he had won from the mysterious Ray. On a whim, he quickly replaced his own irons with Ray's sticks.

Playing the first hole, Sticks thought he had died and gone to heaven. On the 490-yard, par-5 first hole, he hit Ray's three-iron onto the green with his second shot. He two-putted for a birdie. And then, *it got better!* Ray's sticks were the sweetest clubs he had ever swung. His drives using his own woods were average. His putting with his own putter was okay. But when he used Ray's irons the balls flew like magic. He finished the front nine at three under, a stroke better than his previous low of two under which he had only done once three years ago.

Imagine, with all this turmoil and upset, that this would suddenly happen to his game. He stood a little off from his group waiting to get on the 10th tee and play the back nine. Sticks looked at the plain unmarked metal heads of Ray's irons jutting out from his bag. It was a mystery. Why were these clubs so perfect? Who was Ray? Why did this happen now?

"We're up," Randy said, suddenly breaking the spell.

Sticks shrugged. Well, let's see how they do on the back nine.

Meanwhile, Howie Howard sat alone on his large, empty deck staring at the fairway and green of the first hole of The Candlesticks. He watched a parade of hackers and weekend golfers march by—the majority of them hoping that they would at least break a hundred. A few balls came perilously close to Howie's deck. The left side of the fairway was staked so Howie's yard and deck were both way, way out-of-bounds. Only the worst golfer hitting the worst second (or maybe third) shot imaginable could come near the deck. Most of these fools decided against retrieving their balls—especially when they spotted Howie staring at them from the deck. But one twosome in a cart drove right up on his lawn, impervious of his presence. Howie didn't say a word and just stared.

He was about to go in the house when he saw Sticks and Randy go by. The father and son were unmistakable. Randy was a hulk. And Sticks had an odd hitch at the very top of his swing. Of course, he had grown up with Sticks and probably could have picked him out of a crowd at twice the distance without the golf swing. And Randy...well, Randy might very well end up being his son-in-law.

Howie finished his tall glass of tonic water. He didn't even have the energy to drink liquor. Julie had finally come home. One of the Professor's former colleagues had driven her and the Professor out to the house that morning from Columbus. There had been a long, protracted scene that the Professor in his obtuse manner had refereed. The drama, however, had not ended in any resolution. They all had agreed to at least "get through Julie's high school graduation." Then they would do some more "talking." But the main issues of Randy and college were still hanging fire.

Julie, though, was only a part of Howie's depression. He had taken phone calls for more than four hours about Stick's speech. Some from The Candlesticks' Board whose members suddenly realized they couldn't slip by, just being interested bystanders. They all knew about Sticks's speech. The guy had played his card. And Sammi as well. Howie had actually been somewhat amused by Bruce who called just after Sammi left his office. Everyone knew Sammi had always carried the load at the agency. Bruce would have to work harder now. And he would have to pay attention to The Candlesticks' development and not just dump the day-to-day work off on Sammi so he could go screw some babe in Columbus.

Nevertheless, this was not good news. This was exactly what Don Morgan from Cliner feared, local organized opposition. But if Cliner pulled out, so what? Maybe that would actually be good. Howie figured that he and his allies would be rid of that carpetbagger label. They could lay contracts on some locals. For example, Bergman Lumber. Who gave a shit where you bought lumber and nails? Howie bet that Hal and Paul could make their brother Sticks shut up quickly if substantial business was on the line. They'd stick it to Sticks.

Howie smiled, but his smile quickly faded. He didn't feel like smiling. He felt contemplative. Howie was in a mood similar to Sticks's mood earlier in the day when Sticks was standing over the grill and thinking about ethics and selfishness. But Howie was thinking about loneliness and isolation. He seldom thought this deeply. He tried to think metaphorically, although he did not know that was what he was trying to do. First, he thought of himself as a captain going down with his ship. But that was far too depressing. Then he remembered a few months before going to a Harry Conick, Jr. concert. It was a benefit concert for the Columbus Zoo. Howie knew the Director of Development at the Zoo—a college fraternity brother—who volunteered to introduce Howie and Margaret to the singer.

After the concert, Howie and Margaret were ushered with three other couples into a long, narrow room behind the stage. The room had scattered tables and old folding chairs. Maybe it was used as a lunchroom. Harry was sitting at a table by himself all the way at the other end of the room. His coat was off. His tux tie was untied. He had a white towel around his neck. He was drinking a large glass of clear liquid. Water? Gin? He stared straight ahead at a blank dirty white wall and did not acknowledge the four couples standing nervously at the other end of the room. The Development Director had ducked out of the room to hurry up an elderly couple lagging behind.

Nothing happened for exactly one minute. No one moved or said anything. Time for Howie seemed to stand still. He would never forget that tableaux—that was what Margaret later derisively called it. The moment thoroughly annoyed her. But Howie interpreted it as the classic lonely man—hero?—who had done something (or was about to do something) great.

That, Howie thought, was his situation now. Beset by problems, but on the verge of greatness. There, on his deck, Howie Howard decided that he was Harry Connick, Jr.

chapter twelve

EXPERTS

As managing partner, David Canello had a very nice corner office in the firm. Large windows overlooked a portion of downtown Columbus—not quite in sight of the capitol, but there was a passable view of the Scioto River. The furniture was mahogany with contemporary use of teal and rose for the fabrics. There was a big screen Sony TV in one corner ostensibly for CNN, although ESPN—especially Thursday and Friday afternoon golf coverage—was a more popular channel choice. He never turned on his IBM Aptiva that sat poised for action on the credenza behind his desk.

Canello was expected to spend time managing the firm's business and take care of nasty little personnel problems that cropped up among the secretaries, paralegals, and junior partners. In truth, he spent no more time than he ever had to spend in the office, leaving most of the management to his long-time Administrative Assistant, Bonnie Wicks. Bonnie was affectionately known among the firm's employees as the Wicked Wicks of the West.

Bonnie knocked discreetly and opened Canello's office door for Tom Duke, Jr. It was almost 6:00 p.m. and Bonnie gave a quick wave of her hand indicating to Canello that she was *out of here*. Canello gave her a wave back and greeted Tom like a long-lost client even though they had just played golf together at The Candlesticks four days before on the Saturday of Memorial Day weekend.

"Tom, Tom, good to see you. Cocktail hour, I think. Long past. How about...Canadian Club, right?"

"All right, you twisted my arm. Cindy will be with those art queers for another hour or so."

Canello opened up his liquor cabinet and poured drinks. The junior Tom Duke was bigoted, sexist, and a general asshole. Too bad he was on The Candlesticks' Board and David had to be civil to him. Otherwise, he'd kick his ass *out of here*.

"Well, you may not realize it, Tom, but it's quite an honor to be appointed to the Central Ohio Arts Council. Especially for someone as young as your wife."

Tom grunted and accepted his drink: "They're still a bunch of fuckin' queers." He limped over to Canello's long couch and eased himself down.

Tom Duke, Jr., had been on his way to a career as a major league pitcher. But he blew out his knee fielding a bunt in his first month of playing Double A ball. He had jumped right to the Double A level coming out of Arizona State where he had gone to college to play baseball year-round. He already had had three wins in four starts in Double A. He was labeled a "can't miss" major leaguer. But when he blew his knee, he blew it so it couldn't be fixed. Still could hit a golf ball farther than most, although it was painful to watch him swing on his gimpy leg. The leg caused about one out of every five shots to either end up in the woods or an adjoining fairway.

Canello sat down on the other end of the couch. "As a lawyer and friend, Tom, I have to tell you that they aren't a bunch of fucking queers. They're rich arts patrons, most of whom can call up the governor whenever they want and use his first name in the conversation. You keep saying that type of stuff out loud and somebody important is going to hear you. And that will end up hurting Cindy."

Tom grunted again and took a drink. He eyed the lawyer balefully. Canello always talked to him like that, but he didn't care. Canello was friends with his father and it was important to Tom that he be friends with his father's friends. Tom had no intention of working for a living even though he officially was employed as an executive in his father-in-law's restaurant corporation. Cindy's Greek immigrant father owned 11 McDonalds franchises in the Columbus area. Cindy's father, however, worked his ass off and she also had sisters who would no doubt someday split up the inheritance when the old man died of a heart attack from overworking. Hard work and the sisters were both problems for Tom, although her father made a hell of an income and was generous to a fault with his money. The restaurant business did very, very well. Plus, Nick Poppullas loved baseball because it was so American and viewed his son-in-law as a brooding, tragic figure because of his aborted big league career. As a result, he cut Tom a lot of slack.

"I suppose you saw the paper," Tom said.

"I never liked Sticks Bergman," Canello replied.

"The son-of-a-bitch."

"Ironically," Canello mused, "it was always Howie who defended Sticks when some issue would come up at the course. You know, they were high school classmates and then their kids were dating. Maybe they still are dating. I don't know."

"Well, what are we going to do?"

Canello laughed. "You sound like I should arrange to have him rubbed out. Put a contract out on him or something."

Tom stared moodily into his drink and didn't respond to the

lawyer's ribbing.

Canello sighed. "Look, Tom, this was Howie's deal. All you guys on the Board gave your approval because Howie promised you a big payoff in the future. Howie didn't bother talking to me beforehand and then just sprung it on me at the Board meeting in May. You were there. When I tried to ask some questions, he adjourned the meeting and you guys all bailed. You heard him say he didn't need our firm's legal representation even though I'm the goddamn lawyer for the golf course. He didn't bother talking to Bip, the club pro. He didn't bother talking to Warren, the general manager, or the staff. Now that's his prerogative. He's the head of the Board and he has the power because of the Accord."

"I know, that's what Dad said. But..."

"But nothing, Tom. You're the third Board member who's talked to me. Did you call Howie first?"

"Yes."

"The other Board members called Howie as well. I'm sure he told you the same thing that he told the others. Everything is under control. The newspaper article doesn't mean a thing. He expected some opposition around town. He'll talk to everybody at the next regularly scheduled Board meeting."

Tom nodded. "You're right. That about sums up what he said."

Canello gestured with open palms. "Well, at least you talked to him," he said. "He hasn't even called me. But like I said, I'm *just* the lawyer for the goddamn course."

"I know..."

"You guys can't come to me now and start whining. My hands are tied." Canello looked at young Tom Duke in disgust. If his distant ancestor had had the same lack of guts, he thought, the North never would have won the Civil War.

⌐

Late afternoon the next day, Thursday, the three Bergman brothers, Sticks, Hal, and Paul, sat on crates in the nearly empty room at the front of their lumberyard building. The room was just off from the main store. It had two regular-sized windows that looked out onto the front sidewalk. There were two doors, one leading directly into the store and one leading into a hallway that led out back into the lumberyard compound. The room measured about 18 feet by 22 feet. For some unfathomable reason, the room had always been a pain in the ass.

Over the years, the room had been an office, a paint store, a home decorating "center" (run by two ditzy women who drove everyone nuts), an employee lounge (bad idea), and, for the last two years, a locked and mostly empty storage room. Now Paul was on the verge of achieving his dream of turning the room into the "Stowe Towne Wine Shoppe."

"I've always wondered," Hal mused, "if you pronounce the final *e*. Is it just shop or shop-*pay*? I mean, it's an important question. We're going to have to *tell* people."

"Believe me, Hal, it's just plain shop," Sticks advised.

Sticks and Hal had long ago agreed in principle to their younger brother's desire to create the wine shoppe. But now the cold reality of actually laying out money and stocking the store was setting in. Minor problems that had been glossed over were now looming larger. Like hiring sales clerks who at least had some knowledge about wines. You couldn't hire high school kids for the job. And Paul couldn't be around all the time every day.

Paul's interest in wines was in and of itself an anomaly. Of the three brothers, he was the least educated and most boisterous. He had always been a bit pudgy, but now as he neared 40, he was almost fat. In the lumberyard business, he was in charge of the yard. He managed inventory, stacked doors, sawed two-by-fours, and hoisted fence posts into the back of pickup trucks.

Instead of following his older brothers to college at Kent State, Paul had joined the army. By chance, he had gotten hitched up with a con-struction unit and had spent his four years touring the country mostly closing and tearing down military bases, but occasionally working on the construction of new buildings. After he was discharged, he went to Florida with a buddy whose father owned a construction company and a small chain of four lumberyards across northern Florida. He only stayed there three years before coming home to marry Cathy (who was seven years his junior) and start the lumberyard business with his broth-ers. It was all pretty mundane, a story like a thousand other stories except for one unusual event.

Near the end of his stay in Florida, Paul got put on a construction crew, outside Jacksonville, assigned to build an elaborate wine cellar for a retired guy from upstate New York named Hersholm. Hersholm had been a successful beverage distributor until his kids took over and kicked him out of the business. But he had a lot of money and he knew his wines and he spared no expense to build a fine wine cellar. He was also a fanatic about detail. For some reason he took a liking to Paul and, because he was so hard to get along with, sometimes Paul was the only person working on the project. Hersholm didn't care. He would stand over Paul for hours while Paul did some grouting or worked on some strips of wood. He would lecture Paul about wines and then eventually open a bottle that they would share in the late afternoon. By the time the wine cellar was finished, Paul had become a wine connoisseur.

When Paul quit construction and left Florida, Hersholm gave him two cases of very expensive wine as a going-away present. They corre-sponded and Paul would send the old man odd bottles of wine from obscure wineries he would find in Ohio, Michigan, and Pennsylvania. When Hersholm died in 1990, his will left Paul more than 300 bottles of wine. Paul and Sticks drove down in a van to collect the bottles. The wine became the basis of Paul's own wine collection. Soon, Paul's wine cellar was the finest in Stowe Towne which was saying something since a number of the families had pretty good wine cellars that went back for more than a hundred years. Paul and Cathy had gone wine-tasting to France, twice to the Napa Valley, and numerous times to the vineyards of upstate New York.

"I went to the bank this morning and they're ready with the loan," Hal said. "Jack still has reservations, but our credit's good. He just doesn't think that people will buy wine here."

Hal took care of the lumberyard business matters. In his heart, he didn't think the shoppe would make it either. But Paul had lobbied for three years for the project. He had finally worn down Hal and Sticks.

"Well," Sticks said, "Jack is sometimes too conservative for his own good." There was some truth in the statement. Sammi had had a long and frustrating history trying to get mortgages past Jack Schultz.

"He cut the loan back 20%," Hal said.

"What?" Paul responded jumping off his crate (which was just as well since the crate was about to burst under his weight). "He can't do that."

"Of course he can," Hal said. "He could cut it 90% if he wanted and we couldn't do a thing about it. Look, you know we figured in some wiggle room. If you could pare down initial inventory just a little bit more, then..."

"Come on, Hal. What do you want to sell, just gallon jugs of Taylor Chablis?"

"Well, Paul, we could put off doing the outside entrance here for now. Just have people enter through the store."

The outside door for the shoppe had been the subject of a long debate.

"No, we have to go with the door," Sticks said shaking his head. "Women just won't come through the lumberyard to buy wine. But they will pull up on the street if they can walk right in." Sticks gestured at the wall where they would knock the hole through for the door.

"Fine, then it's inventory," Hal said holding up his hand to check Paul's protest. "For now. Just to get started."

Paul shrugged and grumbled, "I don't think the wine shoppe should get screwed because of Sticks's situation."

"What's that suppose to mean?" Sticks asked, surprised by Paul turning on him right after he defended Paul's door.

"Well, Sammi's situation and what's going on out at the golf course. We were talking about this and I don't know if we can squeeze more money out of the lumberyard for you."

Hal protested: "Who's we? You and I haven't talked about this."

"Cathy and me, she was talking to Sammi on Sunday," Paul said. "I mean Sammi's going to lose a lot of income."

"Hey, I'm not sure that's true. Besides, that's not really your problem, Pauly," Sticks said, annoyed.

"It is if you come around here for more money."

"What are you talking about? You act like I show up begging for money. Jesus Christ, I was working my ass off here when you and Cathy went out to Vegas. I cover for you all the time."

"All right, fellows," Hal interjected. "Let's calm down." Hal eyed his two brothers for a moment. "We're too far down this road to stop now. We've been talking about this wine shoppe for a long time. Let's grab the loan before Jack gets cold feet. I've worked out the finances. We can manage it. Just a little less inventory to start, all right, Paul?"

"I'll work on it," Paul said sullenly.

"Great," Hal said. "Sticks, you still okay with being in charge of remodeling the room? We go with the door. Shelves, counter. The Bavarian motif like we agreed on."

Sticks nodded. "I'll do it."

"Randy can help you. Give him a few more hours."

"Sure, that's great."

"All right, then," Hal said standing up. "Jack said we can start drawing on the loan next Monday. Looks like the Bergmans are in the wine business."

~

On Friday morning, Howie teed up his ball on the first tee of The Candlesticks and slammed his Burner down the middle of the fairway.

It was going to be a hectic couple of days. Tomorrow morning, Howie would conduct a news conference on the deck of the clubhouse in which he would formally announce the creation of Candlesticks Acres, introduce the developer, Don Morgan representing Cliner, and introduce the golf architect, Sean Donaldson, who would redesign the course. Tomorrow afternoon at 4:00, Julie would graduate from high school.

Joining Howie in his foursome were the three people who would be on stage with him at the press conference: Donaldson, Morgan, and Tom Duke, Jr. representing the rest of the members of The Candlesticks' Board. Howie had chosen the younger Duke strictly for public relations purposes. He didn't like the guy any more than David Canello liked him. But besides flirting with the Major Leagues, Duke was well-known in Stowe Towne because in high school he had led the school to its only sustained success in any sports. The success was 10 years ago and it included a final four appearance in the state basketball tournament when he was a junior (lost by two points in the semifinal game) and a championship game appearance in the state baseball tournament when he was a senior (lost one to zip on an error in the eighth inning to a kid from a Catholic school in Cincinnati who now was pitching in the majors with the Twins). Ironically, Tom had been forbidden to play football by his father who didn't want him to wreck his knees. Still, despite his wretched personality, Tom was a hero to most of the townspeople.

The match this Friday morning had a couple of purposes in Howie's mind. Donaldson (who had come in late Thursday evening, but had still gotten up at dawn to walk the course) needed to familiarize himself with how The Candlesticks played. Morgan needed to meet and be impressed by Donaldson. Tom Duke, meanwhile, had been thoroughly coached to be supportive and to minimize any local opposition to the project. This was a "team" plan. Howie even went so far as to discourage any betting on their golf match. He knew Morgan wasn't a golfer in the first place, but he also wanted to avoid any competition or hard feelings that might result from betting. This was business about the course itself. Just hit the ball and talk.

Except for how he viewed his daughter's sexuality, Howie Howard had seldom been so naive.

The first problem came on the first hole as the foursome walked off the green to their carts. Howie and Donaldson had scored pars. Tom had missed a five-foot par putt and threw a cursing fit as a consequence. Morgan, meanwhile, announced that he had scored a seven.

"A seven?" Tom questioned as he got in the cart he was sharing with Donaldson. "I think you had an eight."

"A seven, son," the fat man said as he heaved his body into the passenger side of the cart next to Howie. His weight almost grounded the side of his cart into the gravel cart path. "If you're keeping score, I got a seven."

"Well," Tom persisted, "it took you two shots to get out of the sand and then..."

Morgan swung around in his seat so violently that the cart almost tipped again. Howie frantically grabbed the steering wheel. "I got a seven, fella. You got a problem with that?"

Donaldson, laughing, stepped on the gas, swerved across the grass, and sped past Howie and Morgan toward the second tee. The rush of air carried away Tom Duke's curses.

The second and third holes passed in tense silence as Morgan sliced

balls into the large pond between the last half of the second hole's fairway on one side and most of the third hole's par-3 fairway on the other
side. Finally, on the fourth hole, Morgan caught a break. He hammered
a drive into the trees down the left side of the course (overcompensat-
ing for his previous slices), but the ball ricocheted off a trunk back into
the middle of the fairway. He then hit a three-wood onto the green and
was on in regulation. In fact, all four of the golfers were on the large
green in regulation.

As the men prowled around the green like golfers do, reminding one
of caged animals, Donaldson leaned over to repair a ball mark. As he did
so, Morgan barked, "What do you think you're doing?"

Donaldson, from his bent-over position, looked up. "Huh?"

"You can't do that," Morgan said pointing a finger at the golf architect. "That's on your line."

"So what?" Donaldson said straightening up.

"You're improving your line."

"You can repair a ball mark anywhere, Don. I just saw you repair one."

"But it wasn't on my line," Morgan said defensively.

"That doesn't matter. You can't repair spike marks. But you can
repair ball marks."

"No you can't."

"Golf is my job," Donaldson said with heat now in his voice. "I know
the rules. You build houses as I understand it. I don't tell you how many
nails to use."

Howie jumped in: "Hey, fellows, it doesn't matter. This is just a
friendly..."

Morgan interrupted Howie: "If he cheats in golf, Howie, how do you
know he isn't going to cheat us in business?"

"Me cheat?" Donaldson erupted. "You've been the one shaving
strokes. If you're as bad a developer as you are golfer, I don't want anything to do with you."

"Sean. Don. Let's not let this get out of hand," Howie pleaded.

"Get him off the fucking course," Tom chimed in, pointing his putter at Morgan like a rapier. "He's so goddamn fat, he's ruining the greens just walking across them."

It was true. For four greens now, Morgan had left a trail of scuffed spike marks. Howie cursed the fact that the Board had refused to enforce a soft spike only rule for the course.

Morgan took a step toward Howie. "Do you really expect Cliner to partner with these types of people, Howie?"

Howie quickly held up a hand, squelching an immediate response from Donaldson and Tom. "Don," he pleaded, "you have to understand. Tom is a Board member and one of Stowe Towne's leading citizens. Sean Donaldson is just about the hottest golf architect in the entire country." He paused and tried to collect his thoughts. "Look, everyone, I guess it wasn't a good idea to come out here like this. We got along fine over coffee and doughnuts. Maybe we should have stopped there. Why don't we just call this a day? Don and I'll go back to the clubhouse, you two can finish if you want. Let's say we'll get together about 4:00 for cocktails at my house and plan out the press conference then."

Mostly because no one knew what else to do, heads slowly nodded in agreement. Morgan swung his putter and sent his ball in the general direction of their cart, gouging the green in the process. He shuffled off the green, leaving a trail like a slug.

Howie took a deep breath, shrugged at the other two men, and followed. Golf had never been this hard before.

⌐

The Stowe Towne Memorial Library was a squat, unattractive red brick building located on the southwest corner of the intersection of Jones Street and Mitchell Street. It was just east of the Maple Lodge restaurant. If you stood in the library door looking out across the town square you could see the back of the Memorial to the Seven Heroes through the tall trees. The library's window boxes on each side of the door overflowed with red, white, and purple petunias.

The library owed its existence entirely to the Daughters of the Union Army. The library originally occupied the attic-like third floor of the county courthouse. It was hard to reach—the stairs were very steep from the second to the third floor—and was always too hot or too cold. A new library was finally built as a WPA project in 1935. The building's only remarkable feature was that the WPA artist's project created a large mural on a wall in the library's main room. The mural depicted the history of Stowe Towne in rather lurid, exaggerated figures. The DUA ladies at the time, while polite to the artist, soon managed to cover up most of the mural with bookshelves. After all, it was a library.

In the 1970s, the *Bugle* published an article noting that the artist, one Alexander Smith, was recognized as a disciple of Thomas Hart Benton. The mural was uncovered and declared a town treasure. Everyone had known the mural was there. But most town citizens had grown up with partial views of arms and hats and gun barrels and sunrises and cornfields sticking out from between and above the bookshelves. One particular set of bare legs had for generations elicited prurient speculation among the town youths. The legs and bare feet, in fact, belonged to Ruth Hanover, an actress who had gone to Hollywood and had made a number of silent films before marrying a director and never making another movie (or returning to Stowe Towne). She was posed in the mural in her most famous role as an oversexed Anne Boleyn.

Will Boyd haunted the library. He spent hours and hours doing research for the historical articles that he published in the *Bugle*. He always sat in the same oak captain's chair at the head of a long table with books and bound newspapers spread out in front of him. There were boxes of papers and personal artifacts mostly related to various members of the original seven families. The library functioned as an unofficial depository for records and documents from the families. There had always been hopes that someone would come forward to write the history of the town. But no one had.

This was a bit of a dilemma. The family members down through the generations had been leery about an outsider writing the history. There were, after all, some skeletons in the closet. Bootlegging and bathtub gin in the '20s, for example, that the DUA actively participated in because the ladies realized that they had to have something unique to attract Ohio Society. Offering a safe haven and quality Canadian liquor (without any gangland connections) was a real plus. And the strategy worked successfully up until the Depression.

Yet, no one from the families ever stepped forward to write a sanitized town history either. May Miller had tried on numerous occasions, but had never progressed beyond three paragraphs. She was secretly thrilled by the interesting histories published in the paper by Will Boyd, although he was such a scruffy looking character that she would never acknowledge the articles in public. Plus, Boyd occasionally was quite critical of the families. In an article in March, for example, he had written about farming and had noted a history of poor conservation practices that were directly attributed to the families since they had always been the major land owners in Pottawa County. Yet, on the whole, even a booster like May Miller had to admit that the articles were reasoned and accurate and always very, very interesting.

Now, Will Boyd was finishing up his latest article. He had originally intended to write about horses and polo. But with the developing conflict over The Candlesticks, he had changed his mind and authored the article that appeared in the next edition of the *Bugle*:

THE LAND BEFORE THE CANDLESTICKS

On a misty morning in early October, 1860, Josiah Percy met with four men at his hunting cabin located approximately where The Candlesticks Golf Course clubhouse now stands. One of the men with Percy was Thomas Hanover who was engaged to Percy's daughter Sarah.

Percy, Hanover, and the three other men (their names are not mentioned in Percy's diary although it's probable that one of the men was Job Jones who had attended Ohio University with Hanover) were not primarily interested in hunting that day. Instead, they were responding to President Abraham Lincoln's call for troops to form the Union Army.

Josiah Percy was too old for command, but he was willing to finance the formation of a company. Hanover would be appointed Captain, later Major, and through that association and his subsequent marriage to Sarah, Stowe Towne would be founded just east of the crossroads of the north-south Pike and the east-west Columbus Plank Road after the Civil War.

What happened to the land between the fateful meeting at the hunting lodge and more than 60 years later when construction began on the golf course in 1923?

The land, roughly enclosed by a loop in the Pottawa River that includes the waterfall known as the Cascades, has always been a gathering place. Legend has it, although archeological evidence is sketchy, that Indians considered the area sacred ground. In 1892, the *Stowe Towne Bugle* reported that an elderly Indian claiming to be a Medicine Man of the Potawatomi Nation camped out on the land waiting to die. He stayed for four months in the fall of the year and became a curiosity for townspeople who traveled from town by horse and buggy to see him. At Thanksgiving, he disappeared from his camp and no trace of him was ever found.

It was in the early 1890s that the Hanover family fell upon hard times. Thomas and Sarah Percy Hanover had had three sons, Josiah, Jefferson, and George, as well as a daughter, Sally, who was born with a deformed leg and never married. Sally started Hanover Grocery that remains in business today. The two older boys, Josiah and Jefferson, were wild youths who spent money and drove their indulgent parents into debt. When Josiah was killed in a fall during a horse race, his father was devastated. Thomas's health soon failed and he died in 1890. Jefferson, the next oldest son, badgered his mother to sell off most of the Hanover's extensive land holdings for cash, including The Candlesticks' land. Finally, George, the youngest son who had gone East to school (eventually earning a Harvard law degree), was forced to come home and take control of the family. George formed Stowe Towne's first law firm of Miller, Duke, and Hanover with two other sons of the original Stowe Towne Civil War heroes.

The Candlesticks property was sold by Sarah Hanover to Andrew Jackson Howard, son of Civil War hero Major John Howard. The Howards were horse people and the popular Andy Howard and his wife Mary Mitchell turned the area into a large horse farm. A racetrack was constructed on land directly behind the present location of the house owned by Howard and Margaret Howard. Although some public races were run at the track, the track was mainly a training facility and for a time became the best-known racehorse training facility in Ohio. Later, after 1910, Andy and Mary's son Sheridan became interested in polo and trained polo ponies. The racetrack grandstand and a large horse barn were destroyed by a fire in 1952 and the land reverted to farming.

Sheridan, who often traveled to England (one time an unexpected business complication kept him in London or he would have been a passenger on the Titanic), became enamored with golf. However, the credit for the idea to build The Candlesticks Golf Course correctly goes to his wife, Louisa, who served for many years as President of the Daughters of the Union Army.

The land in question borders on what is now known as the Pottawa State Forest. Until an official state survey in 1922, the exact southern boundary of the forest was unclear. The stone ridge that runs the length of the forest made the land mostly unsuitable for farming. Even the trees were unsuitable for lumbering although small portions of the forest were clear-cut during the nineteenth century and some government cutting was done during the Depression for employment purposes. Unprofitable attempts at strip-mining took place at the north end of the forest near the village of Granite City.

Besides the sliver of land that was used for part of The Candlesticks Golf Course, the only extensive use of the state forest was for hunting. Deer and bear were prevalent in the area throughout the nineteenth century. The area was the largest refuge for bear in Ohio. Bear attacks on horses owned by the Howards during a drought in the summer of 1903 were national news. Today, the bears are gone, but deer are still prevalent.

chapter thirteen

PROMPT AND CIRCUMSPECT

The High School Graduation Parade was to step off precisely at
1:00 p.m. on Saturday. The unusual parade, surely the only one of its
kind, was a bizarre Stowe Towne tradition that had begun in 1968. That
year the high school band, the Union Generals Marching Corps, had
won a state marching competition for the first time. The high school
principal then, a Mr. Eldon Goodman, came up with an idea to honor
the Marching Corps and the high school seniors in a parade. (Principal
Goodman had aspirations to leave high school administration and get
into a cushy job teaching in a college education department, which he
did two years later when he became an assistant professor at Northern
Kentucky University, where he only taught in the afternoons on MWTh
and made $5,000 a year more.) Of course, the fanatic parents who com-
prised the Band Boosters jumped on the idea since they were anxious
for the band to show off at any opportunity. More importantly, this new
parade allowed the Boosters to start their new uniform drive three
months early.

The townspeople and merchants rallied behind the idea of a parade because those were the years of the hippies. Merchants happily sponsored the various school floats. Any wholesome patriotic/school event was deemed "super" before some of the students went off to be corrupted by college. Plus, it was a great send-off for those boys who were going directly to serve their country in Vietnam. Or, *die* in Vietnam as Bob Redford pointed out in a very unpopular front-page editorial in the *Bugle*. In any case, the parade was led by the Marching Corps and featured a string of tractors pulling flatbed trailers (like a hayride without the hay). Each trailer was devoted to a club, sport, or activity and each senior could ride on the decorated trailer-float that represented the activity he or she had participated in the most. There was the senior Marching Corps float (the seniors did not march in the parade and were replaced in the Marching Corps by 8th graders—it was a big thrill), the football team's float, the basketball team's float, the *Sentinel Yearbook* staff float, the Future Farmers of America float, and so forth, stretching for about three blocks.

Senior participation in the parade was mandatory for graduation. It was inspired decisions like this that made Principal Goodman think he was ready for college teaching. However, there was one hitch. There were about 15 students who didn't belong to anything. The number remained constant over the years. They were the losers, poor, pimply, occasional farm migrant kids who just didn't *participate*. It was a dilemma because the other students didn't want a kid on their float who didn't *participate!* Principal Goodman resolved the problem by designating the last float as The General's Own Float. The kids who had to ride The General's Own Float seldom decorated it, although occasionally some chubby girl who was either three months pregnant or on her way to college out of state would run blue and white crepe paper around the edge. Bob Redford always thought that the kids on The General's Own Float looked like the French nobility stripped of all dignity being led to the guillotine by the Republican crowd through the streets of Paris. Wisely, however, he never put *that* thought into an editorial. Besides, he had noted over the years that quite a number of The General's Own Float's students had gone on to successful college and business careers. A member of the current Stowe Towne Town Council had even ridden that float, although Bob suspected the man would not now like to be reminded of that fact. Redford, however, made a point from the very first parade to have the *Bugle* sponsor The General's Own Float.

The parade started in the small high school parking lot, ran a torturous traditional route through the streets with emphasis on the more prosperous southwest corner of the town, and eventually ended up, of course, at the Civil War statue in the town's square. There the class president laid a copy of the *Sentinel Yearbook* at the feet of the seven heroes. The Marching Corps then played the school fight song and the alma mater, a dirge that no one knew. Immediately after the ceremony, according to tradition, the town librarian (always a volunteer from the DUA) scooped up the copy of the *Sentinel Yearbook* for safekeeping at the Stowe Towne Memorial Library.

Howie and Margaret turned down a jammed Howard Street right on time, 15 minutes before 1:00 p.m. Parents always saw the seniors "off" for their parade. However, a thunderstorm also arrived precisely at 15 minutes to 1:00. It had been threatening all morning, although the weather reports were cautiously optimistic. But at 15 minutes to 1:00 it poured and it thundered and the lightning flashed as if Noah was launching a second ark.

Howie and Margaret sat immobilized in their car in the midst of a parental traffic jam near the main high school driveway as kids, teachers, and the farmers who drove the tractors sprinted for safety from the parking lot into the high school. Crepe paper and signs and the floats in general were decimated by sheets of driving rain. Thunder reverberated overhead and the June day became as dark as a December night.

"Holy shit," Howie muttered peering out of the windshield, "I hope we don't have a tornado. I remember a tornado coming through here when I was a kid and wiping out all the big trees in front of the school." He turned on the car lights, but the beams were swallowed up in the rain.

Margaret lit a cigarette and was very glum. A tornado was the least of her worries.

Meanwhile, Julie and Randy, who had been hanging out near one of the gym's outside doors, had managed to get inside before they were thoroughly drenched. The senior English teacher, Mrs. Ackermann, who was always in charge of graduation, was horrified to see her nicely arranged and decorated gymnasium invaded by soaking wet students and farmers. Coming down the front steps of the temporary stage at one end of the gym and brandishing whip-like a three-foot-long lilac branch that she had been arranging next to the podium, she herded everyone into the west bleachers where they could do the least harm.

Thunder rolled overhead and rain drummed like a rock concert on the roof. Everyone expected the power to go out any second. Julie and Randy sat off by themselves near the top of the bleachers staring at the sea of folding chairs in front of them on the gym floor. Julie was relieved the parade would probably be canceled. Besides the fact that most of the seniors thought that the parade was a stupid and unnecessary event, it also made it very tough on everyone, but especially the girls, to get home and dressed and then back again to the school for graduation at 4:00.

"You know, after graduation, the cease-fire is over," Julie said.

"What do you mean?" Randy asked. He looked down and noticed his sneakers were leaving watermarks on the bleachers.

"The war will start again. Isn't that what usually happens when the cease-fire ends?"

Randy shook his head. "I have no idea what you're talking about."

"At home, dummy. You. College. Everything. They want some

decisions."

"Call up your grandfather," Randy advised.

Julie made a small noise in her throat that sounded like a growl to Randy. "That worked once," she said, "but I don't think it will work again."

"Why not?"

"Well, for one thing, I'm not sure gramps will be so supportive this time. If push comes to shove, he wants me to go to college. And since he was a teacher at Ohio State, he probably wants me to go there. That's logical, isn't it?"

"I don't know. He seems like a pretty reasonable old guy."

"He can be just like Mom sometimes."

"So, what's going to happen?"

"I'm thinking about going to France," Julie said calmly.

"What?" Randy exclaimed, trying to sit up from his almost prone position leaning back against the bleachers.

"You've heard of France, perhaps?"

"Your parents won't let you go to France."

"Mom might. Mom might think it's a good idea. Get me away from you!" Julie poked at Randy's stomach with a finger.

"Well, I think it's a rotten idea."

"All right, then I'll just break up with you like they want."

"I think that's a sucko idea, too."

"Then I'm all out of ideas."

"Come on, Julie," Randy pleaded. "You know, I bet I could get you a job. Like, my uncles and my Dad are opening up that wine store at the lumberyard. Dad was telling me how they can't find people to help. People who know about wine, I mean."

"I'm not 21, you idiot. I think you have to be 21 to sell liquor. And that store is a stupid idea anyway. 'Give me a bottle of French Bordeaux and, oh, I'll take one of those hammers, too.'"

"It's not a stupid idea," Randy said defensively.

"What, my working or the wine*yard*?"

Randy settled back against the bleachers again. Sometimes the words "spoiled brat" seemed a very appropriate description of his girlfriend. He worked his ass off in the lumberyard. Had for years. She'd never earned a penny in her life. She thought playing golf was work.

Then a crack of thunder seemed to echo right inside the gym and both of them jumped in their seats. A couple of girls screamed. And the lights went out. It was practically pitch black in the gym. It was so dark outside that little light came in the bank of narrow windows above the east bleachers. They were the only windows in the gym and Mrs. Ackermann had pulled the blinds on all of the windows anyway to keep out the morning sun and keep the gym cool for the ceremony. The wind blew a door open and then sucked it shut with a bang that echoed like a shot around the gym. More screams. Some feet clattered on the wooden bleachers. Some kid yelled, "Bart! Bart!" The rain swept across the roof and drummed even harder, drowning out all the screaming and yelling and nervous giggles.

Julie reached over and grabbed the crotch of Randy's jeans. "Let's do it," she whispered.

"What? What?!"

"Now, right here. I know you've got a condom in your wallet. They won't fix the lights until it stops raining. They never do."

Randy felt his erection starting. "We can't do it here!" he whispered back furiously.

"Sure we can. I've got my panties off already." She groped for his hand and pressed it against her breast.

A kid yelled "Bart!" again, but he sounded a long ways away to Randy. He thought about edging away himself, but instead his other hand somehow found Julie's other breast.

Holy shit, he thought, *right in the middle of the gymnasium full of people.* Another crack of thunder. His zipper was unzipped. Julie's hot breath was in his face. All he could think was that Julie was the Valedictorian of Love. *Oh! My! God!*

              ⟿

At that moment, miles away in an apartment on the north side of Columbus, Peter Onear was lying naked in a strange bed waiting for cub reporter Mara Fish to come out of her bathroom. A thunderstorm had rolled over them on their drive back from Stowe Towne where they had covered The Candlestick Acres housing development press conference. But now sunlight and fresh air streamed through the open window. Pale yellow curtains billowed into the room. There was the scent of lilacs and a naked woman in the air. This was the very last place Peter Onear expected to spend the afternoon when he had come by to pick up Mara that morning.

So far—with obviously more to come—it had been a day of revelations. Some even had to do with the golf course.

Most had to do with Mara Fish.

Since 8:30 this morning, he had found out that Mara's mother was Susan Stein, the *New York Times* feminist columnist who had written the infamous feminist history of the U.S. Supreme Court entitled *The Backless Bench*. Her father was Leonard Fish who had coauthored among many other books the Shermann and Fish *Modern Journalism*—the basic journalism textbook used in most university journalism schools. He was *that Fish*. The book was always referred to by students and faculty alike as "Shermann Fish" instead of its given title. Her older sister was a CNN anchor (yes, they did look alike now that he knew that fact) and her older brother was a foreign correspondent in Asia for the *Miami Herald*.

The litany of her pedigree had actually cowered Peter, a feeling he seldom experienced. His nearly 200-year-old, one-eared Napoleonic ancestor wasn't much of a match. "Why Ohio University? Why Ohio?" he had blurted out.

"My uncle is the Dean of the Journalism School there," she replied matter-of-factly. "Besides, it's one of the best J schools in the country, don't you think?"

Peter didn't think much of journalism schools. Had often made fun of them. Had probably made fun of them to Mara's face sometime in their brief relationship.

His mind raced as if he was on amphetamines or three shots of Absolut vodka. He did not really want to be involved with another woman. He had finally extricated himself from Polly after their trip up to Pottawa State Lodge. Polly was not much of an intellectual challenge and was always complaining about something. Mara was the complete opposite of Polly, but Peter did not know if he was ready for that either. His "maleness" easily convinced his intellect to wait until after sex. Mara wasn't that attractive. A little bit frumpy. A little too dark-complected with short black hair for his taste. But one could never tell. Just getting in the apartment door had been an experience.

They had fallen into each other's arms as Mara finished unlocking the door. She lived on the second floor of a house not far from the northern boundary of the Ohio State University campus. The apartment was obviously a converted upstairs with high ceilings and narrow windows. The kitchen was tiny, converted from a walk-in closet. The bathroom had old-fashioned white porcelain fixtures including a high bathtub with claw-shaped legs. But Peter was unaware of any of this at first. He pawed at her and she pawed at him. He lost his sports coat, tie, shirt, and shoes. She lost her blouse, belt, and one shoe. Then she called time-out.

Perplexed, he stumbled after her. She led him to her computer pushing him down into an old battered desk chair, sitting on his lap, and turning on the machine all in one deft move. "We've got to do the article first," she panted. He grabbed her breasts and said something about fucking the computer. But before he could right himself to peer over her shoulder at the computer screen, she had expertly logged on and had written the lead. He groaned.

She hadn't removed his hands from her breasts.

Eventually, she had made him disengage and retrieve his notepad from his inside sports coat pocket and her notebook from her shoulder bag (both by the door) as well as lock the door (she was both efficient and security conscious). The nonsweaty story on the monitor quickly took shape from their sweaty fingers and minds.

Here, throw this in, he had said: "Architect Donaldson pledged golf fans that the course would not be substantially changed. Quote. It's one of George August's finest designed courses and I am honored to have the chance to redesign it for the next century. End quote."

Then she wrote about Morgan: The rotund developer from Cleveland bristled at a question about environmental concerns. Morgan said, quote: The houses will be on land that has been farmland for decades. No wetland. No trees. We'll add trees. It'll look a hell of a lot nicer than it does now. End quote.

"That guy gave me the creeps," Mara said as Peter unsnapped her bra. Braless typing suddenly appealed to him.

Peter added to the screen: A sketchy rendering indicated that most of the houses would be on property adjacent to the golf course. The property is owned by Howard Howard who is also the head of The Candlesticks Golf Course Board.

Phil Jadocak, a *Dispatch* photographer, had also been at the press conference and had taken back a copy of the rendering to the newspaper. The editors would decide if the paper would run one of Phil's photos or the rendering of the layout with the story. Probably a photo, Peter thought, because the rendering was awful. The two Columbus TV stations that were at the press conference would probably try to do something with the rendering anyway. For some reason, TV guys always liked to shoot blurry photos of architect renderings. It was all part of the visual crap mentality.

Mara, breasts unfettered, typed: Mr. Howard refused to comment on a question related to the fact that the golf course is on land that is part of Pottawa State Park. *Forest, not Park*, Peter corrected. He stated that an announcement would be forthcoming, but declined to give details.

"We should follow up on this park angle," Mara pouted.

But Peter reminded her, "It's Saturday afternoon. State government is shut down for the weekend." He squirmed around and slipped off his pants. Maybe she needed some visual encouragement to wind up the story.

Maybe it worked. She finally punched out the story and sent it via e-mail to the copy desk. Let the copy editors have at it for the Sunday paper. Wasn't much of a story really. She measured each story she did against what her father would have thought. After all, his whole goddamn textbook of examples loomed over her. Although, actually, she thought as she fondled Peter on the floor next to the desk chair, she knew what the real story was. It was the golf architect. She knew zilch about golf architects and golf course architecture. Although the idea of outdoor, natural architecture suddenly appealed to her. Big-scale landscaping. She had never thought of it before, but that's what those formal European gardens that she had toured those summers in college were all about. Interesting. European gardens. American golf courses. This Sean Donaldson would have been the right story. Maybe as a follow-up. Whoops! Things were progressing a bit here. She'd have to make a bathroom stop.

And so, that's how Peter Onear came to finally be lying naked in bed with his hands clasped behind his head waiting for this young woman he knew a tenth as well as he thought he did to come out of the bathroom and make love.

The world, he concluded as he heard the bathroom doorknob turn, is full of surprises.

⌒

Sammi Bergman always went to high school graduation even though she usually failed to get Sticks to go along unless some very close relative was graduating—like a son or daughter. Sammi went because that's what she believed a good real estate agent did. People had civic pride. People loved their kids. Therefore, they liked real estate agents who had the same values. She had argued endlessly about this with Bruce who believed that people wanted real estate agents to be ruthless hired guns. Go out and find me a buyer and screw them to the wall. Who knew? Maybe they were both right; they just catered to different sensibilities. Both Sammi and Bruce were successful in their own ways. The difference, now that she had made the break, was that she did not have to see or talk to him. It was such a relief!

The weather had cleared, but the senior parade had still been canceled. There had been rumors of tornadoes and when the rain had stopped the farmers had all left with their tractors to make sure their homes were intact. The electricity eventually came on and Mrs. Ackermann had commandeered several seniors and their friends including Julie and Randy to mop up the gym floor and bleachers and do a bunch of other last minute things that had fallen behind schedule because of the rain and power outage.

Ironically, even with the parade canceled, Julie barely made it home in time to get dressed and turn around and come back for the ceremony. Julie went to graduation with her parents. Dressed in a new and very expensive white dress, her blue graduation gown across her arms.

Randy went home to put on a sports coat and pick up his mother. In the gym, Sammi and Randy sat in the west bleachers since the floor chairs were reserved for graduates and immediate family members. They sat uncomfortably close for Randy's liking to where he and Julie had been sitting just hours before. Of course, he didn't let on and his mother wasn't there much anyway.

Sammi flitted around the back of the floor seating saying hello to old friends and congratulating families of the graduates. It was chatter, chatter, chatter. Everyone talked first about the storm blowing through. Of course, many people had heard about Sammi and Bruce splitting. Sammi had a stock answer:

It was time. Stowe Towne can support two real estate firms. We have the national firms coming in here anyway. My office is going to be where Winthrop Loans used to be. They've been gone about a year, I think. Perfect office space. Sticks is making me a sign: Bergman Realty. Bruce is taking it hard, of course. (Only to a couple of close friends did she add, *He finally realized who was doing all the work!*) *Be sure and drop by. I'm going to have an open house. You bet. If you ever want to sell that lovely home, just give me a call.*

Delia Long heard Sammi chatter. Delia was attending because her nephew Jason was graduating; he was the youngest son of Delia's younger sister Ruth and would have been one of the riders of The General's Own Float. Delia steered Sammi aside and made an appointment to come in and see Sammi at the new office on Monday afternoon. She acted very mysterious and gave Sammi a big wink. Sammi did not know what to make of the encounter as the Union Generals Marching Corps struck up *Pomp and Circumstance*. She wended her way back to the bleachers as the graduates began marching in.

Howie, Margaret, and Margaret's father stood as the familiar music filled the gym. It had been quite a day already for Howie. After the disastrous round of golf yesterday (and the subsequent "chilly" planning meeting), he couldn't sleep for fear of what would happen at the press conference. Fortunately, they got through that all right with no further interpersonal problems. But then there was the storm and the aborted parade. On the way home, he got a frantic call from the golf course on his car phone. One of the larger oak trees on the course, the one just beyond the putting green and to the right of the fifth tee had blown over and, in fact, had wiped out the women's tee and blocked the men's tee. Another smaller tree had split and fallen partially across the Barnes's Knob fairway. The course was littered with limbs and leaves and debris. Howie had dropped off Margaret at home to wait for her father who was coming over about 3:00 from Columbus. Grandfather had wisely decided to skip the parade. Howie then spent a couple of hours at The Candlesticks with Bip and Warren Alexander dealing with the mess.

Now, Howie was tired and nervous, but at least Julie was going through the graduation ceremony. He had always been sure she would. Nevertheless, there had been times over the past month when he would not have been surprised if she had just run away. Devastated, yes; surprised, no. Still, the situation was hardly resolved. In fact, as far as he knew, no progress had been made. Margaret brooded constantly and smoked like a chimney. They suspected Julie was still seeing Randy. There still was no decision about college. Maybe getting this high school stuff out of the way would help.

In front, the stage was decorated with lilacs and white carnations, as close as possible in floral terms to mimic the school colors of royal blue and white. Howie took comfort for some inexplicable reason in the fact that the stage looked identical to when he and Sticks had graduated. The large glittery cutout sign pinned to the back stage curtain was the same, CONGRATULATIONS CLASS OF ____, except for the year. Same stage, same sign, same podium, same chairs—except back then everything was newer. Now the only thing new was the band uniforms, because the Band Boosters were so damn aggressive. (He thought: if the School Board really wanted to build a new high school, they should just put the Band Boosters in charge of the levy. No one would dare vote no just like no one dared turn down a band uniform drive which seemed to happen with unnecessary rapidity and desperation.)

Howie, Margaret, and Grandfather Emerson found their seats in the parents' section four rows in back of the chair section reserved for the graduating seniors. They were right on the middle aisle. Perfect seats.

People were turning now to look up the aisle toward the back of the gym. You could see flashes of the royal blue gowns of the graduates. There was some applause. Cameras flashed. Men hoisted camcorders to their eyes. Someone yelled, "Heather! Heather!" Someone else yelled, "Bart, over here." The music seemed to swell. Howie felt Margaret's hand find his. He glanced over at her. Tears rolled down her cheeks. Margaret was not one to cry very often. He gave her hand a squeeze.

In a moment, the graduates were whooshing past them down the aisle toward their seats in front. Their gowns created a breeze. Faces smiled, beamed. Occasionally, someone reached out from the audience and touched a robe. Then Howie saw her. His daughter. His little Julie. And the emotion caught in his throat. She looked so beautiful. Her hair framed around her face underneath her blue mortarboard hat. Her blue eyes smiling. They saw at once that she saw them. As she swept past she reached out to them smiling. And for that moment—just that moment—everything was all right.

chapter fourteen

DICK OUT

Ray Gunther, the second term state representative from the north part of Hamilton County, walked into Justice Summers's office carrying a brand new seven-wood that he had just made for the judge. It was an unmarked, knockoff Heaven Wood. It was beautiful. Ray, at the next election, would run with the Governor's Party for the State Senate representing a large portion of Cincinnati. The election was greased. Now he was just putting in time in the lower house. Learning the ropes. Helping out when he was needed. Always voting as the Party leadership wanted him to vote.

Ray was a lawyer with a privileged clientele. He was partner in a boutique firm specializing in managing estates, trusts, and old money. Twenty years ago he had graduated from law school at Northwestern and had come back to Ohio and Columbus to clerk for the judge. Summers had introduced him to the members of the firm in Cincinnati that he would join immediately after his clerkship.

Justice Richard Summers trusted Ray explicitly. Ray Gunther was very loyal in return.

When Ray had first met the judge, he had never played golf in his life. Was not interested in athletics of any kind. Came from a nonathletic family. His mother and father were devoted to the arts, especially opera and ballet. Vacations, when Ray and his sister Natasha were children, consisted of going to New York City for the ballet and theater. However, one summer day in 1989, Justice Summers showed up in Ray's office in Cincinnati and took him to lunch. It seemed to be a spur of the moment thing, although, in truth, the judge never did spur of the moment things. Only later did Ray find out that the lunch was the culmination of nearly two years of planning involving, among others, the soon-to-be-elected governor and Ray's own senior law partner. At the lunch, the judge laid out Ray's political future and in the course of suggesting a number of life changes informed Ray that he would learn and master the game of golf.

Being an overachiever, Ray overachieved. Golf became an obsession. One cynical law clerk said that Ray was simply intoxicated with fresh air and sunshine—neither of which he previously knew existed. It turned out that Ray had one tremendous advantage per his golf education. He had never swung a baseball bat or tennis racquet. He had no bad habits. He took lessons the first day and learned how to play golf correctly right from the beginning. He never overswung. He never mishit a ball. He never lost his cool. But he also had one fatal flaw. He had no passion for the game. No competitive spirit. He was the best scrambles player in the legislature. He could always be counted on for a shot when needed. But one-on-one, he was vulnerable. Even to a lesser player who played with a little luck and pluck.

Judge Summers swung the seven-wood easily in his high-ceilinged office as Ray sat off to the side in one of the judge's red leather wing-backed chairs. "Did you see the *Dispatch* article about the press conference at The Candlesticks?" the judge asked.

"Yes," Ray answered, "and I caught a news report on one of the TV stations. Looks like they're moving the project ahead. Not only that, but they seem to be going down the right road. I've seen articles in the golf magazines about that golf architect Donaldson."

The judge shook his head. "I didn't think Howie was that smart. That was something his father might have done. His father was a smart son-of-a-bitch before he went nuts. I didn't think Howie had it in him. Bringing in a golf architect with a national reputation who will supposedly preserve the course takes away some of the criticism that the course will be ruined by the development."

Ray shrugged. "Maybe, but sir, the course is still on public land."

The judge swung the club and it just clipped the rich brown carpet. *This club will work*, he thought. He leaned the club against the front of his desk and went around to his desk chair. "But, our Senator Barnes is introducing an amendment to the strip-mining bill that will allow for development of a tiny parcel of the state land for the public good. It doesn't seem to be much of an opposition rallying point."

"Even for environmentalists?"

The judge frowned. "Ray, half of southeastern Ohio is being surface strip-mined. Do you think putting up some luxury homes on a few acres of scrub forest is going to get anyone's attention?"

"But it's the principle..."

The judge waved off his protégé. "I've already made some calls. It's a no go. The leadership isn't going to slap Kenny's wrist for that little amendment." Summers paused and chuckled. "I guess I didn't think Kenny was that smart, either."

Ray smoothed his dark blue Geoffrey Beene tie. It had tiny white dots and looked very conservative with his dark blue suit. "Well, what about your Accord then?"

Judge Summers eyed the Candlesticks Accord in the gold folder on the corner of his desk. "It's a bit ironic, you know. I wrote the Accord so the people who managed the course wouldn't have their hands tied. I didn't think I would be on the other side. Truthfully, I haven't really decided."

"Isn't time running out?" Ray watched his mentor fidget behind the big desk. Ray kept quiet and kept his composure. In truth, the Cincinnatian could give a rat's ass about the damn golf course. But if the old man cared about it, he had to care about it. Still, it was annoying to have to think about. And a bad outcome—meaning a bad outcome from Summers's point of view—would not be good. He knew the judge. It would just eat at him and that meant continuing problems.

The judge eyed Ray. "You still think Sticks Bergman is a good golfer? Even an exceptional golfer?" After Ray had lost his irons to Sticks, he had called the judge that afternoon and given him a stroke-by-stroke account of the match.

Ray answered: "We had a hell of a game. On that course, he's tough competition. He made a long putt to win. I missed a short putt. However, on a neutral course, I might beat him 60 or 70% of the time."

"But, you're saying at The Candlesticks..."

"He knows the greens. He knows the trouble spots. He knows the course."

"Well, so does Howie," Summers mused out loud.

"I can't help you there. I don't know the gentleman."

The judge shook himself free of his speculation. "Nevertheless, there are still some cards to be played. The game's not over yet. Anyway, Ray, thanks for coming by with the club."

"My pleasure, sir," Ray said as he stood to leave.

The judge got up and came around the desk to shake hands. "I'll call you in a couple of days. We'll keep at this. Remember, we have that outing up in Sandusky next week."

"It's on my calendar."

Ray left the office and the judge leaned back against the front of his desk. He gripped his new seven-wood and thought about golf. Most people thought golf was recreational. Weekend duffers. Take an afternoon off and relax. Hell, they even deliver beer to you right on the course. Do they deliver beer to a center fielder in the middle of a baseball game? No. Most people just didn't understand that golf was a very serious sport. It had implications. Serious implications. It was all about life. People—golfers—needed to understand that.

There was a discreet knock on the door.

He turned and laid the new golf club across the front of his desk. Today, everyone who came into his office would see it and have to deal with it. Maybe some would even realize its importance. He walked around his desk and sat in his chair before he called for the person to come in.

~

As promised, on Monday afternoon Delia Long, dressed in a flowery blue and yellow dress that was much too young for her, stopped by Sammi's new office and whisked Sammi away in an old red Ford pickup truck. In doing so, she saved the newly independent real estate agent from washing the office windows. The windows needed washing badly. But the agency needed business even more—although Sammi was suspicious about what the eccentric Delia Long might have in mind.

Still, Sammi was experienced enough to know that you couldn't judge a book by its cover, a house by its last coat of paint, or a woman by the dress she wore. A good real estate agent always worked under the premise that there was more to the story than appeared on the surface. It was all tied up with plumbing, for example. Do the toilets flush? Is there hot water? Is the septic tank functioning? Sammi had poked her head in more than a few septic tanks. Sort of.

Nevertheless, Sammi was about to learn that lesson all over again.

They were cruising on County Road 8 headed southeast out of Stowe Towne toward George Long's Golf Course. Delia, who had carried on a running conversation about the rainy weather, the high school graduation, vegetable growing, grass seed, and so on and on, suddenly said: "Sammi, take a guess at my annual income."

Sammi was startled, but not surprised. Real estate agents had to be very, very good at estimating annual incomes. "Well, let me see," she began giving herself a moment to think. In her mind, she made estimates. The golf course income couldn't be more than $20,000. Maybe less than $15,000. She knew Delia rented out some land for farming. Maybe another $10,000. Possibly more. George probably had life insurance. Some investment income: $5,000 or $6,000 at most. She did some mental addition. "I would say $32,000 or so. I know you own some extra land around the golf course. Maybe a little more?"

"Add a one in front of that, honey," Delia said laughing.

Sammi looked over at the woman as the truck hit a pothole and they bounced in their seats. "A one? You have an income of $132,000 a year?" she asked incredulously.

"It's down a little the past two years. I've been playing it safe in the market. Building up a little reserve."

"A little reserve?"

"All right, you got me there," Delia said laughing again. "A lot of reserve."

Another pickup truck flashed by in the other lane. Sammi found this a little hard to believe. Certain professionals who talked among themselves like real estate agents, bankers, accountants, real estate lawyers, and others of that ilk almost always knew where there was serious money. Not that you couldn't hide money. You could do your business in Columbus or Cleveland or Pittsburgh or even New York City. And, Sammi speculated, if you had this veneer as an eccentric old lady...

"Where did you get that much money?" she asked not even considering that it might be an inappropriate question.

"My late husband was pretty shrewd. More than people gave him credit for. He kind of liked to play the farmer. Plus, there was some old family money from Pennsylvania. George invested wisely. It was his hobby at night. In the daytime, the golf course was his hobby and that's what people saw. George out on the mower cutting the fairways."

Sammi considered this information as Delia turned into the parking lot of George Long's Golf Course. There were about a half-dozen cars in the lot. A couple of old codgers were getting ready to tee off on No.1. Delia drove through the parking lot and off on a dirt driveway that led to the Long farmhouse. The course's first hole ran along the house property, although quite a bit of land actually separated the house from the fairway. After the first hole, however, the course's other eight holes went off in the opposite direction from the house. Delia pulled up next to a dark green car that looked vaguely familiar to Sammi. Then Sammi spotted Bip Jordan sitting in a lawn chair underneath a large oak tree that dominated the house's front yard.

Three lawn chairs and a small white plastic table were arranged in a circle near the trunk of the tree. "Look," Delia said as she and Sammi approached Bip across the plush lawn, "let's stay out here and talk. It's such a nice day after so much rainy weather. I'll go in and get us some iced tea. Just don't talk business until I get back."

Delia veered off at an angle toward the house to get drinks while Sammi went forward to shake hands with Bip and make small talk. She had known Bip and his wife Dorene for years, although not as well as Sticks knew Bip. The Jordan's youngest son—she couldn't remember his name—had been a couple of years ahead of Sissy in high school. A wild kid, if she remembered right from Sissy's tales at the dinner table. But she knew that Sticks was very fond of Bip. She thought that Sticks almost considered Bip a father figure since Sticks's father had died quite young. Sammi certainly didn't know that Bip and Delia even knew each other, although she guessed that it was logical that Delia and Bip would circulate in certain "golf" circles whatever and wherever those circles might be.

A beautiful collie suddenly ran around the corner of the house and nuzzled up to Bip as if he were an old friend. Delia had probably just let the dog out of the house. Bip called the dog Sandy and rubbed her long, golden brown fur. It was curious, Sammi thought, now that I know Delia is rich or at least relatively rich everything looks more expensive. The dog. The lawn chairs that were much nicer than the ones she and Sticks had on their deck. The windows on the house (something a real estate agent would notice) were absolute top of the line. The roof was very new. Even the bushes in front of the house on both sides of the front steps that looked from a distance like ordinary green shrubs up close were expensively shaped and landscaped.

Delia came out with a tray of glasses and a pitcher filled with iced tea. They sat down with their drinks in a little semi-circle in the shade with their backs to the house and facing County Road 8, a good pitching wedge away. A breeze stirred the oak leaves. Sandy, after a quick run around the yard, sat alertly on her haunches next to Delia's chair.

"You must be wondering why we dragged you out here, Sammi," Delia began.

"I am a little curious," Sammi admitted. "But it couldn't be more pleasant sitting here. Much nicer than washing windows and scrubbing floors in the new office."

"Well," Delia said, "to tell the truth, we weren't quite ready to move ahead. But certain events including your announcement have forced our hand, so to speak."

Sammi glanced over at Bip who smiled back and nodded his head almost imperceptibly at Delia's statement.

Delia continued: "I am prepared to turn George Long's Golf Course into an 18 hole golf course and housing development. It will be called Long Lake Estates. Medium to higher priced homes. The financing is in place. I have partners. Bip will be the club pro and head of golf operations. You're sort of the last piece of the puzzle. For the real estate agent we obviously could not go with Bruce. We were thinking about going with Martin down in Lancaster. But we haven't talked to him. Rather stay local here in Stowe Towne. Then you split from Bruce and the timing was almost perfect."

Sammi realized she was staring at Delia in open-mouthed amazement. She abruptly closed her mouth and sat back. She leaned forward and then sat back again. Finally, all she could think to say was: "There's no lake."

Delia laughed. "Not now, but there will be. It'll be pretty damn impressive, too."

"How long have you been planning this?" Sammi asked. "Is this just a reaction to The Candlesticks' development?"

"Oh, goodness no," Delia said. "George and I were planning this for at least two years before he died. His death, of course, set things back. And I had to learn about some of the things that he knew about and I didn't. In addition, we were buying up contiguous land for more than 10 years. If you remember, you were the agent involved in a couple of those transactions."

Sammi nodded. "I remember." She thought: Location, location, location. A $10,000 scruffy land purchase might now turn into a dozen or more $50,000 half-acre lots. Commissions, commissions, commissions.

Delia set down her iced tea and leaned forward. "Obviously, Sammi, we want The Candlesticks development stopped. It's a beautiful old course. You know all the arguments. But we also don't think that the area can sustain two new housing developments."

Sammi stared at Delia. She no longer looked or sounded like an eccentric old woman. The collie beside her yawned and stretched her paws forward on the grass. Delia reached down and scratched the dog behind the left ear.

"Well, Sammi," Delia said glancing back at her guest, "what do you say?"

"I don't know what to say. I'm in shock. *Good* shock but still in shock."

Bip spoke up: "We thought you could devote full time to it, considering you're a new agency."

"Oh, of course," Sammi quickly agreed.

"I have our business plan, some schematics, and so forth in the house," Delia said. "Let's finish our teas and then go have a look."

Delia gave Sammi a big smile and all Sammi could see were dollar signs flashing out of her eyes.

⌐

Bip drove Sammi back to town and dropped her at her new office. However, instead of going inside to see how Laura was getting along with the cleaning, she walked the block and a half east down Duke Boulevard to the Bergman Bros. Lumberyard. As she approached, she saw her husband and son standing side by side on the sidewalk, arms folded across their chests (*They looked so much alike!*) surveying the new hole in the wall that would be the front door to the Wine Shoppe. They greeted her merrily, exhibiting great pride in their destructive accomplishment.

"When will we be able to *shop-pay* in the *shop-pee?*" she asked with a smile.

Sticks laughed. "You can be the first customer, my dear. We're featuring Thunderbird on tap."

He bowed with a flourish and Sammi stepped past her husband and son and into the darkened room. Dust hung in the air. Lumber, light fixtures, and power tools filled the room.

256

"Needs just a little work, I think," Sammi commented as the men entered behind her.

"Well, we're just getting started," Sticks said. "I'm not really sure why we did the door first. Now we're just going to have to board it up or somebody will steal our tools. But we enjoyed hacking our way through."

"Plus the counter tops," Randy added.

"That's right. We do have some stuff that'll be easier to haul through this door instead of hauling it through the rest of the store."

"How long?" Sammi asked.

Sticks shrugged. "Three weeks or so. End of June maybe. It's not that big a room, really. It won't take all that long."

"In time for the Fourth of July?" Sammi asked. "Wouldn't necessarily have to have a Grand Opening on the Fourth. Still, that's a big holiday for drinking."

Randy laughed. "I think Uncle Paul is going after the wine-tasting crowd. I bet they don't celebrate on the Fourth."

"Hey," Sticks admonished, "don't say things like that. He might hear. He's pretty sensitive."

Sammi rolled her eyes and sat on a bench. "Well, your Aunt Cathy is pretty *in*sensitive. She doesn't think I can make it in the real estate business."

Sticks nodded. "I know."

"Well, I feel like telling her about the meeting I just had. Then see what she has to say."

"What meeting?" Sticks asked.

Sammi lowered her voice to a conspiratorial whisper. She would have preferred that Randy wasn't in the room. But he'd find out about it sooner or later anyway. "I'll tell you," she said, "but you can't breathe a word to anyone. I mean you, Randy, to Julie. You have to swear. This is important to me."

Randy shrugged. "Sure, I swear."

"What's going on?" Sticks asked.

Sammi took a deep breath. "I was just out at Delia Long's house. Bip Jordan was there. Delia has the money and intends to turn her golf course into a housing development."

"And get rid of the golf course?" Sticks asked.

"No, turn it into an 18 hole course. Do a housing development. Just like Howie's proposing for The Candlesticks. Can you believe it?"

"And Delia has the money?" Sticks asked incredulously.

"Gobs of it, supposedly. And she wants me to be the chief real estate contact."

"What's Bip got to do with it?" Sticks paced up and down kicking up sawdust from the floor. This was too much information for him to handle.

"I guess he's jumping ship. He drove me back into town. He said that Howie wanted him to retire anyway."

Sticks nodded. "That's true."

"Delia is interested in having Candlesticks Acres stopped. She doesn't think Stowe Towne can support two new upscale housing developments. I completely agree with that."

All of a sudden, Sticks started to laugh.

"What's so funny?" Sammi asked, feeling slightly offended.

With a nod to Randy, her husband controlled his laughter and said: "Sammi, when the kids were little, you had a favorite phrase you used to tell them. Remember? You don't use it now. I haven't heard you say it in years. But it sure applies now."

"I haven't the foggiest idea what you're talking about."

"Well, you always told the kids that you can't have your cake and eat it, too."

"I remember that," Randy chimed in. "It never made any sense to me. If you had a cake, why wouldn't you eat it too?"

Annoyed and feeling like the butt of a joke she didn't understand, Sammi scowled at her husband and son. "What's your point, Sticks?"

"The way it's working out, you have your cake and you'll eat it, too. No development at The Candlesticks which will save our house, but you'll still have a new development at George Long's Golf Course." Sticks laughed again. "But Delia will have to do something about that stupid name. George Long's Golf Course Housing Development doesn't exactly roll off your tongue. Who would want to live there?"

"Well, I don't know why I should feel guilty. I don't know why you're trying to make me feel guilty, for that matter. Anyway, for your information, she's naming it Long Lake Estates," Sammi said.

Sticks shrugged. "I wasn't trying to make you feel guilty. But it's just interesting how this all is working out, don't you think?"

Sammi wasn't about to let Sticks off the hook quite so easily. She still felt insulted. "Maybe, Sticks, it's because I'm a good real estate agent. Maybe it's because I've earned the trust of people in town like Delia. Maybe..."

"Maybe, Sticks interrupted, "it's because I'm best friends with Bip."

Sammi closed her mouth and stared silently at her husband for a minute. Then, abruptly, she twirled around and left through the hole in the wall.

Sticks stared wide-eyed at his son. "What did I say?"

Randy raised a hand. "Don't get me involved when Mom and you are fighting."

"We weren't fighting. Were we fighting?"

Randy picked up a scrap of wood from the floor. "Sounded like fighting to me. Are we starting on the shelves at this end or that end?"

Sticks stared at his son and then turned and stared out the door into the empty street. *Well, this is a fine mess you've gotten us into, Ollie,* he thought.

⌣

State Senator Kenny Barnes of Granite City lived when he was legislating in Columbus in a very nice apartment in a development on the far north side of the city called The Swedish Market. The apartments were above, behind, and around little shops and restaurants. The place once was a popular yuppie hangout, but now it was a comfortable locale where middle-aged couples came to eat at overpriced quaint restaurants or buy odd kitchen utensils from Ye Odd Kitchen Utensil Boutique. The apartment besides Barnes's was occupied by two stewardesses, one of who was named Beth. Beth was not very attractive, but she was home at odd times as was the senator and they struck up a relationship. Barnes was utterly in awe of himself for having a sexual relationship with a stewardess even if she wasn't "a looker" as his raunchy grandfather (on his mother's side) used to say. Kenny recognized that he wasn't very attractive either. But, it didn't matter since the sex was as good as he had ever had. Which, admittedly, wasn't saying a whole lot.

In any case, self-deprecating as he could be, Senator Barnes lay in Beth's bed while she took a shower. She had to leave in 30 minutes to catch a plane. After all, that's what stewardesses did—catch planes. Kenny lay with his hands behind his head and the pink floral sheet pulled up just over his paunch. He should lose some weight or maybe have more sex. He was sure he read somewhere that having sex was great exercise and you always lost weight.

Be that as it may, State Senator Kenny Barnes turned his thoughts to the deal he had just made with the loyal opposition. He had gone behind his Party's back to get support for The Candlesticks' amendment in agreement that he would support a comprehensive Water Reclamation Act that was actually an anti-strip-mining bill. He got considerable campaign funding from strip-mine owners even though there wasn't much strip-mining in his district. He was still from what most people considered the southeastern part of Ohio and strip-mining interests had considered him a loyal supporter.

Except, Barnes knew, that wasn't enough. Not any more. Specifically, it wasn't enough to get elected. He had commissioned a small private poll and had paid for it with his own money. His district was changing and attitudes were changing. He had to react. To change slightly. Widen his base of support. It was complicated. It was a balancing act. He didn't quite understand it, but he knew it wasn't politics as usual. The boys in the backroom didn't want change, but it was already here. He had talked, for example, to a young woman farmer who was taking over the family farm from her father. He had talked to the new black doctor in his own hometown of Granite City. He had attended an Hispanic Festival in his home district. There was even a *Habitat for Humanity* crew building houses in his district. Imagine all that!

Beth sprung out of the bathroom naked and startled the senator. She started rummaging through her dresser looking for this and that. Kenny knew it was time to leave. He slipped on his red Adidas sweatsuit that he had conveniently worn when he made the 30-foot trek from his apartment front door to Beth's apartment front door. He pecked her on the cheek and promised to call Friday when she got back. He hurried away, his dick flopping under his sweatpants. He was the type of guy who always should wear underwear.

chapter fifteen

PICK IT UP

Usually, after the high school graduation ceremony and the occasional senior rowdiness that accompanied it, Stowe Towne settled down into sleepy summertime until the festive events surrounding the Fourth of July. But this summer, the town was jumping and twitching and that was without many people knowing yet about Delia's proposed Long Lake Estates. There was still enough gossipy news to keep the ears burning. For example, the Candlesticks Acres deal was hotly debated around dinner tables. If the men golfed, they opposed development. But if the men didn't golf, they viewed the development as progress (and a new customer base if the men were businessmen). If the women were older and/or associated with the Daughters of the Union Army, they opposed development on historical principle. But if the women were younger and maybe were thinking about a new home, they favored the development.

There were other happenings as well stirring the gossip pot. The Bergman name was on everyone's lips. Sticks was now perceived as a leader of The Candlesticks' opposition even though he had not done a thing since his impromptu speech in the town square. The new Bergman Realty and the new (still under construction) Wine Shoppe were both welcomed and high profile additions to the downtown business district where there had not been much new business development for some years. But speculation ran wild that one or both enterprises would spectacularly fail. At Abe's Tap, which happened to be located just across the street from Bergman Realty and was the chief watering hole for just plain folks in town, the regulars speculated that they didn't think they would trust selling their home through a woman working alone. As for the Wine Shoppe, the Bergman Bros. weren't no Gallo Bros. for sure. If they wanted to make money, they better be certain there was a big cooler stocked with Bud and Miller Genuine Draft right next to the checkout counter.

On a more juicy topic (although not much was juicier than the fanciful recreations of Sammi Bergman quitting and telling Bruce Dean to zip it up and go to hell), was the prevalent rumor that Gettysburg Café waitress Donna Dougall of the big breasts was pregnant. The rumor was false and Donna kept trying to abort the rumor (so to speak) by wearing tighter and tighter uniforms that only, of course, pushed her large breasts out further and promoted the rumor. Logic notwithstanding.

The month of June, though, for May Miller had honestly never been very sleepy or peaceful. For almost as long as she could remember, she had been actively involved in the Fourth's Arts Festival sponsored by the DUA. In addition, of course, the new DUA junior members and permanent senior members were initiated into the organization on the Fourth. This was a throwback to the DUA's post-Civil War founding. The ladies weren't called the Daughters of the Union Army for nothing. Patriotism reigned.

Mostly, the new senior member initiation was a routine process since there was such a long junior apprenticeship in the organization.

Few, if any, women were turned down at this point in time. The DUA did not want to lose membership, of course, nor did they want an angry cadre of blackballed women in the town bad-mouthing the organization. Women who had put in their time waiting for their 45th birthdays just so they could join the elite of the DUA, weren't going to be denied. Still, the DUA was no pushover. There was a thousand-dollar full membership application fee. There was a mumble-jumble initiation script to memorize filled with patriotic pledges and late nineteenth-century romantic hocus-pocus. The DUA was originally closely aligned with Eastern Star until the DUA members realized that there were not going to be enough mature ladies around for both organizations and therefore quietly and effectively dismantled the Eastern Star from the inside out. But the DUA ladies had integrated much of the Eastern Star memorized mysticism into their own ceremony. In addition, there was a major commitment for the new soon-to-be senior members to work practically around the clock on the Arts Festival.

May usually enjoyed the camaraderie of the senior initiation process. She had been doing it for so long on the "initiator's" side that she had no sense of the agony of the "initiatees." She didn't bother about junior member recruitment or initiation. A subcommittee of junior members took care of that so that senior members did not have to dirty their hands. Initiation into senior membership was cleaner and somehow more elegant. However, this year, May's anticipation was somewhat dampened. Margaret Howard turned 45 just before July 4th and so was eligible to make the leap to full senior membership in the DUA. Obviously, this created a dilemma. Not that Margaret would be turned down. *Oh, heavens no!* May thought. Margaret was exactly what the DUA needed. A wife of a name-carrying member of one of the original families. A blue-blood herself from out East. A long-standing, dedicated junior member of the DUA. DUA presidential material certainly in another 20 years or so. Except, that darn Howie had proposed destroying The Candlesticks. If he had just waited until July fifth...

May, Emma Mitchell, and Joyce Thompson sat in Joyce Thompson's music room in the Thompson house at the corner of Hanover Street and Jones Street. The Thompsons had gutted the old Victorian house and turned the inside into an ultramodern living area. It was bizarre. There was no other house with such a split personality. Outside, the house had gables and turrets and shutters and a large rose trellis in the front yard. The type of house Nathaniel Hawthorne could have written an entire novel about (and did). Inside, however, the house had modern Danish furniture, white throw rugs on polished oak floors, missing rooms (some rooms were completely removed to create *open, gallery space*, in Joyce's words), and very, very modern art. One painting was just a huge square of red and was worth $50,000 according to Joyce.

The music room was all electronic, but today it was mercifully silent. In any event, the Senior Committee was interviewing two candidates for membership. The first had been Mary Schultz, the mousy, unassuming wife of the banker, Jack Schultz. Mary's only accomplishment in life was the bearing and raising of two gigantic sons. Mary brought nothing to the DUA except her husband's banking. She was from Cincinnati and her maiden name was even *more* German than Schultz, if possible. The committee let Mary grovel before them for an hour, then gave her mild encouragement and sent her on her way.

Now, with their iced teas refreshed and the late afternoon sun bending into the tall un-curtained windows, the ladies sucked it up and invited Margaret Emerson Howard into the music room.

Margaret, in truth, had been through too much over the past month or so and should have taken a rain check. Plus, dealing with her uncooperative, unsympathetic, and obtuse father had definitely put her off dealing with older folks. Margaret didn't *do* anything during the day. It wasn't that type of stress. She just needed to get away. Go to Moon Lake up near Traverse City in Michigan where they used to vacation in the

A few days later, Howie Howard sat alone in a golf cart along the narrow stretch of woods on Barnes's Knob that separated The Candlesticks' seventh fairway from the meandering Pottawa River. The day was overcast and a cool breeze was blowing from the west. The weather reflected his feelings. His wife's depressed mood following her disastrous DUA interview had gradually wormed its way into his psyche. Even her "cool" acceptance letter into senior membership in the DUA (waiving the need for a further interview considering Mrs. Howard's "considerable and conscientious service" as a junior member of the organization) failed to change the atmosphere around the Howard household. Margaret curtly informed Howie when he tried to congratulate her on receiving the letter, that the letters were usually effusive missives welcoming the new senior members and were signed by all the current DUA membership instead of a curt note signed only by May Miller.

On the other home front, there had been a couple of flare-ups with Julie about her future. What did they call them in Vietnam? Howie tried to remember. Firefights? Brief shouting matches about her not seeing Randy Bergman or about her finally making a decision about college. The arguments were over almost as soon as they started. Nothing resolved. Howie and Margaret both felt too psychologically whipped to pursue the arguments to a resolution. And maybe too afraid as well, Howie speculated. Afraid that Julie would jump in the wrong direction and out of their control and maybe even out of their lives forever.

Howie sighed. He had to admit that this was where he truly missed Bip Jordan's advice. He and Bip would come out on the course and just sit and watch the golfers and talk over things. He knew he had sometimes treated Bip shabbily. But the club had also provided the old pro with a good living over the years. And Howie really did listen to everything the guy said even though he didn't always follow his advice. Now, Bip was in semiretirement, using up some vacation days. (Howie was surprised Bip even got vacation days—how did you earn vacation days when you spent all day, everyday on the golf course?) Bip just wasn't around.

If Howie had paid just a little bit more attention in college, he might have come across the term Pyrrhic Victory. Or, at least he might have remembered the U.S. general's Vietnam explanation of saving the Vietnamese village by destroying it. Even if he didn't know either reference, he still sensed their meaning in terms of the golf course. The Graduation Day storm had inflicted spotty but serious damage to the course. Although the damage was all cleaned up now, the metaphor still persisted. Howie was having his way in terms of the Candlesticks' Acres housing development. He had overcome the obstacles. The legislation was on track. The Candlesticks' Board was in his pocket. Cliner was still committed. Local opposition seemed to have spent itself. (Sticks Bergman was apparently obsessed instead with building his stupid wine store.) No real environmental problems had surfaced. Sean Donaldson had even sent a short—but brilliant, Howie thought—initial plan for course redesign. So, why didn't Howie feel better? Why did he feel like Pyrrhus, King of Epirus?

The cool breeze picked up and swirled through the golf course. Would more revenue be lost to rain? Howie wondered. It had been a wretched spring, weatherwise and otherwise. Clouds rolled across the sky above him. Almost time for league play to start, he thought idly, when he noticed a golf cart speeding along the edge of the fairway up from the seventh tee. It looked like someone was trying to find him in a big hurry and within seconds he saw that Bruce Dean was driving the cart. Bruce was only an occasional golfer and, besides, he was dressed in a business suit. In a moment, Bruce squealed to a stop next to Howie. Howie could not remember ever hearing a golf cart squeal to a stop before.

"Did you hear about Delia Long?" Bruce demanded. He sounded

out of breath as if he had been running instead of just driving a golf cart.

"Delia Long?" Howie scoffed. "Is she still alive?" He paused when he saw Bruce wasn't laughing. "I'm just kidding, Bruce." Howie's mood had been momentarily lifted by the sight of Bruce's wild ride in the golf cart. He also liked to see Bruce upset. Why was that?

But Bruce wasn't in a kidding mood. "Believe me, Delia's still alive, Howie. And she's turning George Long's Golf Course into a housing development. And I'll give you one guess on who's going to be the real estate agent for the development."

Howie laughed. "Who'd want to live on George Long's Golf Course?"

"All right, wise guy, go ahead and laugh. Bip Jordan is her partner. Did you know that? All our favorite people. Sammi Bergman, Bip Jordan, and Delia Long."

Howie stared at Bruce. "Bip? Are you sure?"

Bruce paused. "Well, no, I'm not sure. But that's the rumor. I'm really not sure about anything. But that's what everyone's gossiping about. You know Stowe Towne. There must be some truth to it. I do know that Delia Long owns a shitload of land around that golf course. I can remember our office selling at least a couple of properties to her."

"You mean Sammi sold it to her."

"Well, yes."

Howie glanced up at the rain clouds. "So, what does it matter? I still say, who would want to live out in that neck of the woods anyway? Especially when they can live here. Just look around."

Bruce shrugged and didn't look around. "Five years ago I guess I would have agreed with you. But things are changing. South of town is easier to get to the highway, to get to Columbus. If you remember, when Allied Pipes was built, everyone thought it was stupid to build the plant out there. Now the town is growing right out to meet it. The new McDonald's. Kroger's."

"Maybe," Howie responded, "but I'm not convinced. George Long's

Golf Course has been there since before I was a boy. Sticks Bergman and I grew up playing together there. People move away from that area of the county. They don't move toward there."

"They might if there's a huge new housing development."

Howie shook his head. "No they won't."

"Jesus Christ, Howie," Bruce said in exasperation, "what do you think we're trying to do? We're trying to lure people to live out in the country. It's just different country!"

"And that's not a major factor, the different country? It's a hell of a factor. Besides, this might be just a rumor. For instance, I'm sure what you said about Bip isn't true. He still works here. I don't know if he even knows Delia Long."

"Everybody knows Delia Long," Bruce said ruefully, "and that may be our biggest problem."

"How so?"

"If there's a cheaper alternative than living out here while still being in a new development with a golf course. No controversy. No state forest. No destroying of an historic landmark?" Bruce was reflective for a moment. "Although that course does back up to the old Creed Marsh. Or, what we used to call Creed Marsh when I was a kid. Remember?"

Howie nodded. "I remember. I haven't heard that name for years."

Bruce shrugged. "I'll check it out."

Howie felt a few sprinkles of rain. The wind picked up and swirled around. "Goddamn rain," he said. "It's fucking up everything."

"What else are we going to do?" Bruce asked.

"Get out of the rain," Howie said, and without another word he pulled his cart around Bruce's cart and headed across the seventh fairway oblivious to a drive streaking over his head from a golfer on the seventh tee.

⌐

As Howie sped off like a maniac across his golf course with no real goal in mind except to see if Bip Jordan was around, Bip was teeing off at George Long's Golf Course with Sticks and Randy. The Bergmans were taking a break from the Wine Shoppe construction that was coming along well except that Randy kept calling it the Wineyard and the name was catching on among lumberyard employees. Bip wanted to run some course design ideas past Sticks. Part of Bip's deal with Delia was that he would do the course design including building the nine new holes. It was like a dream come true for him.

On the first green, however, the nightmare of that dream was evident. This was the notorious hole where George Long had keeled over and Delia had refused to move the pin placement so now it drained like a dirty sink. It was great for wayward putts that trickled in. But the hole literally was under water with the least amount of rain. Such as the rain that was now threatening their outing. Delia had assured Bip that she was over her sentimentality and he could make appropriate changes. But the green was ruined and would have to be rebuilt. Bip was seriously thinking of just wiping it out and linking the first hole with the par-3 second hole into a par-5 dogleg left.

"That's not a bad idea," Sticks agreed as they walked off the green after all three scored birdies. "Problem is that it leaves you sort of a layup second shot. It's odd to have a layup second shot. An ordinary three-wood will carry across what I assume will be the fairway. And, if you have a house there..."

"I thought about that," Bip said, "and if we took out about five trees here on the corner we could curve the fairway more dramatically."

"Sure," Sticks answered, "but then it's hardly a par 5. As long as your drive is on the right side of the fairway any of the three of us, for example, could get to the green in two."

"You could move the first tee back 30 or 40 yards," Randy suggested.

They all turned and looked back down the first fairway toward the first tee.

"Well, the clubhouse is in the way," Sticks said.

"That's not a problem," Bip said. "We're tearing it down. It's just an old cinder block shell. There has to be a new clubhouse. And then we'll make room for the first tee."

They arrived at the second tee to the short 128-yard hole. Randy still had honors and hit a nice wedge to the center of the green.

"You know, you got a problem already, Bip," Sticks said as he teed up his ball. "We've just walked the first hole and already you've knocked down the clubhouse, decided to build a new first tee, wiped out the first green, and, in effect, wiped out the second hole by combining it with the first hole. So, now you have to build 10 new holes instead of nine. I'm not sure Delia can afford your design services."

Bip watched glumly as Sticks landed his ball inside Randy's on the green. "You've got a point, Sticks," he admitted.

Sticks and Randy walked away from the second green with their second birdies. This was not so unusual for Sticks, but it was a first for Randy. Bip scored a double-bogey now that he was thinking about the course design. Still, on the third tee, he brightened a bit. The third hole was a dogleg right par 4 of 390 yards. It was by far the nicest hole on the course and Bip could easily avoid any changes. You could even put houses up along the slight ridge that ran along the right side of the fairway. The ridge and its thick scrub brush along with the length of the hole prevented all but the most foolish of big hitters from attempting to cut the dogleg. It all functioned better than using the dreaded out-of-bounds stakes.

The trio played the hole conventionally and all walked away with pars and praise for the layout. No changes here. The fourth and fifth, though, were something else. They were parallel 450-yard par fives. The fourth played straight out and the fifth played straight back. The trio pounded the ball down the fairway to the fourth green. Watching his son roll in a 12-foot putt for par (Randy was beside himself with joy, he had never been two under par at the end of four holes), Sticks commented that either the fourth or the fifth hole would have to go or (he emphasized dramatically) the new front nine could veer off from here and the current number five would then become the number 14 of an 18-hole course.

Randy retrieved his ball from the cup. "You mean, Dad, that you wouldn't build a second nine to go with this nine, but you'd split this nine and tack on holes?"

"I wouldn't use *tack on*," Sticks responded, removing his Cincinnati baseball cap and wiping his brow. "But what are you going to do here? Look, what if you put a lake over there where the fifth tee is now? Move the fifth tee up and make that hole a par 4 and bring the edge of the lake right over here to the edge of this green. That makes this hole a lot more interesting with water to the left of the green. What do you think, Bip?"

Bip had just made another double-bogey. He was having a very emotional round. "I could see a lake here," he agreed. "And I had thought about splitting the course myself, although I was thinking between the seventh and eighth holes. Still, it's a good idea here."

They walked over to the fifth tee, in the middle of the nonexistent lake. Bip worried out loud about how much money he could spend on course design. Stick reassured him that you couldn't separate course design from housing layout. "The houses primarily have to be in attractive settings, Bip," Sticks explained. "They have to overlook lakes and fairways or preferably both."

All three men ripped drives, although Randy's hooked back into the fourth fairway.

"I assume Howie still doesn't know about you and all of this?" Sticks asked Bip as they strolled down the fairway toward their drives.

"If he hasn't heard about it, he's the only person in Stowe Towne who hasn't. I was having coffee in the restaurant this morning and three people asked me about it. They all said they'd heard a rumor. You know."

"Well, we haven't spilled the beans to anybody. I hope you know that."

"Sure," Bip answered. "We knew this was going to happen. Delia's talked to a bunch of people. She had to get some things done."

"So, what about Howie?"

Bip sighed. "I got to tell him. He's not going to be happy. Frankly, I don't blame him."

"But he fired you, didn't he? Or, forced you into retirement?"

They reached Bip's ball and the pro selected a three-wood. He hit it long and straight and the ball appeared to stop rolling just short of the green. The pin was way up front so Bip would have a chance at an eagle. As he replaced his club, he said, "Howie and I still go back a long time. He'll still feel that I betrayed him."

Sticks walked ahead to his ball and dropped his bag after pulling out his five-wood. "Well, I don't get that at all," he said, "not at all." He banged a shot straight at the hole, but it rolled all the way over the hard green and fell off the back of the putting surface. "Damn," he said.

On the green, Bip missed his eagle, but got a birdie. Sticks recovered for a par. And Randy, after mishitting his three-wood that at least rolled into the proper fairway, bounced a six-iron down the rough fairway, onto the green, and within three feet of the cup. They stood on the green looking at Randy's ball for a moment and then Sticks said, "Pick it up, son, it looks like a birdie to me."

Randy, three-under after five, finished up with three bogeys and a par on the last four holes and ended up shooting even par for nine for the first time in his life. He couldn't wait to tell Julie. It would be a more pleasant conversation than the one Bip would have with Howie.

⌒

The problem was that Randy couldn't find Julie. Finally, he called Heather's house and Heather Miller's mother told him that Julie had picked up Heather and Heather's little sister Stacey and had gone shopping at a mall in Columbus. Randy ended up working late with his father on the Wine Shoppe. They got home after dark even though it was almost the longest day of the year. Randy thought Julie might be home; she and Heather wouldn't go partying if they had Stacey along. So, he took a quick shower and slipped out the back door and decided to do something that he had not done since before he started driving.

He walked across the backyard and then along the edge of the soybean field toward The Candlesticks' 18th green. There was a half-moon that peeked in and out of large fluffy clouds. Randy could see fine and knew the walk by heart anyway. He walked past the cart barn where a couple of kids he knew who were still in high school were washing down golf carts under the light from a pole lamp. He gave them a wave and they waved back. Passing behind the clubhouse, he could hear laughter and music from the bar. Sounded like quite a few golfers had stuck around to suck down some beers. He then walked down the long first fairway. However, where the dogleg bent right to head for the first green, he stepped through the short row of pine trees which often swallowed up the tee shots of long hitters who weren't careful and overhit their drives through the fairway.

The Howard's deck was not at the back of the house, but off to the side so it overlooked the first fairway. There was a wide expanse of lawn. There was no one on the deck and Randy could see through the sliding glass doors that there was no one in the family room. A single lamp was turned on, but the large TV was dark. He knew that Julie seldom watched TV in the family room, preferring to watch TV in her room. There was a light on in her room, which was on the back wing of the one-story, ranch-style house. Howie and Margaret's master bedroom was on the other side of the house away from the golf course.

Randy walked up to Julie's window. Light glowed through her pale blue curtains. He paused and listened to make sure he didn't hear voices. He knew that Julie's parents seldom, if ever, came into her bedroom. Still, it was wise to be prudent. Finally, he rapped a knuckle on the window. "Julie, Julie, are you there?" he said as loudly as he dared.

In a second, the curtains flew apart and Julie yanked up the window. She was dressed in a blue Kent State T-shirt he had given her and pink panties he had not given her. "Didn't you ever hear of a telephone?" she asked.

"Can't see you on a telephone. What have you been doing?"

"Heather and I went to Columbus, but we had to take Stacey along. She's such a brat."

"I shot par out at George Long's Golf Course. I had three birdies."

Randy's remark seemed to soften Julie and she knelt down and rested her arms on the windowsill. "Remember when your father followed you over here because he thought you were window-peeking?" she asked.

"I *was* window-peeking. Fortunately, when he got here, you had put your clothes back on."

Julie laughed. "Stop it. That's not true. I saved your ass."

"You loved me even back then."

Julie ignored him. "Why were you playing at *that* course?" she asked.

"Well, my Mom didn't want me to tell you, but I think everyone knows now. You know the woman who owns it? Delia Long? She's thinking of turning that course into a housing development, too. Just like The Candlesticks. My Mom might be the real estate agent."

"Does my Dad know?" Julie asked in amazement.

"I think so. My Dad said that my Mom said that she heard that your Dad knows. Maybe Bip told him. He's going to work over there when he retires from The Candlesticks."

"Hmm, maybe if Dad worries about that, he won't worry about college for me," Julie speculated.

"He's got a lot to worry about. Come on, put some shorts on and we'll go for a ride."

"I think I'm still grounded. Not that *that* matters. Where are we going?"

"The drive-through at McDonald's. I didn't eat dinner because we were working on the wine store."

"Poor baby," Julie said and she hurried to find a pair of shorts and her sandals.

chapter sixteen

STICKS IT TO 'EM

The copy of the filing of a motion for a preliminary injunction halting further development of The Candlesticks Golf Club was delivered to David Canello at his Columbus law office on Monday, June 15th. The source of the filing was the Central Ohio Chapter of the National Golf Course Owners Association. The president of the Central Ohio Chapter was, of course, Delia Long.

Canello scanned the paperwork quickly and let it fall back on his desk. All those years thinking Delia was an eccentric fool. Delia and her goofy golf course. Delia ordering double Cuttys and glad-handing assistant pros and green superintendents. Handing out Association plaques to club owners for managing the local United Way campaign or promoting environmental responsibility. Always working the crowd. Making friends. Shouldering the Association's work. And now, when she needed a favor: *Bang!*

Canello sipped coffee from his favorite Cleveland Browns coffee mug. Scotch tape held together the cracked handle that still threatened to fall off. The mug featured the old team's plain orange helmet and the word, *Browns*. Considering that the old Cleveland Browns were now the Baltimore Ravens, the mug might someday become a collector's item. Or not. Just being old and decrepit didn't necessarily make something valuable. Although that was exactly the contention of the legal mumbo-jumbo contained in Delia's preliminary injunction.

With a certain detached irony, the lawyer scanned the short document. Essentially, it requested that all development at The Candlesticks be halted because the course was an historical landmark that should be preserved. *Like my coffee cup*, Canello thought and smiled. The document very briefly reviewed the golf course's history. A bit thin on historical significance! George Patton didn't practice tank maneuvers on the fairways prior to WWII. Ike and Khrushchev didn't debate the Cold War over a cold one in the clubhouse. Dick Nixon or even Bill Clinton couldn't be accused of taking a mulligan off the first tee.

Canello didn't sweat the legal ramifications. In fact, it was sort of amusing, even quaint. Although one could never be certain, he seriously doubted any judge would issue a temporary restraining order halting The Candlesticks' development. Especially if it was pointed out that Delia Long had a financial interest in seeing The Candlesticks' development halted or delayed.

Canello had heard the rumors about Delia developing her golf course. Tom Duke, among others, had called him. Tom Junior had sworn like a sailor and all but threatened to do mayhem on Delia. Canello had toyed with him a bit before finally soothing the asshole. He had explained that George Long's Golf Course was a poor man's course. A farmer's country club. The houses would be Caddy Shack shacks. Relax, Tom, he had advised, this won't affect us at all. Delia just wants a little publicity.

This latest delay tactic was only a clever ploy. Amusing at best. And even further amusing, for Canello, because he knew it would upset

Howie. He wouldn't lie to Howie. He wouldn't make it into a bigger deal than just a nuisance. But he would at least be serious in presentation. Let Howie sweat a little. Canello would exact just a little revenge after being shut out on practically this whole deal.

The phone rang and Bonnie Wicks told him that a reporter named Mara Fish from the *Dispatch* was on the line. About The Candlesticks' restraining order, Bonnie said archly. The woman acted like a wife who didn't appreciate golf. She considered this furor over a golf course a *Tempest in a Teapot!*—one of her mother's favorite phrases. Bonnie thought it detracted from more serious legal matters. Her sanctimonious attitude pissed off Canello. He took the call more to spite her than any great desire to speak with Mara Fish.

"Mr. Canello? This is Mara Fish from the *Dispatch*. I've been following the housing development controversy out in Stowe Towne."

"Well, I don't know if I'd call it a controversy, Mara. And please, call me David."

"Right. There are people, though, opposed to the development."

"I think people, let me say *some* people, were initially opposed until they started to see that we weren't destroying the course. In fact, we're enhancing the course and at the same time giving a big boost to economic development for Stowe Towne and the surrounding Pottawa County."

"I understand a temporary restraining order has been issued to stop development."

"No, you're jumping the gun quite a bit here. A motion has been filed for a preliminary injunction. I just got it on my desk before you called so it's too early for me to comment on. But a judge has to act on the motion before anything is halted or delayed."

"It has to do with, ah, let me see, historical preservation."

Canello laughed. "It sounds like you have a copy of it there, Mara. I would say that the motion has even more to do with publicity than historical preservation."

"I don't think that's true, Mr. Canello," Mara said icily.

"Well, be it as it may. We're talking, here, about a golf course. We're not talking about a Civil War courthouse or Abe Lincoln's log cabin. I'm not aware of, nor does the paperwork refer to, any valid historical reason at all in terms of The Candlesticks. It's a nice old golf course. But it's just that; it's a golf course."

"All right, so what do you think will happen?"

"I have no comment on the action a judge might take."

"And what's happening now at the course?"

"Mara, if I may make a pun on your name that I'm sure you've heard before, I think you're on a fishing expedition. I really have nothing more to add."

"You're right, Mr. Canello, I have heard it before. Thank you very much then."

"You're welcome. Thank you, Mara. Good-bye."

Canello hung up the phone and smiled. He felt very pleased with himself and amused by the whole situation.

⌒

Mr. Miller, not yet knowing about the injunction, was not having a good Monday. The last couple of weeks in June were often chaotic around the house as preparations for the Fourth of July Festival approached. May stored craft items or other Festival gear in and about the house. One year, he remembered, the ladies had a kite design contest and the dining room was filled with kites of all shapes and sizes. Colorful but very awkward to handle and store. This year there was none of that, although the garage was filled with boxes of commemorative Civil War plates that the DUA was pushing. The Seven Heroes were pictured in an action sequence in full color. Just what a dinner guest wanted beneath servings of fried chicken, broccoli, and baked potato. Silly, May had chided her husband, you would never *eat* off these plates! This is for *collecting!* Plate collecting is *very* big!

Ironically and coincidentally, it so happened that Mr. Miller was this year's chairman of the golf outing at The Candlesticks. Every year, the DUA men (there was no official men's auxiliary) sponsored a golf outing for all the husbands who had to accompany their wives to the Festival. A trip to the Stowe Towne July Fourth Festival for DUA women from around the country was somewhat akin to a pilgrimage to Mecca. At some point, each member was obliged to make the trip since the DUA had been founded in the town. The Stowe Towne chapter was always dedicated to making its visitors welcomed.

The women more than the men, however. The "scramble" was the only planned men's event and it had become a short but welcomed refuge for some veteran male attendees who otherwise had to meekly follow along behind their wives for the rest of the weekend. (And often worked their butts off on various Festival jobs from cooking bratwursts to setting up and taking down tents.) The position of golf chairman rotated each year among the senior Stowe Towne DUA husbands who played golf. It didn't involve a lot of work. The event was just a straight four-man scramble with a few nice prizes, a few goofy prizes, a raffle (so the ladies got some money), and then lunch. There was a shotgun start at 8:00 in the morning and there were usually as many as 30 foursomes. Playing The Candlesticks was an attraction for some old farts, especially when they were first-time attendees from out-of-state.

But, simple or not, the damn thing still took some planning. Plus, the atmosphere was a little frosty at the course, although the date had been reserved for a year and the event was a solid moneymaker for the club. The Candlesticks' staffers—guys like Warren and Bip and Chet—were friendly enough. That wasn't the problem. But Mr. Miller felt awkward and even a little bit embarrassed during the routine planning meetings. He actually considered changing the venue. But he would have to go considerably far out of town to find a suitable substitute course and it was unlikely that any course would want to reserve a Saturday morning that happened to be July Fourth for an outing. Besides, many players looked forward to playing The Candlesticks. Plus, May wouldn't hear of a change. She would neither break with the tradition of the men playing at The Candlesticks nor allow Mr. Miller to show any sign of giving in on any issue to Howie.

Nevertheless, sitting with May at their kitchen table over coffee in the late morning, Mr. Miller sighed nosily. He took a sip of coffee and pushed aside the registration forms for the scramble. They were ahead of last year's count with more than two weeks still to go and would probably fill the full field of 32 teams. A sudden light shower splashed against the kitchen window above the sink and Mr. Miller remarked that he felt a little like the cruise director on the *Titanic*.

May stared across the table at her husband, neither amused nor informed by the remark.

"Well," Mr. Miller explained defensively, "next year with the new housing development underway, the course probably won't want to host an outing, especially on the Fourth of July weekend."

"We don't know that and we don't know that there will be a housing development," May responded primly. She was using graph paper to place craft booths around a diagram of the town square. "Besides," she continued, "golfing is not the main purpose."

"The *raison d'être*," Mr. Miller mumbled.

"Pardon?"

"Listen, May, all I'm trying to say is that it looks like our Candlestick effort is lost. Howie has the thing locked up—or so it appears from everything I can tell. Contractually. Legally. Hell, I'm not even sure we have much public sentiment on our side."

"I thought the fund at the café was doing quite well."

"A few hundred dollars. But for what purpose?"

"Well..."

"I mean, what are we doing?"

May carefully set aside her graph paper. Booth mapping would have to wait for a minute. She suddenly realized that this was a moment of truth. A moment of truth that she knew had been lurking just around the corner. Margaret Howard as much as slapped her in the face with it a week ago at Margaret's senior membership interview. Although it really was not Margaret's fault. Nevertheless, May now saw clearly that this issue was larger than just the golf course. Indeed, the DUA itself had to change. The organization could no longer cling so rigidly to old values, old traditions, and old rules. Or, old history.

The Candlesticks Country Club and Golf Course was lost. But in reality, it had been lost for years. Decades, really. No one went there to dance or to dine. Now it was simply a sports place. Another sports place like all those that dominated the newspapers, magazines, and television.

Give it up, May, she thought.

She caught Mr. Miller looking at her from across the table. The faintest glimmer of worry seemed to pass across his face. Just a hint. *Worry for her*, she thought. *About her!* She felt a catch in her throat.

"I don't know. I don't know for what purpose," she said softly.

"Well, me neither, May. I guess, on the one hand, it's progress. I've never been against progress. But it won't be the same, will it?"

"No, it won't be the same," she agreed.

"Us old fellows going out and playing. But then, us old fellows won't be going out all that much longer either."

May reached across the small table and rested her hands on top of her husbands' folded hands.

"I'm sorry, Groucho, I truly am," she said.

She seldom used his given name; hadn't maybe for two years or more. It had always been a secret sign of endearment between them.

But a source of pain for him growing up. A lifelong ironic gift from a father who loved Groucho Marx and had grown to dislike the Miller family tradition. He wanted to stick it to the tradition so he goofed up his son's name. Mr. Miller insisted on the nickname Butch as a kid, but then, as an adult, he simply became Mr. Miller.

Mr. Miller stared at his wife. Her response took him by surprise. So much so he felt his eyes tear up. "Just a small sign of our mortality," he said quietly.

She smiled and they sat that way for many minutes as the rain continued to beat against the window.

⤸

That Friday night, Sticks and Sammi Bergman decided to go to the Maple Lodge on the south side of the Stowe Towne town square for dinner. They had both been so busy—Sticks with completing The Wine Shoppe and Sammi with establishing her real estate office—that they had barely even seen each other, much less had meals together. So they made a date of sorts and mutually agreed to take some time and relax and talk through their disagreements and the tension between them. It wasn't serious. It could be worked out quickly if they just talked about it.

The Maple Lodge was always crowded on a Friday night, but this Friday night it was particularly packed. Maybe it was because the week had been cloudy and drizzly, although today had been beautiful. People were ready to get out and do something. Jennifer, who was serving as hostess tonight, suggested they wait for a table in the bar, but warned them that it was probably standing room only. They shrugged, trying to maintain their good humor, and moved off to their left around the edge of the dining room toward the entrance to the small bar with its woodsy, western motif of deer heads, antlers, and a painting behind the bar of a voluptuous, partially clad woman reclining on a lounge. She was nicknamed Mae—after Mae West not May Miller.

As they neared the entrance to the bar area, they ran into a group of people being escorted out of the bar to their table by a waitress. Sticks and Sammi stepped aside and when they did, they found themselves looking directly at Howie and Margaret Howard who were seated in a booth just to the left of the entrance to the bar. There was a moment of shocked silence as the Howards also caught sight of the Bergmans. To another diner glancing over, they looked like old friends running into one another. Two couples, 40-something, well dressed in summer country club clothes of whites and pastels. The tension beneath the surface was not evident, although more than a couple of sharp-eyed ladies around the dining room would take note of the encounter.

Finally, Sammi managed, "Hi, oh, pretty crowded tonight."

Margaret's hands fluttered up to her face. "Yes, it certainly is. Well, uh, are you meeting someone?"

"No, no," Sammi answered.

"We, Howie and I, we haven't ordered yet. Do you want to join us? Otherwise you'll be waiting for hours."

"We don't want to impose," Sammi demurred. Sticks also started to beg off, but Margaret responded before he could speak.

"Oh no, not at all. Here, I'll move over next to Howie. You sit here." Margaret scooted out of her seat wondering what she was doing. Being polite, of course. But she knew as soon as she saw the Bergmans that she had to talk to them. Because of Julie. Her conversations with Julie had just ground to a halt. Ever since the graduation ceremony, their daughter had almost become a ghost in the Howard household. Most of the time she stayed in her room. There was no college decision. They didn't know where she was most of the time, although she always slept at home and, in fact, often was home early. They suspected she was still seeing Randy, but they didn't know. Maybe, just maybe, the

Bergmans knew something.

The Bergmans slid into the booth and the women fidgeted with the silverware, napkins, and water glasses. Howie managed to flag down their waitress, red-haired Kimberly Meyers, and Sticks and Sammi put in their drink orders and took their names off the waiting list. For a few nervous minutes they small-talked about the restaurant crowd, the rainy week, and the upcoming Festival. Howie mentioned that Margaret now was a senior DUA member which elicited congratulations from Sticks and Sammi. Mercifully, the Bergmans' drinks arrived and the four of them managed to relax a bit.

Well, Sticks thought as he looked over his drink at Howie, *here goes nothing.* "Read about that injunction or whatever in the *Dispatch*. Sammi and I didn't know anything about it."

Howie smiled a thin smile and ran a hand through his black hair. Delia's injunction had preoccupied him all week. Canello had hedged and flip-flopped. He had driven Howie nuts before assuring him that legally the injunction didn't have a prayer. Howie said to the Begmans: "Our legal counsel says not to worry. Bit of a stretch going for historic preservation, I think. We're not changing our start date."

"Which is?" Sticks asked.

"August first, maybe. But that will mostly be on the land behind our house. The course itself won't be touched until mid-October at the earliest. That's the preliminary schedule. I don't really expect to meet it. I mean, this is going to be a five-year project. Isn't that what you're projecting at Delia's, Sammi?"

Sammi reddened a bit. "Maybe, four or five years," she finally said. "We may have a couple of houses up a lot earlier than that."

"Well, that's right," Howie replied. "You need a demonstration tract. Something to keep people's interest. You want them driving by and looking. Or you want them golfing and looking. That's what I told Bip."

"You talked to Bip?" Sammi asked.

"We had a little heart-to-heart. You know, we had to. God, we've known each other all these years. Anyway, I told him not to wipe out his golf holes too quickly. You want people to keep playing and watching the houses go up as they play. Gets them in the buying mood. Don't you agree?"

"So, your conversation with Bip went all right? He was nervous about it." Sammi knew she was getting into personal territory, but it seemed to her that they had already crossed the line just by joining the Howards for dinner.

"What was I going to do? Fire him? We had already worked out his retirement. I mean I think it's more power to all of you. Two new housing developments just goes to show that Stowe Towne is twice as prosperous. Delia getting the Association to do the injunction is just a little dirty politics. But that's Delia for you. George was like that, too. That's how he made his money."

Sammi's eyes narrowed a bit and she ignored Howie's remarks about Delia and her late husband. "I'm not sure I entirely agree with the theory that the more housing developments the better," she said.

"Well, up to a point at least. The town's changing. Christ, Sammi, your husband's building a wine store. Did you ever imagine Stowe Towne could support a wine store? A beer carryout, sure. But a wine store? Even if it is part of the lumberyard. What do you think, Sticks?"

Sticks held up a hand. "Hey, I'm not the real estate person. I just wanted to save The Candlesticks."

"Save it? We're going to make it better!"

Kimberly returned and effectively stopped them from going down *that* road toward an argument. They ordered dinner. They had all eaten at the Maple Lodge so often that they didn't have to even glance at the menu. Margaret had the broiled scallops. Sammi had the chicken Caesar salad. Howie had the halibut steak. And Sticks had the house filet. The food really was pretty good.

Kimberly retreated and Margaret thought that it was as good a time as any to bring up the children. "What has Randy been doing this summer?" she asked tentatively. "Working at the lumberyard again?"

"Helping me remodel that front room for the wine store, actually," Sticks said.

"I saw the new door," Howie responded. "Are you making the room bigger, too, or..." He felt his wife's hand on his wrist and paused.

"I'm sorry, dear," Margaret interrupted, "but I wanted to ask if Julie has been over at the Bergmans' much. Recently, perhaps?"

Both Bergmans squirmed a bit. "Well, no," Sammi said, "she hasn't been over. Sticks, has she been over?"

Sticks shook his head. "Randy and I saw her drive by one day, yesterday maybe, when we were crossing the street to the Tap to get lunch. She honked and Randy waved. I'm sure it was her, although we didn't talk about it. You know."

Howie, finally taking the cue from his wife, said, "We're a little concerned. She hasn't made her choice about college yet. Getting late. More than late. She still has this 'after graduation' thing. We weren't like that, were we, Sticks?"

Sticks smiled, but he remembered that he and Howie were exactly like that. The summer after they graduated from high school, they didn't do a thing. In fact, although they were never close friends, they did more together that summer—mainly golfed together—than they ever did before or since. He knew that Howie was being ironic. But he also knew he was getting at something else.

"Well," Sammi said, "Randy was a little like that last year. Even though he was working at the lumberyard. Of course, he knew he was going to Kent State. That was never an issue."

Margaret sucked it in and asked the $64,000 question: "Are they still dating, do you think, Randy and Julie?"

Howie added: "You know, we just don't know."

At that moment, Kimberly swept in with salads for Margaret, Howie, and Sticks. "I got them extra fast for you guys," she explained. Kimberly was a friend of the Bergmans' daughter Sissy and always treated Sticks and Sammi special when she waited on them at the Lodge. She had been married at Christmas to one of the guys at Allied Pipes and Sissy had been in the wedding.

Everyone thanked her profusely and then left the salads virtually untouched.

Sammi spoke first: "I don't know if they're still seeing each other. To tell the truth, we told Randy that perhaps he shouldn't date Julie. Not that we don't like her. Please don't get me wrong. She's a wonderful girl. But he needs to concentrate on college. He doesn't need a girlfriend now. He did all right last year, but he certainly is capable of doing better in his studies."

"That's right!" Margaret jumped in enthusiastically. "Exactly right. We told Julie the same thing. She doesn't need a boyfriend now. She needs to think about *college*. She needs to *focus* on college."

So, the topic was out on the table.

After a long moment Sticks said, "Of course, we're not sure Randy actually does anything we say." He forced a small laugh. "Like today. We're almost done with the wine shop, but he insisted that he had to take off and go to Cedar Point."

The large amusement park he mentioned was near Lake Erie and famous for its roller coasters. The park was a two-hour drive north of Stowe Towne.

Howie and Margaret paused, forks in midair over their salads.

"Cedar Point?" Howie asked.

"That's right," Sammi said. "He told me he was going with a few friends. He mentioned Heather Miller."

"Julie went with Heather Miller to Cedar Point today," Howie said.

"Oh," Sammi responded.

"Well, I wonder if they came back early then," Margaret said icily. She pointed with her fork: "Because Heather Miller is right over there eating dinner with her parents.

Howie and the Bergmans followed the direction her fork pointed and sure enough, there was Heather Miller sitting at a large round table with her parents, Keith and Rachel, as well as her little sister Stacey and her grandparents, May and Mr. Miller. Kimberly was just serving the table a cake with a sparkler on top shooting off tiny sparks. Someone must have been celebrating a birthday or anniversary.

"They wouldn't have come back early," Sammi speculated softly. "No young person comes back this early from a day at Cedar Point."

"If, indeed, they even *went* to Cedar Point," Howie said morosely remembering Julie's sojourn to see her grandfather in Columbus.

Margaret set down her fork. She didn't have much of an appetite anymore.

Finally, Sticks said, "What do you think we should do?"

But before anyone could answer, Kimberly, who had come directly to their table from the Millers, asked breathlessly: "How about another round of drinks?" She thought it odd that the four parents, whom she knew pretty well, just looked at her and nodded their heads dumbly without saying a word.

Just before their entrees arrived, Sticks excused himself to go to the men's room. After the four of them had come to grips with the fact that their children were probably off together at Cedar Point and there probably wasn't anything they could do about it, they relaxed somewhat and ate their salads and drank their drinks. Even Margaret relaxed a little bit.

In the john way back in the corner of the restaurant, Sticks glanced at the man standing next to him at the adjoining urinal. He looked slightly familiar. Maybe Sammi had sold him a house. The man was in his late 30s and wearing a tan summer suit with a light blue tie. Suddenly, the man glanced over at him and said, "You're Sticks Bergman."

It's always awkward to meet someone with your dick in your hand, Sticks thought. "Yes, I am," he responded.

The man vigorously shook his own dick dry as if substituting the action for a handshake. "My name's Alan Newport. I'm a vice-president out at Allied Pipes. One of my responsibilities is community relations."

Sticks shook his own dick dry wondering if he was participating in some sort of primitive male ritual. They both zipped up and stepped away from the urinals and over to the sinks.

"I have to be honest with you, Mr. Bergman," Newport said as they both ran water over their hands, "that I'm not very happy with your opposition to these new houses out at The Candlesticks."

"Why's that?" Sticks made eye contact in the mirror above the sinks.

"Well, Stowe Towne needs housing. We have a hard time recruiting at the plant because there isn't enough housing around here."

"It's my understanding that the houses will be pretty upscale," Sticks said. "Out of the price range for most of the people who work at Allied Pipes, I would think."

"You might be surprised, Mr. Bergman," Newport said as he pulled out paper towels and handed a couple to Sticks. "I would say from the supervisory level on up, our employees would probably be able to afford houses out there."

Sticks shrugged. "You know better than I do. Anyway, I don't think you have anything to worry about. In fact, my wife and I are having dinner with Howie Howard and his wife right now. I don't think there's much opposition left to the housing development."

"There's that injunction I read about in the newspaper."

"Howie just told me that their lawyer has it all taken care of."

Newport tossed away his paper towel. "Well then, no hard feelings." He offered his hand.

Sticks would have been happy with just a little wave. But he sucked it up and gave a firm handshake. "You know," he said, "my brothers and I are putting in a wine store. My one brother Paul is quite a wine connoisseur."

"Is that a fact? I heard about the store. In the lumberyard."

"That's right. We should be open the beginning of July."

"I'll make a point of stopping around."

"Maybe you can use it as a recruitment tool," Sticks suggested.

Newport, not knowing if Sticks was kidding or not, smiled, nodded, and left the restroom.

Sticks, not sure if he was kidding or not either, wended his way back through the restaurant to his waiting steak.

⌒

Later that evening, at the end of the bar under the gaze of the thinly clad Mae, Bob Redford nursed the last of a long line of Beefeater martinis. Very, very dry. One olive. He was morosely thinking about his failure to take an editorial stand on The Candlesticks' development. His son and wife had opposed any editorial at all, either for or against. Too volatile an issue, they claimed. No need to anger any advertiser. Remember, they warned, subscribers now read the paper for the ads, school news, police reports, and real estate transfers. Not for the editorials.

Bob knew his wife and kid weren't being cruel, just realistic. And they would not have outright forbade him to write an editorial. He wasn't that far gone. Still, he recognized it as a meaningless gesture. Full of unsound sound and furry fury!

He wondered how life had just slipped away. He always became morose after his sixth martini. Happy after two, angry after four, morose after six. He could write a book.

The odd thing, though, was that something gnawed at him about this whole situation. Sober or drunk—it didn't matter. Ever since he had first heard about The Candlesticks' development, something had tickled the back of his memory. But so faint. So slight. So ephemeral.

He ate his last olive completing the solid food portion of his evening meal. The thought would come to him. Those lost thoughts always did. But probably too late to be of any journalistic use. Still, who was a journalist anymore? Certainly not one Bob Redford, editor-in-chief of nothing. But the lost memory still bugged him. What the hell was it?

Suddenly, like a ghost materializing out of the ether, Will Boyd was sitting beside him. "Will, my man, good to see you," Redford said, happy to see his friend. "What are you doin' here?"

"Oh, just stopped in for a Coke," Will answered.

Will Boyd did not drink. Some people mistakenly thought that he looked like a drinker. But the fact was that he never touched a drop of alcohol. In addition, he had made it known to the bartenders who worked at the Maple Lodge and Abe's Tap and even, although much more rarely, The Candlesticks' bar, that he was available by a simple phone call to take home fellows that had drunk too much and were becoming unruly or couldn't be allowed to drive. He often got calls for Bob Redford.

"Well, then, have a Coke on me," Redford said, slightly slurring his words.

"Sure, Bob." Will nodded. Since Bob did not ask for a drink himself, he didn't press the issue about cutting him off. He was more than willing to sit for a while and let Bob sober up.

"Did I tell you how much I liked that story you wrote about The Candlesticks before it was a golf course?" Redford asked.

Will laughed. "Actually, you've told me that three or four times. Glad I hit a nerve." Will had been surprised how many people had commented on The Candlesticks' article. Usually his historical articles for the *Bugle* only elicited a few random responses.

Redford leaned heavily on the counter. He was getting tired. "You know, Will, that story reminded me of something, but I'll be damned if I can remember it."

"Really?"

"Yeah, really. But I just can't 'member. Can you 'member?"

Will shrugged. "You got me there, Bob." He drained his Coke. It looked like he better get Bob up and walking. "Come on, let's get some fresh air."

"It's not raining?"

"It wasn't ten minutes ago,"

"Damn," Bob Redford said, "I thought I heard it raining."

chapter seventeen

JACK'S TREE

The only really famous modern era golfer to play The Candlesticks was Jack Nicklaus, and that was only because Jack attended Ohio State University for a while. At the start of the golf season one year, the OSU alumni sponsored a practice at the course featuring the Buckeye golf team. Well-connected alumni could play a round with a member of the team. On the par-3, 160-yard 15th hole, Jack yanked an eight-iron into a tree at the left front of the green. The tree was at the end of a line of boulders that separated the fairway and green from the meager flow of the Pottawa River after it came out of the rush of the Cascades. Jack's ball hit in the branches of the young (at that time) oak, came out in a high arc, landed in the middle of the green, and rolled into the hole for an ace. Forever after, the tree was Jack's Tree.

Late in the afternoon on Thursday, July 2nd, Howie Howard and Bip Jordan sat in a golf cart off to the side of the 15th green looking at Jack's Tree. A threesome of ladies was putting out on the green. Bip had been clearing stuff out of his desk when Howie stopped by the office and asked him to take a ride out to Jack's Tree. The tree was a red oak and had matured into a magnificent specimen worthy of its name and notable early distinction. But now, it too, had been a victim of the Graduation Day storm.

"No one spotted the problem at first," Howie explained. "The tree looked fine. Still looks fine from a distance. About two weeks ago a branch fell off during an ordinary rain shower. It was the week when we had all that rain. No one thought much of it, although it was a pretty big branch. Then last night, no wind or rain, *this* fell off."

Howie and Bip got out of the cart and walked around the tree and the first boulder. The ground was overgrown and sloped slightly down to the Pottawa. The river was much higher than usual. Normally, by midsummer the stream was reduced to a trickle. Bip bent down and picked up a new Slazenger. He tossed it over the boulder and down the fairway for some lucky golfer to find. But in the space between the rocks and the river, the grounds crew that morning had dumped the large limb that had fallen from Jack's Tree. The limb itself was the size of a small tree. Its branches brushed the rocks on one side and the water on the other.

Looking back at the tree from this angle, they could distinctly see where the branch had split off from the trunk. "Jesus Christ, this is huge, Howie," Bip said. Now, almost into retirement, Bip had dropped the Mr. Howard and reverted to calling Howie by his first name.

"Harry thinks that it must have been split during the first storm. On graduation day," Howie said. Harry Knowles was The Candlesticks' greens superintendent.

"I see," Bip said inspecting the downed branch. "Look at the number of dead leaves. Part of it must have been dead for a while."

"But it's worse. Harry got a ladder and climbed up in the tree this morning. Couple of more dead branches. Trunk splitting. Anyway, he's recommending it should come down. Sooner the better. Or, it'll fall on someone."

"Sure it will," Bip agreed.

Howie leaned back against a boulder. There was a light wind and the river babbled by. It was going to be a very pleasant evening. "So, Bip, here's my problem. I need a ruling from the pro. And I still consider you The Candlesticks' pro."

Bip nodded. "I hear what you're saying, Howie."

Howie continued: "We can't take a tree this big down in a day. Especially since tomorrow is the start of the July Fourth weekend for a lot of people. But we can't let golfers go wandering under the tree. Of course, I can't close down the hole. What am I going to do about play?"

Bip walked between two boulders and back to the fairway. No one was playing the hole at the moment. Howie followed. "Does Harry think the tree will fall over?" Bip asked.

The two men eyed the tree. If it fell completely over toward the green, it appeared that the top branches would cover the bunker to the left of the green and maybe a few top branches would reach the edge of the green.

"I asked Harry that. He didn't see anything wrong with the trunk, but he couldn't be sure. It looks solid. Most of the tree's still green. The trunk must still be living. I was thinking that we might pare away all the dead stuff and save the tree. May look a little odd."

"Well, you could rope off an area to keep people from going under the tree," Bip speculated.

"Hell, I'd even be willing to pay a kid to sit out here and stop people. But is the hole even viable?"

Bip walked a couple of dozen yards back toward the tee. Howie was right. There was a problem. The hole was a difficult hole anyway. Jack's Tree protected it on the left side, and on the right side the fairway sloped away plus there was a tiered series of three small traps. For the experienced Candlesticks' golfer, the safe play was actually to hit long to the upper right-hand quadrant of the green that opened into a flat area of very light rough. If you hit a little too long, you were still safe. But the fact remained that many golfers didn't know or couldn't figure out to hit there and couldn't hit an iron that far anyway. So their tee shots often came up short and often drifted left under Jack's Tree. If you restricted the area around the tree, those golfers would even be more confused.

A pair of golfers approached the tee and Bip waved them on and retreated back to where Howie waited between two of the boulders. They watched as the first golfer launched a beautiful shot to the back of the green. But the second golfer, who appeared to be an older man, hit a short drive that bounced along the left side of the fairway, past where they stood, and stopped underneath the tall branches of the tree. The shot wasn't a bad shot and the golfer had a short, low pitch to the pin that was placed near the front of the green. But it was exactly the type of shot that was now a problem.

"First of all," Bip advised, "let's move the pin way back to the upper right corner of the green and keep it there all weekend. That'll keep people aiming right. Second, we'll rope off the area and put up signs and give people a free drop in the fairway. Third, let's put *all* the tees at the women's tee."

The women's red tee was to the right front of the other tees and measured only 136 yards to the green. The golf purists would not be very happy, but the move shifted the entire hole to the right and shortened it considerably so that more people could make the green on the fly.

Howie nodded. "All right. That's a pretty good solution. And it was authorized by the club pro."

The pair of golfers, obviously a father and middle-aged son, trudged by hauling pull carts.

"Beautiful afternoon," the older fellow said as he stopped and picked up the Slazenger Bip had thrown onto the fairway. He looked around to see what golfer might have hit the stray shot.

"I found it behind the boulders, George," Bip said, "so you can keep it."

"Thanks, Bip," George responded.

"How you hitting them, George?" Bip asked.

"Can't complain. I'd be out of it if Eddie here wasn't such a bad putter."

"I bet he's just trying to psych you out, Eddie," Bip said.

"You got it. Look at this. I'm on the green, but I think he's actually closer to the pin. It's been that way all day. The golf gods are after me."

Everyone laughed as George walked under Jack's Tree oblivious, of course, to any danger. Howie and Bip glanced at one another. George executed a nice little pitch to within five feet or so of the pin. He then made the putt while Eddie, apparently true to form, three-putted.

On the way back to the clubhouse in the cart, Bip was quiet and Howie thought about the conversation Bip had had with the golfers. Howie didn't recognize the men. But the old pro knew them both. Of course, that was his job. But how many of those type of golfers would he entice over to Delia's course? How many would look at those houses as well as The Candlesticks' houses? It was a worry despite his bravado to the contrary to the public in general and specifically to Sammi Bergman. Howie wished he could do some things over. He should have kept Bip on here. He could have used him to reassure The Candlesticks' golfers that the course was not going to change that much. But that was all water under the bridge and nothing much could be done about it.

At that moment, Margaret Howard, Howie's better half, was also contemplating water under the bridge. Or, to be more precise, all the missed opportunities they had had with their daughter. Margaret used the staple gun to attach more blue cloth bunting to a craft booth just off to the side of the Memorial to the Seven Heroes on the town square. Well, at least she had not yet put a staple through a finger like she had a few years ago. Still, each time she squeezed the staple gun it was like squeezing a staple into her heart. *So dramatic!* She sat back on the crate she was using as a stool and took a drink from a can of Diet Sprite. The DUA Festival was the only time during the entire year that Margaret submitted to the indignation of physical labor. All for the love of the DUA. Although now that she was a Senior Member Elect, she didn't seem to love it so much anymore.

After a minute, Margaret sensed someone over her shoulder and looked around. May Miller was just standing there a few feet away. She wore a simple blue dress obviously worn for today's hard work of Festival preparation. There was a large brown dirt stain on the left side of the skirt. A green leaf was stuck to the dirt like a decorative pin. She also had on an oversized straw gardening hat and carried a clipboard. Since her interview, Margaret had only seen May a couple of times at Festival organization meetings and had not talked to her privately.

"Hello, Margaret," May said in greeting.

Margaret stood up and summoned more bravado than she felt. "May, how are things going? Are we on schedule? It's getting late in the afternoon."

"Oh, yes, I think we're doing fine. The rental tables for the booths haven't arrived. They were supposed to be here about 1:00. I just called and they are 'in transit' whatever that means. At least it wasn't like three years ago when the bratwurst people claimed they didn't even have the order."

"I remember. I'm sure everything will go fine. I noticed a lot of the exhibitors are here already."

Margaret and May both glanced at the parking around the square. There were an inordinate number of vans and recreational vehicles. Some sported signs such as **Mildred's Quilts** or **Don's Duck Decoys** or **Cider by Kalida Farms**. Technically, Friday morning was reserved this year for setup and the Festival officially opened Friday at noon. But many Festival exhibitors still arrived on Thursday to get a head start and sometimes negotiate with May for what they perceived would be a better booth position.

But when Friday noon rolled around, May would ring the DUA golden bell under the large tent in Festival Park in the block behind the town library and the Maple Lodge. Festival Park was actually not a park, but a large block of undeveloped land that was owned by the DUA. Seventy years ago, the area had been used by the polo club sponsored by Sheridan Howard, Howie's grandfather. For decades, the DUA and the municipal government of Stowe Towne had carried on a running battle over the land. The town wanted to turn the land into a real municipal park with walks and benches and maybe some recreational facilities. The DUA maintained the land—kept the grass cut and bushes pruned, but there were no improvements. Basically, the DUA wouldn't release control of the area because of the Festival. The town had even offered to build a permanent pavilion dedicated to the DUA, but to no avail. The DUA preferred the traditional huge circus tent, and the atmosphere the tent created. Food was served all day through the dinner hour in the tent and then both nights of the Festival there was entertainment and dancing in the tent. Most of the rest of the acreage was used for Festival parking—which was the Festival's second largest moneymaker after the food concession.

May spied a woman who looked like a bag lady near the corner. "Oh, there's Katrina. She does those yarn designs you hang on the wall. Awful-looking things, but she's told me she does more business at our Festival than anyplace else all year."

"Well, I hope she keeps her yarn dry," Margaret said. "It was a nice day today, but the weather report isn't all that encouraging."

"Oh, don't worry, dear, it's never bad weather for the Festival, no matter how bad it gets. I must run. Mr. Miller is eating pie at the Gettysburg. He had to find out the latest about that waitress."

"Who?" Margaret asked.

"Donna Dougall. You know she went to see her sister in Chicago."

"So?" Margaret didn't know what the old woman was talking about.

"Well, she told everyone that she was going on vacation, but you know."

Margaret nodded, but couldn't figure out how she was supposed to respond.

"You know," May repeated emphatically. "Very convenient vacation for someone in her condition, wouldn't you say?"

"Her condition?"

"Absolutely. Well, I must hurry. Mr. Miller will be filled with the latest."

Margaret watched May rush away. Margaret certainly knew what the euphemism "her condition" meant. But she didn't know anything about any waitress at the café. Still, the conversation disturbed her because it touched on an unspoken, deep-seated fear she had about Julie. What if her daughter was pregnant? It was just as likely to happen in a good family. They had done all the precautions. Margaret, in fact, was rather proud of the way she had handled that portion of their relationship. But when you lose control, you lose control of everything.

She shook her head and tried to clear her mind. She went back to stapling bunting and tried to forget that now she had one more thing to worry about.

Meanwhile, miles away in Columbus, State Senator Kenny Barnes was hoping for one *less* thing to worry about. The State Senate was about to vote on the bill that included his amendment to allow The Candlesticks' development on Pottawa State Forest land. The comprehensive Water Reclamation Act was greased. There wouldn't be a problem except for the holiday recess. If the parent bill didn't make it through, then anything could happen. The legislative rule of thumb was that when something got dragged out and postponed, then something bad would happen.

A procedural matter was tying up the President of the Senate for a few minutes, so Barnes decided to stretch his legs. The senator walked out of the newly refurbished nineteenth-century ornate Senate Chamber into the marble hallway and was startled to see Justice Summers sitting on a bench like a nineteenth-century solicitor waiting for a patronage interview.

"Senator Barnes," the justice said with a sly smile on his face.

"Judge Summers, how are you? Are you waiting for someone? Can I get them for you?"

"Oh, I wanted to talk to you, Kenny. Can you sit here for a minute?"

"Of course." Barnes plopped his hefty body down next to Summers on the bench. The nervousness of being near the Supreme Court Justice suddenly made the senator need to take a piss.

"One of those messy sessions before vacation, isn't it?" the justice asked with a knowing wink. "The legislature will debate a boil on a gnat's ass for two months and then pass a half-billion-dollar transportation bill in an hour. The public should be outraged."

Barnes nodded silently. Summers was of such stature that he could insult the legislature to a legislator's face and in the Senate Chamber itself. But the legislator could not turn around and ask the justice what the hell the State Supreme Court was doing messing in this or that legislative matter (i.e., K-12 school funding). Political facts of life were, after all, just that, political facts of life.

"I was wondering," the justice continued, "if you might join me Saturday morning for a little golf at The Candlesticks. It's your district."

"Well, uh, I have the Lions' Annual Barbecue in Granite City and I promised people I'd be at the Mason Township fireworks..."

"Oh, we'll be done before noon and you'll be on your way. This is the DUA men's golf outing. Part of that July Fourth Festival they always have in Stowe Towne."

Barnes knew the Festival well from campaigns. "I guess I could make it," he said meekly.

"Fine, we tee off at 8:00. Be there a half-hour early. I don't like to get nervous on the first tee."

"All right, I'll be on time, for sure."

Summers slapped his knees and stood up abruptly. "Well, Senator, since the Court keeps regular hours, I don't have to stay here like you do. See you the day after tomorrow."

Barnes stood. "All right, sir, I'll be there."

The justice started to leave and then turned back. "Remember our bet? Our bunker bet?"

"Yes, I do."

"You owe me. But the golf invitation, that's not worthy of a political favor. Instead, I want you to withdraw your amendment allowing The Candlesticks to expand into Pottawa State Forest."

Barnes felt himself start to sweat. "It's a little late for that, sir."

The justice looked surprised. "The bill's passed?" he asked.

Barnes shifted his weight from one foot to the other. "Well, not yet. But it will be in minutes. An hour at the most."

"Then it's not too late."

Barnes took a deep breath. "I won't withdraw the amendment."

"So you're welshing on our bet?"

"It's economic development in my district. New housing. Construction jobs."

"You're welshing on the bet, Senator." The justice raised his voice just a notch.

Barnes tried to act indignant. "If I hadn't happened to take a break, I wouldn't have even met you out here."

Summers waved his hand. "Just a coincidence. It just saved you the embarrassment of me having to come and get you."

Barnes said nothing in response. He stood transfixed.

Finally, the justice shrugged. "Well, fine, Senator. But we'll still see you at the golf course. Now it's more important than ever."

Summers turned and Barnes watched the old man retreat down

the hallway of power until someone hissed at him from the door and told him to return to his seat in the Senate Chamber.

⤜

On Friday morning, the day before the Fourth of July and the day the DUA annual July Fourth Arts Festival began, Bip Jordan was hiding out in the nearly complete Bergman Bros. Wine Shoppe. Bip's hobby was woodworking and he had taken over fashioning some of the ornate scrollwork for the new store's Bavarian motif. He and Sticks worked on the shelves behind the checkout counter at one end of the store. The rest of the store was chaos as brother Paul and wife Cathy with their unhelpful, whining daughters tried to finish the painting. Sticks knew from experience that the family who tried to paint together was not necessarily the family who survived without bloodshed.

After gluing on a last section of scrollwork to the bottom shelf (they had actually done the jigsawing out back for these final pieces), Sticks decided to take a break and buy Bip an early lunch. They excused themselves under Paul's nasty glare and walked down Duke Boulevard toward the town square. All the parking spaces were taken and the town already seemed flooded with visitors. It was also hot and going to get hotter with a glaring July sun.

"I thought it was going to rain," Bip remarked idly.

They crossed the street in front of Sammi's clean and prosperous looking Bergman Realty. Laura Robinson was sitting at her desk and gave them a wave through the large front window. Sticks noticed that Sammi's car wasn't in her usual spot tucked next to the building off the alley that ran between the realty and the Scotland's computer store. Maybe she was out at Delia's. Sticks knew Sammi was spending a lot of time out at Delia's going over plans for Long Lake Estates.

Sticks and Bip sat at Sticks' favorite table in Abe's Tap near the back under a large, old-fashioned framed picture of John Brown—the classic arms akimbo drawing of the fanatic abolitionist with wild hair flaring like the sun's rays. They ordered burgers and fries that pretty much comprised the entire menu of Abe's Tap. The owner, Tony, brought them a pitcher of Budweiser. Bip had told Sticks bits and pieces of his encounter with Howie at Jack's Tree, but they had been interrupted several times by Paul and Cathy. So Bip hadn't gotten around to the most important part that he now started on as he poured them both glasses of Bud:

"So, we get back to the clubhouse and I want to just finish getting my stuff out of my office. Now, truthfully, Howie has been a real gentleman. I mean, he asked my advice in a very professional manner and I told him what I thought. We talked about this and that. No problem. So I'm about to say good-bye and he says that he wants me to play golf at the Saturday morning DUA men's outing."

Sticks nodded as he finished off his beer. He'd been working since 6:00 a.m. Paul wanted to have the Shoppe opened for business tomorrow. He didn't know how they were going to make it unless they worked all night. Anyway, Sticks was glad when Bip had shown up at 9:00. He had been a great help.

"Sure," Sticks said, "I've played in that tournament a couple of times. Filling in for somebody or other."

"Well, we're a foursome tomorrow. You and me, Randy and Doc Parsons."

"Why?"

"Howie asked us, that's why. He said it would be a favor. He said somebody specifically requested that you play. And it was somebody important, but he wouldn't say who."

"So what's Howie getting out of it?"

"I don't know, Sticks. Mr. Miller is the general chairman of the outing this year. Maybe it's him."

"Mr. Miller would have just called me himself. But that's good to know because I'll just call him and see what he says."

Sticks poured himself another glass of beer and pondered what was going on. But he could come up with no obvious reason why Howie Howard or anyone else for that matter would want him to play in the DUA men's outing.

Mara Fish, meanwhile, also was having an early lunch at her desk at the *Dispatch*. No beer and burgers, however. She had a very nice onion bagel and pastrami. She was mildly curious when and how the baby would start affecting her diet. Of course, she didn't smoke and drank only moderately which she had already given up. Fortunately, Peter didn't smoke and it didn't matter if he gave up drinking. He didn't know about the baby yet. Mara wasn't sure if she'd tell him before she started showing.

She fingered the pink "While You Were Out" phone message one of the receptionists had taken for her earlier. It read: *Caller—didn't leave name, I asked—suggested you show up at Candlesticks golf course Sat. at one.* The receptionist, Katy, had put a little happy face at the bottom of the slip. Mara really hated little happy faces.

Nevertheless, the young reporter was intrigued by the anonymous phone call. She remembered Peter telling her that another anonymous phone call had first alerted him to the whole Candlesticks' development controversy. Well, she thought, she could roust Peter out of bed in the morning and trek over to Stowe Towne. They had nothing better planned.

Late that afternoon, someone else who had lots of better things to do, nevertheless sat in his own family room smiling and nodding to two people he did not really like very much.

"I had no choice," Howie told Don Morgan and Sean Donaldson. "He told me to call both of you and have you play in the DUA tournament early tomorrow morning. He said the whole deal hinged on your playing."

"What's the DUA again, Howie?" Donaldson asked. He had seen a client in Pittsburgh that morning and had an appointment in Chicago on Monday so this weekend stay at Howie's expense was no big deal. July 4th wasn't a big holiday for him anyway. All it really meant was that his pristine golf courses were overplayed and abused.

"Well, the DUA stands for Daughters of the Union Army. But it's not them, it's their husbands. The ladies' husbands. Look, it's just an old farts' scramble. I swear I don't know what the big deal is. But I've had to line up all sorts of guys to play."

"Fuck him," Morgan said mildly. He was glad to get out of Cleveland for the weekend. His wife had invited their boys over—all three of them—and they would invade the house with their whiny wives and even whinier little toddlers. Morgan had never enjoyed being a father or grandfather. It was surprising his boys turned out so well. He said, "We got to do what we got to do. That's what you said, Howie. We got to humor the old man. I can do that."

Morgan took a sip of gin and tonic and then added malevolently: "But only for a while."

"Aye," Donaldson said softly. "Only for a wee bit."

Howie shrugged and wished he were someplace else.

Near midnight, the party at Matt Pawlicki's apartment was almost out of control. The music was loud and the doors and windows were open. Some of the guys were out in the parking lot setting off cherry bombs. There was some good grass circulating and lots of beer and vodka. Heather Miller was really drunk and Julie knew that she and Randy would have to take her home and try to smuggle her into the Miller house. Might not be too hard what with both of her parents so involved in the Festival. May Miller always made her son and daughter-in-law in charge of Festival parking. May long ago concluded that it was the only good thing that ever came from her son's love of cars. Actually, the Festival was the only reason this party hadn't been shut down by the cops. They were all too occupied with crowd control and adult drunks downtown around the square.

Julie and Randy were sitting on a low cement wall that ran along the back of the small apartment complex, the first apartment complex that had ever been built in Stowe Town. It was just south of Allied Pipes and housed many of the single, male plant employees. Julie lit a cigarette and flicked the ashes off toward the grass.

"I'm beat, we gotta go home soon," Randy said. "I gotta play golf tomorrow in the DUA tournament." He rubbed the sweat from his eyes and rubbed his hand across his green *They Might Be Giants* T-shirt. He was hot and dirty from working all day. He did not want to be here at this party with these people.

Julie turned to her boyfriend. "Why are you doing that? I don't get it. Dad said that tournament's just for those old DUA guys."

"When did he say that?" Randy asked.

Julie shrugged in the dim light filtering out from the living room. "I don't know, whenever. Why?"

"Because Bip said that your father specifically set up a foursome with my Dad, me, Bip, and Doc Parsons."

"Don't ask me."

"Anyway, I'm tired, let's go. I was working in the yard this morning because they were short of help. Then Uncle Paul had a fit, so I had to work in the Wineyard. He's working all night just so he can have it open on the Fourth. My Dad refused to work all night. He went home the same time I did. My uncle's crazy."

"So, is it going to be ready?"

"I think he'll open it, but there won't be much of a selection of fine wines."

"Well, we can go if you want," Julie conceded. "Besides, we'll have to take Heather home."

"Oh, Christ, who said so?"

"I said so. Come on, Randy. Let's go find her. Bedroom first. Then backseats."

Randy gulped down the last of his Sam Adams and set the empty bottle next to others on the wall. "So when are we going to tell your parents? It's getting late. Or are you going to tell them without me?"

Julie stood and ground out her cigarette on the top of the cement wall. "I think you should be there, don't you? But I don't know when's a good time. Maybe tomorrow. I'm getting a little bored seeing them so uptight."

Randy laughed. "They might have other things to be uptight about than your decision about going to college."

Julie took a step toward the patio door of the apartment. But she paused and looked back at Randy and said simply: "I don't think so."

chapter eighteen

ACT V: BUT THIS TIME JULIET LIVES!

There was a loud clap of thunder and Bob Redford woke with a start.

〜

It had rained hard towards dawn. But even though everything was soaked and there were pools of water in the bottom of some of the bunkers and the greens were very spongy, the DUA men's scramble began as scheduled. That's the way the judge wanted it.

Seventy-five-year-old Ohio Supreme Court Justice Richard Summers, author of the Candlestick Accord, was playing out his hand. He knew exactly what cards he held and what cards all the other players held. It had only been a matter of getting them all to the table. Now, as he stood in his expensive scarlet and gray Ohio State Gore-Tex rain suit on the clubhouse deck sipping overly sweet coffee out of a Styrofoam cup, he could pick out the principals milling around in front of him. The deck was about four feet or so above the ground and gave the judge a good view of the golfers and the wet golf course.

It was almost the 8:00 a.m. tee time. It was hot and humid under a low gray sky. Definitely a threat of more rain. Club boys were running about, handing out white towels so the golfers could wipe off golf cart seats and steering wheels. Old fellows were dragging their clubs around. Bags of all colors, but mostly black and deep, leather brown. Some were labeled Callaway or Ping. One dark blue bag had *Pebble Beach* in white. The men (also all of whom were white) shook hands; some greeting friends they only saw here once a year.

Golf, the judge thought slyly, *at once the most democratic and least democratic of all games.*

He spotted his group getting together and he gave them a wave. There was State Senator Barnes (who had arrived *extra* early), State Representative Ray Gunther, and, of course, Howie Howard. He noticed that Howie was looking over his shoulder and keeping a close eye on another foursome. Let's see, the judge speculated. That must be the real estate agent Bruce Dean, the golf architect Sean Donaldson (with the striking plaid golf bag), the corpulent Cleveland developer Don Morgan, and the young Tom Duke from The Candlesticks' Board. The judge knew the elder Duke well and much preferred him to his son.

The judge's gaze next fell on a group of old farts like himself. There were actually many groups of old farts. There were old Candlesticks people like Lincoln Jones and Paul Mitchell. He knew those fellows from the old days as well as from years and years of golf.

Finally, the judge saw Bip Jordan whom he had also known for years at the club. That tall, middle-aged man talking to Bip must be Sticks Bergman with the hulking look-alike son beside him. The judge wondered if this fellow Sticks was really the golfer Ray Gunther said he was. *Well, we'll soon find out*, he thought.

A voice behind the judge said, "Hello, Dick."

The judge turned and looked at the speaker. "Hello, Butch, how are you?"

Mr. Miller, wearing a clear plastic rain poncho over his clothes and carrying a bullhorn, said: "I wish we were 20 years old, the sun was shining, and we were teeing off on the first hole at St. Andrews."

"Aye, laddie," the judge replied and winked.

No one except the judge and Mr. Miller remembered that it had been Mr. Miller, and not Mr. Miller's father, who had first talked with the young Supreme Court Justice Dick Summers about helping to solve a management crisis—a legal quagmire, actually—at the improbably named Candlesticks Country Club and Golf Course 40 years ago. Mr. Miller, not long out of law school back then, had been acting in secret on behalf of the golf course's board.

Mr. Miller stepped to the railing next to the judge, raised the bullhorn to his lips, and announced: "Gentlemen! Gentlemen! If I may have your attention, please!

"I have it on the best authority possible, my wife May, that the rain will hold off for us." There was general laughter; everyone connected with the DUA knew May.

"As you know, we always play a straight scramble with no handicaps and no flights. However, with the help of club pro Bip Jordan who most of you know, we've added a new feature to provide some equity and give everyone a little more of a chance. Based on what Bip and I know about each foursome, we have assigned you different tee colors. The tee color you're to hit from is written on your scorecard. This will give the short hitters a little break off the tee. Also, this year, you must use at least three drives from each member of your foursome."

There was a stirring among the golfers as they commented to each other about these new rules and checked out which color tees they would be using.

Mr. Miller cleared his throat and glanced at the judge before starting again: "When you finish, we'll have lunch for you and you can buy some raffle tickets. We'll announce the golf winners at the end of lunch, and then we'll draw the raffle winners. Remember, the raffle is our way of making a contribution to the Festival, so be sure and be generous in buying tickets. We have a couple of nice raffle prizes including a new golf bag.

"All right, Gentlemen, a shotgun start, of course. Your beginning hole is highlighted on your scorecard. Head out in about five minutes. We'll blow the horn to start.

"Oh, by the way, with the weather. If you hear three short blasts on the horn, that means get back here pronto. Lightning's in the area.

"Thank you and hit 'em straight."

There was renewed bustle as the older men headed for the can one last time. For a moment, the area below the deck looked like a bumper car rally. But the carts soon sorted themselves out and started to head out onto the course.

The judge reached over and touched Mr. Miller's arm. "Butch, before they get away, ask my group, your group, Mr. Bergman's group, and Mr. Dean's group to come over here."

Without hesitation, Mr. Miller put the bullhorn to his lips and repeated the names. With quizzical expressions, the men either drove their carts over or walked over to the deck railing. When they had gathered, the judge spoke without the use of the bullhorn.

"Gentlemen, for those of you who do not know me, I'm Ohio Supreme Court Justice Richard Summers. More than 40 years ago I wrote the Candlesticks' Accord which governs the operation of this golf course. As you know, there's been some debate over the future direction of this course. I intend to resolve that debate once and for all this afternoon immediately after the lunch and raffle. I am asking, no I must insist, that all of you meet me up here on the deck at that time."

"What's this about..." Morgan started to say, his belly flapping under a tent-like white golf shirt.

"Mr. Morgan, please indulge me. All your questions will be answered then. Enjoy your golf this morning. I know I will." With a wave, the judge walked over to the short wooden staircase and descended to join his foursome. Mr. Miller followed, still carrying the bullhorn.

The game, of course, became incidental. The judge's dramatic balcony declaration reminded some of a South American dictator lording it over his subjects. Others, like Morgan, expressed out loud that the judge was full of shit and hot air—a contradictory metaphor that those around him chose to ignore. A couple people, like Senator Barnes, became very nervous. And at least one of them, Sean Donaldson, thought it was a joke. But Howie and Mr. Miller realized right away that it was no joke.

Sticks, meanwhile, didn't know what to think. He was still getting over the new knowledge that the Ray of Ray's clubs was actually a state legislator.

In an odd way, time seemed to suddenly back up. Life had gone on. Sticks had been immersed in the Wine Shoppe construction and Sammi's new agency. Bip had joined up with Delia. Mr. Miller and May had devoted themselves to the Festival. Howie had gone right ahead with planning the development. Even though unresolved issues like Delia's injunction or Randy and Julie dating were still a reality, they somehow seemed to hang out there in a sort of twilight zone that didn't really matter in day-to-day life.

It was like voting for a school levy. Whatever the outcome, the day after you voted you adapted to the result and went on about your business.

For the shotgun start, Sticks's group was assigned first up on the

18th tee. Ironically, with everything about The Candlesticks flooding back over him, he had to play the hole that ran along his property and looked toward his house. They heard the horn blast and Sticks teed up the ball and sent it into outer space down the middle of the fairway. He had almost come to a point of reconciling losing the golf course. Maybe giving up their house. Giving in to Howie and selling out. Building a new house out at Delia's place. But perhaps that wouldn't be the case now.

Meanwhile, Howie, the judge, and the state legislators had the privilege of teeing off on the first hole, the par-5 dogleg right whose green was as close as anyplace on the fairway to the edge of Howie's property. Howie was having the reverse of the feelings Sticks felt. He had thought everything about the development was sewn up except for some minor loose ends. But now, the cryptic judge had shaken his confidence. He had tried to pry something out of the old man as they had walked to the first tee. But Summers had just waved him off and told him it would all be settled this afternoon. Now they had to concentrate on golf and Howie complied because he knew the judge took his golf very seriously.

Balls were whacked around the course. The sounds of the *whoosh* of clubs and the *twart* of balls seemed to carry in the humid air. Occasionally, men would *Whoop!* as long putts curled into holes. The game, as Sherlock Holmes used to say, was afoot.

⌒

The fact that it did not rain seemed to be a miracle. The clouds got lower and it got darker, but then it seemed to brighten as the clouds scuttled away. Reprieves, though, were temporary as even darker clouds moved in. It always seemed to be raining out there toward the west. But no one heard any thunder or saw any lightning. And no one felt any moisture except from the dripping of sweaty brows in the humid air.

At the end of their round, Sticks' team headed in with a 64 consisting of nine birdies, eight pars, and a disastrous bogie on the long par-3 third hole where they had all failed to put a ball on the green and then all failed to get a chip close to the hole. "I don't think a 64 will win it today," Sticks said to Randy as they left the 17th green, their last hole.

"That's a hell of a score," Randy argued, pleased that he had just rammed home a 15-foot putt for birdie.

"If it was the regular DUA scramble crowd, I'd agree. No problem. But there's some ringers playing today. Like Howie, for instance. Or, that team with the golf architect. Tommy Duke's not a good player, but he can hit a ball a ton and that's what you need in a scramble."

Randy glanced over at his father sitting beside him in the passenger seat of the golf cart. He knew his father was nervous about this announcement. He had speculated about what the judge was going to say the whole round. So much so that as soon as they reached the clubhouse, Randy was going to call both his mother and Julie to have them come over for the announcement. He hoped his mother wouldn't be at work. He knew Julie was home. She and Randy had decided to lie low until after the Festival was over because Margaret was so uptight.

They pulled up to the clubhouse in another chaotic mass of golf carts, like a gathering of Scottish clans.

Inside, in the dining room, Mr. Miller and Bip sat at a table next to a portable bulletin board where scores were being posted. They accepted scorecards and started figuring out the winners. May Miller sat at an adjoining table selling raffle tickets. On the table were the golf and raffle prizes which included a Taylor Made golf bag, a Ping putter, 12 boxes of a dozen Slazenger golf balls, blue and green Candlesticks' golf towels, and a dozen coupons for free rounds of golf at The Candlesticks (expiration date was September 1st).

Golfers turned in their scorecards, dutifully purchased raffle tickets from an overly shrill May, and then went to the far end of the dining room and helped themselves to the fried chicken buffet. More than a few golfers detoured into the bar. It had been a long weekend already and most of them still had the rest of the Festival to get through.

Don Morgan was beside himself. He wasn't used to mysteries or being ordered around. Things were cut and dried in the development business. This entire Stowe Towne project hadn't been right from the beginning. Yet, it seemed like a no-brainer. Something you should be able to handle by only devoting a couple of hours a week. And the area was ripe for picking. Yet it just hadn't been clean. And now this judge had interjected himself. Morgan thought: *I'd leave in a minute. They need me more than I need them.* Yet, his team shot a 64 including an eagle. He'd never been near an eagle before. In fact, they could have been two or three shots lower—he discovered that Bruce Dean and Tom Duke had as few scruples as he did about shaving a stroke here or there or taking an extra putt. But that Scot asshole played strictly by the book and they couldn't get away with a thing. Still, the team members speculated coming in from their last hole that they might be in first place.

Howie's team also shot a 64, very conventional eight birdies and ten pars reflecting the staid, conservative play of Howie, Ray Gunther, and the judge. No chances. Always made sure there was a safe shot. Their major problem had been working in three of Senator Barnes's drives. In fact, they were forced to use his drive on their last hole, the 18th. His drive turned out to be a hundred-yard worm-burner. They were damn lucky just to make par.

When they got back to the clubhouse, again under the judge's direction but using the weather and course conditions as an excuse, Howie ordered the staff to close the course that had been scheduled to reopen to public play at 1:30. The order sent the staff scurrying to make phone calls to afternoon players canceling their rounds and put up "Closed to Play" signs at the parking lot entrances. Howie's nervousness increased.

Mr. Miller and Bip sorted the scorecards. The three 64 scores from Howie's team, Sticks's team, and Morgan's team were set aside in first place. There were two 66s and three 67s. Bip could tell as he sorted through the cards that the wet conditions and the overly-long rough had taken a toll on scores. He recognized a number of names of good golfers who had not scored well. His own group of veteran Candlestick players had shot an embarrassing 70. They even had to use not one but two different bunker shots. *Choosing* to use a ball in the sand when you were playing a scramble always was bad news.

About the time they thought they had all the cards, a younger fellow hustled up and tossed a damp scorecard on the table: 62.

"Sixty-two!" Bip exclaimed looking up at the blue-eyed, sandy-haired young man.

"Yeah, my Dad was disappointed. We only eagled two of the four par 5s. But it was awfully wet out there."

Bip nodded. "Well, son, this still puts you in first place."

"Great."

Bip looked at the names: McGinnis, Hartman, Porter, and Porter. "You fellows from around here?"

"We're from Toledo. My grandma's in that group that's doing the thing here," the kid said.

"The DUA, Daughters of the Union Army?" Mr. Miller volunteered.

The kid nodded. "I guess so, anyway, she made us bring her this year because she's having a harder time getting around." He paused and then said, "Ah, I was wondering...?"

"What do you need?" Bip asked.

"My Dad said that if we were going to get any prizes, could I pick them up? You see my grandma and my Mom are expecting us to meet them for lunch. You know?"

"Well," Bip said glancing at Mr. Miller, "we aren't quite done figuring here."

There was an awkward pause as the two men and the kid looked around. Everyone was at the other end of the room near the buffet. Even

May had taken a roll of raffle tickets and was working the buffet line.

Finally, since it was embarrassingly obvious that they were done, Mr. Miller shrugged. "I guess you fellas are the winners. Wished you'd stay for lunch and meet everyone."

"Dad says we're late now. Sorry."

Mr. Miller got up and went in back of Bip's chair over to the prize table. The kid followed him.

"Okay," Mr. Miller said, "first prize team gets a dozen balls each, a Candlesticks' towel each, and coupons for a free round here." Mr. Miller loaded up the kid with the prizes.

"Thank you very much," the kid said politely.

"Plus, you're obligated to come back here and play next year." As soon as he said it, Mr. Miller wondered if there would be another year at The Candlesticks. He shook off the thought. "And, tell me your grandmother's name. My wife is the president of the DUA. She'll want to know."

"It's Martha Washington," the kid said without missing a beat. He abruptly wheeled about and was out the door in two seconds.

Mr. Miller turned and looked at Bip. "Did you hear that?"

Bip shook his head. "I guess that makes me Ben Franklin. I don't know. But here's the master list. They paid their money and started on number six. Which, let me see, they birdied. Come on, let's get the rest of the names on the Board and go get some food."

Mr. Miller nodded, thinking that they just might need nourishment for the afternoon.

A half-hour later as May supervised the raffle drawing, Mara Fish with Peter Onear in tow peered into the room from the front doorway. The two reporters watched a petite, young waitress named Melanie Swift pull the raffle tickets out of a fishbowl. But the two reporters weren't paying much attention to Melanie. They were a little on edge because on the way over from Columbus Peter had asked Mara to marry him.

Why is everything that happens between him and Mara somehow connected with The Candlesticks Golf Course? It was something he had been wondering about, even as he had surprised himself by popping the question.

Mara had accepted Peter's proposal as she maneuvered around an Allied Pipes' truck hauling raw steel to the plant in Stowe Towne. She hadn't told him yet about the baby. No sense in ruining the moment. Of course, she didn't love Peter, but this was certainly a useful first match. Truthfully, though, she was kind of thrilled about this sequence of events. It was like her life suddenly was a series of breaking stories on CNN. First baby. Now marriage proposal. Soon wedding. Then birth. Back in five after Headline Sports!

"So, allow me to ask for the 10th or 20th time," Peter whispered to Mara in the clubhouse doorway. "What are we doing here?"

"I got a tip."

"A tip? How very cub reporterish."

"You got me to accept your marriage proposal. What more did you want from the trip?" Mara asked impishly (an adverb not often applied to her conversational tone).

Someone named Hockenfelder won the golf bag. *Hardly page one news*, Mara sighed. Someone named George Smith won the Ping putter. *Whoo-de-do*, Mara thought. *Maybe Peter is right: What are we doing here?*

"Well, isn't that interesting," Peter whispered in her ear. "Over there along the windows near the front. Baby-faced guy. That's State Senator Kenny Barnes. And that guy next to him...ah, he's Gunther, I think. A rep from Cincinnati."

"How unusual is it that they're here? I mean, it's guys playing golf."

"True, but not at an event like this. At least I don't think. This isn't for a politician. A fund-raiser or anything like that. Although it is Barnes's district so I suppose..."

A round of applause brought the raffle to a close and, apparently, the event as well. A few people were still eating a chicken wing or drinking a beer, but most of the men got up to leave, exchanging hearty handshakes and good-byes for another year. Mara and Peter moved into the room to get out of the way of the exodus out the door.

"Ms. Fish and Mr. Onear," a voice said, pronouncing Peter's name correctly.

The reporters recognized Justice Summers.

"Justice Summers," Peter said extending a hand. The judge took his hand and then also shook Mara's.

"Glad you could make it," the judge said. "We're just about to start. Out on the deck."

Within 10 minutes, all of the principals had gathered on the deck. They shuffled their feet and didn't have much to say to one another. Lincoln Jones and Don Morgan had gin and tonics. Many of the men carried sleeves of Slazengers, the insufficient second place prize. Sammi arrived and was greeted with surprise by her husband. Randy explained that he had called. Julie arrived with her mother in tow who had coincidentally gotten home to change clothes from morning duties at the Festival as Julie was leaving. Julie had explained that something was up at the golf course according to Randy. Margaret had no choice but to accompany her daughter. A couple other fellows had wandered out to see what was going on. Mara and Peter hung in the back. All in all, it was an impressive crowd for the judge.

He spoke without introduction or formality:

"Gentlemen, and Ladies, I see. As you all know, the proposal to redesign The Candlesticks Golf Course to accommodate a housing development has been greeted with controversy and, clearly, opposition from some segments of the local community. Indeed, some of us from outside the community such as Mr. Morgan and Mr. Donaldson and even myself have become involved in this question.

"Mr. Howard, as head of The Candlesticks' board, however, has effectively moved ahead with the development. He has done so based on his authority granted to him by the Candlesticks' Accord. For those of you who might now know about that piece of paper, the Accord is a legal document that I wrote 40 years ago. At the time, it clarified ownership and devised, for want of a better term, an arrangement to manage the course.

"It worked pretty well. In fact, it's still working pretty well. I have gone through the document with a very sharp pencil and I was not able to break it. Let me say that it's quite unusual in contractual law for a lawyer to find himself in the odd position of trying to find a flaw in his own work. It was an interesting exercise. I was a damn fine lawyer 40 years ago."

A sudden gust of wind blew off a couple ball caps. The judge swallowed his words and paused for a moment to drink some iced tea. Faces looked up at the sky, but there was still no rain.

The judge continued:

"The Accord gives Mr. Howard, Howie, the right to do whatever he wants because he is the current head of The Candlesticks' Board of Directors which is made up of members of the families who own The Candlesticks. As you may know, those families are the families that originally founded Stowe Towne. So, we have a lot of history here.

"Now, there have been other efforts at opposition. The Candlesticks is technically on Pottawa State Forest property. Some thought that the course couldn't be altered because of that. But our friend here in the audience, State Senator Barnes, recently attached an amendment to a strip-mining bill that allows for not only the golf course to be changed, but actual development to go on further up into the forest. The bill was passed late yesterday. It was a well-done piece of political maneuvering. Even though I'm on the other side of this issue, I congratulate the senator."

Barnes turned red with embarrassment and wanted to crawl in a hole. He knew that this type of congratulations was like a Mafia Don giving someone a kiss. Little did he realize that two Columbus newspaper reporters were now furiously scribbling notes on the back of Candlestick placemats. Mara and Peter had forgotten both tape recorders and notepads. They had not anticipated that a story would practically be dictated to them.

The judge continued:

"Then there was the court of public opinion orchestrated by our old and dear friend Mr. Miller and by Mr. Bergman and by a couple of other unnamed persons. Although obtaining some newspaper and TV coverage, it's my opinion that this campaign, too, failed. Despite the love of history professed by our Daughters of the Union Army friends, The Candlesticks is no great battlefield. Many current residents of Stowe Towne don't care that a housing development will go up here and frankly might see some economic benefit for themselves.

"Finally, in the great spirit of American competition, we suddenly had a new competing housing development begun by a lady whom I have never had the pleasure of meeting."

"Believe me, it's no pleasure," Bruce Dean interrupted with a laugh he shared alone. He shut up and wished he hadn't said a word.

The judge frowned, made no comment, and continued:

"Delia Long has filed a motion for the issuing of a preliminary injunction to halt development of The Candlesticks' housing development. Now, let me present very briefly a rule of law. Something like this filing—whether or not it is completely meritorious or completely lacking any merit—can be dealt with in either a few days or, conversely, a few years. Regardless of merit. Do you understand, regardless of merit? Especially, if some people of influence take an interest."

"That's blackmail," Morgan said.

"It's the way the law works," the judge replied smoothly without missing a beat. "Yet, I ask you, why would someone waste years of effort on something so insignificant unless delay is the only purpose?

"None of us want that. We want to get on with our lives. Some of us are in a hurry. Here's the deal then. This afternoon we will have a golf match. Straight up. Low score wins, just like on TV. Sudden death play-off from the first hole if there's a tie. Mr. Howard will play Mr. Bergman. If Mr. Howard wins, the housing development here at The Candlesticks will proceed with all due speed. I guarantee that there will be no opposition. However, if Mr. Bergman wins, a new Candlesticks' Accord will be adopted. It's laying right there in this gold folder on the table in front of me. Essentially, it says that the golf course cannot be changed or developed for 50 years."

There was a stunned silence. People edged away from Howie and Sticks as if they were two gunfighters in the Old West.

"Gentlemen," the judge concluded simply, "you tee off in 15 minutes on the first tee. By the way, just so it's pure golf, no carts for anyone."

Justice Summers left the new Accord laying on the table, walked through the circle of people, and disappeared into the clubhouse. He had to pee real bad.

～

There was a minute of astonishment, panic, confusion, outrage, amazement, and general chaos on the deck until Howie and Sticks, facing each other, both held up a hand for silence. The crowd quieted.

"I don't want to do this, Howie," Sticks said. "I don't want houses built here and I don't want The Candlesticks to change. But I gave it my best shot. I mean, I have no business or right to play you for all the marbles."

A smile crept across Howie's soft and tired face. "Sticks, I *want* you to play. Justice Summers calls the shots and it's come down to this. If you don't play, he'll be mad at you and me and then Stowe Towne. The

Candlesticks and everyone will suffer sooner or later. He'll find a way to make everyone's life miserable."

"He's right, you know," Senator Barnes said. "This will settle the issue in a way he finds acceptable. Believe me, I want it settled, too."

"I find this utterly ridiculous," Don Morgan chimed in.

"What do you care?" Howie turned and spoke sharply to the Cleveland developer. "Three hours from now and it's settled."

"Fine," Morgan said, "then just to make it personal, I've got a thousand dollars that says you'll win. Who'll take my bet?"

"I'll take it," Mr. Miller said stepping forward.

"Wait a minute," Howie said. He turned back to Sticks. "Sticks, is there going to be a match?"

Sticks stared at his neighbor. For more than 40 years he had known Howie Howard. Liked him and disliked him. Grew up playing golf with him. Graduated from high school with him. Grew up envying the fact that he was from one of the seven families. More money and prestige. Yet, Sticks realized that he hadn't really had that much different a life than Howie had had. But now, it had all come down to this.

"Sure, Howie," Sticks said, "let's play a little golf."

Howie went into The Candlesticks' pro shop and got himself and Sticks new golf shirts on the house. He chose a white one for himself and tossed Sticks a dark blue one. Each bore The Candlesticks' logo, Howie's in red and Sticks' in white. The men went into the small locker room to change and use the bathroom while news of the match raced through the club. Phone calls were made. People seemed to materialize out of the air. By the time the two golfers had finished up 10 minutes on the putting green, there were upward of a hundred people in a semicircle behind the first tee.

The only people on the putting green with Sticks and Howie had been Randy and Julie. The four of them agreed that the children would act as caddies for their fathers. Randy tossed a tee up in the air and it came down pointing in the general direction of Howie. He'd hit first.

On the first tee, Justice Summers held up a scorecard. "I'll keep score, Gentlemen, with the help, I'm sure, of the gallery. This is tournament golf. No mulligans and no gimmees. Announce provisional balls. Mr. Howard, I understand you're up first."

Howie put his tee in the ground and then his ball on the tee as it began to rain lightly.

Both golfers scored nervous, but routine pars on the first two holes. However, on the third hole, the long par 3 which featured the pond running along the right side of the fairway almost up to the green, both golfers were extra careful. They realized that they were playing gross score and not match play. Every bad shot counted against you and wasn't wiped out by just losing one hole. In addition, they had both played a scramble in the morning, which encouraged taking risky shots as long as one player in the foursome hit a safe ball. So, on the third hole, both players overcompensated to avoid a disaster in the water. Consequently, Howie landed in the deep left-side bunker and Sticks was so far left that he was almost on the adjoining fifth green. They both managed to get on the green and down in two for bogey.

On the fourth hole, both men hit their shots in the bunkers (on opposite sides of the green) and took bogey again. Then on the short, par-4 fifth hole, Howie blinked. While Sticks scored a routine par, Howie pushed a short three-foot putt and took his third bogey in a row. He was down one as he walked with Julie and Margaret to the sixth tee, a very short par-3 hole ranked as the easiest hole on the course. His confidence was shaken.

"Don't worry, Dad," Julie advised. "The ball just slipped past the hole because of the wet green. It's going to happen to Mr. Bergman, too."

"I'm not exactly used to playing in front of a gallery."

"I can't believe I'm out here," Margaret chimed in. "This seems so...childish."

"Mom," Julie pleaded, "Dad needs our support."

Margaret shook water off her golf umbrella that also had been hurriedly supplied from the pro shop. She was supposed to be working a booth for the DUA, although she knew there were plenty of people to cover for her. Besides, the rain would certainly cut down on the crowd around the town square. "I'm sorry, Howie, Julie's right."

Howie glanced at his wife. She was wearing an Ohio State sweatshirt and her hair was soaked. She looked 20 years younger. He was surprised and pleased that she was out here. He gave her a smile. "Thanks, honey. Glad you're here."

Both men hit high wedges that plugged in the soft green. The judge allowed both to lift and place their balls and both made 10-foot putts for birdies. On the next tee, however, they faced The Candlesticks' hardest hole, the long, 420-yard uphill par-4 Barnes's Knob whose green was next to the top of the Pottawa River's Cascades. Sticks was still leading by one stroke.

The crowd slogged over to once again form a semicircle behind the tee. The rain had not increased; it was still steady but light. However, the course itself couldn't absorb too much more water. There already were a few pools on the fairway. If it started pooling on the greens, they would have to stop play. Bip had grabbed a few dry towels from the locker room and he took the opportunity to toss the golfers dry ones.

As the crowd quieted while Sticks teed up his ball, everyone paused and listened. Sticks too turned away from his ball. There was an unusual sound. "It's the river," Doc Parsons finally said. He was right. Behind the wall of trees that ran along the left side of the seventh fairway, the Pottawa River was suddenly making river-like noises. No one ever remembered the so-called river being more than a stream that produced a picturesque trickle of water over the rocks affectionately called the Cascades. *What was going on?* everyone wondered. Well, they'd get a view when they got to the top of the hill.

Sticks was careful to stay out of the trees and left his drive short, barely 200 yards down the right edge of the fairway. Howie saw a chance to make up a stroke and powered a drive over 250 yards down the middle of the fairway. Sticks had to overhit a three-wood uphill that drifted to the right and short of the green. Howie hit a six-iron safely to the back of the green above the hole. Sticks scored a bogey and Howie a par to even up the match. But their scores were incidental to the spectacle of the Cascades that had turned into a raging white rapids. The increased volume of water...well, *cascaded* down the rocks slamming into the boulders at the bottom and turning an abrupt left. The roar was almost frightening. No one had ever seen anything like it.

The judge (who had never visited a national park and was not in the least impressed by natural phenomena) hurried the golfers to the next hole. The match now was even. Both golfers scored pars on the 530-yard par-5 eighth hole. But on the ninth hole the tall and wet rough finally got them both. The grass grabbed Sticks' seven-iron second shot and the ball barely rolled 20 yards out onto the fairway. Howie's eight-iron, on the other hand, flew out of the grass and over the green by 30 yards into even deeper rough. Both men took double-bogeys and were lucky to score those.

People dashed from the ninth green into the clubhouse to dry off, buy a towel or umbrella, and use the bathroom. Rain can sometimes have the same effect on a bladder as a running bathroom faucet. Sticks and Howie, however, stayed on the course huddled separately under umbrellas held by their children. Sammi joined her husband and son.

"How you doing, Sticks?" she asked. She hadn't spoken a word to him during the round.

He smiled a big grin. "It's way too wet to play. Even for a fanatic golfer."

Sammi laughed. "Lucky I don't know any fanatic golfers, just crazy golfers."

The judge carrying his red OSU umbrella—now he was completely outfitted in his non-alma mater's colors—came over. "Ready to go, gentlemen, let's head out."

Holes 10 and 11 played back the way they had just come so they would soon have another view of the raging Cascades. "Sure is getting dark," Randy said as he wiped off and handed his father his driver. "I think you have to be a little more aggressive off the tee, Dad," he said. "Mr. Howard's really outhitting you." They watched as Howie hit another long drive down the center of the fairway. Sticks took his son's advice, but ended up in the rough again and again had trouble getting out. But Sticks' rough trouble was balanced when Howie again missed a short putt and both men made bogey.

The 11th hole was an uphill 160-yard par 3 to a small elevated green that overlooked the bottom of the Cascades. A long tee shot was death. But the hole was balanced by not having any sand around it. The problem was if the golfer hit too short, the ball could roll back down the fairway. Both golfers flirted with that possibility, but their balls held in the soft grass. They chipped on and both made soggy 10-foot putts as it began to rain harder.

The judge picked up the pace, hustling people away from again gaping down at the raging Cascades. The 12th hole was the tricky dogleg left that had been Ray Gunther's downfall. The hole suddenly reminded Sticks that he was playing with Ray's clubs and that got him to wondering if Ray had planned to lose so Sticks would have these clubs for today. Or, was Ray sent just to see if Sticks might be a worthy opponent for Howie. The club bet might have been meant to put pressure on Sticks' game and see how he would respond. In any case, both golfers now played the hole expertly and parred it easily. They also made pars on the parallel back-to-back par-4 13th and 14th holes. The only odd thing about the two holes was the tiny ditch stream that ran from the base of the Cascades across both fairways to the large pond near the clubhouse had changed from a trickle that you could step across to a 10-foot wide torrent. Everyone had to use the cart bridge to cross the water; all remarking that they had never seen anything like this.

The golfers in the crowd were now speculating about the game. Since neither player had broken out, it looked like it might come down to one bad hole or even one bad shot. The last three holes after they played the par-3 15th, which featured the cordoned-off Jack's Tree, were relatively flat, long but easy holes that occupied the land between the clubhouse and Sticks' property. Maybe, the gallery speculated, it wouldn't be a bad shot that lost it, but a good shot that won it. Maybe someone would chip in from off the green or curl in a 40-foot putt. Everyone knew that something had to happen. The golfers were running out of holes and it was raining even harder.

Mara and Peter plodded along. The story was rapidly losing its appeal. They were soaked since they had to share one small umbrella that Mara fortunately had had in her shoulder bag. They didn't know golf enough to understand the nuances of what was happening. *Where was a sports reporter when you really needed one?!!* Plus, this was taking hours! Still, it was a hell of a story if they could put it all together. When you came down to it, millions of dollars were on the line. Jobs. Housing. Economic boom. All hinging on a few golf swings.

The crowd proceeded to the women's tee on the 15th hole. The river roared out of the bottom of the Cascades and ran along behind the row of boulders that edged the left side of the short fairway. People glanced nervously over in the direction of the river; they were so unused to the sound of the rushing water. The sky actually grew darker. The light was like an October twilight instead of a July afternoon. But it was still hot and humid and the breeze that gusted occasionally was far from cool.

Sticks waited under the umbrella that Randy held protecting his clubs. Bip came past and gave him a dry towel and then went on to toss another to Julie. They all watched as Howie teed up a ball and used a pitching wedge to put the ball on the green in the upper right-hand corner, just where he was supposed to be. Sticks sucked in his breath and stepped toward the tee. He congratulated Howie on a nice shot as they passed. He teed up his Titleist and stepped back to line up his shot.

"Put it in the hole!" someone yelled from the crowd, one of the few times anyone had yelled during the course of the round. Sticks smiled. Maybe it was Mr. Miller trying to protect his thousand-dollar wager.

Sticks stepped up to the ball and started to take his club back when lightning struck the center of Jack's Tree. The lightning exploded in a crown of fire at the top of the tree and the noise and shock spun Sticks away from his ball, made everyone else recoil, and knocked down a half-dozen people. At that moment, the river roared like a bear waking from a long sleep and water suddenly gushed between the boulders and across the fairway.

There were screams and people yelled *Get out of here!* and *Get back to the clubhouse!* Suddenly, and belatedly, the recall siren from the clubhouse shrieked and shrieked across the golf course. People scrambled up the incline behind the 15th tee and headed straight across the 16th and then 17th fairways toward the clubhouse, now almost obscured by the driving rain. Off to their right across the course, they could see that water from the river was flooding onto the grounds. It was plunging out of the Cascades and rolling out of the woods above the front nine.

Let's go! Hurry up! people yelled.

The Bergmans and Howards brought up the rear. Margaret had been one of the persons knocked over and had twisted an ankle. Howie on one side and Randy on the other now more or less carried her between them. Sticks had picked up his clubs when Randy had thrown them down to help Margaret, but now he saw Julie struggling with Howie's clubs.

He threw his clubs back on the ground. "Julie, Julie," he yelled, "forget them." He grabbed her arm as she slipped on the slope. She let go of the clubs. Sammi was just ahead of them and Sticks grabbed her arm with his free hand. "Come on, come on," he shouted over the rain and thunder.

A long line of people stretched out ahead of them. Now lightning danced over the clubhouse and all around the course. The two families hurried together. Even the old men in the crowd sprinted out ahead of them. Water seemed to be literally pooling out of the ground. They were close enough now to see people on the deck of the clubhouse jumping up and down and waving them in. The siren kept screaming. It seemed to be taking them forever.

"The shelter?" Sammi yelled in Sticks' ear, pointing at the small structure behind the 16th tee. But as they got closer they saw why no one else had taken refuge there. The water from the ditch stream had already flooded the shelter to a depth of two feet.

"No, no," Sticks shouted back. "We have to get to the clubhouse."

Ahead, people were detouring around the pond that was overflowing its banks. But at least people were reaching the clubhouse. Sticks glanced behind him and water was everywhere. Flooding behind them. Catching up to them. Lightning struck in the woods behind the Cascades and there was an ear-shattering clap of thunder. The water now was so far out of the pond that they had to veer across the 18th green. They rushed the last few yards and people reached out from the door and helped them up the short flight of stairs and into the main dining room.

Bob Redford and Will Boyd just made it across Bryce Bridge in Redford's battered green pickup truck before a tree carried along by the cresting Pottawa slammed into the bridge's ancient supports and caused the bridge roadway to buckle and bend. The buckling made a loud crack causing both men to look back through the truck's rear window.

"I can't believe you didn't tell me about the flood," Redford said accusingly to his passenger. Rain slanted against the windshield and it was almost impossible to see The Pike.

Will shrugged and picked up Redford's cell phone from the seat between them and calmly called the Stowe Towne police reporting that Bryce Bridge had just been washed out.

"You must have known about it," Redford continued. "You did the research for the article about The Candlesticks' land."

"I knew about it," Will finally said. It was practically the first thing he had said to Redford since the newspaper editor had come pounding on his front door demanding Will go along out to The Candlesticks *before it's too late!*

"Why did you leave it out?" Redford asked, hunched over the wheel staring out at the driving rain through the whip-like action of the pickup's large windshield wipers.

"You would have cut it out of the article," Will answered calmly.

"What? Why?"

"Because it queers the deal. No one with any sense would put a housing development in a floodplain. However, a flood once every hundred years is a little hard to believe. So, if you had published it, you would have been accused of malicious speculation. Scare tactics."

"But it's a fact. I have the paper right here." Redford gestured to the hundred-year-old copy of the *Bugle* that lay on the seat between them.

"I know. I've read it. But my point's well taken, Bob. Except for Haley's Comet, predicting events that happen every hundred years is very speculative."

They rounded a curve and came up to another small bridge. This bridge was still intact because the riverbed was a little wider and no tree had rammed the supports. However, the water had still risen enough to cover the roadway. Redford crept through the water trying not to splash it up into the engine more than necessary. He got through and sped along the mostly clear road the last two miles to the golf course. The Pottawa looped off into the fields and woods to their left. They could occasionally see water rising out of the river.

"What else didn't you tell me, Will?" Redford asked.

Will laughed. "I know lots of things, Bob. But most of them don't matter."

"Tell me one."

"No, I don't think so."

"Come on, just one."

Will glanced at Redford. The man was clear-eyed and aggressive. Just like he should be if he wasn't drinking or depressed. "All right," Will said. "I know what happened to Billy Barnes."

"Who?"

"Billy Barnes. You know, Barnes's Knob. The ghost of Billy Barnes."

"That happened a long time ago."

"1923."

Redford glanced at his companion. "Who cares?"

"State Senator Kenny Barnes might care. Billy Barnes was his grandfather."

"So, what happened to him?"

Will pointed. "Your turn's coming up. And to answer your question, nothing happened to him. He just walked away. Walked away from his life."

They sped by Howie Howard's house and could see in back that the Pottawa River was flooding The Candlesticks. Redford turned hard into the golf course parking lot and stopped right in front of the door. He leaped out of the pickup, grabbing the old copy of the paper. Will followed behind without as much haste.

Wet and exhausted people were sprawled everywhere in the dining room. May Miller (who had not gone out on the course) was ministering to her husband. Mara Fish and Peter Onear stood in a corner, soaked through. All their notes and car keys and everything had been in Mara's bag that she had dropped sometime during the sprint back to the clubhouse. Don Morgan was sitting on two chairs huffing and puffing as if he were giving birth. He had not moved that far that fast in 30 years. A number of people including Kenny Barnes and Tom Duke sat with their heads in their hands. They had never been so frightened in their lives.

The Howards and Bergmans tried to pull themselves together at the table that had been used by Bip and Mr. Miller at noon to add up the scores. Julie and Sammi looked at Margaret's ankle to see how badly it was injured. An eerie silence took over the room as everyone tried to catch his or her breath.

Bob Redford took the opportunity to step up on a chair so everyone could see him.

"Can I have your attention everyone? Please, everyone," he shouted above the sound of the rain beating on the windows.

People turned to look at the tall man standing on the chair. He hardly looked like the old Bob Redford. He looked sober and more alert than most people had ever seen him.

"First of all, is everyone accounted for? Is anyone hurt?"

"My Mom twisted her ankle," Julie volunteered.

Margaret waved her hand. "I'm all right. I'm all right."

People strained their necks to see how Margaret was doing. Doc Parsons made his way over to her to see if he could help.

"Just to tell you what's happening," Redford continued getting back the crowd's attention. "I wish I could have gotten here earlier to tell you what was going to happen."

"What do you mean, Bob?" Lincoln Jones asked. Lincoln felt about dead. He hadn't exerted himself that much in years.

"I've been going through old newspaper files all morning," Redford responded. "It was something I remembered, but I had to confirm it. I'm talking very old files. Way down in our office basement..."

"Get to the point, man," Don Morgan yelled.

"All right, I'm sorry. It's the hundred-year flood. Every hundred years on July Fourth, the Pottawa River floods. Look at this." Redford held up a folded yellow paper. He opened it carefully and held up the front page of the *Bugle*. The headline read: *RIVER FLOODS* in huge type. Underneath in type still big enough to read: *Pottawa Floods County North of Village.*

"The date on the paper is tomorrow, July fifth. The flood was exactly 100 years ago on the Fourth of July."

"Is it just a coincidence?" Mr. Miller roused himself to ask.

Redford shook his head. "No, apparently there was a well-known Indian legend that the river floods every hundred years. This edition of the paper speculates that that's why this area wasn't settled until after the Civil War. In the first half of the nineteenth century people remembered or were told by the Indians that the river flooded. But then they forgot, just like we forgot at the end of this century."

Everyone paused to absorb this incredible new information and then they began to wonder how much land up and down the Pottawa was flooding.

Suddenly, Howie stood up from bending over to watch Doc Parsons manipulate his wife's ankle. "Where's Judge Summers?"

People looked around. On the course, it had been hard to miss the judge in his distinctive scarlet and gray rain gear. But in the excitement of the dash back to the clubhouse, he was forgotten. "Look!" someone suddenly yelled. "Out the window!"

Everyone rushed to the dining room's wall of windows. Below, outside in the downpour, stood the judge supported by Will Boyd. Obviously, Will had dragged the judge out of the water the last few yards. They were both soaked. The judge's gray hair was whipped by the wind. The judge and Will were facing the golf course that now resembled an inland sea. Waves of water washed back and forth. Most bushes and shrubs were underwater. Treetops stuck up like isolated sentinels. The pin on the 18th green was still stuck in the hole and the yellow Candlesticks' flag flapped in the wind in front of the judge.

The judge must have sensed the faces that were pressed against the windows. He slowly turned and stretched out his arms in a gesture that at once indicated defeat and an embracing of the natural elements. We lost, he seemed to be saying, all our plans and schemes and games. And the wind and rain and the thunder and lightning have won.

People ran to the door to bring Justice Summers inside before the flood could wash him away. Bob Redford rushed up to Will Boyd to shake his hand. Will shook it reluctantly, but turned away as his friend tried to pull him toward the clubhouse door. Redford released Boyd's hand and Will waved him away and walked in the heavy rain and darkness around the end of the building and out to the truck in the parking lot. Redford hesitated for a moment, but then went inside to see about the judge.

More lightning danced over the course and, within a few seconds, everyone had retreated inside to wait out the century storm.

FIREWORKS

Despite the rain.

Despite the flood.

Despite the apparent disappearance of one heroic citizen.

Despite all the chaos that engulfed the small town of Stowe Towne, Ohio, this Fourth of July, the traditional installation of the junior and senior members of the Daughters of the Union Army took place exactly on time. The stage under the huge tent in Festival Park was festooned with red, white, and blue carnations. On the stage sat the current DUA officers in red blouses. Behind them in blue blouses were the five senior member inductees for this year including Margaret Howard. And behind the senior members, dressed in white blouses, were the 16 junior member inductees.

Every year, the ceremony always lasted exactly one hour and started precisely at 9:00 p.m. Fifteen minutes after the ceremony ended, fireworks would begin over at the high school football field. The DUA installation followed by Fourth of July fireworks had happened annually since the founding of the DUA after the Civil War.

Apparently, Mr. Miller ironically mused from his seat in the first row, there was also a major flood on the day of one of those installations. The one exactly 100 years ago today. He wondered why the flood was not part of DUA lore and legend. Or, had the DUA always been above the whims and vagaries of men and nature? More than likely, he thought, the DUA had always had a knack for suppressing bad publicity.

The Union Generals Marching Corps was seated on stage and played the *Star-Spangled Banner* and *The Battle Hymn of the Republic*. The members were inducted. May made a very nice little speech. Pins and American flags were handed out. Some very tasteful self-congratulations were expressed. The audience, consisting mainly of family members at this late hour, applauded on cue.

Howie and Julie Howard applauded vigorously when Margaret got up from her seat on stage and limped noticeably to accept her pin and flag. She smiled faintly. This day, that she had so long anticipated, had been bizarre. Her home almost flooded. Her husband's business almost ruined. Her ankle almost broken. An Ohio Supreme Court Justice almost drowned on the 18th fairway. She glanced at the audience to acknowledge the applause and caught the beaming faces of her husband and daughter. She realized she loved them so much.

Sticks, Sammi, and Randy, seated beside Howie and Julie, also applauded vigorously. The families had decided to come to the ceremony together after they had spent the late afternoon going back and forth between their homes and the golf clubhouse, watching to see if the Pottawa River would stop flooding before it reached the buildings. The river's water had stopped just short of the back of their houses and their decks. The water got closer to The Candlesticks' clubhouse, actually lapping at the first floor doors and the base of the building. Of course, the flood did swamp The Pike in places and Bryce Bridge was washed out. They had had to drive to town the long way looping around to the east.

The ceremony ended with a patriotic prayer and the Union Generals marched right off the stage and right out of the tent and toward the high school. It would take them 15 minutes to get to the football field and get set up. There they would play *Stars and Stripes Forever* to begin the fireworks and *The 1812 Overture* as the grand finale. Everyone hustled after the band to see the fireworks. May and Mr. Miller waved at the Howards and the Bergmans as the Millers walked by, leading the procession out of the tent. They were followed by the Joneses, Jack and Mary Schultz, the Thompsons, the senior Dukes and junior Dukes, and the Mitchells. All the old gang was going over to see the fireworks, just like they always had for 130 years.

All, that is, except the Howards and Bergmans, who placed their folding chairs in a circle. Within a couple of minutes, they were the only people in the tent except for a few workers at the nearly abandoned food concessions down at the other end of the tent. People would wander back after the fireworks for some late night brats and beer.

Margaret, limping but helped by her husband, trailed down last from the stage and was congratulated by everyone. Randy excused himself for a minute and returned with a small blue cooler. It was filled with ice and beer. He passed around cans of Miller Genuine Draft to everyone, including himself and Julie. Howie and Margaret had never seen Julie drink except for tiny classes of wine at Christmas and on New Year's Eve.

Randy sat down on a chair and was suddenly conscious of all four parents staring at him with open mouths.

"What?" he exclaimed. "Hey, you guys grew up here. Get real." He laughed and opened his can. Beer foamed out of the opening and Randy expertly sucked off the head.

Julie followed suit. After she took a long gulp, she said, "Randy and

I have something to tell you."

The four parents sat stock-still, beers unopened. Apparently, their *very* long day was not yet over. Each instantly fantasized a vision of their children's wedding. Margaret saw Julie coming down the aisle in the century-old Episcopalian Church just down the street. Sammi saw Randy and his best man waiting with Reverend Palmer at the modern altar of the new contemporary Lutheran Church across from Allied Pipes. Sticks envisioned the children getting married in the chapel at Kent State University with the Kent football team acting as honor guard, golden helmets held high in the air. Howie wondered if he might convince them to elope. A free honeymoon and a thousand bucks spending money would be a hell of a lot cheaper than a wedding.

Surprisingly, no one was very upset.

"It took a lot of planning," Randy said, bringing the parents back from their revelries.

"It was my idea," Julie said proudly.

"Really," her mother responded, "*your* idea."

"But Randy was all for it once he knew that I was serious. He thought I was just jerking him around at first."

Sticks looked at his son. "You didn't take something like this seriously?"

Randy shrugged. "Well, I didn't want it to be one of those things that lasted two months and then she'd want out. Why would I want to be part of that?"

"Why indeed!" Sammi said with a quick glance at her husband.

"Plus, other people had to get on board, if you know what I mean," Julie explained.

"Other people?" her father asked.

"Well, we couldn't do it alone, Daddy."

"No, of course not, Julie," Howie said slowly. "So...?

"So," Randy chimed in, "we caught a break. Sheila backed out."

All four parents who had been leaning over farther and farther out of their chairs suddenly sat up. "Sheila!" Sticks exclaimed. "Who the hell is Sheila?"

"Is that one of your old girlfriends, Randy?" Howie demanded.

"Sheila?" Randy said. "Of course not. She's the younger sister of a guy I know on the football team. She turned down the scholarship."

"And so I got it," Julie said proudly.

"What scholarship?" Margaret said, suddenly confused.

"It's a full athletic scholarship to play golf at Kent State, Mom," Julie explained. "That's where I'm going to school next fall."

All four parents stared at their children.

"Isn't that great?" Randy asked. "Mom, Dad? Aren't you going to congratulate Julie?"

Sammi was the first to recover. "Oh, of course, Julie. That's wonderful. Isn't that wonderful for Julie, Sticks?"

"Oh, absolutely. Congratulations. How about another beer?" Sticks reached blindly into the cooler and grabbed a cold one, but instead of offering it to Julie he kept it for himself even though he had yet to open his first beer.

Margaret started to cry.

"Mom!?" Julie said loudly.

Margaret held up a hand. "No, Julie, I'm not angry. I'm happy. I'm so relieved, I can't tell you. It's wonderful." She sobbed loudly again into a Kleenex.

"A full scholarship?" Howie asked his daughter.

"Full scholarship, Dad. I went up and played twice with the coach. I did it on my own. Well, almost, Randy helped." She reached across and Randy took her hand.

"Well, this has been quite a day," Howie said. "I guess we should have some champagne to celebrate." Instead of champagne, however, Howie suddenly seemed to notice the cold beer in his hand and decided to open it. The other adults followed suit and everyone laughed as beer sprayed into the circle.

Finally, taking a deep breath—it seemed like he had been holding it for minutes—Sticks said, "Say, speaking of champagne, my brother called just before we left the house to come here. He managed to open the Wineyard this morning. He practically sold out. He said everyone in town stopped in. People told him it was the greatest thing that ever happened in Stowe Towne. He didn't even ask me about the flood."

"You're calling it the Wineyard now?" Howie asked.

Sticks smiled, "Paul's come around to agreeing that it's kind of catchy."

"I had an interesting phone call as well," Howie said. "You know David Canello, Sticks, The Candlesticks' lawyer?"

"Sure, we've played golf and gin a few times."

"Well, he called to resign. Told me that he was against the housing development. He was the person who kept tipping off the media. I didn't bother to tell him about the flood and the fact that there isn't a golf course anymore. He can read about it in the paper. Good riddance to him, I say."

"I guess he was an ally we didn't even know we had," Sticks mused. "I don't understand."

Howie shrugged. "Well, it's complicated. He wasn't really your ally. He wanted to keep the course the way it was just so he and his firm could have it for themselves. To use. And he was angry at me for not including him in the discussions from the beginning which, I suppose, I might have done. But that's water under the bridge. Literally."

"What in the world happened to Will Boyd after he rescued the judge?" Sammi asked. Sammi had sold Will the Hanover Mansion, although she did not know him well.

Randy spoke up: "I saw one of the Sheriff's deputies just now when I went to get the cooler. Jeff Young, you know. They've been looking for him. Everyone wants to congratulate him. But he's not at his house. He apparently drove Bob Redford's truck back to town and left it at his house. Then took his own truck and dog and skipped out."

"Will Boyd's always been pretty eccentric," Sticks commented. "I can see him just taking off."

"Bob Redford was upset that he didn't remember about the flood," Howie said. "It really bothered him. Said he'd never take another drink."

Sticks shook his head. "Well, that's some good that'll come out of this. That and the fact that we have a new lake in town, Lake Candlesticks."

"But the water will go down. Won't it, Daddy?" Julie asked. "The golf course will dry out."

"Plus, there won't be another flood for a hundred years," Randy added.

Howie nodded. "The golf course is still there somewhere, I hope. But obviously, there will never be a housing development. At least in the lifetime of anyone who remembers the flood."

He paused, and then looked at Sticks. "But that brings up something that we might as well discuss now with everyone here. Sticks, how about coming on board at the golf course? You could help me with the cleanup, plus we'd clean up our own places. Then, maybe, when the course reopens you could stay on. Take Bip's place. Teaching pro. I mean you were going to whip my ass this afternoon if we could have finished the round."

"I'm not sure about that, but are you serious?" Sticks asked.

"Sure, of course I'm serious. I never wanted all that to happen like it did." Howie laughed, "Anyway, we need to find our golf clubs. They're out there somewhere."

Sticks nodded. "Sounds pretty good to me. Let me think about it overnight and I'll stop over tomorrow and we'll survey the damage."

Howie reached across and the two men shook hands. "At least," Howie said, "Stowe Towne still has Delia's housing development."

"Well, maybe not," Sammi said softly.

"What happened?" Margaret asked.

"There's this old farmer down the road. Wrote the Environmental Protection Agency that Delia's development will ruin Creed Marsh. I never even heard of Creed Marsh."

"No kidding! Howie and I know Creed Marsh," Sticks said. "We used to play golf out there when we were kids. We'd go out beyond the sixth hole and hit old golf balls out into the marsh. Remember, Howie?"

Howie agreed. "Sure I do." He thought for a moment and then said: "I'll tell you and it's the truth, golf is not an easy game."

In the distance, they heard the first fireworks go off.

"Come on," Julie said standing up and grabbing Randy's hand. "We can see them over the trees."

Everyone got up, excited to see the fireworks. Sticks gestured in the direction of the high school. "All of you go ahead. Hurry up. I'll straighten up around here and bring the cooler. Hurry before you miss them."

Everyone took him at his word and rushed out of the tent, admonishing him to hurry up himself. He watched them leave. Howie with Margaret, who was holding her husband by his arm and limping along gamely beside him. Randy with his mother on one side and Julie on the other.

Sticks could hear the fireworks whistle and boom overhead. He straightened the chairs back into rows. Wasn't there a prayer service in the morning? Or maybe an antique auction? Life, apparently, goes on. He picked up the beer cans. A couple of the containers were half-full and he poured them out onto the matted-down grass. One stream of beer, he noticed, flooded an anthill. *Well, that would be hard to explain to the queen ant! Honest, your majesty, we were just carrying our load and this flood of beer washed right over us.*

Sticks laughed and tossed the empty cans in the cooler. He lifted it and started down the row of chairs to follow his family and friends. He could see people gathered just beyond the aura of lights from the tent. Chinese paper lanterns were strung around the edge of the open-sided tent. They were four and five feet apart. Light blue. Yellow. Pinkish red. Pale green.

My problem, Sticks thought as he stepped under the glow of the Chinese lanterns and into the darkness of the warm summer night, *is that I always have wanted things to stay the same. And that's not always possible and it's actually better that it's not always possible.*

He paused, looking up into the dark sky, waiting for the next burst of fireworks.

I think it's better not to worry about it, he concluded. And then he was glad to be here in the darkness with his family and his cooler of beer and the unexpected and beautiful explosions of fireworks above his head.

Sticks saw over the buildings and trees of Stowe Towne flashes of red and white, blue and gold, green and purple illuminating the dark, clear sky. You could hear people all over the town *Oooh!* and *Aaah!* as one explosion after another crackled and flashed above them in the sky.

It was, everyone no doubt thought, a beautiful sight.